the ROAD HOME

TOMMY & TENNEY
MARK ANDREW OLSEN

BETHANY HOUSE PUBLISHERS

Minneapolis, Minnesota

Published by Bethany House Publishers
11400 Hampshire Avenue South
Bloomington, Minnesota 55438

Bethany House Publishers is a division of
Baker Publishing Group, Grand Rapids, Michigan.

Printed in the United States of America

ISBN-13: 978-0-7642-0499-9 (International Trade Paper)
ISBN-10: 0-7642-0499-8 (International Trade Paper)

The Library of Congress has cataloged the original edition as follows:

Tenney, Tommy, 1956-
    The road home / Tommy Tenney & Mark Andrew Olsen.
        p. cm.
    ISBN-13: 978-0-7642-0330-5 (alk. paper)
    ISBN-10: 0-7642-0330-4 (alk. paper)
    1. Widows—Fiction. 2. Lancaster County (Pa.)—Fiction. 3. Mothers-in-law—Fiction. 4. Daughters-in-law—Fiction. I. Olsen, Mark Andrew. II. Title.

    PS3620.E56R63   2007
    813'.6—dc22   2007023746

To those who travel

in search of more

than just geography.

Ephrata, Pennsylvania—sometime in the future

70

It's funny where you can be when you finally come to an important conclusion, especially one you've resisted most of your life. I have just made a decision, sitting here in my front-porch rocker with my old afghan clutched against an autumn wind. I've changed my mind about something—something that has bothered most of my family for years. I feel like I'm ready to share these secrets. Actually, I'm just trying to work up the courage to spill it out.

After all this time, I can hardly believe what I'm going to say. The thoughts have been floating around my brain for a while now, but until tonight I haven't felt any urgency about clearing the air. I know some of you have always felt I am a bit too secretive.

Maybe it started with my coming out here to the porch, which is something I haven't done in a long time. Not at this late hour, at my age, and at this time of year. In summertime, maybe. But this is a crisp autumn night, and strangely enough, I felt almost drawn out here by a wind that stormed out of the north and chilled me in my bed, not to mention it rattling the shutters and incessantly flinging dead leaves against the window. And the widest, brightest harvest moon took up station above the familiar granddaddy maple tree and beamed its dusky glow through that bedroom window so brightly I could see the tree's reds and golds.

The coming of fall no doubt has something to do with the choice I'm contemplating. You see, it was fall when I first came here. The season's rich colors and smells wove together my earliest impressions of this place. I came from a part of the country where autumn meant only slightly less scorching days, bluer skies, crisper nights, and maybe a rain shower or two. And before that, when still a girl with my biological family, all I experienced of harvest time was hard work. I never knew people who actually harvested their very own pumpkins for fun and took in such leisurely activities as hayrides and events like apple festivals. Or celebrated the arrival of what they called "sweater weather."

So now, every time fall rolls around to those falling dry leaves, I find myself magically transported to the first time I came here. In contrast, I feel the past come to life in autumn. Sometimes during my ambling sunset walks, I can almost make out silhouettes of the old-timers stomping along with their emphatic gaits, leading horses through the tall grass or grasping rusty old hand plows. I strain to see them, but the figures remain faint in my eyes, gauzy and transparent like the screen ghosts on those old-fashioned televisions. This was back in the black-and-white days when you changed channels with a metal knob, and the see-through remnant of one show sometimes bled off into another. I suppose I see the past a bit differently than most, maybe even the ones who lived it with me.

So I have just now decided the time has come for me to tell the complete story of where I came from and who I was before I arrived here. Yes—brace yourselves—I have changed my mind. After years of resisting all your well-intended requests, there's no one left that my silence protects but myself. I have nothing to hide now. Those I loved so much, whom I had vowed to shelter, no longer care what we know or don't know—are no longer here to protest. And as I live through old age myself, I imagine I won't care either. The greatest risk now is that I will pass on without telling you the truth, and carry my story with me into the hereafter. That would be a tragedy, I'm thinking.

Those loved ones I sought to shield passed away decades ago. First, my dear husband, Bo. Many of you are not aware of the facts surrounding our marriage. Just as my complexion has always been a tad darker than most of yours, thus raising questions, so has my reputation been. But I have managed to outlive all that, I think.

The last person I sought to protect died not long after my husband. Naomi—the only woman who was ever like a true mother to me. All these years after their passing, I no longer need to clamp my history down tight in a hiding place no one can reach. Instead, I now feel the need to give all of you a long-overdue glimpse into my past—the good and the not-so-good.

It may take some time for me to get it all down. I know my lawyer would rather this was a document entitled *The Long-Overdue Last Will and Testament of Ruth Salmon,* as lately I've neglected my estate planning. But first things first.

I write my story for you, my family. I want you all to understand things like why an old 1976 Chevrolet Impala sits in the back of the barn, covered by that blue tarp and gathering dust. And why, even though it no longer runs and is little more than a pile of scrap metal, I cannot bear to part with it. For it is precious to me, and to my memories.

I want you all to understand why I came down to this porch tonight. Without turning on the flood lamps and yard lights that Bo had installed for me, I'm looking out over the farm in the moonlight. You need to know what this farm-house looked and felt like when I first came here and found an Old Order home empty for decades, without electricity or modern amenities.

Most of all, I want my descendants to know the truth about the blood running through your veins, and why I chose to stay so reticent about it all these years.

Don't worry, it's good blood—time has proven that. My story is full of human failing and pain, but nothing absolutely vile. However, it will not be a whitewashed story. You'll figure that out soon enough. Human beings in my story behave like human beings, damaged and fallible, carrying around great big broken hearts. You won't find any angels in this tale. At least none we can see with the naked eye. That's because this story is real and true. And I'm pretty sure you will find it interesting as well as informative. You will learn some things that will certainly surprise you.

I realize my long silence has provoked many of you in the family, and many in Lancaster County, Pennsylvania, to some-times imagine things far more serious and embarrassing than what is actually true. I have both chuckled wryly at some of those rumors and deeply regretted others—though I do have to admit that one of the few remaining joys in life is the inventiveness of the town gossip still being spun about me. I'd hate to see it all die out forever since it seems to provide much entertainment here. Where I came from, such rumors are a dime a dozen. But here they take on a life of their own, stretched and elaborated beyond belief.

Just last week a little boy came up to me at Martin's Market and asked if it was true that I had my husband locked in my cellar, and had I really been keeping him alive on bread crumbs and root beer all these years? His mother looked like she was ready to box his ears something fierce. I bent down and, in the spirit of Halloween, mock-whispered that, no, actually he passed on a long time ago, and I'd stashed his bones under the floors of Ephrata Elementary. Then I gave him an exaggerated wink for good measure. His mom, just the same, didn't appreciate my humor. She flashed me a look that made it very clear where I'd spend eternity, then whisked him away with his eyes still bugging out as he stared over his shoulder at me.

I don't know if my story will ever squelch such stubborn whimsy on the part of the very young and the very old. But I know there's far worse gossip out there, just sitting there pickling the older ones' minds.

I'm going tomorrow to pick up a large notebook to begin chronicling the little-known events of my life.

You know what will be the hardest part of writing all this down? By far, it will be figuring out where to start. I could go back quite a ways, trying to explain everything about my childhood, my husband's family and your aunt Naomi's. There's a lot of story moldering away out there in the sun, like that ghost of a steel mill along the banks of the Lehigh River that launched it into motion. Right here in greater Bethlehem.

But the part of the story that matters most—about that I have no doubt—starts on the worst day of my life. Ironically it's the day I lost two others who were more than dear to me.

And not here in Pennsylvania. It was many years ago, beginning in a place where I'm not even sure you knew I lived.

PART ONE

The Far Country

CHAPTER I

Las Vegas, Nevada

I was thirty years old when I endured the worst day of my life.

The day began with my eyes flying open, followed by a shudder. The face swimming into focus before me, to be brutally honest, resembled that of a ghoul—swollen, distorted, with eerie green-orange skin and eyeballs. The dull stare of a man who could measure the rest of his life in hours. Shallow, staccato breaths rasped in and out between cracked lips.

I remember thinking, *if only this were a nightmare . . .* as my awareness grew.

He looked like death incarnate.

I sighed in despair. Another morning had found me back in the same hospital, slumped in the same, sadistic vinyl visitor's chair in which I had spent so many days and nights, drifting through that disorienting no-man's-land between discomfort, sheer exhaustion, and shallow sleep. Most heartbreaking of all, though, I was back at the same agonizing vigil, watching a loved one slowly die of liver disease.

His name was Mel. The poor soul was not only a dear friend but my brother-in-law—the only brother to Lonnie, my husband.

My *first* husband. Yes, that's right. Some of you may have forgotten, or maybe never knew, that I was married once before. So long ago now that it seems like another lifetime, another world.

Both Lonnie and Mel were kind men, good men by the humblest of street standards, although weak and prone to addictions, which made Vegas the worst possible city for them to inhabit.

Yes, Las Vegas.

I met Lonnie in the cocktail lounge where I was a waitress.

Yes, a cocktail lounge. There will be some shocking revelations, but please don't let those initial skeletons in my closet frighten you off!

I lived with Lonnie briefly and married him in Las Vegas, Nevada. And that, my dear family, is where your esteemed matriarch came from. The city of a thousand nicknames, few of them wholesome.

I chuckle just now, picturing some of your faces as you read this. *Aunt Ruth had a first husband, and was a cocktail waitress . . . in Las Vegas?! How much more shocking can it get?*

I'll tell you how much—for here goes the next truth volley. I was born Ruth Simone Escalante, of the San Moises, Sonora, Mexico *Escalantes*. My family and I were migrant farmworkers in the fields of central California, Arizona, and Nevada. I grew up with my back bent and my fingers in the soil, pulling produce of every kind for the supermarkets of America. Some of my brothers and sisters are probably still out there, somewhere, this very day, though I have not been able to locate a single one.

I am by birth and heritage a Mexican-American migrant

farmworker. I believe my family had immigrated legally, although I was too young to know for sure. But regardless, we definitely occupied the lowest social rung human beings could cling to in these United States. While I'm fairly certain we weren't an illegal immigrant family, we certainly lived like one—including having a fierce distrust of the authorities and the banking system. Of this part, I am quite clear; I missed way too much school in order to work in the fields. Both to make ends meet for my family and out of fear of my father.

Because of things I suffered (which I'll probably reveal over the course of this story, when my courage has gotten some practice) I was removed from my birth family as a young teenager and lost touch with them.

And when my third foster family brought me to Las Vegas, I thought I had died and washed up on the shores of Paradise. Las Vegas shone to me then like a beacon of hope and opportunity as bright as the neon along its famed Strip. Back then, any future that involved being indoors and air-conditioned, standing up straight and not being paid by the filled bushel basket, represented a giant leap forward.

Hours after my eighteenth birthday, I left the constant abuse of my so-called foster family and struck out on my own. My first boyfriend, a sleek blackjack dealer named Darryl and the first truly kind man I had ever known, quickly landed me a waitressing job working the graveyard shift in the casino cocktail lounge where he dealt cards.

Yes, again, my real career began in a bar as a cocktail waitress. I had never even drunk alcohol before then.

The job wasn't on the Strip but on the outskirts of town, in one of those casinos that tried to lure travelers in before they saw the Strip's glitz and glamour. Working along Las Vegas Boulevard represented a higher rung in the pecking order, which I had yet to achieve. But that was okay with me.

I was young, had my energy, and knew how to work. Compared to my lost birth family, or even those foster families, I was in the proverbial tall cotton.

Darryl didn't last. Neither did Leon. Or Patrick. I was seemingly cursed with the ability to attract men. A few good men, more bad men, even some married men—just *men*! I was told so often that I was beautiful that I came to believe it was just another lie. Another come-on.

Until much later in life, when one man caused me to believe it was actually true.

But the job itself lasted. And I survived, out on my own. One day I spotted an open, good-looking face scrutinizing our microbrew list. That face looked up as I approached, and as our gazes locked, so did our destinies.

He brought me home to meet his widowed mother to whom he was unusually devoted. And also his brother, Mel, who was his closest friend in the world. Lonnie became my husband, and they became my family. I finally belonged, and it was wonderful.

Then, only three years later, Mel's vibrant face had cruelly morphed into the death mask now lying next to me, and Lonnie was a crushed soul in a bar somewhere, unable to face either his dying brother, his heartbroken mother, or his disappointed wife.

I looked away, unable to bear the sight on the hospital pillow. Just a few feet away, sitting in the chair beside him, was his mother, Naomi, trying to read a novel. Anytime Mel's wife, Orpah, (yes, that really was her name) vacated that spot, Naomi would occupy it in seconds. Whether Orpah only left for a quick bathroom break or an afternoon shift of unavoidable work, as was the case at that moment, no sliver of time was too short for Naomi to be nearer her son. Orpah would never see her make her way into it, only scurry out as soon as she returned, always with a kind apology. Naomi would then retake her seat and resume what she had done almost nonstop during her long years of isolation in that Vegas apartment—reading voraciously. Naomi was such a prolific reader that both Orpah and I were shocked to learn, not long after meeting her, that the well-spoken Naomi was actually an eighth-grade dropout who had sharpened her mind through the consumption of thousands of library books over the years.

Naomi was losing a son and Orpah was losing a husband. Both of them knew that the two dreadful experiences were only inches apart in the realm of emotional agony. Naomi was doubly aware of this because, not so many years before, she had lost her own husband.

That's right. The wasted body now before her was the next-to-last member of a once-thriving family, including her good-looking husband and a pair of strapping sons—boys she once shook her head at with the bemused smile of a mother barely concealing her pride in the energy and invincibility of *her men.*

Her Eli had passed on just three years before, slumped forward of a heart attack at the massive Hotel Bellagio check-in counter where he had been employed for going on six years. He had worked his way into management, only to die before enjoying the benefits.

Both Lonnie and his brother, Mel, were in construction, helping support themselves and their mother after their father's death. The two brothers were so close they seemed to function as a single unit. If you knew one, you knew the other. That's why my marriage to Lonnie also led to a warm friendship with Mel. In fact, the four of us often went out together, preferring one another's company to all others.

But today, with the liver disease ravaging his brother, Lonnie remained at work on the girders, desperately trying to keep the family afloat. Naomi had become too fragile and emotionally scattered to work. During the day, Lonnie had been too concerned with earning a wage to ask for time off to see his brother in the hospital. Sometimes it seemed he and I merely passed like the proverbial ships in the night, scarcely aware of each other or our marriage any longer.

And yet I knew Lonnie loved me intensely. So intense was that love that I was hardly aware of the pain from my past. He had healed so much with his unwavering affection. Lonnie was a good man with bad faults and an occasional penchant for bad decisions, yet I adored him for the way he loved me. That's one thing I learned from this family. How to love while in pain.

Now Lonnie was drowning in a new pain of his own, and I felt powerless to help him. He could barely make himself look at the wasted shell of a man who was his beloved brother.

Admittedly, Mel was hard to look at by this point. And hard to listen to as well. Toxins had settled into his brain and erupted into full-blown delirium, and his rants had become nearly unbearable. Hepatitis in its last stages is relentless.

Even now, Mel's withered hands reached out and weakly grasped the nurse's as she tried to take his pulse. "What's the frequency, Kenneth?" he muttered at her with the tiniest grimace of a smile. "Kenneth, what's the frequency?"

I couldn't help but grin at his words. After all, few people would remember them as the phrase of CBS anchorman Dan Rather, who, years before in Manhattan, claimed an attacker had growled the phrase at him as he was being mugged. Not long after that, the rock group R.E.M. had mockingly recorded a song with the words as its title and main lyric. It was just the kind of random trivia Mel had been summoning from the dregs of his memory for days now.

I was always amazed by both brothers' ability to remember the minutiae of life. Because they had spent their early years without pop culture, Mel and Lonnie later had developed an excessive admiration for its history. They became fanatical movie buffs. Trivia wizards. Music savants. Their favorite game was peppering their family talk with pop-culture factoids, a foreign language that Orpah and I learned ourselves over time. Naomi, however, from a different place and era, had never been interested enough to master it.

Now Mel's fevered brain muttered one pop-trivia reference after another.

The nurse gently placed Mel's wrist on his stomach and gave me a somber look.

"Any preferences for last rites?" she asked softly.

I glanced over at Naomi. Her eyes were wide open but unfocused.

"No, he's not . . . religious," I said, my voice also low. "Is the end really that close?"

The nurse shrugged, but her expression held genuine care. "It's impossible to say with hepatitis. He could slip further into the coma and stay there for weeks. I couldn't make that call, and of course, I shouldn't, not being the doctor. But his vital signs have gotten much worse, and rapidly. His blood pressure has dropped pretty dramatically. His kidneys are now completely shut down and his urine has turned brown. And his breathing. . . ?" Her voice faded, yet her insinuation seemed to shout at me.

I paused, listened, and realized I'd been tuning out something. It was a soft, steady rattling sound, floating out from between his lips whenever his chest moved. I had been so focused on measuring the ever-lengthening intervals between his breaths, wondering if each one was the last, then sighing in gratitude with each one, that I hadn't noticed it.

With a quick, unexpected hand on my shoulder, the nurse was gone.

Naomi turned to me, her face set.

"Better call Orpah right away," she said, her voice shaky.

Strangely, the directive brought me back to the first time I'd heard that odd name, shortly after meeting Lonnie.

Several things you must understand about Orpah.

First of all, in case you're wondering, I've been spelling her name correctly. It seems her mother, who hailed from someplace like Ethiopia or Somalia, had met and married a visiting Global Aid relief worker The husband's idealistic rescue of a beautiful, ebony-skinned refugee had eventually clashed with the hard reality of multicultural marriages. The union didn't last long—just long enough to produce a child. She wanted to name her daughter Oprah after the famous African-American talk show host with whom she was enamored, and whose daily program had helped tutor her rudimentary English.

But when the baby was born, the woman, still befuddled by equal parts epidural, sleep deprivation, and poor English, had transposed the letters on the birth certificate and been too distracted afterward to return and correct her mistake. Her mother continued to call her Oprah, but school and society called her Orpah, as it was spelled. I guess you can tell which part of her life had the most lasting impact.

Orpah was a stunning example of human beauty, and I envied her quite openly and vocally. Being half Caucasian and half African, she had the creamiest coffee-colored skin and long curly black hair tumbling down a fit, six-foot-two frame seemingly composed mostly of long slender legs. Orpah turned heads even along the Las Vegas Strip, which is where she made her living—as an exotic dancer at the Olympic Gardens cabaret.

I never looked down on her for that. As they say, what happens in Vegas stays in Vegas, at least until this story. Residents of Las Vegas quickly learn an unspoken law of never judging anyone for their choice of profession. If you're going to do that, better to move somewhere more righteous.

Secondly, I'd admitted to myself not long after meeting Orpah that I probably would have been tempted to take up the profession myself, if only I'd had legs "up to here." Don't get me wrong; I'd gotten my share of looks along the Boulevard, and good genes are probably the most valuable inheritance my Hispanic family ever bestowed on me. (Funny, but no one here or in Vegas ever thought I looked Hispanic, and I worked hard to lose the residual accent.) But merely having good-looking bronze skin didn't get you onto the casino stages. Only bona fide genetic mutations have the looks *and* the legs for that kind of work.

Her husband, Mel, had no problem with her occupation. Actually, that is where he first met her. Naomi, however, could never bring herself to say the word *topless*; in fact, she hardly ever mentioned that her daughter-in-law was a dancer. Only that she "worked in a nightclub." But Naomi loved "O," our private name for Orpah, just the same.

Third, and most important, Orpah was my best friend. By marrying brothers, it seemed we'd both washed up on the troubled shores of the Yoder family with baggage that, while quite contrasting, proved equally messy to unpack. But unpack it, Naomi most certainly did—in both of our cases. Unlikely though it might have seemed, we each wound up finding a haven there. Sometimes it was abundantly clear that Naomi was that *haven* more than her two hapless boys. But neither of us was staring gift horses in the mouth.

By then, the name Orpah sounded as ordinary and proper as any I could think of. But she was also the last person I wanted to call, with this message, on this day.

"Make sure Lonnie gets here soon too," Naomi added.

"Orpah's show ends in five minutes," I answered. "And Lonnie isn't answering his phone. Naomi, I'm afraid he's off at a bar somewhere."

"Well, you'll have to find him. He would never forgive himself, not being here for—for his brother's last moments."

"Naomi, you know I can't drive."

Although I had survived my years in Vegas relatively intact, I did struggle against an intermittent problem with drinking. That struggle had resulted in several DUIs and a recent suspension of my driver's license. As a result, Naomi had driven me to the hospital in her old Chevy Impala.

"I know you're not supposed to drive," Naomi insisted with a little shake of her head. "But could you please make an exception? We can't let my two boys miss their last words to each other."

"If I get caught, I go to jail," I said, shaking my own head.

"Please. I'd go myself, if it didn't take me away from him." She was clutching his hand with both of hers like she'd never let go.

Finally, I nodded my agreement. I rose from my chair, leaned over and grasped Mel's other hand.

Looking into his face at that point was more difficult than ever. Every feature that had once made his face appealing was now either swollen grotesquely or turned some foul, unnatural color. Thank God the rest of his body was covered by blankets, for his stomach was now bloated the size of several basketballs. Just looking into those orange-colored eyes swimming in withered, discolored skin made me want to scream, be sick, and strike someone—all at the same time.

"Mel, can you hear me?" I half whispered. "I'm going to

go now and bring back Lonnie. Okay? Will you try to hang in there until I return?"

His pupils turned in my direction, and he seemed to smile.

I lifted my head and risked a look into Naomi's eyes and saw something there which further broke my heart in pieces.

Four miles away, sitting in one of the grim, dimly lit bars that catered to working-class Vegas locals, Lonnie picked up his cell phone, saw the vibration was me, calling for the fourth time, and dropped it back on the table. The shaking caused it to skitter across the surface and nearly fall off. He slapped the phone with his hand and held it there, muffling the sound, and closed his eyes in anguish.

The sinking feeling in his insides told him all he could bear to know. His brother was losing the battle.

He raised a callused index finger to a nearby waitress. The only way he would reenter that nasty hospital room, he told me when I found him, was with a lot more booze in him.

CHAPTER 2

When I found him a half hour later, Lonnie was still at the bar, his mission largely accomplished. He'd added two more whiskey sours in quick succession to an already substantial base of alcohol consumption when I walked in and saw him with his head in his hands, staring ahead at nothing more than the neon light flashing in his face.

"You have to come now," I said, sitting down beside him and laying my hand on his arm. "There's isn't a minute to spare."

"Will he even hear me?" he asked morosely. "Will he even know I'm there?"

"He knew I was there when I left," I replied. "Besides, that's not the point. Like your mother said, you just need to be there. If you miss this moment, you'll regret it for the rest of your life."

He sighed deeply, gave his glass one last longing look, and rose unsteadily to his feet.

"All right, honey. Let's go."

Even drunk he was still my good-looking hero. I knew what was really inside Lonnie. The same inner something that characterized Naomi. They were *good people*. Even with his flaws, Lonnie was a good man.

When we reached the parking lot, he took a look at the classic two-door 1976 Chevy Impala, with its monstrous, gas-guzzling 454 engine. The car had good lines; it just needed a ton of work. His dad had kept it for sentimental reasons. His mom had lost the "good car" to creditors and had been forced to drive this old relic from their past.

But Lonnie turned away for his own car, his pride and joy: a meticulously restored 1967 Mustang. The old Impala, his father's decrepit onetime beauty, embodied all the disappointment he'd felt about his dad. The Mustang, however, represented everything hopeful and enthusiastic in Lonnie. Although he had always lamented not buying a 1964, the earliest and most prized of all pony cars, he nevertheless poured his heart, most of his time, and a good chunk of his spare money into his "'Stang."

I knew that getting him to relinquish the wheel of the Mustang would be a fight. He had let me drive it only once before, and then had pestered me with so many instructions and objections that I had vowed never to touch the steering wheel again.

"Look. I'm not the one with the suspended license and the DUIs," he argued, standing beside the door with the keys held away from my outstretched hand.

And it was true; even though Lonnie was a far worse drinker than I, and a far less careful driver, he had somehow managed through sheer cunning and concentration to avoid getting caught during any of his numerous drunk-driving episodes. I, on the other hand, seemed to attract a police car even thinking of driving impaired.

"That may be true," I told him, "but right now you are hammered. I'll tell you what. Let's spring for a cab. How's that?"

Swaying, he shrugged and did not object.

What we didn't know was that several things were occurring simultaneously in the once-happening, now decrepit, downtown block. The area was frequented by the locals for its cheap prices but avoided by tourists for its well-deserved tough reputation. First of all, police cars and ambulances were everywhere. The evening, as so often happened in Vegas, had slipped out of hand. Secondly, as a result, taxis were no longer running to this block. Things were just too dicey, and I didn't blame them. We waited and waited for a cab over several long minutes.

Finally, Lonnie, drunk and turning belligerent, said "Forget it." He would drive his car to see his brother, not wait around to get mugged and have his precious vintage Mustang stripped bare in this sewer of a neighborhood. I argued, then pleaded with him not to drive. But in the end, only one alternative presented itself. I launched myself through the driver's door, shoved him aside, and started the engine myself.

A block later, Lonnie and I began to fight over the best route to Interstate 15. Still drunk and in a hostile frame of mind, he proceeded to show me the way by jerking the steering wheel from my hands, thirty degrees hard to the right.

"Lonnie! Please let go!" I remember screaming at him.

But he did not relent. Instead, he pulled harder.

I remember little else.

I barely recall an odd hovering sensation when the wheels became airborne, launched by the lip of the sidewalk. Then some sort of horrible sound.

And darkness.

I awoke on a bed, with a bright light close to my eyes and a nurse's face hovering right beside it. The face turned and another appeared. That of a middle-aged man, wearing a clerical collar.

"Mrs. Yoder, can you hear me?"

I formed some kind of a primal groan.

"I'm so sorry to have to tell you this now. But you've been in a very serious accident. You are hurt, but not severely. Your husband's wounds, on the other hand, were far more severe. The staff here labored very hard to revive him, but they were not successful. Mrs. Yoder, your husband has passed away."

I felt the information assault my skin more than enter my ears, like the caustic drumming of a summer sandstorm. For an instant, the words remained aflutter somewhere outside of me, beyond my thought patterns, unwelcome but unprocessed.

I remember shaking my head without much cause or intent. Just to feel my muscles move, to do something purposeful in the face of those last words.

"Mrs. Yoder, can you hear me?" came a voice from some foreign, echoing place.

"I heard you. . . ." My words were autonomous, free from my conscious control and therefore strangely frightening. "I don't know what—why you'd say something like that now. It's not right. Where am I?"

"I am so very sorry, Mrs. Yoder," he said in a practiced tone, ignoring the obvious response. "Would you like for me to pray with you? Or just stay awhile?"

The cruelty of it threatened to steal the breath from my lungs. Truly, for a moment, I either could not complete the reflex or had actually forgotten how to suck air into my throat.

"I'd like to be alone now," I finally managed.

"I understand. If there is anything I can do for you during your stay, please have the nurses call me. I'm here."

My next visitors were the police. It turns out Lonnie's fist was still clenched around the steering wheel when they'd found us, so my faltering account of the final moments was believed. Besides, my blood alcohol level was bone-dry, while his was twice the legal limit. It seemed everyone would prove sympathetic about my dilemma—whether to let a drunk husband drive or defy my suspension. Yet the fact remained that, at least hypothetically, if I had calmed Lonnie down and persuaded him to stay put, we could have waited for a cab or even asked the bar for assistance.

But rather than haul me off to jail, the officers expressed their sympathy. Still, I could read the writing on the wall. When my court date would come around three weeks later, I'd be lucky to escape with a lengthened suspension. I might have my license revoked permanently. I could even go to jail after all—which, while it paled in comparison to my loss, didn't exactly rank as my ideal place to grieve.

CHAPTER 3

I found out later from Naomi that Orpah had arrived promptly from her job, smelling of cigarette smoke and perfume. She spent several hours with Naomi, watching as Mel's body began shutting down. His breathing became shallow and unsteady, with the awful interval between breaths growing longer now. His fingers were stiff and cold to the touch, developing a bluish-purple tinge.

At one point, the regular nurse was assisted by two others, who stood against the back wall, appearing uneasy and wearing somber expressions. Their hovering presence seemed the only official acknowledgment of the gravity of what was taking place in the room.

With anxious eyes Naomi looked up from her son's side.

"Where is Ruth?" she asked no one in particular.

Orpah shrugged. Not only did she have no idea, but in her emotional fog she'd temporarily forgotten about my leaving the hospital.

The regular nurse shook her head. Orpah interpreted the reply as just another sign of the grim moment upon them. But then she noticed the woman was staring straight at her. Meeting her gaze, she saw that the nurse continued shaking her head at her, then toward the door. It then occurred to Orpah that she was signaling for them to meet outside the room.

Feigning weariness and a need for a break, Orpah followed her into the hallway. Only a few yards behind the nurse stood a man in dark clothes, a clerical collar about his neck. Orpah became confused.

"It's about your brother-in-law," the nurse whispered. "Lonnie?"

"Yes," Orpah said. "That's my brother-in-law. Mel's brother."

"I'm so sorry to have to tell you this, but . . . we just got word that he's died."

For a moment Orpah just stood there, dazed. She pointed back to the room and said, "No, he's still alive."

The nurse shook her head again. "No, not Mel. Lonnie. Lonnie has passed away. I need you to be strong for your mother-in-law," the nurse added. "She's facing a terrible blow losing both her sons like this."

"What?" Orpah stammered.

The nurse leaned in, her eyes more focused now. "Apparently your sister-in-law, Ruth, tried to drive her husband over here, but he was impaired and caused them to have a serious traffic accident in which he was killed. Please, would you come and speak to Ruth? She doesn't know what to say to your mother-in-law."

Orpah appeared, her face smeared with tears, walked over and knelt by my bed.

"Is it true?" she asked.

We embraced each other, both of us in a state of shock.

"He's gone," I found myself saying over and over again. I wondered if my mouth would ever be capable of forming another sentence. Yet I couldn't help it; my mind seemed stuck on the phrase and all that it meant.

"Piling on," I whispered at last into her cigarette-smelling hair.

"What?" she asked, pulling back.

"Piling on. You know, like in football. Lonnie was always trying to teach me the rules. When the ball carrier's already been tackled and a couple of defenders jump on top of him for no reason—just because he's vulnerable, just because they can—they call it 'piling on.' It's a serious penalty."

"So?"

"Well, that's how this feels. Like life, or God, is just piling it on. It's too much. Too much. We're already down. He should just quit. Leave us alone."

She nodded.

"I don't know how I'm going to tell Naomi," I continued weakly.

"Don't tell her. Let one of the nurses, or that priest," she said, pointing to the figure in the clerical collar who had escorted her to my room.

The notion seemed immediately wrong. I shook my head. "I don't think so. She doesn't know them. She knows you and me. We're family."

"But it's a cruel thing to ask of you," she said. "You shouldn't have to do it."

"I know," I said, "but still, it has to be done. And better that the news comes from one of us than from them."

"Nonsense," she said. "You just lost your husband, and you're hurt besides. Let the chaplain do his job."

We should have both been beside ourselves with grief, disrupting that entire wing of the hospital, yet here we were calmly discussing how to inform Naomi of Lonnie's unexpected, untimely death. That gives you some hint of how much we both loved Naomi. She'd survived the death of her husband, Eli. She had steeled herself to lose Mel that day to hepatitis. But how could we tell her about Lonnie's death? I was the widow, part of me observed; I should be the one being consoled. Why then did I feel like this?

"No, I can't do that to her." I looked at the chaplain. "I'm going to tell her," I told him. "You can come along if you like. You can help by getting the nurses prepared. I don't know how she'll survive it."

I rose slowly. My right shoulder was bandaged; I had several bruises there and also on my right hand. We walked side-by-side to Mel's room.

As I entered, Naomi didn't look away from Mel and failed to notice my bandages.

I can't tell you how much I hated knowing what I knew. It hung there in my mind like some hateful little pebble, one I would have given anything to reach in, grab it, and throw it out through a window—far, far away. Finally Naomi looked up, and her face fell at the sight of the chaplain behind me. It occurred to me that she thought this was about Mel, that the priest's presence meant the end for her son lying in the bed. The fact that I knew otherwise brought on a sudden feeling of nausea, threatening to overwhelm me.

Instead of resuming my spot on the other side of Mel, I walked over to her and knelt down.

"There's something I need to tell you," I said, my voice sounding strange and unfamiliar.

"I know," she answered, obviously thinking I meant Mel was about to pass on.

"No, Naomi, you don't," I said.

"Yes, I do," she sobbed.

I reached in and forced my arms around her sides, then slid my chin over her shoulder toward her ear.

"It's about Lonnie," I whispered, "and the reason he's not here. The reason I'm all bandaged up like this."

She tried to pull back, to move away from me and read my face. But I wouldn't let her. I didn't want her to see my eyes, and I needed my arms right there under hers.

"No."

"Naomi, I don't have the words to tell you this. . . ."

"No!"

"Lonnie and I had an accident on the way back to the hospital. He's gone. I'm so sorry. . . ."

There. I'd somehow formed the words and forced the air out over them. At least I was fairly sure I had.

Instead of going limp like I thought she would, she did the opposite. She stiffened and began quivering. I feared some kind of seizure might overtake her, until I pulled back and saw her mouth open wide in a silent scream.

Evidently, as she took in the knowledge of Lonnie's death, confirmed by my bandages, while still in my arms she looked down at Mel only to see his chest no longer moving. Mel had just died. Within seconds the machine's incessant beep agreed with what Naomi's eyes and heart had told her. I don't think either the medical or clergy staff present had ever experienced such a cataclysmic collision of grief as what took place in that room. In that instant, everybody's eyes filled with tears.

CHAPTER 4

![70]

Often in families at a time of death there emerges a strong one, someone who bears the brunt of making the arrangements and, despite intense pain, muddles through the indignities of planning the things that have to be planned.

We didn't have such a person. There was no strong one among we three widows—we were hardly able to sign our own names, let alone focus on planning a memorial service or considering carefully a burial contract. But because Naomi was the eldest, with three years' experience as a widow, she emerged by default, even if she was as dazed and shell-shocked as Orpah and me.

So we did nothing but let the day carry us through. It was a small double funeral. Strangely, the event closely resembled Eli's three years before—same funeral home and chapel, including many of the same stricken faces in attendance. Only this time there were two caskets and two widows. Some of the mourners still wore their Bellagio uniforms. They were old pals of Eli's, and their presence seemed to buoy Naomi somewhat. Some of my friends from the casino nightclub were there, as well as a group of construction workers, uncomfortable in their suits, as they were more accustomed to blue jeans. While I didn't know their faces, when they passed by to offer condolences, some of the names sounded familiar.

Lonnie's co-workers were there. Mel's co-workers, too. Their drinking buddies and construction-crew friends. Orpah's friends, with their fake eyelashes and French manicures, looked out of place beside the construction workers in ill-fitting suits. I didn't know whether to be annoyed or comforted. In the end, I followed Naomi's lead and simply repeated, "Thank you for coming."

The other thing that struck me as strange was, for a second time, the absence of any of Naomi's family. We had never met any of them; it was as though they didn't exist.

I remember seeing Mel's face before they closed the casket and thinking that, for once, funeral-home makeup had improved someone's features. Not his real features, mind you, but the horrific mask his face had sunk to in the end.

A nervous teenage girl provided by the funeral home sang a cheesy song about heaven. I remember thinking that she had probably come to sing in the shows but had yet to get her hoped-for big break. A man in a sharp navy suit stood and read some statistics I had never heard before.

"Leonard Gene Yoder, born August 31, 1973, in Bethlehem, Pennsylvania ... Melvin Hugh Yoder, born March 19, 1975, in Bethlehem, Pennsylvania ..."

The words made me frown and glance over Orpah's way. *Bethlehem, Pennsylvania?* Lonnie had never mentioned that to me. All I'd ever heard Lonnie speak of his past, before coming to Las Vegas, was of Moab, Utah. He described it breathlessly, the way a young man talks of his most cherished adventures—campouts on the edge of the world, mountain biking through a place named Slickrock he compared to heaven, and something about running "over the Arches" by moonlight.

But before that, there was only the cryptic phrase, "back East." *"We're from back East."* Followed by an unsettled silence. Naomi was always incredibly kind, but she also had her secrets, her dark silences. She never elaborated on the phrase's meaning, and I never probed.

It wasn't important; it was just the past. Everybody in Vegas had a past. What we had then was the loving present and the future. It was all I needed from Lonnie.

Other than that, I remember little more of the service.

But we didn't get around to burying our husbands for another six months.

I know it sounds terrible that we waited so long—as though three widows sat around carelessly avoiding the inevitable. But for the first three weeks after the funeral, we were too numb to do anything but stumble through our work, then aim ourselves back to Naomi's apartment at the end of our shifts. Before the first week was out, Orpah and I had given up our own apartments and moved in with her. Officially, we were doing so to help with rent, as Naomi had finally depleted the dregs of Eli's $10,000 life insurance policy from the Bellagio. The truth was, nights spent on Naomi's couch and on a narrow old hospital bed had led to an inability, on both Orpah's and my part, to face going home alone.

Not too long afterward, her shifting fortunes compelled Naomi to put her lease in Orpah's name. I had tried to include my own name on the contract, but the credit check had uncovered my driving violations and rejected me. Orpah, with her steady job and decent income, was a much better candidate.

Somewhere during that time—my memory of those painful weeks is as tattered as were my emotions—I appeared for my court date. Fighting back tears and exhaustion, I pleaded with the judge to consider the extraordinary reasons why I had taken the wheel the day of Lonnie's death. Thankfully, he considered this and let me off with only a further suspension of my driving license and a stern warning against driving during the following six months.

Also at that time, I experienced a devastating setback regarding Lonnie's life insurance, or lack thereof. Naomi had long before urged her two sons to sign up for policies. Mel had been promptly rejected due to the detection of a blood-borne infection that turned out to be the early stages of hepatitis. Of Lonnie's policy, Naomi remembered little and I recalled even less. I had signed the papers, then foolishly left it to him to complete the task.

Somewhere during the fifth month after his death, when cash woes had long since prevented us from giving our men a proper burial, I dug up Lonnie's unsigned, unexecuted life insurance papers. He had promised to take care of it, but being the irresponsible, though well-meaning, man that he was, he'd failed to turn in his forms and finish the process. I'm sure his brother's painful outcome had played a role. But regardless of this, his failure now left me at a standstill financially, barely able to cover our bills, let alone move out of Naomi's house after the proper mourning period. This extended even to my own emotions. I felt unable to budge from my ice cube of grief and loss.

To add further injury, Orpah and I now had no idea how to properly dispose of our husbands' remains.

Then midway through the sixth month Naomi had an idea.

We would take a road trip. It would be good for us.

It was one of those days, from its very first moment. You've heard the expression "change is in the air"? That morning, I opened my eyes and smelled change with my first waking breath. And it wasn't just the emotionally charged trip I knew the day would bring either. No, this was deeper, more subtle than just *knowing*. It was a stirring deep inside me, a charged quality to the light, to the dance of thoughts and feelings within. Something so subtle I didn't fully notice it for several hours.

You might say it was the change in seasons. Generations of my family's living in touch with the soil had left its imprint on me. Although you don't really get four seasons in Vegas, the calendar said it was the first day of autumn. And having been raised in the fields of the West, I was more attuned to such changes than most Vegas folks. I may not have known the extreme temperature changes I know now, but I knew more than most desert dwellers did. I seemed to have that temperature trigger programmed into my bones. I felt the residue of nighttime chill on my skin, sensed the tiniest snap in the air, the smell of vegetation edging beyond ripe. I felt it on an almost subliminal level, and it never failed to tell me that autumn was upon us.

The day threw itself upon me just before dawn, with a maddening screech I had never heard before—a sadistic, seventies-vintage alarm clock Naomi had dug out to help us catch an early start. After all, there was driving to be done.

I rolled over and parted my eyelids just enough to see darkness mercifully cloaking the apartment's dingy, cramped excuse for a living room. As I mentioned already, during the final stages of Mel's long deathwatch, both Orpah and I had taken up residence with Naomi. Lonnie wasn't around that much, and Naomi was lonely and needed help getting to the hospital. After Mel's death, Orpah went home only once that I know of, to gather her things. Grief, it seemed, had caused the three of us to gravitate toward each other and form a new family. The apartment's tiny size only magnified our sense of living in a cocoon, sheltered from a vindictive, uncaring world.

Through the window frame I saw more gloom. It was awfully early.

Orpah and I said nothing as we rose. I'm not sure we even made eye contact, although in that tiny living room we were probably within an arm's length of each other, she on the couch and me on the hospital bed. We silently stumbled to our feet and, without turning on any lights, pulled on our best clothes—for Vegas girls. Actually the dresses we wore were gaudily inappropriate for the task at hand. But given what we were about to do that day, it seemed the least we could do was dress up.

Then we stepped outside, carefully cradling, like freshly poured hot Starbucks venti lattes, the uber-cheap urns containing our husbands' ashes. In fact, these were no urns at all.

Now let me explain. Our beloveds' ashes, since we weren't planning on displaying them anywhere, and since all of us were broke, rested inside tall, rubber-banded styrofoam cups. The humble containers reminded me of the big white cups of night crawlers my papa and my uncle Julio would use years ago when heading out to *las playas* to fish for carp.

I know. I *know*. I tried not to think about it. But anything fancier and we wouldn't have been able to afford even the cremations.

The biggest problem the cups presented, as Orpah and I

would soon discover, was the difficulty of transporting them with any dignity. After all, this was styrofoam. Papa and Julio were notorious for tossing their cups into the coolers along with their bottles of Tecate, dirty ice and all.

Orpah was juggling her cup comically while struggling to flick her Zippo and light the day's first cigarette. Naomi didn't allow smoking in her car, thirty-year-old wreck or not. Just as the cup began a disastrous plunge, I chuckled inappropriately and grabbed the styrofoam resting place of my brother-in-law clean out of midair.

Somehow, balancing a pair of cremated corpses in each hand and choking on the tragic but comic irony of it all, I felt myself transported back to every bad movie and TV show I'd seen portray the handling of human ashes. You know, where someone invariably winds up flicking cigarette butts or visiting some crass indignity onto the cremains of a loved one. I've always considered that a pretty feeble attempt at comedy, bent on ramming down my throat the notion that at heart, human beings are little more than glorified dirt because of the similarity between the carbon in our bodies and the burnt ends of dried tobacco. That's a connection I was never willing to buy.

As an ex-semi-migrant farmworker, I've worked with both dirt and people, and I know the difference.

All the same, it struck me that I seemed to be living out one of those absurd plotlines.

Just then, weighing these things, I felt a wave of unbearable sadness come over me. The reality of what we were about to do hit me full force.

CHAPTER 5

70

I glanced around, trying to distract my emotions with an inventory of my surroundings, but Vegas at such an hour held no solace, no unexpected wonders. Even that early, freeway noise roared from somewhere nearby, which struck me as depressing. The air on my cheeks and hands felt cooler than I remembered—although the last time I had been outdoors at such a time was anyone's guess. My recent cocktail-waitress work schedule kept me out very late, until my lack of transportation and hospital vigils with Naomi had forced me to quit. But Vegas never sleeps. The sky overhead consisted of that mysterious shade between black and blue that's nearly impossible, at least in Vegas, to distinguish between half-light and the reflection of neon glare.

I inhaled deeply, trying again to identify what was different in the air. I smelled car exhaust, a trace of pollen, and honest-to-goodness woodsmoke. It was then that I was reminded it was fall. For some reason, the smell of burning triggered it, filling me with a sense of something quiet and potent. With autumn came the powerful feeling that time was growing short, that beauty was fleeting, and the year dwindling away.

Change.

But I didn't want to turn my thoughts in that direction. Not yet. Instead, I turned back to Orpah, and the sight of her provided the distraction I'd been looking for. It occurred to me then—even as she stood there shivering in that iridescent blue strapless number, puffing on a cigarette as if her life depended on it—that she'd never looked more beautiful.

Finally, with her cigarette well under way, I handed Orpah back her husband with as much gravity as I could muster. Then I reached up and rested my hand on her shoulder. A caring touch, motivated more by my own need than anything I sensed in her.

This was going to be harder than I thought. I could already tell.

At last Naomi appeared in the doorway—at fifty-five she was too young to look so old. An aging, slightly stooped woman with graying hair, shuffling pathetically, her eyes more bleary and pain filled than ever before. I took one look at her and sighed in sympathy. Her face read like a study in what tough times could wreak on a woman's beauty, on her sense of self and worth.

Strangely, no single feature of hers betrayed those ravages in itself. Yet, taken as a whole, their bruised dishevelment told the unmistakable story of a woman whom life had singled out for harsh treatment.

Naomi glanced at the cups in our hands. She took a shaky breath, shook her head, then turned and gazed out toward the north.

I noticed she was clutching a letter, its envelope torn.

The styrofoam cup dilemma only intensified after we slid onto the Impala's wide bench seat beside Naomi. I started, for just a split second, to reach out and place the remains of my beloved Lonnie in a flimsy, beat-up cup holder hanging from the dashboard. Thankfully I was yanked back to my senses and halted my forward reach.

So what do we do? I asked with a look to Orpah, whose eyes met mine with a similar plea. Do you hold your dead spouse's ashes on your lap for four hundred miles? Stop and ask a fast-food employee for one of those cardboard drink carriers? Wedge the cup between the seat and the door. . . ?

Next thing I knew, I was laughing.

And weeping.

Not faintly. Not hidden. I'm talking *crying*. Real, full-lunged, makeup-smearing, hysterical sobbing.

A nearby echo told me that Orpah had instantly done the same.

"What is it?" Naomi asked, her eyes awash in confusion and fear.

"The cups! The ashes!" I cried.

"What do we do with the things?" Orpah begged, a single hiccup demonstrating how hard she was trying to control her emotions.

Naomi frowned, as though ready to find fault with our reaction, until she glanced at us again and seemed to realize our strange wails mixed with laughter was mostly made up of enormous pain.

We were already on the Interstate, but that did not deter Naomi. A little short for her steering wheel, she strained to check the rearview mirror and then swerved onto the shoulder. After pressing the trunk latch, she stepped out in the face of traffic. It was just now becoming daylight. A semi-truck roared by in a blast of air that assaulted her face. Unblinking, she accepted the cups and walked to the back of the car, then placed each of the containers into a safe hold inside the cavernous trunk.

That was Naomi. When she knew something had to be done, she stoically steeled her features, turned within herself to some calm, quiet place, and did it.

But by the time Naomi returned, her face was streaked with tears.

She silently got back behind the wheel and just minutes later unexpectedly turned off the Interstate, veering toward a destination we all recognized. The sign *Woodlawn Cemetery* towered above row after row of gravestones. We stopped and walked hand-in-hand with her down toward Eli's gravesite. We had known Eli, during the last years of his life, as a kind soul and a loving family man—even though his front-desk schedule at the Bellagio had conspired with our own night-shift careers to keep us little more than friendly strangers. Between Eli's unpredictable hours, his sons' daytime construction jobs, and the nocturnal working hours of his daughters-in-law, only one person stayed in daily touch with everyone—Naomi, the glue that held our delicate family together. Without her, we would have been little more than a collection of missed meals and brief encounters.

On that day, standing there in the cemetery, Naomi shed enough tears for the three of us.

Naomi had brought her family together again, her husband and their two sons. It was a solemn time of good-byes.

Having retrieved the absurd containers from the trunk, one marked on the bottom with a *L*, the other *M*, Naomi set them on the ground facing Eli's gravestone, carefully and silently, as if not to interrupt a father's last precious conversation with his boys.

CHAPTER 6

70

We drove north out of Vegas, and the source of the woodsy smoke smell soon revealed itself. The barren, shrub-dotted hills northwest of town lay veiled in the pall of a wildfire. Up somewhere beyond floated a hazy, ropy column of smoke. The small dots of firefighting helicopters hovered against the vast landscape.

Getting out of the city seemed to flip some kind of internal switch inside us. The oppressive silence that had reigned over us like that cloud in the north began to thin, then dissipate. Our tongues loosened at last.

"I've always had a creepy feeling about this area," Orpah said. "I mean, just look at it out there. It's so completely empty, and yet you have these power lines going off through the mountains toward the middle of nowhere. It's surreal, like something out of *The X-Files*."

I looked, and had to agree with her. The gigantic transmission towers did in fact resemble huge steel monsters striding across a barren land.

"X-Files?" queried Naomi with a frown.

"It's a science fiction show from a few years back," I explained.

Naomi gave an affectionate roll of her eyes. That pop-culture talk again. It seemed now to come up in the conversation in times of great strain more than in times of leisure.

"But I'm not just joking," Orpah protested. "That *is* the direction of Area 51."

"Or at least Nellis," Naomi conceded.

To Las Vegas residents, such talk was no paranoid whimsy. Nellis, the Air Force base that administered Area 51, was located just outside of town. And it was common knowledge that certain Area 51 employees left McCarran Airport every morning on a secret, unmarked flight. Again, I only knew this because of Lonnie, who was an endless source of trivia.

I looked back at greater Las Vegas, sprawled out across a broad, sun-blasted desert valley. Distance had now reduced the metropolis to little more than a sloping grid of intersecting lines punched through the heart by the jagged towers and garish colors of the Strip. Somehow it seemed all out of proportion. Only the Nevada desert could stretch flat as a board for eternities between mountain chains like this, its featureless wastelands like gigantic serving trays, tilted at angles smooth and vast enough to hold an entire city.

It didn't look right. It wasn't natural—but then, that was the whole point of the place.

Seeing it this way, it felt strange to see my life's stage shrunk to such compactness. A city of a million people, contained in a single flick of the eye. There lay the stage of my existence, that of poor Lonnie and my whole sad life's misfit cast of characters, framed within a gray blot as busy and confined as an overdesigned postage stamp.

Then it struck me that I felt nothing. Las Vegas provoked

no more warmth or nostalgia in my breast than my parents' tales of a Mexico I had never seen.

For so long I had measured myself against its daunting reputation. *Can you make it in Vegas? Surviving in Vegas, girl? Up to Vegas? If you can make it in Vegas* . . . Now it stirred not even a flutter inside.

"Orpah's right," I said, peering over my shoulder. "Look back at the city. It doesn't look like a real place, but more like something out of a bad sci-fi movie, don't you think?"

Orpah turned gamely around from her center position on the seat. Naomi, ever the meticulous driver, ventured a glance in the rearview mirror.

"Reminds me of a cartoon," said Naomi.

"A cartoon starring *us*," I said with more than a little bitterness.

"Th-th-th-that's all, folks!" Orpah said, imitating the animated classic.

Then, with a single wide turn in the highway, the whole panorama disappeared. Just like that. And seeing it go left hardly a smudge, no emotional residue, on what remained of my soul. Out of sight, it was truly out of mind.

"Buh-bye," Orpah said, incorrigible. "Leaving Las Vegas, that's us."

"What do you mean?" I asked, suddenly irritated at the timing of yet another pop-culture reference. "You mean the movie with Nicolas Cage?"

"Yeah. We're getting out of town. We're *Leaving* Las Vegas, get it?"

I practically snorted in disgust. "Orpah, did you actually *see* that movie?"

"I think so."

"No, you didn't. If you had, you'd know that leaving Las Vegas is a euphemism."

"A *what*?"

"A euphemism—saying things in a way that makes something really bad sound tame or vague. The only way the Nicolas Cage character actually left Vegas was by committing suicide. He drank himself to death." *Whoops*. I gave Orpah a quick glance when Mel's drink-damaged face flashed into my mind. But she didn't seem to make the connection.

"Really? Is that right?" She thought for a moment. "Man, that's depressing. I guess I didn't see it after all. Fine, then. We're leaving town in the *non*-movie sense. The literal sense."

"And not for good either," I added.

"That's enough, girls," joined Naomi in her motherly way. "I don't want to hear any talk about suicide. Even from a movie. I've had enough of death for a dozen lifetimes."

We both nodded and stared somberly ahead.

"I'll drink to that," Orpah finally blurted, laughing despite herself. When Naomi frowned her disapproval, her half-African daughter-in-law leaned over and squeezed her in a strong, sideways hug. Things ran deep between those two—especially on that subject.

Mel had brought her home, proud to have "snagged" such a beautiful girl even in the environment where he met her, unaware that Orpah was stumbling through her last few weeks of a terrible alcohol detox. Naomi accepted "O" regardless of where she worked; it was personal character she most cared about. She had voiced her disapproval of the two of them living together, offering that they stay with Eli and her—in separate bedrooms. And it was Naomi—while Eli spent most of his time at the Bellagio and Mel spent his hanging steel hundreds of feet above the desert—who held Orpah's head in her lap, cleaned up the vomit, and whispered into her ear the encouragement that would ease her through.

When Orpah had emerged into sobriety as a strong-willed

yet principled young woman, she'd also discovered a deep affection and appreciation for Naomi. Her mother-in-law became the mother Orpah felt she'd never had.

Naomi shook her head with that affectionate chuckle both of us knew so well. "That entertainment talk—it's become almost a separate language with you two. I wonder if you could have a decent conversation if not for MTV and *Entertainment Tonight.*"

We drove that way for hours, awash in conversation that shifted between giddy humor and shades of normalcy, followed by impenetrable sadness.

That's the way we were together. Comfortable. Three wounded women, trying to laugh and travel our way through pain deep enough to float the *Titanic.*

An unlikely trio.

CHAPTER 7

(70)

Nearly as enormous as the landscape unfolding around us was Naomi's decrepit whale of a car with its vast prow for a hood and front bench seat wide enough for a family of five. Neither daughter-in-law had to be relegated to the back seat, although it was just as cavernous. And so we rode, all three in the front, wheeling our grim little party ever eastward.

Orpah and I both offered to drive, knowing the answer we'd receive, but neither of us insisted.

You already know why I was refused. And Orpah—well, if you wanted to leave Las Vegas in the *movie* sense, the suicide sense, the quickest way to do that was to let her behind the wheel of your car. The girl was incapable of following a lane or obeying a traffic law. Applying the brakes was to Orpah a remote curiosity, a choice as arbitrary as turning on your flashers in a rainstorm. Much of my brother-in-law's money had gone for cabs.

So we were stuck with Naomi as our chauffeur, nodding

off every so often, gripping that wide wheel in both fists, and keeping an unwavering four miles per hour below the speed limit.

The Interstate rose through ever-higher mountain ranges until, in a splash of unexpected beauty, it ushered us through a crinkled mountainous pass, leaving Nevada through a rock gateway and heading into Utah and the green valley town of St. George. Orpah and I stared out the windows, incredulous that a city so beautiful in a normal and all-American way, with thick hardwood canopies and countless Mormon church steeples, could exist so close to the cheap tawdriness of Las Vegas.

We left the freeway to fill up the gas tank. Naomi pulled in alongside the last pump in the lane and stopped. I looked back at the car's absurd length, then at her.

"Naomi, you might want to move forward as far as possible. The car's so long, it's blocking the other pumps behind us."

But instead of moving the car, she gently touched her forehead to the steering wheel and shut her eyes.

"What's the matter?" Orpah asked.

For a long time she said nothing. When she finally spoke, she did so without lifting her head.

"One of the men always did this kind of thing for me," she murmured toward the floor. "Life since they passed has been so much more difficult."

She sighed, slid off the seat and into the hot afternoon sun. Orpah and I looked at each other and shrugged. I offered to help, but Naomi declined. Even after I got out for a bathroom break and returned, we still waited in the car for her to finish pumping the gas.

When Naomi returned to her place on the driver's side, Orpah said, "Anybody gonna pop the hood? I mean, whenever we'd go on a long trip, Mel would always take a look under there. Measure the oil. Check the belt."

I had just washed my hands.

Naomi sat as though one more big motion would consume her last drop of energy. I turned to Orpah, now by the window so she'd have more room for her legs. She gave me a sheepish grin and held up her long painted nails. Those nails had cost her good money. And such was the competition at her job that the loss of even one nail could mean Orpah's position on the dance line.

Orpah climbed out and I followed in resignation. Watching Lonnie tinker with his beloved Mustang had left me knowing as much about cars as most women, although lifting this hulk of a hood was sure to be a challenge. Rather than supporting its weight on a flimsy support rod, the steel behemoth before us was held up by its own set of springs. After a few minutes struggling to get the hood raised, I peered under it and gasped at the ancient relic before me.

Its engine was probably three times the size of any motor I'd seen before. A pale sheen of dust made its components hardly recognizable. Nevertheless, I did figure out the places to pull a dipstick and check the oil, also checking the brake and transmission fluids. And I knew enough to *not* unscrew the radiator cap. Everything was surprisingly full, but it was the dust-encrusted belts that concerned me. I could easily picture a tobacco-chewing mechanic taking one look at them and declaring, "No way will you make it a hundred miles, lady."

Yet to my great relief, nothing seemed to be actually broken. I shut the hood with a bang, so loud it made customers inside the shop turn and stare. Then I returned with a mixed verdict—the car might be on its last legs, but for now the legs were holding.

An hour later, where I-15 joined I-70 and split off east

toward Colorado, Orpah's poise finally played out. I had wondered how many hours those long, restless legs would be able to stay folded under the old Chevrolet's dash space, ample though it was. We pulled over at a rest stop and let her sprawl out in the back seat.

By the time the first fits of light snores began drifting up to us, we were headed east again, the landscape changing from a Nevada desert of high, dark ridges brooding over desolate flats into an altogether different world.

If you've ever traveled it, you'd know that Interstate 70 between central Utah and the Colorado line crosses some of the most unearthly terrain in all of North America. Stretches of this country appear almost alien, as if deposited from outer space. The formation layers don't line up right. Their dimensions look all stunted and compressed, more like a dwarfed, bonsai version of desert, with ridgelines seeming to span towering divides, but then at second glance turn out to limp only a couple dozen feet. The stone looks bulbous and strangely colored. The effect of staring out at such a landscape can prove very unsettling, particularly on the surreal journey on which we had embarked.

Naomi, unaccustomed to driving such long hours, was tired, and her nodding was becoming more frequent. Suddenly the horizon turned gray, then quickly black, and soon large drops began slapping the windshield.

On the third occasion of my leaning over to elbow Naomi in the ribs, I noticed the fuel gauge showed us to be in the final quarter of a tank. I tried to picture the last highway sign I'd seen and how far it would be to the next town. I felt the blood leave my face and my stomach clench. The only sign I could picture had read, *Next gas off freeway 104 miles.* Glibly trusting in the seemingly infinite capacity of the huge tank, Naomi had passed it by without a thought. I would later learn that we happened to be traveling the longest stretch on the American Interstate system without any motorist services.

But for us it was too late. We were compelled to sweat out the final miles before Green River. And the vintage Impala did not help. Every turn caused its needle to slide either toward the plenty-left side or, alternately, into the time-to-panic range, depending on the direction. The anxiety had one positive effect. It awoke Naomi from midafternoon sleepiness once and for all. During the miles to follow she was a hawk, constantly moving her eyes between the highway and the fuel gauge.

Our stress only heightened the otherworldly quality of the landscape around us. We were now glued to its every bend, craning our necks for the first sight of Green River and a service station. With the gray sky and rain, the gargoyle-like rock formations, and our efforts to utilize the last of our fuel, the ride proved to be a harrowing one.

Finally, Green River emerged ahead just as we'd dipped into the truly time-to-panic zone. We turned off and coasted into a station where we fed the steel beast, shocked at how few miles our last full tank had allowed us. At last, we sped back on our way.

About a half hour later, Naomi turned off the Interstate onto a state highway, headed due south and away from the unearthly landscape. We made our way through a series of driving thunderstorms and into the embrace of a majestic red-rock wilderness that looked a lot like the Grand Canyon. The exact opposite of the scorching desert route we'd expected.

Despite the gloomy weather, Naomi was a transformed woman as soon as she turned onto that highway. She recognized the road as one she and her family had taken years before, on a long-ago, late-evening drive out to their new home. She straightened in her seat, her eyes bright and animated, her voice sounding clear and strong.

"I wish you could have seen my boys that night," she said with a smile I had not seen in weeks. "They were at the beginning of their teenage years and just bursting with that wild energy that made you wonder if they'd explode any minute. Especially when the moon came out over this road. They saw the mountainsides around them and started to believe their dad's promise that they weren't moving to the middle of the Sahara but rather to one of the biggest outdoor playgrounds in the whole country. I thought Lonnie was going to bounce off that back seat straight through the roof. Every turn gave the two another reason to *ooh* and *aah* and point to something else. The La Sal Mountains off to the south, Canyonlands, the Arches, the Colorado River, all these beautiful overhangs and rock faces. Their career goals changed with every bend. Pro mountain biker, river guide, rock climber, backpacking guide, photographer. Then morning came, and when they walked outside and took a look around them, their breath was taken away. Look." She gestured toward the windshield. "See what I mean?"

I started in surprise. The rain had ended suddenly, and the heavy clouds parted to reveal the perfect turquoise of a waning afternoon sky. A nearly full moon was inching the crown of its disk past a horizon of red stone beneath which a plunging face of black-stained rock lunged straight into the earth.

"It's such a beautiful place," Naomi mused. "The only tiresome thing I found about it was that after a while you start to long for something green to look at. My boys didn't seem to mind, but my eyes became homesick, even if my heart didn't."

"Where exactly are we going?" I asked, suddenly curious. "I mean, besides just 'near Moab and Arches National Park.'

Will we drive through the town?"
   "No, not until afterwards."
   "So are you going to tell us?"
   "We're going to Dead Horse Point."

CHAPTER 8

70

Dead Horse Point truly was the name of it. In fact, it was the name of a Utah state park, which we veered toward from the main highway, driving for twenty miles through a nearly endless series of grandiose tableaus—valleys and river bottoms surrounded by cliffs and red-rock canyons and petrified sand dunes and vast horizons of soaring and intricately wind-carved stone.

After a while of looking out at one tableau after another, I wanted to say, "Okay, I get it. I'm impressed now. The desert is indeed a majestic place." But the desert didn't bother to relent, no matter how saturated my eyes became. The more my sight was flooded with such visual overkill, the more I remembered that this place neither wanted nor needed to impress me of anything. It had no more use for my applause than it did for my presence.

This great show wasn't about *me*. That was an odd feeling. Even bracing somehow.

I closed my eyes for a moment and, while my retinas rested from the excess, it occurred to me that while living in Las Vegas I'd grown used to being the target of everything around me, the artifice and advertising so woven into my surroundings that I could not tell the difference anymore. Worse yet, it no longer even dawned on me to try to distinguish what simply existed from what existed to *sell* me something. I no longer bothered to tell organic reality from the manufactured kind—the billboards, the neon signs and JumboTron screens, the imitation Eiffel Towers and fake New York skylines and pirates' coves, which may provide my eyes a visual spectacle but were actually board-thin façades designed to seize my attention and brand loyalty.

I'd become so comfortable with this role that I hardly knew how to interpret a natural wonder that existed outside of me, free of any intention to seduce me or sell me *anything*. Here was an attraction that didn't covet a single dime from my pocket. A sight that was quite indifferent to my coming or going or my very living or dying. You can't buy a ticket for things like this. Vistas like this simply *exist*—nature just being itself, for its own sake, its own reasons. Geological glory.

As foreign as this notion was, it shot a liberating thrill straight through me. There *was* something beyond me and my existence, something beyond selling and marketing, a reality into which I might enter on *its* terms, not mine. I could, like all the outdoor types who lived in towns like Moab, apply myself to this wilderness, test my strength against its vastness and challenge, and in the process learn to appreciate its beauty as a gift.

For the first time, it dawned on me that there might be something more important than remembering the happy-hour special at the lounge, or pushing another drink on an already inebriated customer.

Tears had now seeped into my eyes, and I wasn't entirely sure why. I had lived long enough to know that stress can cause emotion to spill out at the most random and inopportune times. On that day I was running on a veritable tank load, not to mention the intense grief, fatigue, and strangeness of a long car trip. But I also sensed something else. I had not thought or felt this way for a very long time. Awe and wonder hadn't been a part of me since I was a little girl. And that long-lost little girl was returning just then for a rare appearance.

Maybe, I considered, my Beulah Land of Las Vegas had fulfilled its promise of saving me from a hard life in the fields yet wound up setting me adrift in a different, but no less entrapping, kind of poverty.

I felt a hand on my forearm, turned and saw Naomi's face, smiling warmly.

"You okay, honey?"

I did not know how to put my thoughts into words. I simply looked over at Naomi and nodded.

"I'm all right" was all I could think to say. "Or at least I will be."

"Just wait," she said, bright with anticipation.

After a series of harrowing switchbacks, we pulled up before the most exquisite wonder yet: a promontory dwarfed before a vast gorge lined with ragged, serrated ramparts of stone. Far below, curled along its distant floor several thousand feet down, uncoiled a gray-blue cord of river. Straight ahead into a seeming eternity stretched Canyonlands, a gigantic moonscape of rock faces and sheer sandstone cliffs. Above, the sun wove its way through torn, horizontal cloud banks that glowed so red, you might have sworn the hills were on fire.

Naomi cut the ignition, we cranked down the windows

and just sat there watching while the motor shuddered and cooled with a series of internal knocks and ticks. The cool air—fresh and moist from the recent rain, thick with the scent of juniper and pine, moist earth and moss, and a subtle layer of woodsy aroma I could not place—flowed into the car and met my face.

Eager to escape the Impala for a while, I opened the door and stepped out. The enormity of the vista before me made my body sway and my head swim with a touch of vertigo. I had never seen so far in all my life. The wind and the smells redoubled and engulfed me. My hair began to wave above my shoulders; my thin Vegas dress flew into a frenzy not unlike that of a kite being flapped about by a vigorous gust. I straightened my back, raised high my arms, and felt my body stretch to life.

How small my world had been!

I turned at the sound of footsteps behind me and saw that Orpah had awakened and silently exited the car, still puffy and softened by her slumber. Naomi too walked forward along the far edge of the hood, which in the Impala's case must have been a good ten feet away.

"This place is incredible," Orpah said through an outstretched yawn. "But it looks familiar. You're sure this isn't the Grand Canyon?"

"Dead Horse Point," repeated Naomi firmly.

"Pretty name."

Naomi pointed straight ahead to a cluster of distant platforms worthy of Monument Valley. "That mesa way out there? It's called Island in the Sky."

"What about Moab?"

"That's a few miles from here."

"I'll tell you why it looks familiar," Naomi said. "Especially to you two. This is the spot where they filmed the final moments of *Thelma and Louise*. They drove their Thunderbird off this edge right here."

Orpah and I shared a disbelieving look. Not only was the information intriguing, but surprising because Naomi had just made a pop-culture reference of her own. Some of her sons' knowledge must have rubbed off on her.

I drew back, suddenly seeing the place through a whole different set of eyes. The landscape seemed to visibly shrink as I mentally fit it with my lingering mental image of the movie scene.

"Yeah, I can see it now," I finally said.

"It's sort of common knowledge around here," she said almost apologetically, as though needing to account for her uncharacteristic observation. "I think in the movie it was supposed to be the Grand Canyon."

"Great," Orpah said, her mouth pulled to one side. "The site of the most famous suicide in American film history. Is that why you brought us here? So we could take the Impala for one final joyride?"

"Hush," Naomi said, probably sounding more cross than she intended. "I told you. Enough of that kind of talk."

"Hey," Orpah continued, ignoring her mother-in-law, "it may not be the worst thing ahead of us. I mean, look at us. Three widows with no prospects—no good jobs, no money. We could go out with a bang of our own. Star in our own highlight reel."

I knew Orpah, and I knew she wasn't seriously proposing such a thing—just letting her morbid, latent depression out for a late-afternoon walk.

"I mean it," Naomi warned. "Stop with that business." She would not look at either of us.

"But if not that," I asked, "why then *did* you bring us here?"

"Because this is my favorite place in the world. The place where my family shared its happiest night."

The nature of Naomi's reply, along with the emotion in her voice, stole all the teasing impulse out of Orpah and me. The three of us took up spots along the car's front grille and stared into the abyss ahead.

"So," said Orpah, suddenly animated, "you gonna tell us about it, or are we gonna sit here and imagine the whole thing?"

Naomi shot her a look, sighed deeply, and then paused as if to recall the memory, every detail of it.

"We camped out, right here on this very spot," she began slowly. "All four of us. It was only our second week in Utah, and we were still fresh with that glow you get when you move to a fascinating new place, exploring everything you can. We had no idea what to bring and what was allowed, but we lucked into everything that night. I remember Lonnie disappearing into the bushes. Eli and I smirked at each other, and I assumed he was taking care of some poorly timed personal business, but as it turned out he came back with an armload of firewood and a triumphant grin on his face. He and Eli started the liveliest little campfire you've ever seen while Mel went and found some logs for us to sit on. By the time the sun went down, we'd eaten our dinner, sung 'Kumbaya' a few times, and even told a scary story or two. We fell asleep by the fire, all snug in our sleeping bags. I woke up at about six the next morning, when the predawn glow had lit up the gorge all pink and orange, and Eli looked at me and whispered, with the most contented smile he ever wore, 'Honey, I think we've found it.' And I smiled back because I knew what *it* meant. We'd been on a quest for *it* a very long time.

"That quest had led us all the way out here from Bethlehem, so far from our hometown and our people. My fantasy then was that our life would stretch on forever like that, one great night and one magical dawn after the other. But it never happens that way. That night was the highlight of our lives in Moab. Our highlight as a family. Some families pass on scores of great memories to their kids. But the only memory Mel and Lonnie could ever refer to when they asked, 'Dad, you remember that night when. . . ?' was this one."

The three of us continued staring out over the darkening canyon, and I felt a deep sadness at Naomi's last words.

Though we had questioned Naomi's decision at first, now Orpah and I knew why Dead Horse Point was the right resting place for Lonnie and Mel. They would be together again—scattered to the winds like the free spirits they were.

CHAPTER 9

70

Her tale over, Naomi turned and walked around to the Impala's trunk. She soon returned with a styrofoam cup in each hand. Looking at us, she colored in embarrassment as it became clear she'd forgotten which cup held whom. With the grimmest little hint of a smile, she lifted one of them, looking for the marked initial on its bottom. Then, holding up the one in her right hand, she said, "Mel always was the heavier of the two." She handed that one to Orpah, and handed the other, Lonnie's cup, to me.

"I'm not ready yet," Orpah said in a voice I could barely hear, softened by emotion and carried off by the wind. "Ruth, say something."

"I don't know what to say," I confessed. But my words fell flat. The longer I waited, the more I realized I had to say something. I opened my mouth, determined to fill the moment with a coherent word or two.

"Most speeches people give at times like this put some

kind of happy, philosophical spin on the person's life. You know, as if the loved one finally won the race or seized the prize, or found Nirvana or finished his assignment, or just got called home by the angels. But I think that's a load of—"

Orpah quickly leaned over and elbowed me.

"As I was saying, it's like they've just gone to some great reward and everything's just peachy. I don't see anything like that for Lonnie and Mel. As for their reward or their destination, I think God must be infinitely forgiving, so I have no idea. But I do know this. This kind of ending stinks. It was premature, unnecessary, and incredibly hurtful. The only thing I can truly say is that we loved both of you, Lonnie and Mel. We're all lost without you guys. . . ."

The galling finality of what I had just expressed rose up from somewhere around my midsection and threatened to choke me. I was left with the bitter aftertaste of my words. Lonely. Hoping. Feeling there had to be something better than this.

"How's that, Orpah?"

"That's just fine, Naomi," she said, turning. "Do we need to say some kind of prayer?"

Naomi's face twisted. "You can pray if you want to. But God and I aren't on speaking terms. He gave up on me a long time ago, so I finally gave up on Him. Tell you what—I'd rather say something to my boys."

Naomi reached out and took both cups into her hands. She opened her mouth as if fully prepared to say something, but the breath seemed to have been ripped from her lungs. She just stared at the cups, shook her head faintly. When she spoke at last, she'd closed her eyes and aimed her face skyward.

"Lonnie, Mel, I want you both to know that I remember. Not the last few years and their . . . disappointments. I remember how you two were here. That night. I remember your handsome faces, your endless energy, your great plans that never, even then, seemed to lie beyond your grasp. I remember later, the stories you'd tell me after coming back from some dangerous trip into this very wilderness, and I'd usually thank the Lord I hadn't been there to see it. Most of all, I remember how happy you two made me. Oh, you two made me smile. And laugh. I don't think there ever was a mother more in awe and in love with her two sons. Or one more sorry that . . ."

Her voice broke, and she hung her head with a stifled sob.

She never finished her thought. Instead, she sank to the ground.

Have you ever been part of a moment so terrible, so painful or mortifying or unbearable that you're not convinced you can live through it? Yet at the same time a voice whispers that for good or bad, you've been invited into someone's defining life moment, and so you'd better show it some respect. And then for the rest of your life you're so grateful you kept your feet in place, your mouth shut, and played the role fate had assigned to you. Because whether painful or not, those are the things we truly hang on to at the end of our days.

That's how I felt as I sank to my knees beside Naomi, Orpah doing the same on the other side, and we all three wept together. Then, many minutes later, we slowly helped Naomi back to her feet. At that moment an inner assurance settled within me and gently whispered that, despite my misgivings about such a long road trip to the middle of nowhere, this little adventure would produce some lasting good.

"You know why they call this place Dead Horse Point?" Naomi asked in a subdued voice, obviously wanting to change the subject.

Neither of us answered her. Obviously we didn't know.

And obviously she was about to tell us.

"Over a hundred years ago, a band of cowboys chased a herd of wild mustangs through this country and cornered them right on this peninsula. To keep them contained against the cliff's edge, they built a fence right behind where we're sitting. After they culled out all the best horses for themselves, they took off and left the others behind. Legend claims the remaining horses tried for weeks to find a way out, but never did. They all died of thirst right here, in sight of the Colorado River they could never reach. And their dried bones are those bleached white things we passed by on the way over here. Some folks say that a few of the horses actually jumped, trying to reach the water right in front of them. But so far away."

I couldn't place exactly why, but her anecdote seemed the perfect rebuke to our flippant talk about suicide. Maybe it meant that hope was right in front of us, and we just needed to keep searching, one more day, to find it.

Just then a strong, sustained gust of wind swept across our backs, and I knew my moment had come. I swallowed back a sob, peeled off the lid, and held my cup high above my head, still leaning back against the car's grille, my arm extended straight above me like the Statue of Liberty.

At first I was concerned that Lonnie's remains might have hardened into some kind of shell the wind wouldn't be able to budge. But the gust grew stronger, more insistent. Suddenly the cup shuddered. Something caught my eye, and I looked up to see a dark gray trail enter the wind stream as I walked gingerly toward the unguarded edge.

I kept my eyes locked on that dark flow as it drifted out across the void and the ocean of air above the gorge. Toward the Island in the Sky mesa. It did not stay together as a narrow streak for long, but broadened and dissipated into the now-dimming light. I smiled to myself. *How apt.*

And then, even though a great many strange thoughts and reactions had already occurred to me that day, I was overwhelmed by a sense that more than my husband's body was floating away. It was *my whole life*. All my aspirations and relationships and attachments were flying off into the wind along with my husband. Just like the dust floating away, I was adrift, unmoored, even more unattached than the day I'd walked away for life from my foster family and into the arms of my then-boyfriend.

The impression of solitude took me totally by surprise, because Mel's gradual decline had caused me to feel such a kinship with Naomi and her grief. But just then I felt completely alone. It was almost physical, a sensation like someone standing on my chest, the weight making it hard for me to breathe deeply. I concentrated on inhaling that wondrous air and keeping my composure.

Naomi turned to Orpah. It was growing dark. Her time had come.

"Do you need help?" she asked her.

Orpah shook her head, withdrawn. She rubbed the sides of the cup, deep in thought. Then she raised it a little.

And began to run toward the gorge.

I cried out and rushed toward her, but she was moving too fast. Those long legs churned and propelled her onward. She accelerated, still holding the cup high. Then she stumbled on a crack in the gnarled stone, nearly falling on her face—yet somehow she managed to keep her balance and ended up in a kneeling position.

One more lunge and she would have reached the edge of the precipice. From where she knelt, she leaned her whole body backward and lowered the cup in her hand almost to the ground behind her. Then, in a single motion, she launched the cup into the void. I followed the white shape for only a second, but just like Lonnie's, Mel's remains blackened the horizon for hardly a moment. I looked again and they had melted into splendor.

Orpah walked slowly back to us, looking a bit sheepish at her own impulsiveness.

"Hey, you did it in your own fashion," I told her.

She laughed and threw an arm around my shoulders. "Can we go now? I'm freezing."

"Hold on. I'll be right back," Naomi said, and she scurried off into the brush.

So we stayed put, leaning against the Impala's grille and shivering in our skimpy clothing, looking off into the vastness of our husbands' resting place.

"Hey, you could have told us it got so cool here in the evenings," Orpah called out.

"I'm so sorry!" Naomi answered back. "I meant to tell you to bring something warm to wear. I just plain forgot."

A few minutes later, Naomi returned, bearing an armful of sticks and kindling.

She dropped the load of wood at our feet. "Anybody know how to start a fire?"

We both shrugged, totally lost.

"Guess I'll have to remember how Eli did it all those years ago," Naomi murmured. "At least, Orpah, I know you have a lighter. Let's see . . . I think we start with a little of the kindling at the bottom, then build like a house of bigger sticks on top of that. I can't believe I remember." She looked up at us, suddenly serious again. "Actually, I can believe it."

Orpah tossed Naomi her cigarette lighter and, to our surprise, soon a bright, cheery tongue of yellow fire began to climb the little tower Naomi had erected out of twigs. The flame engaged the higher sticks, and then Naomi threw on two thicker branches.

We had a fire, thanks to a reprieve from the wind. Neither I nor Orpah had ever started a fire! We were mesmerized.

Looking somehow heartened, Naomi held out her hands and rubbed them together, as though we were in some kind of snowstorm. The two of us knelt and joined her in a tight huddle around our little blaze. The dry piñon wood cracked loudly, burning fast and hot, and sent forth a fierce and friendly heat.

Naomi would not budge her gaze from the flames.

"So does this look like the fire you guys started all those years ago?" asked Orpah.

Naomi nodded.

I could tell she was preoccupied.

"You have something else," I said, overcome by my hunch. "You've got something else to tell us."

Naomi looked at me, appearing for all the world like a trapped animal. Only then was I sure.

Naomi did have something to tell us.

"What is it?" asked Orpah.

"I'm not going back there."

Orpah glanced at me, then said to Naomi, "Not going back *where*?"

"Vegas. I'm leaving—leaving Las Vegas. Oh, you two have got me doing it now! You know what I mean."

"You don't mean suicide?" I said in my most direct tone.

"No, Ruth, I don't. I just mean that I got a letter recently from an old friend of mine back East. Seems the economy has really turned around out there. Eli and I left years ago because there were no jobs. The whole area seemed to be drying up. But that's not the case anymore. So I'm going back. Back to my people. It's the only place for me, really. There's nothing left in Las Vegas for me but pain, and nothing here in Moab but memories. I've been silently debating it during our whole drive out here."

A moment of silent shock washed over me. I felt like I'd just received the proverbial punch in the gut—a palpable sensation of pain filled my midsection. My head was starting to swim, with nausea creeping in to warn me of an even worse reaction ahead. I could hear Orpah huffing beside me, breathless at the news.

"There are plenty of jobs in Vegas," she argued plaintively.

"Not for a woman like me," Naomi answered. "For you, sure. For a fifty-plus-year-old widow with my issues? Hardly. Look, I'm not going back to start a new career. I'm going back because I heard things are better there now, and because that's where my people are. That gives me a tiny bit of hope."

"*Good* people," I said numbly.

"I'm not making comparisons," Naomi said.

"I'm not saying you are," I countered. "I'm just remembering the first words Lonnie used to describe his family to me. His folks were 'good people.' And the way his face looked when he said that, you knew he meant it, too."

"He said that?" Naomi asked with a wistful look.

I nodded.

In the silence that followed, the sick feeling of dread filled my body and mind. Somehow the thought of Naomi leaving felt just as cruel, just as arbitrary, just as unfair as Lonnie's sudden death. Mel's passing was devastating, but at least it was something I had expected, something I had time to prepare myself for. But Naomi was my last pillar of support, my final bastion of hope. Always, in picturing how I would survive the days ahead, I had factored in her continued presence.

Worse still, my sensation of being completely lost, untethered to anything in this world, suddenly returned a hundredfold. My last frayed tie to all that came before was now being cut away for good. The vertigo grew worse, with a carousel of darkening canyon walls starting to spin sickeningly around my head.

Orpah stood up but continued to stare straight into the fire, like someone who could hardly bear to look anywhere else.

"You just can't leave us," she said softly.

Naomi reached out and grasped her hand.

"I mean it," Orpah continued. "We won't survive without you."

"I don't know any other way," Naomi said, her voice full of sadness. "You know I love you both dearly, but there's no other place for me. I'm an aging woman with no immediate family within several thousand miles of me."

"You have *us*," I insisted.

"We're not legally even related anymore."

"Forget legal," Orpah shot back. "You know how we feel about you. You know where we've lived, who we've lived *with*. You think we have family to go back to? I don't even know where my real mother is!"

"I'm a ward of the state," I added. "I came to Vegas with a foster family. My foster father's now in jail for child molestation. And that's the people they gave me to, *after* removing me from my biological family."

"Yes, but you're young," Naomi countered. "You have prospects. You have energy. You have your looks. You're employable. And someday you'll find other husbands. Besides, Orpah at least has family in town."

"Yeah. A brother who never speaks to me and a sister-in-law who won't let her children near me."

"Hey," I interrupted, looking at her directly, "it's better than no one at all."

"Orpah," Naomi put in, "the apartment's in your name

now. You two can go back and continue being roommates. I'll get in touch with you in a month or so to tell you where to ship my things."

"How were you planning to get there?" Orpah asked.

"In the car, of course," she said, with the blank look of one daring her answer to be challenged. "I have a little over two hundred dollars for gas and lodging."

"To get back East? What kind of *east* are you going to? Missouri?" Orpah was nearly shouting.

"Pennsylvania," Naomi muttered.

"You'll never make it," I said, now incensed on top of my discomfort. "You'd never make it even if you had a brand-new car that wasn't a gas-guzzling, oil-burning, bald-tired, radiator-leaking, on-its-last-legs relic from the days of cheap gasoline!" My volume matched Orpah's.

"Speaking of which," Orpah said, "you have enough money for four, maybe five, tankfuls—if you sleep in the car. That'll possibly get you to Kansas. Dorothy, you're dreamin'!"

Naomi's face fell again, which immediately told Orpah and me that we'd gone too far.

"I don't have a choice," she said after an uncomfortable pause. "I have no idea where else to go." The last syllable twisted into a sob. "I only know I can't go back. I don't like what Las Vegas took from me. Where I came from, people are treated differently."

"Don't leave," Orpah said in a conciliatory tone. "Things'll work out. We're all pulling for each other, aren't we?"

"You don't understand." Naomi was shaking with sobs now. "Las Vegas feels like death to me. Everywhere I look, I'll see somewhere I went with Eli, somewhere I picked up Lonnie, some building constructed by Mel. Or even the place Mel died. I'd be better off running off this cliff like Thelma and

Louise, or those mustangs, than going back to that city for even a minute."

"Wait," said Orpah. "Where were you planning to leave from?"

"From Moab, tomorrow morning."

"And what about us?"

"I have enough money—in addition to the gas money—for us to stay in Eli's old motel tonight, and then you can both take the bus back home."

"Oh, how sweet," said Orpah sarcastically. "The bus. Thanks for thinking of us."

"Orpah, I did not make this decision to inconvenience you." I could tell Naomi was making a great effort to keep her voice even. "Either of you. I made it to survive. I actually just made up my mind sitting here, staring at the fire, and remembering the letter I recently got from home."

"What exactly do you have waiting for you?" I asked. "A job? A home? A welcome committee?" I was falling into Orpah's sarcasm.

Naomi took the torn envelope from her blouse, pulled the letter out, and glanced at its contents.

She sighed, no doubt feeling the stress of our interrogation. "Like I said, the economy is getting better, and I have the old family farmhouse on some land we've been leasing out to farmers all these years. Lease is up soon, and the house stayed empty. It's not much, but it's something."

"How old is the house?"

"Over a hundred years old."

Orpah and I looked at each other. In Las Vegas, even twenty-five years is museum time.

"A broken-down house and some land you won't be able to farm. And do 'your people' know you're coming?"

"No. There's only a few of them left, anyway—those who

would even remember who I am."

"Great, Naomi," I blurted. I couldn't help myself. "Sounds like a real promising picture."

Naomi had enough. Reaching down, she threw two handfuls of dirt on the fire, then began stamping out the remaining flames, her anger evident.

"Let's go back to Moab for the night," she finally said, her voice trembling.

As she moved toward the car, Orpah touched Naomi's hand. "I'm so sorry, Naomi, to be acting this way. We don't mean to turn on you. We love you, and we're scared to see you go."

"I know." Naomi nodded, the comforting maternal figure again. "Believe me, I'm scared too, honey. I'm plenty terrified for all three of us. Just because I'm older doesn't mean I'm braver."

CHAPTER 10

70

Our drive into Moab was marked by silence. We all were emotionally spent. Night had fallen, and the once expansive scenery darkened as if a shade had been pulled. We crossed the Colorado River, now placid and accessible, and approached Moab's Main Street, lined with charming motels and restaurants with whimsical and locally inspired names like Back of Beyond Books, Sunset Grill, Peace Tree Juice Cafe, Pagan Mountaineering. After stopping at a convenience store for a few food items, Naomi turned into a place called the Greenwell Inn, a modest-sized motel whose street sign was flanked by a ten-foot-high boulder gleaming under a man-made waterfall.

"We came here when Eli took a job at this place as their desk manager," Naomi explained. "They'll remember me. I'm sure they'll give me a good discount."

I suddenly had an idea. "Naomi, why don't we just sleep in the car? The parking lot's safe, and we could save a nice sum of the cash you took with you. It'll probably be almost the same amount of room, as big as your seats are."

"You and that car." She shook her head, her lips twisted in a wry grin.

So we did. Naomi retrieved a pair of quilts from the trunk and, refusing one herself, handed them to us to stay warm. Orpah resumed her spot in the back seat, and Naomi and I took the front, leaning back against the headrests.

Soon the brightness of morning roused me from a fitful sleep. I straightened in the seat, looked over at Naomi, and saw that she was already awake, staring numbly through the windshield like a woman contemplating the dawn of her execution day. I rubbed my eyes and felt the ghosts of the night past reach up for one last prod at my subconscious. It had been a troubled slumber, afflicted by dreams and anxieties of being lost and abandoned.

I definitely was not at peace with Naomi's decision. In light of day, the idea of her driving alone, in that car, with little money, three thousand miles across America, toward prospects ranging from remote to nonexistent, sounded even more absurd. I felt like I was one of those discarded kids, dropped off by harried parents at some randomly chosen roadside rest area.

That was a feeling I'd felt before, although, thankfully, it had been many years ago.

Despite all that, I was too frazzled, sleep-deprived, and out of sorts to take up the argument once more. We left the Greenwell Inn parking lot, and Naomi treated us to a quick tour through our late husbands' favorite haunts such as Moab High School and the first few miles of the amazing Arches National Park, with sandstone towers reminiscent of Monument Valley and endless vistas of twisted stone. Moab is evidently the mountain-biking capital of the world, I learned as

I looked out at scores of cyclists roaming the wilderness.

The tour over, we drove to a sidewalk eatery called the Slickrock Cafe. There we had Southwest-style breakfast burritos while we gazed blearily through the windows at the town's ring of towering red sandstone. By meal's end, we still had exchanged hardly a dozen words.

Finally I couldn't stand it any longer. "I just can't believe, after all we've been through, that we just ate our last meal together," I said, my tone as petulant as I felt.

"Ruth, please," Naomi said with a soft, pleading tone.

"I'm sorry. It just seems so . . . so wrong."

"Good-byes are like that, Ruth. They're hard. I'm sorry—"

"So are bad decisions," Orpah interrupted.

"Look," said Naomi. "All these years I was a weak and ineffective mother. You might say that I adored my sons so much that I couldn't bring myself to tell either of them *no*. Even when I found out the worst, I could rarely manage more than, 'You boys know you shouldn't be doing that,' or some spineless variation on that theme. I always wished I'd been firmer, and now I have the rest of my life to regret not having had more backbone. But I'm going to try and change that by telling you for the last time—*I'm going back East*. It's what I should have done a long time ago."

Her words did nothing to soothe me. I rose abruptly to leave, and the two followed me. We exited onto the sidewalk, and Naomi did something unexpected, yet utterly like her. She stepped between the two of us and grasped our hands. Tightly. We walked that way to the bus station, looking every bit like a mother, her trashily dressed daughter, and her exotic African adoptee, out for their morning walk.

Although I could hardly admit it, the gesture was like a balm to my heart. Just the sort of thoughtfulness that had so endeared this broken little woman to me.

Orpah, for her part, was beyond rescue. Thank goodness for her Vegas Strip celebrity sunglasses, because her eyes hadn't stopped shedding tears since shortly before breakfast. The first one to spot the bus as it lumbered up Main Street, she spun around and swept Naomi up in her long, dark arms.

"Is there anything I can say," she asked in a shattered voice, "to change your mind?"

Naomi didn't pretend to answer but squeezed her even harder, mouthing, "I love you," over and over again.

Then just as quickly, Orpah released her, snatched the ticket from Naomi's fingers, and ran up the steps into the bus. My turn was next. I truly didn't know what to say, and I told her so. I won't bore you with how hard I cried when we embraced. I don't remember much, to tell you the truth, because that day was so wrought with conflicting emotions. I do remember turning away, stepping up and feeling the rubber of the bus flooring under my feet, and the institutional smell of the bus's interior.

I wasn't going to look back at her. In fact, I wasn't going to look at all. It was already too embarrassing to climb aboard, blubbering like a child. I wasn't about to make things worse by trying to make eye contact with her outside the window. Fighting for breath, I took a seat next to Orpah. The engine growled, bumped into gear, and the front door closed with a *whoosh*. I looked over at Orpah, who, bless her heart, was frantically waving through the window.

"I can't believe this," I gasped out. "I can't believe we're going to let her do this thing."

"There's no way to stop her," Orpah said, still waving.

She had a point. For all her poor judgment, Naomi was still free to make her own choices. There was no way to . . .

Wait. Could there be another solution?

I caught sight of her face just as the bus rolled past where she stood. It was a face wracked with sadness and grief, and the sight seared my brain and drove through my heart a realization I had been fighting ever since the evening before.

Orpah turned to me, her face wet with tears. "You know what we did, Ruth?" she said. "We went and left without getting a way to get in touch with her. She's going to move, and she doesn't do e-mail. If we're not careful, we're going to lose touch with her forever."

CHAPTER II

As the bus began to accelerate, something inside of me—already on the verge of breaking—snapped entirely. I leaped to my feet. *No way was this going to happen!*

"Orpah, good-bye, sweetheart."

"Huh? Ruth, what are you doing?"

"I'm going with her. I have to. I'm getting off right now."

Orpah gave me a look I'll never forget. It was quick, yet incredibly penetrating. So powerful that, without a second's hesitation, she stood and started yelling at the top of her lungs.

"Driver! Stop! Please stop!"

I gave Orpah a kiss on the cheek, then stumbled out into the center aisle.

"Please stop!" I repeated. "I need to get off this bus!"

From where I stood I didn't catch the driver's reaction, but I felt the brakes squeal and the bus turn abruptly to the right. I aimed my body toward the front and tried to stabilize my forward motion. I stumbled through a dozen faltering steps, fighting to keep my balance. Finally, I reached the frustrated, gray-haired man sitting behind the big wheel.

"I'm sorry, but I have to get off the bus," I said, breathless. "Please open the door for me."

"Are you okay, ma'am?"

"I'm fine. I just—Please open the door."

He reached for a silver handle, and the door flew open. I scrambled down the steps and jumped straight to the pavement.

I was already wheezing like a long-distance runner, but if I didn't catch Naomi soon I feared I would miss her entirely.

The bus growled past me as I started to run down the sidewalk. It had only gone a block since Orpah and I had boarded. I weaved between the clusters of tourists, yelling, "Naomi! Naomi! Stop!"

I probably looked silly and cheap in my Vegas-style dress, shouting my head off. But none of it mattered—all that counted now was getting to Naomi.

I spotted the car at once and closed the distance in seconds, my heart racing wildly and my lungs about to surrender. I later discovered she hadn't left immediately but retreated to the Impala for a good, private cry.

Her brake lights blinked on, and she began backing out. *Nooooooo!*

I waved and screamed, but she didn't hear me. Before I could reach her and block the car's path, she pulled out to the parking lot's exit. Her blinker signaled a right turn away from me.

A new surge of determination roared through me. I was not going to let her get away. I forced my feet to move faster and pumped my arms like a madwoman. The car slowed. I thought it was my speed until I looked ahead and saw the red light. I gained on the car, then I threw myself against the driver's-side door and began pounding the window, shouting her name.

She peered at me in amazement and threw the car into park. The door swung open.

"Ruth? What are you doing?" Her face was blotched with tears as she rose to stand in front of me.

"I'm going with you!"

"You can't come with me. That's impossible."

"No, it's not." I was still panting, but my voice sounded just as determined as hers.

"Ruth, this is *my* journey. My end, not yours."

"Naomi, please don't send me away, I'm begging you. I have even less to go home to in Vegas than you do. All I have in this world is you. You're my family now. All my hope is wrapped up in our friendship. I'm coming with you, Naomi. Don't deny me."

A honk blared from behind us. The light had turned green.

"Look, they're not your people."

"That's a load of—" I stopped and began again, trying to keep my tone calm, matter-of-fact. "If they're your people, then they'll be mine, too. Wherever you go, wherever you live, that's where I want to be. It will be my home. You're going back to find something. And I'm going to find it with you."

"You can't, Ruth. I'm simply going back for a decent place to live out the rest of my sorry life. There's nothing there for you—"

"Yes, there is!" I almost shouted. "You need me, and I need you. And God can strike me down if anything but death comes between us!"

The poor woman obviously didn't know what to do in the face of such an appeal. She shook her head, wept, laughed, and fought for words all at once.

The honking resumed, taken up by not one but three cars now. Just under the blasts we could hear the voices of the drivers, yelling.

"You can't turn me away," I continued, ignoring the commotion around us. "I'm here. The bus is gone. I'm alone. I'm stranded. And something else. You can't make it without me. This trip is beyond you alone. And *I* can't make it without *you*. The only way we survive is together."

Those words somehow seemed to break her final barrier. She looked down and sighed deeply, then held out her arms to me, almost grudgingly.

This time I did not step as much as jump into her arms, trying my very best to squeeze all the air from her lungs.

"You're a stubborn one—you know that?" she said, laughing shakily.

"Only when I mean it." I pulled back and looked her in the eyes. "One more thing. I'm driving this lousy piece of junk back East. You've given me my last anxiety attack. If we die on this ride, it's going to be at my hand, not yours."

"But you don't have a license—"

"That's only the beginning of our problems. I'll keep an eye on the rearview mirror, I promise."

And just as I had done to Lonnie on my last drive before this one, I opened the door and slid onto the driver's seat.

"Climb in," I told Naomi. "We're going to Pennsylvania."

PART TWO

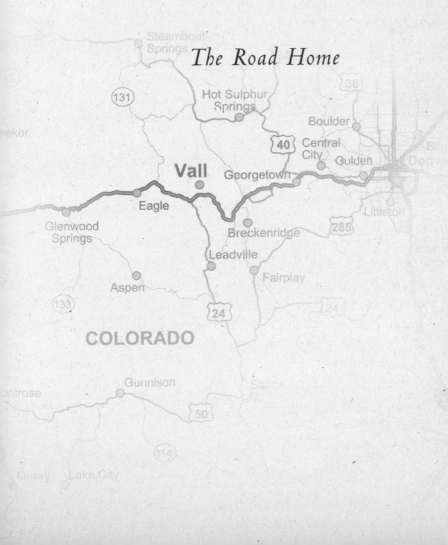

The Road Home

CHAPTER 12

And that, my dear family, explains how and why a desperate young Latina who had only heard of Pennsylvania a few times in her life came to find herself eastbound, lurching and shimmying on the pathetic shock absorbers of a 1976 Chevrolet Impala, holding just a few hundred dollars with which to rebuild not only her own life but that of a mother figure to whom she was no longer legally related, with no material goods other than the rather skimpy black dress that clung to her body.

Of course it explains very little else.

As I'm sure you're aware, it does not explain how a cynical, tough-talking cocktail waitress with an arrest record from Sin City itself came to be the Aunt Ruth you all know today.

Well, it was a long road. A *very* long road.

That road began only minutes after our Main Street shouting match and my leap into the Impala. And not a moment too soon. A squad car met us shortly after I pulled away, presumably on its way to the traffic jam we'd left behind.

Still riding the adrenaline high of my rash decision, I spotted an ATM machine on the way out of Moab and stopped to clean out the last dregs of my bank account in Vegas.

No worries, I told Naomi. We now possessed a grand total of $483. Since my contribution more than doubled Naomi's stash, the total seemed enough to get us through the journey ahead. Provided all went well.

Thinking back, I barely remember our actual departure from Moab. I vaguely recall feeling suspended in a state of both agitation and euphoria. Strangely, the one thing I can picture vividly is the expressions on Naomi's face. She looked scared and intimidated by what had transpired. But I also glimpsed a wry grin when I turned to catch her watching me from the corner of her eye. Almost as if, despite knowing me like she did, she had to reassess me all over again.

"You know, it's okay if you change your mind," she assured me not once but three times during those first miles.

Inwardly, I did give her offer some serious consideration, if only because I was as shocked by what I had done as she was. Shocked by how impulsively I'd acted, and by emotions coming to the surface that I didn't know lay dormant within me. That's why, even as I got used to driving again—and wrestling with that ocean liner of a car along a curving two-lane highway—I, too, was caught up in reassessing *myself*.

But my ultimate answer to her was no.

"I have nowhere else to go," I repeated. "Naomi, if you're really going, then I'm going with you."

"I know this trip is a crazy idea," she said flatly. "I didn't even realize how risky it was until you joined me. The odds are not good that we'll make it all the way to Pennsylvania—

you know that, right? I mean, I don't want to be responsible . . ."

I shrugged. "I figure the odds aren't great that we make it even halfway. But when I look at the big picture, we don't have much of a choice. I'm not sure exactly why I feel that way, but I do. It's strange, but Vegas feels like a door already slammed shut. It's no longer an option. Lonnie is dead. My life there is over. I'm not sure our destination ahead is even relevant. The point is, together at least we have a chance."

"I'm not *that* helpless," Naomi interjected, smiling faintly.

"I beg to differ," I argued stubbornly. "Nearly broke, alone, in your state of grief, in this heap of a car, under the spell of this weird homing beacon that's pulling you back to your *people*, whoever they are—you need me."

"Maybe," she said.

"You need me," I repeated, insistent.

She laughed.

"Besides," I added, "I need you, too."

After the drama of my leaving the bus and joining her, a calm silence fell over us as I turned left along the Colorado River and followed a shortcut from Moab back toward I-70 East. Perhaps we were just spent. Perhaps it's that the decision was now settled for good. No matter how tall the odds and what challenges we faced, being together was a done deal.

Having given up the task of driving, after a while Naomi became restless. In an effort to rechannel her energy, I suggested she take up the task of determining—with a pencil stub and a little spiral notebook in hand—just how far our $483 would actually take us.

I had no real desire for a reality check, or to hear the voice of reason announce that we had no chance of reaching Naomi's near-mythical farm and suggest we would have to turn around and slink back into the city's smothering arms. Ironically, though, her mumbled calculations and the effort of answering or deflecting her questions only helped bring me down to earth that much sooner.

I rested my eyes on the high, black-stained sandstone walls, the Colorado's prodigious quantity of water flowing effortlessly, and the abundance of trees and plants stretching all the way to the distant Entrada Bluffs, awaiting her bad news at any moment.

When we crossed the historic Dewey suspension bridge, the rock turned lighter in color, and the terrain stretched out into a broad valley. In the distance brooded great mountain ranges, gray-shadowed mesas and buttes.

All the sweeping heights led me back to the fate of those poor mustangs all those years ago. The story continued to trouble me. Had they simply given up hope, so grieved were they by their leaders' abandonment? Or were they truly incapable of finding sustenance without help? Regardless, the thought of those noble beasts starving and dying of thirst within clear sight of a deep, grass-lined river that taunted them from hundreds of feet below struck me as unspeakably sad and ironic.

I also wondered if that could have been my fate had I not followed the inner voice urging me to jump off that bus. Staying frozen in my status quo, enduring one moment of longing after another, gazing out at salvation but feeling cut off, no longer able to make the jump. And finally, dying of thirst.

That image slingshot my thoughts to those two film characters who had appeared in that very same setting with a strikingly similar story line.

"Naomi, what did you actually think of *Thelma and Louise*?"

She looked up from her calculations and squinted in the

light. "I hardly remember it, Ruth. It's been so long since I saw the movie. I'm not sure I even saw the whole thing, just bits of it as Mel and Lonnie watched it on TV."

"You don't remember anything?"

"The only part I remember clearly is that final scene—with them driving off Dead Horse Point and grinning like Cheshire cats the whole way down, as if they were on a ride at an amusement park or something. I couldn't accept their being so cheerful at taking their own lives. Besides, I felt cheated. I'd wanted them to make it."

"Yeah. I did, too."

"Call me old-fashioned, but that's still what I expect from movies—or books and stories of any kind. A good ending. Maybe not always a blissfully happy ending, but at least a good one."

"But don't you think the way their story had been going, a happy ending was no longer in the cards? They'd been heading downhill the whole time. They started out these nice, put-upon women with messed-up lives, but then they made one self-destructive choice after another, and ended up vindictive criminals with no way out *but* death."

"Maybe what I wanted for them was redemption. A place of safety where they could return to the women they once were."

"But the film seemed to strongly make the point that there was no choice. That they did their best."

She nodded. "And that's where it lost me for good. Because I always believe there's a choice. As long as I draw breath, I always have the chance to make things right. They had the choice to give themselves up, there at the end. Susan Sarandon could have slammed on her brakes, even after they'd sped away from the police. At any time, they could have turned themselves in. And I don't believe for a second they wouldn't have gotten justice. Matter of fact, the way things are today, they would have gotten better than they deserved. After a trial, they would have been such folk heroes they could have run for president. So their choices weren't inevitable, and they definitely weren't noble. In the end, they were just plain dumb."

"The reason I'm here with you right now is because I feel I have no choice." I said somberly. "Didn't you tell Orpah and me that you were going home because *you* had no choice?"

"No *good* one," she answered thoughtfully. "Of course there's always choices. I know I could go back to Vegas and suffer a thousand deaths." She paused a moment, then rushed on, uncharacteristically brusque. "I could go home and slit my wrists. Why, I could have taken Orpah's suggestion and driven off Dead Horse Point myself. But the right choice, the only choice that has any hope is very clear to me. It's going back to my people."

"Maybe that's the difference between us and Thelma and Louise. You and I are driving *toward* hope, not away from it."

"And that's why our trip *starts* in Moab," Naomi said, sounding relieved, "instead of ending there."

I chuckled and smiled at her. For someone who knew nothing about popular culture, she had a good point.

CHAPTER 13

70

Naomi returned to her calculations, which had now taken so long I wondered if she intended to complete them.

A few minutes later I struck a rough patch in the road and realized it was the last cattle guard before rejoining the Interstate. Steeling myself, I gunned the engine to safely merge onto I-70. Instead of the meandering, deserted highway I'd been driving, I was quickly struggling to keep up on one of the nation's great arteries—a speedway of roaring semi-trucks, thick traffic, and driving speeds that felt downright dizzying after the leisure of the roads surrounding Moab.

"Are we staying on this freeway the whole way there?" I wondered.

Naomi nodded. "I think so, unless they've changed th— Oh no!"

I looked over. Naomi's eyes were fixed on the passenger's side mirror. I glanced at the rearview mirror, and instead of seeing open Interstate falling away behind me, I saw a strangely familiar blue surface, shimmering in the light. . . .

The trunk!

It was bobbing wide open, casting its contents to the wind. That cattle guard must have jarred the lock.

I swerved so hard to the shoulder I feared losing control. Slamming on the brakes, I pushed the shift into park, threw the door open, and jumped out with a shout to Naomi to stay put.

I whipped around and stared. The quilts Orpah and I had used to stay warm were now billowing across the freeway in the wind, forcing a large panel truck and several cars to lurch out of their way. I heard brakes screeching wildly, and several horns blowing.

The lane closest to us, the shoulder, and the median were scattered about with things that had flown out of the Impala's trunk. I saw a Bible, a bound journal, and various cosmetics in the weeds and on the concrete many yards behind the car. I felt an urge to leap heedlessly onto the lane and play daredevil, forcing the vehicles to avoid me and Naomi's things lying there. But I knew immediately that was too risky. Doing so would cause a horrible accident—if not my death. I stood poised to dash across at the first opening in the heavy traffic.

"Ruth! Please don't!" Naomi had disobeyed and was standing behind me. "It's not worth it!"

I didn't answer. Not too far away lay the journal I had so often seen her writing in. The next vehicle was several hundred yards back. With a flash of adrenaline, I sprinted across the concrete, picked up the volume along with the leather Bible lying splayed open nearby, and scrambled back to the shoulder. The vehicle was only a few seconds behind me. In that weird way of remembering things at the wrong time, I recalled never having seen a Bible at Naomi's house. The car's horn was sounding long after it had passed us.

"Oh no!" she screamed behind me.

I wheeled around, my motion helped by the blast of another vehicle.

"The money's out there!"

"*What!* Where?"

"I kept it in that little tote bag full of cosmetics!"

I'd already seen it, lying pathetically at least fifty feet away in the far lane, a small pile of the bag's heavier contents still together near one of its straps. I looked to the left and froze. A monstrous two-trailer semi was headed straight for it, and it seemed the pile was lined up exactly with its churning left tires.

Yet there was time. I could do it.

Without hesitating another second, I threw myself into the gap. I lowered my body, extended my arms, and scooped up the pile with the side of the bag. Clutching my precious cargo, I left my feet, rolled off, and flattened myself against the center cement divider.

Barely in time.

The truck's horn mixed with a scream from Naomi, and it thundered past me, followed by a mass of hot air—brutal and smelling of exhaust fumes.

I crouched there and concentrated on pressing my back against the cement divider and willing my heart to stop racing and my breathing to calm down. I looked down and took a quick inventory of what I was holding. There, right near the top, was a small bank envelope. I could see the edge of a stack of bills peeking out.

"Hey, Naomi!" I waved the envelope over the rooftops of the cars passing between us. "I got it! I found the cash!"

Another scream answered me, though I couldn't make out what she was saying. But the look of gratitude on Naomi's face didn't require words.

Since I was already at the center median, I could make my way backward a few dozen yards and retrieve the quilts. I recalled Naomi talking about them as family heirlooms that carried great sentimental value. *"They're from back East,"* she'd said with a tone of reverence.

Still hugging the divider, I hurried closer to where the quilts lay in heaps that billowed ominously with the passing traffic. Luckily the coast was again clear. I ran and gathered into my arms the first one, then made a dash for the second. A sudden gust of wind whipped it away from my outstretched fingers and blew it high over the median and into the west-bound lanes.

Shaking my head, I'd decided to return to my place of relative safety when a bright red flurry in my peripheral vision told me I had miscalculated. A compact car seemed to come out of nowhere and was bearing down on me, honking its horn. At the last second I felt myself flying backward and realized only an instant later that I had not been hit but had stopped on a dime and leaped backward. My back hit the cement hard, and the pain released a new wave of adrenaline. I glanced backward, gritted my teeth, and steeled my muscles.

Finally. Another break in the flow.

I took off running as fast as I could toward the Impala, where I saw Naomi, her arms frantically reaching for me. I awkwardly tried to combine hugging her with handing off my load, almost bowling her over.

I quickly turned around to resume my task.

"No!" Naomi yelled over the noise of traffic. "This stuff isn't worth you risking your life for!"

I waved off her concern, riding a wave of stubborn determination. "I'm okay!"

"No, you're not! You're out of your mind! Please, Ruth, stop now! You're going to get killed!"

"It'll be okay," I repeated over my shoulder as I ran off toward the next item.

Over the next several minutes I used the same dart-in, dart-out method to retrieve a good deal of what Naomi had packed in the trunk. She grudgingly made herself useful by stationing herself a ways down the lane and gesturing wildly for drivers to beware and give me a wide berth.

Finally, with many more items still blowing off in the distance and my body completely wrung out of energy, I collapsed, heaving against the Impala's back end.

"Welcome to the Interstate," Naomi said with a grim chuckle.

"We're going to have to tie off the trunk door," I panted.

"I thought the cattle guard sprang it open."

"Whatever. We can't afford to have this happen again."

Naomi nodded, then reached over to help me back to the driver's side. As I walked around the rear of the car, I softly kicked the side.

Piece of junk, I thought. *I knew it would be our worst enemy.*

CHAPTER 14

Fruita, Colorado, Interstate 70

"All of a sudden I've got a bad feeling about this trip," I admitted to Naomi when we were well on our way again and entering the outskirts of Grand Junction, Colorado. "If our luck doesn't improve . . ." I shook my head.

"Bad luck follows me everywhere," Naomi replied, refusing to look at me. "It always has. I can still get you back to Vegas, you know. We haven't gone so far yet."

I glanced over and the sight of her caused the rightness of my decision to surge back tenfold. "Meeting you is the only good luck I've ever had," I assured her. "No matter how bad it turns out, my home is with you, Naomi. Which, for now, is right here inside this car."

She looked down, shaking her head.

"What is it, Naomi?"

"I'm grateful, Ruth. Don't think I'm not. But you have to know I barely have the strength to keep myself going. This is the most desperate thing I've ever done. There's no way I can be responsible for carrying us both through this thing."

"Maybe that's one of the reasons I'm here. To help keep us both going." I glanced over at her figures scribbled in the spiral notebook and pointed. "No matter what those numbers say, you have to remember. You and me, we're one plus one makes three."

"Not if you get yourself killed on the first day," she said pointedly. "Not that I'm ungrateful, but you do something like that again, and I *will* leave you behind."

"Four hundred and twenty-five dollars," Naomi said in a low, subdued voice after several minutes had passed.

"Just for gas?"

"Just for gas. It's a rough estimate, and it's likely to be on the shy side of reality."

I looked at her and attempted my best playful smile. "Well, we can go on a starvation diet between here and there. When we arrive, we'll be so elegantly thin that all the men will start fighting over us."

"Have you ever heard of Mennonites and the Amish?" she asked, staring at me blankly.

"Aren't they the people who ride buggies and don't use electricity?"

"Ruth, those are my people."

No doubt the shock showed in my expression. I had pictured Naomi on some kind of farm—but *Mennonite*? I tried to put the jumbled jigsaw puzzle together in my mind, unable to remember what a Mennonite was and what they looked like. I recalled Mormons I had seen walking down the Strip in Las Vegas, gawking at the sights as if they were taking their own personal tour of Sodom and Gomorrah. When I thought of Mennonites, that same picture came to mind.

When I told her this, Naomi laughed at my confusion.

"No. Mennonites aren't anything like Mormons, except that they do dress similar to the conservative Mormons. And those folks drive cars and such. My particular Order was those who ride around in buggies and don't use power—along with the Amish, who are sort of close cousins in their beliefs. Other Orders aren't as *plain* as those. But one of their favorite sayings is, 'A plump wife and a big barn never did any man harm.' Which is to say that most Old Order Mennonites don't care for thinness in their women the way modern men do. There are few size fours among the Mennonites. And these are the people we're headed toward."

I ventured a look away from the traffic and stared at her, incredulous.

"We're going to live in some Amish-like commune?" I asked, then glanced down at my now further rumpled and dirty, yet still sequined, dress.

"No, Ruth," she laughed again. "Not a commune. A community. An ordinary, beautiful country town that just happens to host an unusually large Mennonite community. And you know, now that I think of it, there is something we need to do right away."

"What is it?" I asked, as we swerved abruptly onto an exit marked *Grand Junction*.

Naomi smiled. "I don't know what I was more worried about when you were running out on that freeway—that you'd get creamed by a big truck, or get arrested for public indecency due to that skimpy dress of yours. Even among these *Englisch*, as Eli's grandmother used to call them, you looked a bit immodest today."

I thought back at all the extreme postures and gesticulations I'd made during my recovery of the trunk's contents and felt a blush rise in my face. Then I chuckled, thinking of the free entertainment I'd inadvertently provided to the passing drivers. Living in Las Vegas, a city comfortable with such overexposure to the flesh, I guess over the years I had become immune to it all.

Since Naomi had left Vegas almost certain she would be heading east from Moab, she had packed for that possibility, but she finally convinced me we needed to dip into our already inadequate stash to get me dressed properly. After a half hour of frustrated searching, we finally located the Grand Junction Wal-Mart. There, as frugally as we could manage, we both made a few key purchases, including some snacks for us to graze on during the journey.

I found their cheapest pair of blue jeans on a clearance rack and a passable T-shirt bearing an imprint of floating clouds. Frantic to get the old dress off my body, I wore my purchases out of the dressing room. Walking out with the dirt-stained, no longer glorious, ball of fabric in my hand, I was tempted to go to the nearest trash can and throw it out. But the dress seemed to embody so much—my life in Vegas, which I was now leaving behind—so I tucked it under my arm, later stuffing it into a Wal-Mart bag.

Strange, I thought, how my entire life can fit into my one fist.

I'd also picked up a pair of cheap tennis shoes and several pairs of socks, then met Naomi at checkout so we could tally the damage.

The total came to $44.75, a sizable chunk of our precious hoard.

Making our way back to the car, I felt my spirit pierced by another awful premonition.

This is going to end badly.

The sense of foreboding only increased after we got back on the Interstate and saw the next challenge looming ahead—

the foothills of the Rocky Mountains. Even though Grand Junction was fringed by a curious, horizontal stack of stone columns aptly called the Book Cliffs, behind them soared mesas of pine that promised elevation aplenty.

You have to realize that it had been years, back in my childhood, since I had experienced real mountains. The barren peaks surrounding Las Vegas were high enough, but hardly anyone ever ventured among them, especially when the region's main highways deftly wove the bottomlands between their many gaps.

So the idea of scaling the Continental Divide on my first day behind the Impala's steering wheel filled me with dread. As we passed the bucolic charm of Grand Junction, I glanced briefly to the right and south.

"Look, Naomi," I gasped. "Are the Rockies going to be like those?"

I knew it wasn't our destination, but lining the southern horizon was an almost cartoonish razor's edge made up of jagged peaks. Although they were distant enough to be only silhouettes, the summits seemed to broach no foothills at all but only a breath-stopping leap to timberline and heights beyond.

"I think that's the San Juan range," Naomi said. "I'm amazed I can remember Eli's narrative from so many years ago. They're part of the Rockies," she continued, "but don't worry—they can't make an Interstate any steeper than that slope right there ahead of us."

Sure enough, flanked by the end of the Book Cliffs on our left and, of all things, thick vineyards on the right, the lane just ahead of us rose to leave the valley behind in an initial preview of climbing grades to come.

"The way I see it," I told Naomi, "we could just make it if the Rockies are one quick push up and down, allowing us to coast into the Midwest and never have to climb a steep hill again all the way to Pennsylvania. How far off track am I?"

Naomi merely shut her eyes and shook her head. "Dream on, my girl," she said.

Glenwood Canyon, Colorado

The Rockies' approach had proven more gradual than it looked. The resort town of Glenwood Springs, gateway to the beauty and riches of Aspen and the Roaring Fork Valley, brought us to a breathtaking canyon. Entirely different from the desert chasms of just a few hours before, here was a lush, tree-lined river gorge.

Probably the most remarkable aspect of Glenwood Canyon was the graceful and discreet way the Interstate maneuvered through her winding turns, its ramps painted a complementary shade of brown. At times poised on narrow columns, at times seemingly glued to the canyon wall itself, the highway appeared to glide through with ease. It was unlike anything I'd ever seen before.

The beauty put me in an inquisitive mood.

"What did you really think of me," I asked Naomi, "when Lonnie first brought me to your home?"

"Ruth, why would you ask something like that? That's so long ago."

"Because you couldn't have been excited to have your son bring home a cocktail waitress. It's hardly every mother's dream. Yet I never felt anything but warmth and acceptance from you. Every other boyfriend I had always found a reason to keep me away from his family."

"When I heard where Lonnie had met you, yes, I was disappointed. It didn't sound ideal. But when I saw how in love he was, I made a conscious choice to love you and make the best of it."

"Oh." The reply, though honest, wasn't exactly flattering.

Naomi turned and smiled. "But then I met you," she said.

"What did that have to do with it?"

"It was the way you treated *me*," she said softly. "On only your second date with my son, you brought me my favorite deli food and spent the evening with me. Remember? And I'm pretty good at reading other women—how they really feel under their smiles and surface politeness. I remember you were a little nervous, you wanted to make a good impression, but that you also genuinely cared. And you didn't seem at all frustrated that Lonnie had taken you home to see his mother rather than to a good show or a fancy dinner. For some reason, you were okay with that. It never seemed to bother you that Lonnie was a mama's boy."

"It's because I never had a loving, stable family of my own," I said. "I didn't know what a quiet evening at home was even like. That, and the fact that Eli, Lonnie, and Mel were all you had. I may have worked in a cocktail lounge, but it's a good place to study men. How men treat their mothers is often how they will treat their wives. That much I did learn!"

CHAPTER 15

Vail, Colorado

After the canyon had diminished into another stretch of arid hills, we found ourselves again surrounded by rising slopes and a scattering of condominiums that quickly thickened into a beehive. It was Vail, which meant nothing more to me than one of a dozen elite names dripping with privilege and exclusion. I glanced out the windows, expecting to see all the signs of a swank ski-resort town. What I saw instead were lots of pitched roofs crowded close together, treeless ski runs, and hotel logos.

"If my map is right," said Naomi, "this is where our first really tough grade begins. Vail Pass. Ten thousand feet."

"What do you mean, first?" I demanded. "I asked you if we were in for a straight up-and-down."

"And did I say yes?"

"No. But you didn't say no either."

"Look, if you're so scared, I'll be glad to take over the wheel for a while. You know I'm still very uncomfortable about your not having a license."

"No. That's not the issue. I'm going to be extra careful. I just don't like it."

"Just remember to keep the transmission out of overdrive on the way up. It's going to try and shift into it every minute or so. And on the way down, instead of using the brakes, use the gears. Otherwise you'll burn up the brakes, or at least lose their function. Manage those things, and you'll be fine."

Yeah, sure, I told myself through clenched teeth. Already the grade had steepened dramatically. As my right foot pressed on the gas, I could hear the engine straining to find the sweet spot, allowing it to ease back into fourth gear and out of overdrive. Remember, Lonnie was a good mechanic, and I was a quick study, in case you're wondering.

In my mind I could almost picture those aged transmission gears shredding what was left of their dulled teeth, and the prehistoric carburetor sucking our dollar bills into its overheated incinerator. My blood pressure was rising along with the elevation outside.

"Relax, Ruth, you're doing just fine," Naomi encouraged. "Take a look at that stand of aspens. Aren't they beautiful?"

I was far too tense to follow her instruction, but my peripheral vision caught sight of a shining patch of gold off to my right.

"I suppose so," I muttered.

"Come on. You're not going to do either of us any good holding in all that tension. Even if everything goes bad at the summit, which it might, you'll need to be calm to cope with what comes next."

"What are you saying?" I asked crossly.

"And if we run off the cliff here and die," she continued, clearly enjoying herself, "do you want your last moments on earth to be filled with nothing but fear and panic?"

Catching her morbid humor, I soon found myself laughing, which did help to ease the tension. I reached over and slapped her on the arm.

"Better than driving another mile with *you*," I joked. "Oh no . . ." I felt the car shift into overdrive, this time so strongly that it seemed the transmission would launch itself straight through the hood and into the sky. A few seconds later, prompted by my overcorrection on the accelerator, it slammed us back into a snail's pace that almost flung the car into the front grille of a semi-truck churning close behind us.

For the third time that day came the jolting blast of a Peterbilt's horn at close range.

"Mommy, are we there yet?" I asked, only half in jest.

"Only a mile longer," Naomi said. "I think I can see the pass now."

And just as I'd begun to despair of ever feeling level pavement under me again, the slope lessened as the forest thinned out around us. Then a sign came into view. *Vail Pass, Elevation 10,666.*

A rest area beckoned to me from the right, and it was then I realized how bad I needed to stop. Despite driving now on level ground, I nearly rocketed into overdrive again as I took the exit.

Several minutes later, after visiting the restroom, I was perched on a fence post, glowering down into the valley beyond, when Naomi approached me.

"Naomi, you really did lie to me," I said.

"What do you mean, honey?"

"Look at that down there. Does that look like a level mountaintop stretching all the way to the eastern edge of the Rockies?"

Naomi started to chuckle, until her eyes met mine and she realized I was not joking.

"You really don't know about mountains, do you?" she said. "Ruth, there's no such thing as a straight up, level forever, then straight down and you're done with the Rocky Mountains. It's up and down, up and down again, and so on like that."

"Is that the truth, finally, or just another cheesy life lesson of yours?"

She paused, looking away, and I saw I had wounded her.

"I'm sorry, Naomi. I didn't mean that. I value the things you tell me—I do. I guessed . . . I don't know . . . I thought I'd earned myself a break after making it all the way up here."

"But you did," she said. "You got yourself a bathroom break, a chance to stretch your legs and take in the pretty scenery, plus more great conversation with your favorite person!"

We burst out laughing and walked back to the Impala. With even more trepidation but much less complaining, I got back behind the wheel and pointed the car down the eastern side of Vail Pass, feeling like an Olympic ski jumper entrusting her fate to the forces of gravity.

"Now use that transmission," Naomi repeated for the eighth time. "Slip it into first gear low."

I did as I was told, only to discover that *first gear low* with a car this old, even one on its third transmission, only keeps speeds low when the car's on level ground. For grades as steep as we were traveling, the gear's slowing effect was about the same as if you wedged large sticks under the front fenders. At best, a net resistance of maybe four or five miles per hour.

That left relying on the brakes, which I could smell as I pushed on the pedal, trying to compensate for each sudden steepening of the road and corresponding failure of the accursed *first gear low.*

"Please tell me there won't be a grade like this again," I pleaded.

Naomi couldn't quite remember. It had, after all, been close to two decades since she'd made the trip, and in the opposite direction.

I continued my destruction of the burning brake pads. Traffic was starting to thicken just ahead, despite my driving in the fast lane. I tried to relax as Naomi had urged and began weaving around the vehicles.

Soon I could see a soaring mountain range ahead. The aspens were truly beautiful. So this was what folks meant by "fall colors." I had never seen them before. In the distance I also noticed a dramatic flattening of the grade.

And yet, as close as we were to the finish, I could also feel the brakes growing softer and less effective by the second. The engine, still stuck in low, whined and shuddered worse than ever.

Our descent was taking its toll on the car.

Just as I reached Copper Mountain at the bottom, a large truck decided to move into my lane and apply its brakes. I was forced to slam on mine, and in the process forced the pedal down farther than it had gone up to now.

"We can't do this again," I told Naomi, shaking my head. "Not without giving this car an extended break. It just won't handle any more."

"Why don't we just keep going as long as we can, and when we see a long hill, we'll exit and wait awhile. That'll allow time for everything to cool down—us included."

Exhaling loudly, I agreed with a nod.

The Midwest had better be one long, flat plain, I told myself, or we stood less of a chance than I'd initially feared.

CHAPTER 16

Lake Dillon, Colorado

"Why do you keep your family's past such a secret?" I asked Naomi as we devoured some of our snacks and drove past a large alpine valley cradling a huge, blue body of water identified by a sign as *Lake Dillon*. Now on a fairly level surface, I was feeling much more relaxed.

"What do you mean? I just spent a whole day showing you around my family's past."

"Not *that* past. Moab, I know plenty about. Lonnie couldn't stop talking about Moab. And now I know a lot more. But I'm talking about what came before that—back East. The place we're headed."

"Oh, my," she said in a tone that sounded like I'd just asked her to pick up a 300-pound weight. "I never meant to keep it a secret. . . ."

"Well, you have. And until now, it's been none of my business. But since I'm about to move my whole life there with you, I figure I have a right to ask. It does, after all, make what lies ahead a lot scarier for me."

"There's nothing scary about the place or the people. What keeps me quiet is just the personal pain it all represents for Eli and me."

"Eli's not here, Naomi," I said as gently as I could. "Why don't you tell me?"

She turned to me, her face splotched red with emotion. "It's really not much of a story, I promise. It's just so full of regret and sadness for me, that's all. When you get older, you'll understand."

"Naomi," I persisted, "I'm fully an adult, and what matters to you, matters to me. Don't you see? You're all I have in this world now, so what troubles you troubles me, too."

"Yes, but can you give me some time? I don't think I'm quite ready to unpack all that baggage."

"Okay. It's just . . . I don't get it. If all those memories and those times were so painful to you, why risk so much by going back?"

She laughed ruefully. "Good point. But remember, regret means it's my own choices I'm pained about. The people back there, the place itself, they were fine. They weren't perfect, but in many ways they were wonderful."

She took my right hand, which for the moment wasn't gripping the steering wheel.

"What about you, Ruth? I could ask the same thing about you and your past."

I swallowed hard, because explaining my past to her simply hadn't occurred to me. My life was different, I'd somehow convinced myself. My issues, my memories, were just too personal. Too painful. They existed . . . but in a different category.

"It cuts both ways," Naomi continued. "If you can't tell me these things, who can you tell?"

I let out a loud curse and pointed ahead. Naomi's question had disturbed me so that I neglected to pay attention to the road ahead. Suddenly I was looking up at a looming hill, so long it stretched beyond the mountainside and out of sight.

A sign beside the road said, *Loveland Pass, 6 miles.*

I started looking frantically for an exit, but it was too late. We were already on our way. Instead of an exit, all that lay to our right was a thousand feet of mountain air.

"If I remember right, this climb may be longer than the one before, but it's also more gradual," Naomi said.

"Man, I hope you're right, or we're toast."

"I'm not going to change the subject just because of a hill, you know," Naomi continued.

"You want me to dig up my past, all my old stuff, even while I'm driving for my life—*our* life?"

"You bet. I'd say the old stuff is a lot more important."

I glanced at her, trying to gauge her state of mind. Was she doing this to simply distract me from a distressing situation, or did she really mean to coax my dirtiest laundry out for a quick spin? Yet her eyes revealed nothing but kindness and concern.

"You're right about one thing," I said, more cheerfully now. "This hill isn't near as bad. Yet." I spoke that last word just as I saw several semis pulled off to the side with their hazard lights blinking and steam pouring from between their tires. To the left, across the oncoming lane of traffic, I'd already spotted my second runaway truck ramp.

I took a deep breath. Maybe this pass held perils I hadn't anticipated.

"So what exactly were you asking me?" I said to Naomi.

"I was asking about your deepest, buried secrets."

"You mean like why I left my foster family?"

"No. Before that. Your *real* family. Why were you taken away from your birth parents?"

"Why do you need to know junk like that? Why not just leave it alone?"

"For the same reasons, Ruth, that you want me to dig up my old 'junk.' What troubles you, troubles me."

"No, it's not the same," I countered. "There's a solid reason why I need to know about what happened *back East*. Because we're headed there, this very second. That place is going to be my future, and your problems with that place are going to determine how I come into that future."

"Yes, but as you keep telling me, we're it—you and I have only each other. You even said I've been more of a mom to you than your biological mother. And yet I have no idea what's holding together your emotional well-being. I'm pretty sure you never told Lonnie. Wouldn't it help you to tell someone?"

She was making sense, but I didn't trust myself to decide for certain. I felt myself losing concentration, fighting to maintain focus on the road before me. My concerns about the highway ahead were becoming lost in a swirl of emotions assaulting me from every side.

Finally, I hit some kind of bedrock, and spoke the words I'd avoided for years.

"Because if you knew, Naomi, then you'd have all the cause in the world to write me off as the trash you always knew I was."

There was silence in the seat beside me. The only noise came from the Impala's engine, which continued to growl its way uphill. Then Naomi's hand reached over and rested softly on my wrist. She seemed to wish she could hold my hand but knew I needed to keep it where it was on the wheel.

"Ruth," she said, "I want you to hear me. I know *exactly* what kind of person you are. In fact, I probably know it better than you do yourself. Believe me, if there's anyone in this world who knows that what kind of person you are isn't determined by what kind of job you have or where you live, or what bad things happened to you in your past—sweetie, that's me."

"Yeah?" I asked, feeling myself close to tears. "Then what kind of person am I?"

She didn't hesitate.

"You're a woman of character."

The moment I heard those words, I started weeping. Which I couldn't afford to do because we were now approaching the hilltop, and I had no idea what awaited me there. But I was powerless to stop the tears.

"You are, Ruth," Naomi continued. "Character is how you act when no one's around, when no one's forcing you to act right. And I've seen you choose the right thing, make the loving and responsible choice even when no one expected it of you. I've seen you behave far above what people expect of a Las Vegas cocktail waitress. Without even thinking about it, you treat people the way you want to be treated. You follow the Golden Rule, Ruth—and that's the first rule that gets broken in Vegas."

"That's no big deal, Naomi," I argued through my sobs. "I just know what it feels like to be abused, that's all."

"Yes, but many people take that same suffering and turn it into rage and aggression. You turned it into thoughtfulness. And kindness."

"I don't feel kind or thoughtful. . . ."

"It's how you treated me, Ruth, when you didn't have to! How many other women would have seen a bond as close as between Lonnie and me, and then set their mind to come between it, to break it? How many others make their mothers-in-law their worst enemy? And you could have won, too. You could have taken Lonnie away from me completely, given how much he adored you. I was at your mercy. Instead, you gave him back to me. That's how I know what kind of woman you are."

CHAPTER 17

(70)

Before I return to my story, I have to start this portion with a bit of a warning. If this is being read by a member of my family, especially for the first time, and if there are small ears within listening range, I need to alert you and ask you to please send the young ones away. They can come back, I'm sure, after this chapter is over. But for the time being, what I'm about to relate will be too disturbing for them.

Naomi had just finished telling me something I'd never considered before—that I could have easily distanced Lonnie from his mother, as so many wives do. And that my not doing such a thing showed her what kind of person I was.

Since it had never occurred to me to alienate Naomi from her son, I wasn't all that impressed with myself. But I was glad to hear I seemed to have done something right, for once.

I straightened up in my seat. We'd just driven into a tunnel, and everything changed. The lighting turned dim and yellow, with signs overhead warning me to lower my speed, and the ground was suddenly level again.

"Naomi," I replied, "I decided marrying Lonnie would be a very good idea after I saw how he treated *you*—how much he doted on you and wanted to take care of you. That was, honestly, the one major sign of character I saw in him. So you were never a threat. In fact, you were the opposite. You were the best news in the whole situation. Now you're the only good news I've got left."

The Eisenhower Tunnel stretched on and on. I could no longer see either the entrance in the rearview mirror or the exit ahead. I would later learn that it's the highest road tunnel in the world. At the time, however, it was merely a bewildering distraction.

"Ruth," said Naomi with passion in her voice, "do you want to know the real reason why I wish you'd come out with these buried things about your past? Because the more you stuff them inside of you, the more power you give them. The more you admit they're major, they will continue to define who you are. The moment you let them out, you defuse all that. You tell yourself it's just old junk that can't control you anymore."

"It doesn't control me," I protested weakly.

"Oh, right. Then why did you just tell me it defined what kind of person you are?"

"Because it's the first thing I remember!" I threw at her, just as the exit came into view around a shallow turn and we burst into a suddenly gray and rainy world.

I should have been paying closer attention, because in a heartbeat all the challenges ahead had changed completely. I was suddenly going downhill—too fast, with gravity, velocity, and wet pavement all working against me.

But none of it mattered. The words hung on my lips now, and they wouldn't be stopped.

"My very first memory, Naomi, is of waking up at night with . . . with a man's hand between—"

"Ruth, you don't have to say it if you don't—"

"No!" I interrupted. "I want to. Between my—"

But the breath tore out of me, and I couldn't finish the sentence.

"I was five, Naomi! *Five!*"

I suppose it doesn't need to be said that I was shouting by this point. I even thought I heard an echo in that car's interior, although it had to be my mind playing tricks.

I shifted down into low. It was as I'd feared—a shudder ran through the car, but it hardly slowed a bit.

"Your father?" she asked gingerly, nearly a minute later.

"No. My father was usually too high or drunk to do anything like that. Of course I didn't know that then. I just figured I wasn't worth protecting. See, we lived in shacks the farmers built on the edges of the fields. Because I had two older brothers, we rented two shacks. One for Mama and Papa, the other for me and my brothers."

I focused again on my driving, testing the brake pedal. It was higher than it had been at the bottom of Vail Pass, but not as recovered as I'd hoped. I gave it a long, gentle push to slow us down as we came around a broad turn with a sharp drop-off on one side. When I had pushed the pedal as long as I dared, then released it, we regained speed at an alarming rate. I took a deep breath to staunch my rising panic.

"So your brothers did it?"

I shook my head. "Worse. They charged their friends from across the highway one dollar each for a turn with me."

Naomi lowered her head. She finally asked, "Did you ever tell? Ever say anything to anyone?"

I paused and depressed the brake to change lanes and avoid a bottleneck ahead.

"I told Mama after it had been going on awhile, and she stomped off, found Tonio and Rudy, and started beating the daylights out of them. Only thing was, they were the best pickers in our family. We depended on them. So when Papa saw her about to do serious bodily harm to them, he came and stopped her. With a right slug to her jaw."

"Did—did he suffer any consequences?" She sounded horrified.

I chuckled bitterly. "Naomi, this wasn't white-bread America. No police officer or social worker came to help me and Mama. She just never came to my defense again, that's all. I tried twice more to tell her it was still happening, getting worse even. But she didn't want to hear it. She couldn't. She bandaged me a few times, but I knew not to tell her a word ever again."

"Did your father ever learn what really happened?"

There. She'd reached it. Touched the core. The raw nerve.

My next breath wrenched from me as though I had an anvil on my chest.

"He did. Much later, he caught them doing it. I was nine by this time."

"What did he do?"

A slowpoke was approaching fast in my windshield. I lowered my foot onto the brake, a little harder than before. Perhaps due to the topic at hand.

The pedal sank all the way down. My toes made contact with the top of the rubber mat.

Oh no! The brakes . . .

The bitterness of knowing I had nothing to stop the car seemed to match—to merge somehow—with the bitterness of my reply.

Smiling fatalistically, I turned to Naomi. "Nothing."

"He did nothing about it?"

"Well, he took the money. He took the money for himself, and he . . ."

I couldn't finish. I turned back to the road, pumped my foot violently once, then twice.

"No brakes!"

Naomi's quick intake of air must have been for me, because I couldn't breathe at all. The scenery below, bordered at the bottom by a fir-clad slope and a sharp left turn, was rising faster and faster toward us.

I swallowed and felt the old hatred and rage electrify every inch of my body.

"He took the money, and he bought beers for all of their fathers. With the same money, Naomi. Then later he came home drunk and beat Mama unconscious for not keeping better watch over me."

Naomi was letting out little moans and climbing up in her seat, as though trying to cushion an imminent impact.

What I was doing then is hard to say. I'd entered a state where my fury had become so potent, it burned clean into some sort of suicidal calm. I was beyond tears or shouts now. I was steering for my life through a deathtrap both physical and emotional, and all outward disturbances had left me now. I was as physically still as a forest after a storm.

Inside was another matter.

The low gear was now whining at an alarming level, but it was hardly stopping us at all. Our car and its contents had become an out-of-control projectile.

My fingers gripped the wheel so tightly I thought my knuckles would break. And I stared so furiously at the road ahead that I anticipated blacking out at any moment.

"He sold me, Naomi. Sold me for a six-pack of beer."

I swerved to avoid yet another car, and the tires squealed in protest.

"Did you hear me, Naomi? He *sold me*!"

Naomi's hand touched my shoulder. We were turning now, and the centrifugal force tugging us to the right was exhilarating. Her hand gripped my shirt now, trying to keep herself upright. But the effort only pulled me with her. I braced myself with my free foot, grimaced and held on. Still, I could feel myself leaning and then sliding sideways, away from my position.

The tires squealed madly as the car drifted to halfway between the stripes toward the cliffside guardrail. I'm sure it was less than a foot from the guardrail when finally we began to ease back into our lane.

"You sold me! You *scum*!" I shouted at the top of my lungs, picturing my father's face in the windshield before me. "How could you do such a thing?"

Naomi was right—the catharsis of unleashing those words into the air did release something inside me. I felt infused with strength, with the power to steer my course anywhere.

So I did. I edged the car back into traffic, the broad turn now behind me, and began to serenely weave around the cars in front of us. I was doing ninety on a two-lane mountain highway, and I didn't care. The bottom was approaching and the slope flattening again, with an exit approaching quickly on the right.

Then I looked ahead.

Traffic on the Interstate was stopped. A sea of red brake lights met my gaze.

"Naomi, we have to take this exit, no matter what. Or we're dead."

As it neared, I could tell it was a typical exit with a near-perpendicular turn not far after leaving the highway. No way could I make that turn and follow the lane—I simply was going too fast. What if I stayed straight? It was too early to tell where such a trajectory would lead us. I quick made up my mind and started moving to the right well in advance of the exit, knowing I would need the extra room. Which turned out to be a good choice.

I careened onto the exit ramp like a jet fighter down a runway, still pumping the brake pedal in a surreal display of futility. The road sank down and so did the car, striking the underbody loudly, still flying at sixty-plus miles per hour.

Just ahead of us, past the cross street and both its lanes, was a gas station and convenience store. I slammed my hand down on the horn.

Thankfully, the light just ahead glowed green. We sailed through, bounced up savagely at the curb of the pavement. Only then did I see that if I steered hard to the right, I could weave between the building and the pumps. Open space lay beyond the gap, beckoning me.

If I missed, Naomi and I would strike the pumps, ignite the fuel, and—

The car's tires squealed when I made the turn, but they held. Thank God no one was crossing that convenience store parking lot, because we blew through it like a tornado. We bounced on the warped pavement, the impact throwing me sideways as we hurtled toward the building's corner. Somehow, in a wild instinct I turned the wheel at the last second. The brick corner sheared off my driver's side mirror, mere inches away, but we passed by. Amazingly the building was left totally unscathed, we saw later. We shot over a sloping rear parking area and into an adjoining, unpaved road. Victorian façades raced past our window. I jerked the car to the side, hoping to follow the road, pitting such force against our momentum that our left wheels actually left the ground. But we held and stayed on the road's bumpy surface. We sped through a stop sign unharmed, through the intersection, then another span of roadway.

I looked ahead and saw that the road ended in a cul-de-sac! All around us were more Victorian-style homes. There was no other way out than to try something I'd seen demonstrated on TV on a sleepless night several years before.

"Hang on, Naomi!" I shouted. "'Cause this is the end of the line, no matter what. . . ."

If we hadn't been losing speed rapidly, I would never have dreamed of trying this. But as we bumped and bounced into the cul-de-sac, I jerked the steering wheel to the right as hard and as swiftly as I could.

Sure enough, the Impala's rear end swung out wide and began a broad slide across the pavement. I started straightening the wheel almost immediately, and before we could do a 360, we were pointed back the way we had come, finally at a stop.

Neither of us had the energy to say a word during that moment of immense relief after the car stopped moving and it became clear we had actually survived. We both hung our heads and exhaled, long and loud.

I flung open the door with as much strength as I could muster, shut it behind me, and sank against the side of the car, down to the ground, and threw up.

"I've got to hand it to you," I said to Naomi without looking up when I detected her coming around to my side. "For a layperson, you sure put on one doozey of a therapy session."

"If that's what it was," she said in a tired voice, "then I pardon you now for the crime of trying to kill your therapist."

CHAPTER 18

Georgetown, Colorado

We had landed, almost literally, in Georgetown—a small, Victorian village of a thousand people, perched on the eastern foot of Loveland Pass.

If there was one fortunate turn in our life-threatening descent, it was that we came to a stop less than seventy-five yards from Brantley's, the largest truck stop in the state. The car was towed there while Naomi and I sat down to give a statement to the officer in charge of the scene. A half hour later, we found ourselves standing at the truck stop's main counter, waiting to hear the news of what our little episode had done to the Impala. Brantley's service manager—a tall, potbellied, grease-stained, middle-aged man with the name *Kenny* stitched above his shirt pocket—delivered his verdict.

"Well, you ladies are lucky in a whole lotta ways. What you did is ride your brakes so hard that you caused the brake fluid to overheat. It got so hot, it started boiling. And when fluid turns to gas, it compresses where liquid won't. That's why you lost your pedal height so quick."

"So what's the damage?" asked Naomi. After the wonder of finding ourselves still alive, we had both come to realize our journey was now hanging on a knife's edge. What we didn't know, and anxiously wanted to find out, was the cost.

"Well, you didn't burn up your brakes entirely," Kenny answered, staring at a clipboard. "But you did do a pretty good number on the calipers and pads. You're gonna need a complete brake job. We can get you back on the road for about four hundred."

Naomi looked like she'd been struck by an invisible blow to the midsection.

She looked at me. We both knew this was the end. Our Wal-Mart run and a gas stop had left us with just under four hundred total.

We both turned away from the counter, reeling. I don't think I've ever felt more trapped in my life. We couldn't leave without getting the work done, but getting it done would make it impossible to buy enough gas to return to Vegas.

Going forward? That was completely out of the question.

"We have to get it fixed," I whispered to Naomi, "or we're stuck right here. Wherever *here* is . . ."

She nodded, her face ashen with the accumulated shock of our ordeal, followed by such discouraging news.

"How quickly can you do it?" I asked the manager.

He glanced back at his clipboard. "If all goes well, we should be able to have your car ready as early as tomorrow afternoon."

I nodded numbly, trying not to think about how Naomi and I would survive until then. One catastrophe at a time, I told myself.

And yet the thoughts haunting me since the start of this trip had now grown deafening. *You'll never make it. It was doomed from the start. A fool's errand . . .*

Inwardly, I kicked myself. I'd always been known for having a good head on my shoulders, able to heed and abide by my keenest instincts. But in the last two days I had ignored them in a fit of emotion and stepped off the deep end. I looked around me and experienced a head-clearing, cloud-parting kind of epiphany—seeing my surroundings with fresh eyes, I asked myself, *What in the world are you doing here, Ruth? Hundreds of miles away from home, stuck in some little town in the mountains—and at a truck stop of all places?*

I shook my head, more to rid my mind of these thoughts than anything else. No matter what I was wrestling with, I knew there was a harsh reality at hand, one that absolutely demanded my attention.

"We're stranded here, sir," I said. "Trying to get to Pennsylvania with just about the amount of money than what you just quoted us. Is there any kind of deal you can cut us?"

"How much d'y'all have?"

"We have about three hundred and ninety, but that's supposed to last—"

"I'll do it for three fifty, cash."

I froze, taken aback by his abruptness.

"Look," he said, "I can see you're in a tight spot here, but that's the best I can do. You won't find a better deal on a brake job this side of Denver."

I knew I should seal the deal without delay, but somehow I could not picture myself handing him almost all our remaining money.

"What're you gonna do?" he asked, his eyebrows raised.

Just then, like a clarion call of salvation, came the sound I needed—a sound very familiar to my ears, straight out of my recent past.

The sound of a half drunk, irate bar customer.

"Hey! I need a drink! When's that hag gonna come back and serve me?"

Kenny rolled his eyes and turned toward the bar area, which began in a dark room immediately to our left.

"Sorry, buddy. Radonna had to go home sick. I'll be with ya in a minute." Then he turned back to me and said, "Well, what's it gonna be?"

I had an idea.

"Watch me," I said.

I stepped into the bar area, walked over to a nearby corner where I saw an empty tray and a pad and pencil, picked them up and hurried back to the customer.

"I can help you, sir," I said in my most composed, business-like voice. "What'll it be?"

The man looked me up and down, confused.

"Who are *you*?" he said with a smirk.

I could read a customer like this in my sleep. He was one step away from belligerence, requiring what my old boss would call a "forcible removal," maybe even a call to the police.

"I apologize for the delay, sir," I continued. "This one's on the house."

The man leaned back, an exaggerated look of appraisal on his face.

"Fine. Another scotch. Neat."

I hurried back to the bar, which was also unoccupied. Sizing up the liquor display, I picked out the Chivas and poured him a small glass, straight. I brought the drink to the customer, then walked back to where Kenny stood, his eyes wide.

"Sounds like you had a defection today," I said. "How about, while our car's in the shop, I sub in your lounge?"

"Do you rent rooms?" asked Naomi. "I spent twenty years in the motel business. I could do some housekeeping."

Kenny's face softened, the old brusqueness gone. "We don't have motel rooms exactly, but we have a shower area and some small rooms where drivers can change and catch a nap. Matter of fact, it's gotten pretty nasty. . . ."

"How much do you pay your housekeepers?"

"Tell you what—how about a lump sum? You clean the place up and down, catch me up on the backed-up laundry, organize the place, and I'll comp the brake job."

"The brake work will be free?"

"In exchange for what I just said, sure."

"If that includes letting Ruth keep her tips from the bar"—she extended her hand to shake on the agreement—"you've got a deal."

He thought for a second, shook her hand, then mine.

And that's when, for the very first time, I began to catch the first stirrings of an inner voice quite unlike the discouraging one I'd been hearing all throughout the day.

You're gonna make it, the voice said, low and confident. *You two are gonna muddle through after all.*

You'd think it would have been completely depressing to spend two days stuck in a small-town truck stop, slinging booze for under-the-counter cash. But during that first afternoon, while I plunged into the challenge of making that bar run like a top, I felt a sense of purpose and determination I hadn't felt in years. This was something I knew how to do, and I'd stepped back into it voluntarily, with a clear knowledge that it would end. Soon.

We'd made it through one of the worst disasters imaginable, and survived. I had endured those moments of helplessness, of total shock and dejection, of feeling sure the end of our journey had come. And together, Naomi and I had not only survived but overcome it.

I met Naomi for a break outside, after our first two hours, and she felt the same. We walked awhile, breathed in the cool mountain air, our arms folded against a pine-scented breeze, and drank in the view of mountaintops on every side, the late-afternoon light, azure blue and aspen gold, with sunbeams pouring down between the peaks.

But we didn't return to my revelation while careening down the mountain and through town. For now, it seemed off-limits. She knew it, and I knew it.

"I can't believe our luck," Naomi said with a grin.

"Wait a minute. I thought you said you had no luck."

"That's what I meant, Ruth. I can't believe I had *good* luck."

"Hey, I told you that together we were gonna make it. Remember?"

She laughed, and the sound of her laughter had me smiling deep inside.

"How's your job doing?" I asked. "Is it as sloppy as it sounded?"

She shrugged. "No worse, I suppose, than cleaning up after a teenage boy. I'll live through it. Especially if it puts new brakes on the Impala. How about you, Ruth? How does it feel to dip your toe back into that old life?"

It was my turn to shrug. "It's not so bad. I mean, mentally I'd so enjoyed putting my whole Vegas life completely behind me. I was sure I'd never strap on a bar apron ever again. But it's only for a little while. Like one final tour of what I'm leaving behind."

"Hey, look," Naomi said, pointing toward the Interstate. I looked but only saw the echoing roadbed as it rose up toward Loveland Pass.

"No, dear. Above it."

I raised my gaze to a huge rock face rising above the highway. I focused my eyes upon the faraway stone. There, almost completely camouflaged against the granite, rested a small herd of bighorn sheep. Their lead ram, his horns curled almost into a complete circle, stood at their head, staring out over the valley from an outthrust boulder.

"Wow. Sheep."

The sight pulled my thoughts back to Dead Horse Point. I couldn't help but revisit those horses in Utah, standing there until they dropped from malnutrition. The ram brought to mind some rogue mustang, left behind for his unruly nature, staring out over the Colorado River, the fringe of green grass surrounding it, and wondering if he could survive the leap.

We returned to the truck stop and worked several more hours. Actually, Naomi finished before I did, and she came into the bar, walking like an old woman, and sat down in the back. She stayed there for nearly three hours, munching on peanuts and watching TV, while I continued to rack up the tips and count the hours till closing.

As it turned out, both the truck stop's bartender and the waitress had skedaddled together, apparently for good. Yet I was able to handle both tasks without too much trouble. When dinnertime came around, I slipped Naomi some of my tip money, and she walked to a nearby convenience store. She returned bearing an assortment of sandwiches and junk food, which I gratefully gulped down during stolen moments at the bar.

We spent the night in an old, rusted-out RV that Kenny had parked out back. I felt my way in after midnight and found a couple of moldy blankets and a stiff mattress Naomi had pulled out and saved for me.

It didn't matter. I had never been so exhausted in my life, and with cool mountain air drifting over me from an open window, I fell into a deep, heavy slumber.

In a way, this brief return to my old occupation was good for me—what I would later think of as my Georgetown interlude—because it allowed me to make my peace with that past. I also resolved never to go back to it ever again, no matter what.

The next morning we woke with the sunrise, and a chill that made my bones ache. For a second, still groggy and sleep-addled, I forgot where I was and imagined myself back two dawns before in Naomi's tiny living room, rising in the silence with Orpah. Then I felt the pain in my back and legs, the nip in the air, and saw the dirty apron at my waist that I'd forgotten to remove the night before.

Focusing my eyes and seeing instead Naomi huddled in the corner gave me an unanticipated pang of nostalgia. I wondered what Orpah was doing, how she'd weathered the trip home alone. Whether she'd harbored any second thoughts about not joining me in that impulsive final moment. Somehow, though, when I thought about it, it seemed fated that this particular journey wasn't for her. Nothing personal, because she loved Naomi as much as I did, yet she didn't seem to need her as completely.

All the same, I missed her, and decided that as soon as I could charge up my cell phone minutes, I'd give Orpah a call and check up on her.

Naomi and I stepped out into the truck stop's grungy backside just in time to hear some of the early rising truckers fire up their engines and see the morning crew arrive for breakfast shift.

The cocktail lounge didn't open until ten o'clock, and since Naomi had no time card to punch, we explored Georgetown with a refreshing sense of aimlessness. Eventually, after walking half a mile along unpaved roads that looked as though they hadn't changed much in over a century, we reached Main Street. The three-block downtown district consisted of an 1880s Currier and Ives streetscape of Victorian storefronts and streetlamps kissed by rosy, early morning light. A block away, a strangely triangular white tower bore the markings of a long-defunct fire company. One of the storefronts was an authentic general store, unchanged since the nineteenth century. *Kneisel & Anderson*, the hand-painted sign read.

"You want to go in?" Naomi asked. "By the way, how did you total out last night?"

"Thirty-three bucks—after the snacks."

"Not bad."

"No, but I doubt that added to our stash will get us to Pennsylvania."

CHAPTER 19

70

Following Naomi across the threshold of the general store, I felt like I had traveled back in time. The wooden floor, the solid oak shelves and icebox displays filled with European cheeses and delicacies, the smell of pine boughs and cinnamon tea and coffee all convinced my senses I was in Scandinavia at least a century ago.

We had to be careful with our money, but this was the first place for groceries we'd seen on our walk. In the spirit of frugality with a hint of extravagance, we bought a day-old baguette and a tiny jar of Nutella, the chocolate and hazelnut spread we'd heard so much about. Sitting out on a curbside bench, we coated our bread and enjoyed what was, for us, an extravagant meal. Washed down with generic mineral water, the spread tasted every bit as delicious as we'd always been told.

"So, young lady," Naomi said after finishing her first piece, "do you think we're going to make it?"

I almost groaned. I had been so relieved to finally take my mind off the subject and all its stresses.

"Oh, Naomi," I sighed, "I don't know. I have these moments when I'm certain we'll muddle through somehow. Like yesterday, when we worked out our problem with the car and got the jobs. Then there are other moments when I hear that voice of reason jumping back in to tell me we're both out of our minds. That loonies like you and me are liable to end up in unmarked graves, because there's no one within a thousand miles to identify our bodies."

"Thanks, Ruth," she said glumly. "That was quite uplifting."

I laughed so abruptly that I spit out bits of Nutella and bread on the sidewalk. Immediately a pair of fat, gray pigeons flew down upon my offering with enthusiasm.

"What about you?" I asked. "What do you think?"

"Ruth, I didn't pose the question in order to confirm my own mind. I'm truly confused. I cannot see or feel the outcome right now. I'm completely in suspense. Which is why I asked you."

"One thing's for sure. If my tips don't pick up, we'll be pushing that car past the Mississippi."

We began walking again and crossed over a fast-running mountain creek.

"At times it kind of feels like we're on vacation," I said. "Do you know what I mean?"

She turned to stare at me. "I feel like I'm in that bad dream of a vacation that ends with my alarm clock going off." Then she smiled. "We'd better start walking back. Kenny is probably wondering where we are."

We arrived at the station and launched into the day as "Brantley's magic cleaning team," something Naomi came up with. Her dry sense of humor could catch you off guard and make you laugh to the point of tears.

Naomi kept the showers off-limits for two hours while she washed them clean again, scrubbing like only a Pennsylvania Dutch woman could. As for me, I sleepwalked through the soul-deadening early hours at the bar, serving a group of truckers and some locals and waiting for a big spender to come along and save the day.

He walked through the door sometime around two in the afternoon. Jimmy was built like a linebacker gone to seed, wearing a Peterbilt cap, knee-stained jeans, and dirty shirt. He began quizzing me on exotic drinks I had no problem mixing and, once impressed, moved on to a one-way conversation on the evils of the United Nations.

I was in rare form, succeeding both at making him think I was actually conversing with him and agreeing with his views. When he asked about food, instead of sending him over to the diner area, I forwarded his order and served as his waitress.

Later that afternoon, after he left, I found a twenty-five-dollar tip next to his empty plate. I smiled as I pocketed the cash. It brought my day's take close to fifty dollars.

I found Kenny and asked for an update on the car. He laughed and said, "Well, it's been ready since eleven this morning, but you and your friend Naomi have done such a good job, I didn't want to lose you. I've had five compliments on the condition of the showers, and lots of positive comments about you as the new waitress *and* bartender. Oh, and I still haven't made any headway on replacing you in the bar."

"Thanks, but, I mean . . . we're square, right?" I asked. "We can go now?"

"Yeah, yeah, we're square. But I'd appreciate it if you'd help me out through close tonight. I'll throw in fifty bucks."

"And another night in the Taj Mahal?"

With a chuckle he said, "Tell you what—I'll even throw in a room at the All Aboard Inn, our best B and B."

"That sounds great! You got yourself a deal."

My consolation for a miserable evening in the bar was that Naomi got to enjoy a leisurely evening at the bed-and-breakfast up the street, soaking in a claw-foot tub and reading a passed-along novel for hours on a comfortable mattress.

For me, it was a profitable evening. At around ten o'clock, a dozen bikers on a tour of the Rockies invaded and turned the place from a quiet haven into a louder, more dangerous version of a frat house. My tips went through the roof, but at the cost of several pats on the rump, the creepy yet familiar feeling of eyes staring at my body, and shouting matches with angry customers. The bar—which had previously been quite manageable all by myself—had quickly gotten out of hand, and I paid the price.

The low point came just before midnight, when a bald, beady-eyed character who seemed to be the leader of this bunch decided he'd waited long enough.

"I want to see your manager!" he yelled.

"I'll call him, sir," I said, trying my best to sound cooperative. I walked over to a telephone and punched in the numbers given to me.

But no one answered. I left a quick message for Kenny on the answering machine about the problem with the man at the bar, then returned to work.

The biker man didn't give up his rant, and the atmosphere started to seriously deteriorate. After so much experience, you learn to read the vibe generated by customers the way you feel humidity or air pressure. And this room was on its way to blowing its top. Curses echoed across the tables, and their angry eyes were fixed on me.

Walking past the biker, I felt his hand clamp on to my arm in a vise grip.

"I'll tell you what you're gonna do, sweet thing," he said through clenched teeth. "You're gonna refund every dime my buddies and I have spent here tonight. And you're gonna do it now."

You should know that after a lifetime's worth of taking abuse from men, I'd taken measures to educate myself and in the process learned a few moves. First and foremost, I don't let any man scare me—or at least see that I'm scared.

"You know what *you're* going to do?" I said in my huskiest voice. "You're going to let go of my arm. Then you're going to pay your tab. Then you're going to leave this place before the cops arrive."

"Oh yeah," he said, rising to his feet to level his sweaty, grimy face with mine. "And who's gonna make me?"

Just then, to my complete surprise, I heard a metallic click and a male voice growl, "I am, dirtbag."

Suddenly something shiny appeared between me and the biker. A chrome .357 handgun, its hammer already pulled back by a very big thumb.

I glanced at a familiar face, but the clothes were all wrong. Standing there was my big tipper from earlier, now wearing a clean pair of pants and a fancy button-down shirt.

The clamp on my arm released, and I stepped away from the table. From behind me came the sounds of chairs and tables scraping the hardwood floor, of boots hitting its surface as their owners quickly backed away.

The bald biker's features twisted into an ugly, inhuman expression.

"Son, you better have some ammo in that thing," he snarled, "because you can bet I'm gonna make you use it."

The gun's barrel shoved hard against the biker's temple.

"Fine with me." The biker grimaced and flexed his neck muscles. "Tell your buddies to settle up and leave. *Now*. I wanna hear hogs firing up and squealing out of here."

The biker-leader screwed up his face and spit on the floor. "This place stinks anyway. Let's go, brothers!"

After an unsettling pause, the group of bikers started pulling out wallets, tossing down bills, and walking toward the exit with exaggerated slowness, a murmur of curses uttered under their breath, mixing with their cigarette smoke.

Their leader leaned away from the gun at his head and pointed an index finger at my rescuer. He said nothing but mercly held the finger level for a moment, the threat clear. Then the biker swiveled on his heels and pointed the same finger of revenge at me.

The first hog roared to life outside, mimicked immediately by a whole flurry of others. The biker-leader left the bar, punching the glass door open with his fist on his way out.

The man holding the gun lowered it and let out a sigh. I looked around and realized that, except for the two of us, the bar was empty. The angry bikers and the sight of a gun had driven out all the other customers.

"Thank you," I said to the man. "The gun might have been a little much, but I really appreciate you getting them out of here."

"You're welcome. I hate seeing those scum come through our town. Makes me wish the Interstate wasn't so close."

"Where do those guys come from?"

"They come through every ycar. From somewhere back East."

Back East. The words flooded my veins with ice water. This gang could be on the road ahead of us.

I sat down, unsteady, and felt my head swimming. "I'm

sorry. Did you want a drink? I'll be glad to whip you up something. On the house."

"No, thank you, miss." He shot a glance toward the exit as if to verify the bikers had actually left. "If I might give you a little piece of advice—you might wanna call the police and make a report, and then shut this place down for the night."

I did just that. I also called Naomi at the bed-and-breakfast to tell her I'd be coming back sooner rather than later and could she ask that the front door be left unlocked for me. Then I spent the next hour getting interviewed by the police, along with my armed savior. Toward the end, the officer received some kind of emergency call about something happening on the Interstate and rushed out.

"Now there's an anticlimax," said the man, whom I'd heard identify himself as James. "Could I give you a ride to the All Aboard?"

I gulped and frowned. "How did you know where I'm staying?"

He smiled apologetically. "I didn't actually come here tonight to have a drink. I came here because I ran into Kenny downtown. He told me about your situation. Said if you'd done such a good job, I should be embarrassed to tip you as little as I did. So I came here to see you . . . well, to give you this."

He pulled out a hundred-dollar bill.

"I-I can't accept this," I said. "I appreciate it, though. It's very kind, but—."

"Look. After what I saw you put up with tonight, you earned this ten times over. Please keep it along with my best wishes and admiration."

"I don't know what to say. Thank you . . ." I closed my hand over the bill and smiled at him. Now out of his work clothes and without a gun in his hand, he looked like a nice, attractive man. A man I might have gone out with, back in my former life.

"I'm sorry the police left so soon. They should've given you a ride. Sure you don't want a lift?"

Still wary, conditioned by years of working as a cocktail waitress, I hesitated. But then I pictured walking four blocks in the middle of the night with the possibility of vengeful bikers lurking around, and found the prospect less than desirable. I smiled, then stopped again. Those instincts—the oldest and most well-worn of them—were blinking. Full red light. The man was hitting on me. Obviously out for something I didn't want to give.

"Look, I'm . . . I'm not looking for—"

He waved his hand. "Just a ride. From a gentleman to a lady."

"Promise? Because I buried my husband not too long ago."

His face fell. He seemed sincere. "Promise," he said.

I walked out into the night after him. All told, despite its trials, it had been a good day for tips. I now had a nice wad of cash to count later.

I climbed into James's oversized pickup, still scanning the bushes and nearby street corners for lingering bikers. I saw nothing to fear.

"Do you think they'll come back?" I asked.

"Hopefully by the time they do, you'll be long gone. I know Kenny and his crew will be ready for them."

"Well, that makes me feel better."

A couple of minutes later we drove right by the All Aboard Inn in a surge of speed.

"That's my stop," I said, pointing.

He turned to me with a boyish expression. "Oh, you don't want to hit the sack so soon, do you? After all this excitement?

Why don't we prolong the party just a little bit?"

The fact that he hadn't asked until after speeding past the B and B told me all I needed to know. I sighed as every muscle in my body tensed again.

"Because I don't want to, James. Please take me back right now."

He turned, smiled indulgently, and kept driving straight. Then, with a heart-stopping suddenness, he threw the massive truck into a turn, pulling into a parking spot off to the side of the road.

"I just figured we could help each other, you know," he said smoothly. "I've got more cash than I do companionship. And you, well, I know you're in dire need, and I've been glad to help out. But there's another bill like the one I gave you, just waiting for you if you'll . . . party with me a little. Please. I'm still a gentleman, just one who's willing to pay."

"No. You stopped being a gentleman when we passed my bed-and-breakfast."

His smile melted into an expression of regret.

"Now, don't be that way . . ."

I reached for the door handle, but his hand was quicker, pouncing on the lock button before I could jump out. I went for the lock lever, but it was smooth and barely protruded beyond the door panel. As I fiddled with it, I felt my arm grabbed tightly for the second time that night.

CHAPTER 20

70

"Look." The charm had turned into irritation. "That place wasn't Tavern on the Green in Central Park, New York, and you're no Julia Roberts. So why don't we drop the pretenses and just get down to business?"

I need to remind everyone that I'd learned how to handle myself a long time before this. You don't make a career as a cocktail waitress in Vegas without learning self-defense. And I had taken a year's worth of classes, plus several years of real-life practice. Truth was, James had shut down a dangerous situation with that handgun of his, but I wouldn't have been helpless if he'd never arrived.

"Because," I told him, "I'm *not* in the business. I've never been for sale."

My hands flew into action. My left fist drove out sideways and connected with his face. Not a great blow, but I knew it had thrown his nose into a state of agony, giving me a couple of seconds. Before he recovered, I plunged my other hand along his belt where I'd seen him holster the gun. In a flash I unbuckled the strap and whipped out the gun.

In case he mistook me for a helpless female who couldn't handle the weapon, I slapped off the safety with my free hand, cupping it over my gun hand to form a two-handed revolver grip. Despite my distaste for firearms, I fervently thanked Lonnie for all those Saturdays he'd insisted I accompany him to the pistol range outside Vegas. Togetherness time, you know. As a result of those hours spent shooting with him, I now handled the weapon with an ease that surprised even me.

The man roared into action, trying to slap the weapon away from his face. Yet I held on, and as he threw himself on me, I brought my right hand back to press the barrel hard against his temple.

I made sure he heard the hammer cock back.

"James, you will drive me home. Now."

I slid back across the seat all the way to my door, keeping my feet outstretched between us, the gun aimed at his forehead. Breathing heavily and shooting me homicidal looks, he threw the truck into gear and peeled out in a cloud of burning rubber. Less than a minute later he screeched to a halt in the middle of the street, directly in front of the B and B.

"I have a question for you," I said, one finger poised on the door latch. "Were you really going to pay me for sex, or just rape me?"

He rolled his eyes and started fishing in his front pocket. He pulled out a hundred-dollar bill, which he dangled before me with two fingers.

"So, James, I have another question. What's it worth to you for me to leave town tomorrow without ever speaking to my friend at the Georgetown Police Department, the officer we spoke with tonight?"

He released the bill and it fell into my open hand.

"Good answer. You're in very good luck, James. This bill is all tonight's criminal behavior is going to cost you, instead of an arrest and trial, a fortune in legal bills, public humiliation, the loss of your job and whatever family you may have waiting at home, not to mention jail time. And all you have to do in exchange for such good fortune is to walk away. And trust me when I tell you that I have no interest in making a further stink about this. So if you leave me alone, you'll never have to deal with the consequences of trying to assault me. This night goes away. Consider it a second chance on your part. Okay?"

In response, he spat out a curse.

"See, James, that wasn't very polite. Do I need to show you how good my aim is?"

"No, you don't."

"Because it's good. I can shoot, James. And with so many people mad at me tonight, I think I'll keep the gun, too."

I backed out of the truck, still aiming the gun in what Lonnie used to call a "modified Weaver stance." All I knew is it looked intimidating. Strange what you'll remember at such times. Going with Lonnie to the shooting range had never been my favorite way to spend an afternoon, but now I was truly grateful.

Naomi was sitting up in bed, wearing the bleary-eyed stare of the newly awakened, when I walked in. Anxious that she not see the state I was in, I left the lights low. That didn't work. Naomi sprang out of bed and flipped on almost every light in the room.

"Ruth, are you all right?" she demanded. "You look like you just fought World War II single-handed! And what is that you're holding?"

I looked down. I'd been too distracted to hide the gun or

let go of my earlier grip. Now I did, allowing my fingers to straighten and go limp. The gun fell heavily to the room's antique carpet.

Without meeting Naomi's gaze, I went over and plopped onto the bed. Naomi followed, taking a seat next to me. I turned and burrowed into her arms, releasing all the muscles I had clenched so tightly for the previous three hours. Not crying really, but sort of whimpering like a child who doesn't know which emotion to choose. I leaned my head on her shoulder.

"Are you all right, sweetie?" she asked again.

"No, I'm not, Naomi," I said shakily.

"Please tell me . . ."

"Naomi," I said at last, feeling incredibly weary and overcome, "are there any bath salts left in that open box over there?"

"Oh, yes," she answered. "I thought of you and saved half of them just for your return."

"Do you think they're strong enough to wash off the last residue of who I've been all these years? At least from my own eyes? I'm ready. I'm ready for it to all be gone. I'm ready for men to see me as a woman, not prey. I wish I was as ugly as I feel."

"I understand," she said, patting my back lovingly and parting my still-disheveled hair to look into my face. "It's all there waiting for you. You go into the bath and scrub it all off, every bit of it."

And so I filled the claw-foot tub with steaming water and, even though it was almost two-thirty in the morning, took a long, indulgent bath, emptying every container of spa suds and minerals in the process.

At one point Naomi tiptoed in and coaxed the evening's story out of me. She wept with me and told me that I was beautiful and clean. She reminded me that my past was sitting all bunched up in a Wal-Mart bag in the trunk, and said I'd been very brave to stand up against my attacker—something she rightly guessed I'd learned to do after leaving my birth family to enter the "protective custody" of not one but three foster families in a row.

Then she counted my wad, which came to $287.

Holding the cash, she sat on a wicker basket, looked at me, and cried.

"I know it's just money," she said in a wavering voice, "but for us right now, this, added to what we already have, is miles toward our journey. And toward hope, when we reach the end. The first hope I've had that we might actually make it. I know it'll still be very tight, and we're going to have to pray the Impala doesn't throw us another curve. Literally."

CHAPTER 21

70

Strangely, my long bath had the effect of stimulating me instead of the usual sedative impact on my senses. My mind sharpened, my spirits lifted, along with my energy level.

But when I finally stepped out of the tub, wrapped a thick towel around me, and began drying my hair, a sense of danger swept over me and seized me by the throat. I stood still and looked around. The shades were drawn over all the windows, the door to our room securely locked. For the moment, Naomi and I were safe.

But my thoughts moved outside the walls of the room and the B and B in which we were spending the night. I suddenly realized how naïve and foolish I'd been. I'd enraged not one but two evil and vengeful men, and at least one of them knew where I was right now. My heart pounded and my knees went limp.

It was going on four in the morning when I walked over and gently roused Naomi with a hand on her shoulder. She shot up, instantly awake, and I wondered if she shared this same feeling of lurking danger.

"Naomi, I'm so sorry to do this, but I think we ought to go. As in now."

Her expression grew fearful. "Is there someone. . . ?" she whispered.

I shook my head. "No, but I'm coming to grips with how vulnerable we are here. How about we leave quietly, and you get the rest of your sleep on the road?"

"And what about *you*?"

"Me? I'm keyed up enough to drive a thousand miles."

Without turning on any lights other than the bathroom's, and making as little noise as possible, we gathered our few things and slipped out into the dark hallway.

In my right hand I held James's gun, feeling its weight like a heavy burden. Leading Naomi into the B and B's vestibule, I peered out the windows to see if the coast was clear.

I turned back to a frowning Naomi, who was staring at the weapon gripped at the ready in my hand. "Remember, Ruth," she said with a finger upheld in my face, "we're not Thelma and Louise, okay?"

"I know. But just in case . . . I refuse to be a victim."

"Just don't forget. And we're traveling in the opposite direction, aren't we?"

Maybe.

I nodded soberly, then turned to face the windows again. Since there was no sign of James's truck or any motorcycles outside, we made our exit from the old Victorian B and B, cautiously stepping into the cool, early morning air while scanning the surroundings cloaked in darkness still.

The streetlamp closest to us revealed nothing threatening. Behind the house loomed the bank holding up the Interstate as it rose toward the lower approaches of Loveland Pass. All that could be heard was the occasional whine of an engine-braking semi as it slowed down the incline.

Still, a sense of something menacing oppressed every inch of my body. I tightened my grip on the gun, took a deep breath, and gave Naomi an *all clear* with my chin. We scurried over to where she'd parked the car the day before, popped the trunk, and crammed our few items inside. Then we climbed in and I turned the ignition.

Two things happened next, which, together, made my blood run cold.

First, the engine responded to my cranking with only a sluggish churn.

Second, I spotted a large pickup truck parked in the deepest of shadows, a hundred yards down the road. And a cowboy-hatted silhouette, sitting motionless behind the steering wheel.

I cranked again, channeling all my panic into the muscles of my right foot. It turned over—eight times and without success.

"Don't flood it, Ruth," Naomi whispered urgently from the right seat, prompting my first unkind thought of the day.

"Look," I said, pointing forward with my chin for lack of a free hand, "You see that truck down there? I think that's my pervert. Waiting for us."

I cranked again. The starter had become whiny and tired, yet I could feel it within a millimeter of springing to life.

"Are you sure they improved your car?" I asked sharply.

"Before handing me back the keys, Kenny read off a laundry list of things he said needed to eventually get fixed to make this thing 'road safe.' Sure, the brakes are okay now, but the tires are bald, the—."

I waved my hand impatiently and gave her an *okay already, I get your point* look, steeling myself for what I was sure would be the last attempt to start the motor.

Just before I stomped my foot down, the pickup truck's headlights blinked to life. Its brake lights glowed red. He'd put the truck into gear and was moving toward us.

"Come on!" I demanded.

I stomped on the gas pedal, held, pulled back a little, and waited a few seconds. Then I turned the key again. The motor cranked and cranked, and finally, just when I was about to quit, it turned over and sputtered to life. With smoke from the exhaust billowing up all around us, I shoved it into gear and lurched forward.

The truck was closing in.

I swerved around his nose and punched the accelerator for all it was worth. Other than the generous trunk space, the Impala was good for one thing only—once you got the thing started, it could get up and go in a real hurry. I straightened my tires and we roared ahead, leaving a cloud of smoke.

Thankfully, since we were parallel with the Interstate and moving in the right direction, entering the freeway was just a matter of racing down a long straightaway, then making a quick dogleg at the exit where we'd nearly killed ourselves on our way into this town.

I entered I-70 at seventy miles per hour and continued to build speed. Less than a minute later I was doing eighty-five.

I could feel, in my peripheral vision, Naomi's anxious gaze. But I had no patience for her words of caution. James and his pickup had followed us onto the freeway. In fact, as I glanced again in my rearview mirror, I saw the pickup's headlights surging ahead and gaining ground.

"Naomi, I know you don't like going this fast," I said, staring through the windshield while trying hard to stay calm, "but we don't have a choice! He's still on our tail. See him back there, in the other lane?"

She twisted herself in the seat, looked and turned back again. She said nothing, which I took as a sign of her assent.

I pushed farther down on the gas, and the speedometer's needle passed ninety. With it being so early in the day, the traffic was fairly light. For once, I felt grateful for Naomi's antiquated speed demon. The ride actually felt smoother the faster we went.

But then a swerving set of headlights in the other lane dropped the sobering truth back onto my shoulders like a weight. James had a big engine too, and he obviously wasn't afraid to use it.

Moments later he came up alongside the Impala with his interior light on. I looked over, and his hate-filled eyes met mine and sent shivers across my body.

I took a deep breath. "Hang on!" I shouted to Naomi. "I think he might try to run us off the road!"

I glanced in the mirror to make sure I was alone in my lane. The moment had come to test what we'd received in exchange for two days of hard labor.

I pressed down on the brake pedal, quick and firm. It felt as if a giant hand had grabbed the Impala and yanked its body backward. Relief swept over me as James's truck shot ahead like a rocket. I caught a split second's glimpse at his snarling face as he sped past. His sudden move to ram us from the side now met only thin air, sending him nearly careening off the freeway.

"Thank you, Kenny," I whispered.

Yet now he was directly ahead of me, and a pair of red lights told me he was braking, trying to slow himself and make me rear-end him.

So I sped up to make James think he was succeeding, followed by a desperate move. I swerved into the fast lane and floored it. It was our turn to race ahead. Despite its age and wear and tear, the Impala's motor rose to the challenge, shooting forward with hardly more than a shudder.

James fell away like he was driving in reverse. I must have reached a hundred. I'm unsure because I was too nervous to take my eyes off the road and check the speedometer. But regardless of the terror of trying to stay on the road and outrun a madman, it was the most exhilarating moment I'd ever lived through. The surge of speed suddenly bolted through my emotions like a rocket thrust out of my past, flinging the last particles of my old life off into the distance. With every second that passed, I felt freer, more alive. I wanted to shout, to pump my fists in the air.

My elation was interrupted by a swirl of bright blue and red lights filling the car. I glanced at my rearview mirror and saw flashing headlights of another kind.

"It's a trooper," I said, slammed back to sobering reality.

"What are the odds?" Naomi asked. "We've only been on the freeway a little while."

"Yeah, but at this hour of the morning, the cars on the road tend to be either police or people who need to be caught by them."

"Where's that gun?" Naomi suddenly demanded, wild-eyed, then started searching the spot where I'd placed it on the seat.

"What are you doing?" I said.

"Hiding the gun. We can't be found with *that* in here."

"Naomi, I'm pretty sure having a gun is only illegal when it's concealed. As long as it's in plain sight, we should be okay."

"All right, then. As long as you're sure."

I slowed down, moved over onto the shoulder, and stopped the car. It occurred to me that getting pulled over by a trooper might actually save our lives.

I turned and focused on the adjoining lanes. James's truck raced by, and as it did, I caught sight of his license plate's first three characters—*BM5*.

After what seemed like an eternity, the trooper's face appeared in my side window. I wasted no time. "Officer, I'm so glad you pulled me over. The reason I was driving so fast is because a man who tried to assault me last night, well, the same guy followed me onto the freeway this morning and almost ran us off the road. We were trying to get away from him. I promise that's the truth."

The trooper—a thick-faced, mustached man in his forties—squinted in disbelief and then gave our front seat a once-over with his eyes.

"Is that the reason for the firearm, ma'am?" he asked.

"Yes, sir. He tried to rape me."

My voice broke when I said that, and although I hated betraying such weakness, I knew the involuntary display of emotion would help to convince the trooper I wasn't making this up. Which, thankfully, was what happened. The officer's face relaxed, and he looked forward up the road.

"All right. What can you tell me about the man who's been after you?"

I gave the trooper the truck's description as best I could, reciting for him half the license plate number I'd just spotted. "He drove by just as we were pulling over," I added.

"I'll put out word about this vehicle. You say he's from Georgetown?"

"I believe so."

"You know, I still ought to write you a citation on the excessive speed. For good measure."

"Oh, please don't, Officer," pleaded Naomi, leaning almost into my lap. "We have barely enough money to get us to Pennsylvania, which is where we're headed. Please have pity on us. A ticket could make the difference between us getting home or not."

"Home? Your registration says your home is Las Vegas."

"Officer, do you live in the town where you were born?" Naomi's matronly appearance and kind demeanor penetrated the trooper's professional façade.

"No, ma'am," he said with a chuckle at her persistence.

"Well, neither do I. We're going *home* home."

He looked up at the mountains surrounding the Interstate, apparently in a moment of reflection.

"All right, ma'am," he chuckled. "You talked me out of it. You stay safe getting home, you hear, and we'll keep the madmen here in Clear Lake County. How does that sound?"

"Thank you, sir," Naomi said, and I echoed her after taking an elbow to the ribs.

So we pulled back into traffic, not only free of our pursuer but spared a major new expense.

Thank God the officer hadn't thought to ask for a look at my license.

Better still, only one steep hill and descent remained in our drive through the Rocky Mountains. For some reason, the Impala, whether from a side effect of the repairs or a difference in the incline, now seemed less interested in downshifting to overdrive. Instead, it purred smoothly uphill.

Just when I thought the upslope would never end, all of a sudden the summit burst upon us and, without warning, like some invisible hand throwing open a pair of grand, wide doors, one of our journey's most magnificent sights unfurled before us.

Both Naomi and I gasped as our faces were bathed in light.

Swathed in shadow, yawning so far ahead that it may as well have been the sea, stretched the Great Plains, all the way to a perfectly level horizon. Spreading upward from that flat edge was an expansive, clear, pink and orange dawn.

I know that I was quite tired and sleep-deprived at that moment. And my emotions remained at a fever pitch after the fear and stress of the chase just ended. Not to mention the high toll of this entire journey. But the sight triggered a whole new wave of emotions and sensations inside me.

I felt a physical rush of freedom and openness, probably something akin to that first lungful of fresh air after being trapped for a long time in some oppressive space. Relief washed over me like a bucket of spring water tipped over my head on a hot summer afternoon. I felt a shedding, a spreading of invisible wings across my arms and chest.

I felt liberated.

"Oh, isn't that some view?" sighed Naomi. "So open and spacious . . ."

"You'd think we'd timed our whole drive just to reach this spot at this second. It's perfect."

"That's the Midwest," she added pensively. "Plain as day."

I tried to mentally capture and inventory all the images evoked by the word *Midwest*. Lemonade stands, ropes hung over swimming holes, tractors swallowed up in corn. Ruddy-faced children in weathered overalls. Rusted weather vanes on copper-stained barn roofs. Hard work and wholesome food.

I knew they were stereotypes, but for me, just then, it all sounded as inviting and as impossible as a Tahitian beach-front. I had never seen either.

CHAPTER 22

70

Still basking in the relief of breaking out onto open and level ground, we swept through Denver's industrial north side and, after sloughing off its last layer of suburbia almost an hour later, found ourselves driving across the plains. The trauma of our mountain passage lingered, though mainly as an exhausted, reflective silence that hung over us until the prairie's monotony spurred me back to conversation.

"Naomi, do you feel yourself getting closer?"

"Closer to home, you mean?"

"Yes."

She breathed in deeply, thinking. "Physically, no. But emotionally, yes, I do. Just being out on the prairie puts me in mind of the farm. The life of the soil. Midwestern values. It's not quite the same, but it's a giant step closer to home than where we've been."

"I'm finding it all so strange," I said. "And that word *home*—in some weird way, I feel like I'm going home, too.

Only I've never been where we're going, so of course that's impossible."

"No, it's not impossible."

I ignored her reply, anxious to describe for her what was going through my mind.

"I've never really experienced anything like home. Never had a place of my own or a real house, certainly not one with a picket fence. I grew up moving from one nasty, rat-infested shack to another. Nothing that belonged to me or my family. Until I met you, I never even knew what *home* meant."

I paused to watch a red-tailed hawk look at us from where it was feeding on a carcass in the center of the road ahead. The bird seemed to weigh his chances before quickly taking off out of the way.

"So now here I am, years later, risking everything to drive to a place you call home. And I keep catching these strange, fleeting glimpses of what it means—this place we're headed— as though I once had a home but erased it from my memory for some traumatic, forgotten reason. Like there's a place ahead of me where home could have been, should have been, only it's just a void—haunted by snapshot fragments of something that used to be there. Also mixed in, I think, is that movies and books have given me a sense of what I've missed. But only a sense . . ."

I drifted to a stop, and Naomi said nothing, peacefully allowing the moment to wash over us like the warm breeze blowing in from the car's open windows.

"You know what?" I continued. "It reminds me of what people say who've lost a limb and are haunted by these sensations of the part of them that's no longer there. 'Phantom limb,' they call it. Maybe I have *phantom home*. Only with a twist. I'm haunted by the lost memories of a home I never had." I laughed at myself.

"And I feel like I want to go there, but I'm afraid it'll turn out to be just another dashed hope or crushing disappointment. Then again, I'm probably speaking psychobabble. Or maybe I just need coffee, or a whole lot of sleep. But it's all very weird, and very emotional for some reason."

"No, Ruth," said Naomi in a low voice. "It's neither weird nor impossible. Home is a powerful thing, and it has a hold even on those who've never had one. Maybe *especially* on those who've never had one."

"Maybe you're right. Well, Naomi, in honor of our being out here in the openness of the Midwest, I think it's time you started spilling out your own story."

She said nothing, but turned her head toward the green wall of a cornfield whipping past outside.

"What? What part do you want to know?" she asked testily, turning back to me.

"Don't give me that, Naomi. I want to know, in the same way you've put that question to me a hundred times. I want to know the parts that hurt you. The parts that drive you. That you'd rather not talk about. *That's* what you need to tell me."

"Well, it's nice to know you plan on making it comfortable for me."

"All right, I'll start, then," I said. "At the funeral I heard two words that I'd never before heard Lonnie mention. *Bethlehem, Pennsylvania.* Can we start with that? Is that where we're going?"

She leaned back against the headrest and arched her back, long and hard. It was starting to get stuffy in the car, so she laboriously rolled the window all the way down.

"I suppose we could start with Bethlehem. After all, that's where the boys were born. It's also the place that launched us out West, after its steel mill shut down. After *everything* shut down. But Bethlehem wasn't the starting place. It wasn't our real home. It was just the place we fled to when we decided to walk away."

"Walk away from *what?*" I asked.

She nodded forcefully. "Now *that* is the real question. And answering it could take us all the way to Pennsylvania."

So Naomi began to speak. One sentence flowed into five, then fifty, and soon swelled into a verbal flood. Thus we entered what I call the second phase of our journey home.

Naomi's Story.

Here, to the best of my recollection, is how her account unfolded.

CHAPTER 23

"Eli and I actually grew up near Ephrata," Naomi began, "a town in northern Lancaster County about an hour and a half southwest of Bethlehem. Now, if you knew a little more about the East, you'd recognize the name Lancaster County immediately. It's famous for being home to more Amish and Mennonite communities than anywhere else on earth."

"It might be where they filmed *Witness*," I interrupted, relentless in my habit of relating everything to modern trivia.

Naomi rolled her eyes. "Maybe, but it's where tens of thousands of real-life Plain folk who aren't movie actors actually live and breathe to this day."

"Tell me again who the Mennonites are, besides that the men don't favor skinny women."

"'Mennonite' is one of the names for a dozen or so Christian groups, all of them from a broader tradition called the Anabaptists. They range from conservative types like the Old Order Mennonite and Amish, those that live Plain and separated from the world, to modern Christians known mainly for strong pacifist beliefs and a concern for helping the poor and needy. Not only are the Amish also Anabaptists, but so are the Hutterites and Brethren. And within each group are sometimes hundreds of different subgroups and even sub-subgroups. Some of them are separated from each other by as little as whether to use steel-wheeled wagons inside a dairy barn as opposed to only outdoors."

Surprised by Naomi's knowledge of all this, I asked, "So you grew up in one of these groups? And what do you mean by *plain*?"

She nodded. "Ruth, just like there's lots of different kinds of Baptists, there's also many different kinds of Anabaptists. They all try to live simple lives separated from society so as not to become corrupted by its sin. It can create strange beliefs. Such as barns can have electricity since cows can't sin, but people can't have them in their homes because electric power opens the door to temptation. It's hard to explain; it must be even harder to understand. Anyway, I grew up a Pike, also known as Stauffer Old Order Mennonite. Probably the most conservative in lifestyle of all the Mennonite groups. If you think the Amish conservative, many people consider the Stauffers even more so."

Confused by all the terminology, I could only summon a simple picture of women in headdresses. "You're kidding! So you grew up wearing one of those bonnets?"

"I did," Naomi answered, chuckling.

"I can't picture you in one of those."

"Many things were different for us. For instance, we were pacifists, who refused to belong to the army and bear arms, and people married very young."

"Then you went from riding one of those horse and buggies to driving *this* thing!"

She laughed outright. "You're correct. When we left the church, we didn't just go halfway, did we?"

"Did you have electricity in your house?"

"No electricity or telephone until I was in my teens, and even then only sparingly. Our farmers could use tractors, but no tires or rubber of any kind on the wheels."

"Why? Who cares about that?"

"Someone a long time ago felt that having tires would tempt farmers to take their tractors on the road, which is against teaching. They're only for work and farming, not transportation."

"Did everyone in the group speak English?"

"That was a huge issue. We spoke Pennsylvania Dutch at church, English at school and at home."

"How about you and Eli? Did the two of you speak English on your first date?"

She took a deep breath. "That's a thorny question. First of all, we didn't date. Even if our parents had approved of us, we still wouldn't have dated. We *courted*. You see, Eli and his family didn't belong to the Pike group. He belonged to a car-driving group called the Weaverland Conference."

"Ooooh, car-driving," I said, making a face to go with my bit of sarcasm. "That sounds really sinful."

"The Weaverland group were still Old Order Mennonite, but they used motor vehicles, so in our eyes they were suspect. Even the fact that they painted over the chrome to avoid vanity didn't redeem them in our eyes. Our two groups used the same meetinghouses yet managed to stay separate. One group met one week, the other group the next, and so on. That way we didn't have to come too close to each other."

"Apparently you and Eli came close to each other."

"That we did," said Naomi with a nod and smile. "Eli lived just down the road, although I didn't know it for the first ten years of my life. I know it sounds crazy by today's modern way of living, but I was nurtured in a world completely hemmed in within the cocoon of my family and the local Stauffer community. I had four brothers and sisters, which was a modest-sized clan by Old Order standards. I had nearly seventy cousins of different levels within ten miles of the farm. I had parents who might have seemed strict and never failed to punish us, but they also never failed to give us hugs and kisses and maintain a close and devoted family. Just packing up to leave the farm and go to church was a huge deal. And riding into Ephrata to buy the odd item or sell vegetables at the Green Dragon, the town's farmers' market, felt like a journey to the outer ends of the earth."

"Seventy cousins?" I repeated. "That's unbelievable. I hardly know about anyone beyond my immediate family. How did you manage Christmas?"

"We only exchanged gifts with those in our immediate families. They were our whole world anyway. I still remember when Kurt, my oldest brother, came of age and went off to court a girl miles away. I cried all night, certain he'd gone forever, because I was so unaccustomed to anyone I loved leaving at evening time. That's how close we were. I grew up with a sense of togetherness that people today in the modern world could never imagine."

"Do you miss it?"

"You have no idea," she said, looking up with a sudden glistening in her eyes. "I-I miss my family so much. What hurts even more is that I spent my last two years in that house resenting every moment of it, feeling trapped and close to being smothered to death if I didn't get out of there. A few times I had anxiety attacks and needed to run out of the house and into the fields because I felt so oppressed and hemmed in.

"Yet just look at where I ended up, at this point of my life, now coming up on sixty. In an apartment, essentially alone, and in one of the most physically and emotionally isolated cities in the world! How I've wished for a little of that closeness back, especially these last few years."

"But you know something?" I said with as much earnestness as I could convey. "You obviously brought those qualities to your own family, in spite of its challenges. I'm sure that's why I was so drawn to Lonnie's devotion to you, why I enjoyed the time we all spent together. Orpah felt it too, even though she had her own relatives nearby. You radiated this intense warmth and loyalty. In one of those therapy groups I had to attend after my DUI, they loved to use the word *centered*. You're the kind of person they were talking about. I think it means you carry your own center of gravity around with you. You're a family unit of one or two or three, or however many people you happen to be with. You made it fun to be together, talking, laughing, joking. I never had that. The only memories I have of being together with my birth family is either riding in the back of a truck to some new place, or helping Mama nurse Papa back to consciousness after he'd drunk too much or gotten into a fight. I know Hispanic culture is known for being family-centered, but mine was just too stressed and afflicted for that."

I breathed out slowly and heavily, as though the effort would purge the very thought of those days from my mind.

"By contrast, your apartment in Vegas was a haven to me. I hate to admit it, but during most of my marriage, I actually craved getting together with you far more than spending time alone with Lonnie. He was a better husband when he was around you. More good-natured, relaxed, kinder, gentler. Away from you he could be sad, pessimistic, even depressed for long stretches of time. Not always, but for long spells, yes.

Being with you brought us a sense of hope and optimism. I don't know why, because I know you were going through a lot of hard stuff yourself at that time. But being with you brought us this feeling like clouds clearing after a long overcast."

"That's why it's called *family*, Ruth. You guys did the same for me. You lifted my spirits too, just by being with me. We all buoyed each other."

"Yeah, but you had a special knack for pulling us together and creating that feeling. And I think it must be this heritage of yours. Maybe it's even one of the reasons I'm here. You've been my home, and wherever you are is home even if it's the middle of nowhere. It's that center of gravity again. It turns out to be portable, at least in your case."

"Well, the middle of nowhere is about to become the middle of a storm."

"Oh? Are we in Kansas yet?" I couldn't resist referencing Dorothy to lighten the mood. "If so, the tornado looks like it's about to hit! Where's Toto?"

As if on cue, a loud clap of thunder made us jump and quickly roll up the windows.

CHAPTER 24

70

In just five minutes' time, the sky had darkened and a thick barrier of low clouds had overrun our splendid view. Now a straight, gray-black front was dropping a veil of rain over the prairie. A gust of wind struck the window next to me as sharply as a fist striking the glass. The entire car shuddered. All at once, the road ahead was nearly erased by a solid wave of water as it pounded the road. I impulsively jerked the wheel to avoid a tumbleweed that blew past the windshield.

"Wow, this is some storm," I said as I slowed to a safer speed. "Do you see anything that looks like tornadoes out there?"

Naomi peered around from side to side. "No, but there are lots of dark clouds dancing around that worry me." She leaned over to fiddle with the radio dial, but all she got was static.

Then something round and dull in color struck the windshield, dead center.

Hailstones.

I could make out the dim hulk of an overpass just ahead, and as the pelting turned into a roar, I gunned the motor and pulled up under its shelter in the very last available space.

The drumming ceased with an almost jarring suddenness, and a sense of relief washed over me. I looked over at cars forced to keep driving for lack of space under the shelter and felt an immediate surge of sympathy. What lay ahead did not resemble an opening so much as a solid wall of white and gray.

I glanced over at Naomi. The forbidding scene outside the car combined with what we'd just discussed created a heart-warming sense of refuge and solace.

"Well, it looks like we'll be here awhile," I said. "Why don't you tell me more about Eli."

I strained to hear over the noise of the storm as Naomi picked up the story.

"As I said before, Eli lived within a quarter mile of my house, but I had no clue. One day I accidentally spotted him in the next field while out catching butterflies near our back fence. I can't tell you how terrified and fascinated I was at the mere sight of him. He seemed to come from Mars, or worse, because everyone outside our fellowship was alien and there-fore seemed vaguely dangerous. But I was intrigued at the same time. He had the features of a handsome grown man but on a boy, baked brown by the sun. And he had this shock of hair right in front that he could never control, that insisted on falling over his eyes in the most beguiling way.

"He walked over, and I froze with fear. I think if he'd said 'boo,' I would have sprinted back to my house, and ten minutes later my father and two brothers would have been out searching the farm with pitchforks.

"But he didn't. He came almost to the fence, wiped the sweat and dust from his face, and said, 'Hi. I'm Eli Yoder.'

"'Hello, Eli Yoder. I'm Naomi Kauffman.'

"'Whatcha doing all the way out here?'

"'Chasing butterflies.'

"It was one of those conversations. One of those awkward childhood exchanges made up of blunt, short sentences that hide a mountain of feelings.

"Despite our communication failings, we became friends almost immediately. He took off at breakneck speed and caught the biggest, most beautiful monarch I'd ever seen. He held it out in his hand for me, and my studying it had the unintended consequence of my index finger brushing against his palm. I quivered right to the very core of my being.

"I fell in love with him right then and there, and effectively ruined my life at the tender age of ten."

"What do you mean?" I asked.

"I mean it's your classic Romeo and Juliet. Not that our families actually hated each other like the . . . Who was it?"

"Montagues and Capulets." Of course I only remembered because I'd seen the movie version of the Shakespeare classic—the one starring Leonardo DiCaprio.

"Right, that's them. No, there was no hate between the groups, just a bone-deep, ingrained distrust. And therefore separation. In the Stauffers' eyes, Weaverlands didn't care as much about staying Plain or about keeping the old ways. They were considered less spiritual. So marrying one of their boys meant leaving the only community I'd ever known. And did I tell you about the practice of shunning?" Naomi gave a shudder and muttered, "I'll save that for later.

"I was keenly aware of that dreadful potential from the very beginning. Because marriage often came early in our society, so did my questions. I would spend most of my preadolescent and teenage years pleading with not only my parents but every church official I knew, even the bishop himself. 'Please,' I'd beg, 'how can I be banned for marrying an Old Order Mennonite boy who loves God with all his heart? He simply grew up thinking it was all right to ride in a car to church instead of a wagon. I know it's not our way, but how could such a thing condemn him to hell? Or me, if I spend my life with him?'

"The day I posed this to the bishop, at age fourteen, I was told that nobody was being condemned to hell. No one was sending me away. It was *me*, I was reminded again and again, who spoke of leaving the fold by marrying outside of its membership. Not the other way around. And weren't there some particularly handsome young Stauffer men in the district? But surely I didn't expect two large groups of people who had hardly spoken to each other in a century to suddenly reverse history itself and reconcile? Somebody had to be right and somebody wrong!

"'No. That would be entirely too Christ-like,' I said under my breath as I shook his hand and walked away.

"I can't imagine he took too well to that remark," I noted.

"You're right," she replied. "That comment cost me everything. The bishop took exception not only to what I was asking him to do, but the rebellious attitude I had displayed toward him. The very next day he was at our front door in his long black coat, standing there with four other elders, asking to meet with my father. Waiting for the outcome while sitting on the porch, I died a new death with every passing second until the door opened. My father looked out, his face a different color than I'd ever seen it. His expression was grim. I can still hear the strain in his voice as he called me over. So vivid is the memory, I feel as if it were only yesterday. 'Naomi, would you come in here?'

"Dreading what awaited me, I stood and followed him inside. The bishop demanded that I apologize to him and publicly confess my disrespect to the congregation at the next meeting. I came within a hair of telling him that I'd never apologize for criticizing division between believers, and that it was he who should get on his knees and beg for *my* forgiveness. It's a scenario that has replayed in my mind for decades. But I took another good look at my father's expression and realized there could be exceedingly dire consequences to my refusing to obey."

"No way!" I exclaimed. "You actually did it? You got up in front of everyone and—"

"That's right. I completely buckled under. I apologized on the spot, and I stood up and confessed the following week, before everybody, my sin of contrary speech and lack of respect for my elder. And this made me sort of an antihero in the eyes of the older children and teenagers in the rebellious phase of their lives.

"You see, there's another part of Old Order life you have to know to understand this. During their later teenage years, even the plainest young Mennonites are allowed to sow their wild oats—at least wild by Old Order standards—and experiment with the ways of the world. Parents pretty much look the other way at their children's behavior, hoping a disappointing encounter with the modern world will drive the youth back to the Old Order fold again. And most of them do return. They're usually turned off by the impersonal and rootless nature of the world and the fleetingness of its attractions. This period in a young person's life even has a name. The Amish called it a 'wilding.'"

"It didn't work on you, though," I interjected.

"No, it didn't. I had more issues than that. From the day of that church confession and onward, I kept up outward appearances and my parents hardly suspected my true feelings. But during the years between that day and my entering my own *rumschpringe,* I was in a constant state of confusion."

"Room . . . what?" I asked.

Naomi laughed. "Boy, I am reverting back to my youth. I haven't used that term in over twenty years. It's a Pennsylvania Dutch word that means 'running around.'"

"Well, I don't know about 'rumschpringe,'" I replied, "but I do understand running around. In my days as a waitress in Vegas, I saw a lot of men *running around* on their wives."

"Yeah," said Naomi, "and my temporary wilding turned into too many years of wandering in the wilderness. I never fully embraced all the Old Order insisted on. I never stopped seeing Eli. We met in barns, in the woods, sometimes down by the creek. And our constant refrain was the same one held dear by every adolescent with a persecution complex. *When can we fly this coop? When can we spread our wings and leave this place and these people?* We could sit around forever, when we weren't *knoatching und schmutzing*—our parents' lingo for hugging and kissing—and we would dissect everything wrong with our community. We were merciless. In our minds it was all backward and stifling and too embarrassingly stupid for words. That's how, one afternoon, one argument at a time, we began to lay the groundwork for a grand new life someday, as far away from Ephrata as we could possibly travel."

CHAPTER 25

70

The late-afternoon hailstorm had passed now, leaving in its wake a pale white sky, while the cars around us began pulling back onto the highway. I'd enjoyed the break from driving, laying my head back, relaxing and listening to Naomi's calm voice as she recounted her early years, intrigued by the people and the community in which she grew up.

Watching carefully for my fellow drivers, I eased the Impala back into traffic, and we were soon speeding on our way again across the prairie.

"So, obviously," I said, pulling Naomi back into her story, "you did exactly that, at some point."

"Exactly *what*?"

"Flew the coop."

"Ah, yes. We did. I was seventeen, only two months into my official wild-oats phase. I told my parents I was going to Ephrata to see a movie with my cousin Deborah and a few of our more distant relatives. Going to a movie was certainly wild enough to shock my parents. I never came back. I left a note telling them that my future lay with Eli, and that the church's refusal to make a place for us had forced us to leave. I was safe and no one should come looking for me. I remember filling the letter with verbal jabs at the Old Order world and how ridiculous and backward it all was. Eli and I were going to find our happiness somewhere where people wouldn't tell us who to love on the basis of hundred-year-old catfights between a bunch of old men.

"I can't tell you how excited I was that night when I met Eli behind the public high school. I jumped into his arms, and together we piled our most precious possessions into the back of a pickup truck of an English friend Eli had recently met. By the way, everyone not Old Order was called 'English.'

"I'll never forget the moment I scooted up onto the seat of that pickup, the first powered vehicle I'd ever sat in, and smelled gasoline and carbon monoxide. The lurch of an engine kicking into gear made me nearly jump out of the cab. Then it whisked me away at a speed that made me dizzy. I gripped Eli's knee for support, feeling the world yank itself out from under me."

"You'd never been in a car before?" I asked Naomi.

"No, Ruth," she said with a frustrated chuckle and shaking her head, no doubt at the snail's pace of my understanding. "You couldn't have sent me on a scarier leap into the unknown. It might as well have been a trip to the moon. I wasn't just leaving the home of my parents for the very first time; I was essentially running away at a young age, leaving my family's embrace forever. The feeling of being unmoored, adrift in the universe, keyed up and ready for anything at all was both exhilarating and shattering. But most of all, I was stepping out of the only world I'd ever known—into another I only knew existed from distant observation and the jaundiced descriptions of my parents and our church. Yet.I couldn't wait to plunge into it. To become a citizen of my century. To sample prosperity, strange foods, sexy clothes, movies, and pop music—the endless laundry list of things that had been denied me my whole life.

"The year was 1969. I'd never heard of the Beatles. I'd heard there was a terrible war somewhere overseas but only because some of my male cousins had been forced by the Selective Service—because of their conscientious-objector status—to join alternate social-service projects in large 'English' cities.

"We drove at what felt like lightning speed to another side of town, where a place had already been arranged for us. Eli had a cousin, Bo, who was quite wealthy and well respected as a community businessman. His father had been excommunicated from the Stauffers for bearing arms in a past war, and he, the son, had seriously injured a man for insulting his mother. So even though the community knew the two of them as heroes of sorts, they'd been banished somewhere in the countless layers separating the world of the English from the plain existence of the Old Order, which they'd still managed to respect in spite of everything.

"Bo fixed up a cozy little corner of his basement for us, on the sole condition that we find a way to let our families know we were okay. Which we did. We dutifully composed letters of reassurance to our families sometime in our second week away. Writing the letters, I must admit, caused me to shed more than a few tears.

"I wish I could say we ventured into our brave new world with gusto and relish, but the fact is that we hardly ventured from our love nest in the cousin's basement. Our reclusiveness was so excessive, and worrisome, that even Bo after the third week suggested that if we wanted to continue staying with him, perhaps we should find a way to get married. He might not have been a Stauffer in good standing, he grumbled, but despite being pretty wild himself, he doubted that his tattered reputation could survive harboring a couple of fornicators.

"Bo put us in touch with other Mennonite groups who didn't go by the label of Old Order. 'Conservative,' they were called, which seemed an ironic label to me then, as they seemed miles removed from the stringency of the Old Order. After all, they never used Pennsylvania Dutch, they drove cars and used phones and electricity, and in many ways they lived much like the worldliest of Englishers. To me, in those first few days, I couldn't have imagined anything more liberal."

"Still, not exactly Vegas," I laughed. "I can't imagine how they'd judge me and Orpah."

"Oh, I know," Naomi said. "I now realize that by any other standard, let alone those of Vegas, they were incredibly conservative. But my upbringing explains why I had such a hard time adjusting to life out West."

"So, did these *conservatives* take you guys in?"

"Yes and no. Eli and I visited the local Conservative pastor and explained our plight. We told him that we wanted to be married in as much of the Mennonite tradition as possible, given that we both came from such separate groups. Although this wasn't really truthful, since we were fast becoming completely disenchanted with so many facets of our faith. But this man was only our second potential ally in a great big hostile world, and Eli felt we should at least give it a try.

"The pastor expressed many misgivings, such as a desire that we join his congregation before he performed the ceremony. He talked about Eli's lack of employment, and a wish not to sow needless discord with what he called his 'Plain brethren' in the area. But at last, recognizing our good intentions and the fact that getting married was a necessary first step in our moving ahead with our lives, he finally agreed. We were married in cousin Bo's backyard, with my older cousin and the pastor's wife as our witnesses."

"Did you guys have a honeymoon?" I asked.

Shaking her head, Naomi said, "Our honeymoon, for the next several months, was that basement. In the absence of the normal pile of wedding gifts from our new community, which didn't quite know what to do with us, the best wedding gift we could get was hospitality. Eli's cousin sheltered us, counseled us, was wise enough to answer our questions, and knew enough to mostly leave young newlyweds alone.

"But there was something else Eli had completely failed to plan for. Our wedding paper work somehow alerted the government to his presence and his location, and within a month he received an ominous letter from the Selective Service. He could either register for the draft or present himself for conscientious-objector service within the month. Eli was confused about whether pacifism was one of the Mennonite beliefs he was ready to reject. He spoke about it at great length with my cousin, who told him from his own experience that many sincere believers didn't see it the Old Order way, that the Bible showed many godly men, including David, engaging in warfare. But since Eli owed so much to the Conservative church, which had just embraced us, and which, like other less-Plain Mennonites, was almost totally defined by its strong pacifist tradition, he took the latter route.

"And so I watched Eli board a bus for New York City, where he spent the next two years as an orderly at NYU Hospital. With him away, I could no longer live in the same house as Eli's single cousin. Even the most liberal of Mennonite groups would frown on a newlywed young woman living with an older bachelor."

CHAPTER 26

Hutchinson, Kansas

That night we ran out of gas, literally and figuratively, in a small town nearly halfway across the rectangular span of Kansas. I don't mean we actually drove our tank dry, but that night grew long, our stomachs grew empty, and the needle on our gas gauge said it needed attention, too. After filling up, we bought some groceries at a convenience store—a loaf of bread, baloney, a small jar of mayo, a can of peanuts, carrots and celery, and a case of bottled water.

We then found the largest chain hotel in the area and parked in its lot, close enough to the front entrance to sit under an outdoor light and feel safe from harassment, yet far enough away to feel reasonably private.

Energized by the food and elated at a solid day's progress, I pestered Naomi to return to her tale. It was strange, but I'd begun to feel the unraveling of her story as somehow linked to our progress in the opposite direction. The more she described her gradual estrangement from home, the closer it seemed we came to completing her return. So even though we stopped for the night, it felt as if our journey was continuing forward as she picked up where she left off.

"Ironically," Naomi said, "what saved me was yet another of the Mennonite faith's traditions. Caring for the vulnerable and needy is one of their hallmarks, and so in short order I found myself hired as a live-in housekeeper and baby-sitter for one of the church's large families. I maintained my friendship and fondness for Eli's cousin Bo, who in a way had become his mentor. The wife of the charitable family turned out to be only five years older than myself—a tall and vivacious blonde by the name of Herte. We soon became best friends, and she turned into an excellent mentor and guide, teaching me all about Conservative Mennonite life. The busyness and camaraderie in Herte's home helped me to forget, at least partly, the sudden separation from not only my beloved Eli but also the family I'd always known and, despite my rebellion, continued to love dearly."

"And you were only seventeen?" I interrupted.

"Exactly. It was a time of major growth for me, and quite painful. Even while weeping into my pillow each night, grieving Eli's absence and fighting back a gnawing sense of loneliness, during the days I could feel my independence stretch from embryo to adulthood in the span of only two years.

"In just a few weeks' time I'd gone from the teenage daughter of a large family to what you might call a 'single newlywed.' I mean, Ruth, try to imagine the contrast in my life. I went from living in a constantly crowded, thriving family home, filled with brothers and sisters and relatives by the dozen, to living in a dark little basement room, cut off from all but one of the human relationships I'd ever known. Without Herte and her family, some days I was certain I'd go out of my mind. With few exceptions, that's how I spent the next two years."

"Did you see Eli at all?"

"Once. It took me over a year to work up the courage, but eventually I got on a bus to New York and went to surprise Eli on his birthday. It was the scariest trip of my life."

"Scarier than this one?" I asked, laughing.

"Well, second scariest," she acknowledged. "But remember, I'd never seen a big city before. Not in a book, not on a television, certainly not in person. The incredible size of the place, the noise, the crush of people. And it took me three hours after arriving to find where Eli worked. I had no idea about the subway or taking cabs. By the time I got to his hospital, he'd left for the day. Someone took pity and rang him up for me, and he quick hopped a cab to come fetch me. By that time, I was in tears, and I vowed never to visit a big city again as long as I lived. Another reason why I had so much trouble adjusting to Las Vegas.

"Then one day—after my life at Herte's had begun to seem like it would last forever and Eli would continue to drift into the recesses of my memory—the doorbell rang, and some wild instinct compelled me to rush to answer it before any of Herte's children did. A strange apparition greeted me from the doorstep—a handsome man whose overall features were already ingrained in my mind, yet whose eyes seemed altogether different from the Eli I'd known most of my life. He would later tell me of having a similar reaction to the sight of me. I appeared to him as grown up and saddened almost beyond recognition.

"But none of this prevented us from falling into each other's arms—me with a bright, piercing squeal, and he with a long, ringing laugh. Minutes passed before he allowed my feet to touch the floor again.

"I had fully intended to greet him at the bus station, maybe even before the bus reached Ephrata. But he'd managed to catch a bus a day earlier, deciding then to surprise me.

"It was that second gaze, the one after the kiss, which revealed the most of our new selves to each other. We had both matured and learned a great deal. Two years spent not only in the world's largest city but in one of its busiest hospitals had changed him so much. He seemed to carry a whole different demeanor. Although he was ecstatic to see me, I could tell that the light in his eyes had changed. His rebellion and idealism were no longer based on just his beefs with Old Order traditions and his notions of a better life with me. They'd been honed against some of the harshest realities of the Englisher world—death, sickness, the coldness of life in a modern city, and the challenge of making one's mark—let alone surviving—in a country much bigger and harsher than he'd ever imagined.

"While my own experience had been much less difficult and closer to home, in two years I had learned quite a bit about how to handle a family home with electricity and a car.

"Unfortunately, Eli's newfound maturity did not translate into his finding employment. We had turned into a pair of pariahs around Ephrata. Neither of our respective groups wanted anything to do with us. Besides, this was the early seventies, and with only the usual Mennonite eighth-grade education, Eli was relegated to menial work around town.

"That's when Bethlehem Steel entered our lives. Eli came home one day with word that 'The Company,' as everyone in the region called it, one of the state's largest and most respectable employers, was still in its booming stage. One of its periodic upturns had caused the behemoth to seek young and brave men for some of the grunt work the union guys weren't anxious to try. He hopped a bus to Bethlehem and wound up, in a stroke of what we considered miraculous good fortune, getting the job.

"So we said our good-byes to Ephrata and to Lancaster County. It was much harder than I had anticipated. Being geographically if not relationally close to the world of our childhood was the last link we had left. Now we were moving an hour and a half away, and again it felt like a whole universe in distance."

"It was a city, though," I said.

"Yes, but a small one. One I could handle. And there were distractions. After we moved to Bethlehem and rented a second-story apartment on the city's south side, another life-changing event came right on its heels. I woke up one morning nauseated, thinking it was nothing, that it would pass. So I didn't bother to tell Eli. Then after a few days of feeling this way, I called Herte to confirm what I suspected. I was pregnant."

"Lonnie?" I asked brightly, as though I were experiencing his birth right there with Naomi.

"Of course. Lonnie's birth did for me what it does for most mothers, I suppose. It gave me a real sense of purpose, and at a time when I needed it most. When his brother was born two years later, and Eli began moving up through the ranks at the plant, it seemed we were starting to achieve what we had so much wanted to build—our own family success story, independent from the Old Order structure.

"'We'll find it, someday,' Eli kept telling me, referring to that strong sense of family the Stauffer and Weaverland families carried around so effortlessly simply by virtue of their size, their close-knit manner of living, and the air of tradition that followed them. That's what Eli talked about the night of our campout at Dead Horse Point—about creating our own family tradition, our own world with our two boys. A feeling that seemed to rest on us for a single night and then disappear, never to return.

"At times, early on in Bethlehem, it looked as though we might achieve a little of that. My two brothers ran away from the Selective Service and appeared at our door one day, sheepishly asking for food and shelter. They eventually fled to Canada, a choice that would dictate the course of their lives for decades to come."

"No one ever saw them again?" I asked.

"Basically," she replied. "It was only the beginning of a series of setbacks for my folks back in Ephrata, which later resulted in the collapse of our whole family unit. For several weeks my brothers stayed with Eli and me and the baby, and it seemed a blessing from God, that a fragment of what I'd left behind had come to bless me at a time when my own young family was just starting to grow.

"Speaking of God, our efforts to cobble together some kind of compromise with our faith wound up falling flat. We searched out a Conservative Mennonite church in Bethlehem, but soon started to accumulate the same complaints we'd built up in Ephrata. Despite not being Old Order, the church seemed afflicted with the disease of 'it's always been done thataway.' Certain activities drew the church's opposition just because they were timesaving and efficient, not because of any discernible moral deficit. Rules once meant to clear out the debris between us and God now became the debris itself. As soon as Eli and I discovered some new wonder of modern life—not to mention the counterculture at the time, which we'd never before experienced—the church rushed in with a lame objection to the effect that it was too modern, too nifty, or just too easy. To us, it was the same old narrow-mindedness all over again. And we were too enamored with this bright new world of the 1970s to just give it up again. I'd fallen in love with the Rolling Stones and the Beatles, Eli with the Mustang and Pony Cars and Pink Floyd, both of us with McDonald's hamburgers and Kentucky Fried Chicken, all the conveniences of fast food and supermarkets and so much more, and we saw no reason to abandon it.

"So instead of giving up the pleasures around us, we checked out a new variation of the church—the General Conference Mennonite Church. The final layer of Mennonite, the one rarely spoken of during our youth, whose members were hardly distinguishable from the world's heathens."

"Had you even heard of other religions like the Catholic Church, Judaism, or even Islam?"

"Sure. But groups like that, the way I was raised, were like second cousins to Satan. The Pope may as well have had a goatee and a pitchfork, for all I'd heard. We felt like we'd backed off the end of the world when we settled on General Conference Mennonite. We were at the height of our material-appreciation phase, and it didn't seem right that God or any of His ways should stand in the way of that.

"In celebration of a raise at work, Eli came home with a shiny new present to himself that represented the epitome of all we'd gained through our experiment. This very car we're riding in! Which explains why we could never bring ourselves to sell it. A brand-new, metallic green, 1976 Chevy Impala Sports Sedan with Magic Mirror lacquer paint and the famous Comfortron air-conditioning system. You should have seen Eli's face when he stepped out to face me on the front lawn. He was all aglow with the knowledge that he could actually do this. He'd joined the ranks of Americans who could simply walk into a dealership, pull out their wallets, and drive home in the latest and greatest. Not only that, but as our first car, this purchase symbolized freedom's mobility—we could spend Saturdays cruising the LeHigh Valley or running errands all over town instead of taking the bus. His first choice would have been to buy a Mustang or Camaro, but after thinking it through, he'd happily compromised on a four-door Impala with plenty of room for a growing family.

"But like all the golden periods in our life, this one was quite short-lived. A few months later, I received a distressing call one morning from Herte back in Ephrata."

CHAPTER 27

🛡️70

"What was it?" I asked, completely engrossed now with Naomi's story.

"My younger sister Katie, only weeks into her wild-oats phase, had gotten drunk the night before and, after coming home late from a party, accidentally set my family's barn on fire with a carelessly tossed cigarette. My father had rushed out in the cold of night to try and save his livestock. A falling beam struck him across the shoulders and knocked him into the blaze. He wasn't expected to live.

"Suddenly the Impala and its mobility took on a whole new importance.

"Eli had always intended to drive me in our new car back to Ephrata, to cruise into the old hometown in this blaze of glory and give everyone a lump of envy. This return turned out to be anything but triumphant. We were now racing, yes, but only in order to reach the hospital on time.

"No one who saw us drive into town felt anything like

goodwill as Eli thoughtlessly darted around black buggies and broke every traffic law in existence on our way to the hospital.

"We pulled up near the entrance, parking alongside other modern cars mixed in among *dachwaggeli*, the square, black buggies of the Old Order. I noticed the stares of the few Stauffers walking by and instantly felt like a desecrator of everything good and holy. But ignoring the discomfort, I gathered up our baby boys and hurried into the hospital."

With the finishing of Naomi's sentence, my worst nightmare burst to life and jerked me into the present in the Impala's rearview mirror.

Police lights flashing—approaching fast, right behind me.

This time I knew there would be no cover story to excuse me, no drama about a would-be rapist stalking me to deflect scrutiny away from my suspended license. I tried in vain to slow my galloping heart, to ignore the inner voice that had immediately begun telling me how stupid I'd been to tempt fate for so long, to recklessly disregard the odds.

I looked over at Naomi and found no comfort. Her expression was blank with fear, her body rigid in the seat. I took a couple of deep breaths as I started edging the car toward the right shoulder.

Then, as my right front tire passed onto the shoulder, the police car roared past us with a crescendo of its sirens and disappeared around a curve. After a brief pause, Naomi turned and looked at me. Something about the look in both our eyes touched each other's funny bone.

We didn't stop laughing for several minutes.

"Eli and I were never shunned or excommunicated," Naomi continued when the hilarity had finally passed. "Shunning is the cruelest of Old Order legalisms. After you're baptized as an adult, if you turn your back on the church, they *shun* you. You are instantly cut off from everybody you know, your family included! They act as if you don't exist, as if you've died. Thankfully, that would only have happened had we been baptized as church members before marrying. Nevertheless, I'd become the source of great disappointment for my family, and the stares that followed me through the hallways of that hospital were proof of that.

"Old Order Mennonites, contrary to their backward reputation, do not oppose the use of modern medicine. Yet they only frequent hospitals for emergencies. Nothing like this had ever happened in my family before. So with the boys in our arms, Eli and I approached the door to my father's room. Predictably, my aunt Leah, as strong and broad as an ox, stood guarding the door, keeping away unworthy visitors. I smiled at her in greeting and walked right in without waiting for her permission. She nodded and did nothing to stop me. Apparently the topic of my coming had already been discussed.

"I hardly recognized my father's face. The sight of him ripped the breath from my lungs. And yet my eyes would not leave him, even though my peripheral vision noted half a dozen familiar family members standing all around me.

"Finally I turned back to Eli and asked him to take the boys and wait for me outside the room. No wonder Leah had been stationed outside his room. My father's face was burned the color of eggplant, his hair all but gone, one of his eyes bandaged over. The rest of him lay mercifully hidden under blankets.

"When I stepped through the ring of praying folk around his bedside and knelt, my mother caught sight of me from the other side of his bed. She hurried over from her spot and, whimpering sorrowfully, threw her arms around me and burst into weeping. All the hurt and alienation between us was immediately forgotten.

"In the moments that followed I learned that my family had basically imploded. Of course my two brothers were already fugitives in Canada. My sister who had caused this tragedy was now missing and being sought by the state police. That left my youngest sister, Rachel, who was only fifteen and utterly devastated.

"I was devastated as well. I'd left home believing that my family was a rock that would remain, flawed but indestructible, until long after I was gone. I'd never dreamed it would prove less solid than my own precarious grip on survival in the modern world. To make matters worse, I also learned the Stauffer Mennonites were filling out a new settlement in Tunas, Missouri, and nearly all of my close relatives would within the next three months leave behind forever Lancaster County.

"Late that night, my father slipped away. I helped my mother through the funeral as best I could, given that I had two young boys in tow and a husband who was unable even to visit his own family in Ephrata, an awkward experience in its own right.

"The last conversation Eli and I had with my mother concerned the farm. She'd already decided to take Rachel and follow her sisters and extended family to Missouri. That left no direct family to work the farm. But when she mentioned the prospect of selling it to a neighboring Stauffer family, Eli came to life. Without consulting me, he leaned in close to her and offered to keep up the taxes on the place, making sure others within earshot wouldn't hear him. After all, it was a long-standing tradition that farms be kept in the family. We would find someone to work the land, he pledged, if she agreed to sign it over to us. 'Why would you want such a thing?' she asked with an edge of bitterness to her voice. 'You risked so much to leave the farm, in complete disdain for our feelings.'

Eli shook his head and tried very hard to formulate his response. 'We just think it should stay in the family, that's all. And maybe someday, when we're both old and gray, it will be a nice place to return to.' I stared at Eli when he said that, because I'd never heard him express anything other than the desire to put as much distance as humanly possible between himself and Lancaster County. This sudden nugget of good-will toward his hometown surprised me to no end. Even so, I nodded as if we'd discussed it earlier between ourselves.

"So that night we signed the papers. That was the last time I saw my mother.

"As the Old Order usually keep no mortgage on their properties, all that needed to be done was to make sure the taxes were paid and that someone trustworthy cared for it. Eli's brother, Hans, agreed to farm the land and maintain the house while we lived our modern lives in Bethlehem. We never visited. The memories were just too painful, and the visits would have been too awkward. However uncomfortable, this arrangement laid the cornerstone for the destination that now lies ahead of us."

CHAPTER 28

🛡️**70**

In August of 1977, over 7,000 blue-collar workers were laid off   though it was, tellingly, the September 30 layoff of 2,500 white-collar workers that is remembered as "Black Friday." Billy Joel's 1983 single "Allentown" made the Bethlehem layoffs infamous:

> *"Out in Bethlehem they're killing time*
> *   filling out forms*
> *   standing in line."*

—**Jeff Pooley,**
"Historic Preservation: Will Bethlehem Turn Steel into Gold?"
The Next American City magazine. Fall 2006.

Naomi interrupted her story when we stopped for the night. Soon we were both snuggled under our blankets in a hotel parking lot, she in the back seat and me in the front, coats and other blankets rolled under our heads for pillows.

We had pulled farther away from the front entrance so as not to attract attention.

"So the house you were talking about is the house we're hoping to find waiting for us when we get there?" I asked. "This hundred-year-old house?"

"That's the one," Naomi said. "Except there's a slight problem."

"I think I figured it out," I said. "If it's a Stauffer home, there's no central heating, no electricity, no running water."

I heard a chuckle drift over the seat back. "Well, yeah, actually that could be a problem, too. But there's something else."

"Oh, great."

"I haven't been able to keep up the taxes since Eli passed. I know there's a grace period, but I think it's either expired or is about to very soon."

"Wonderful! So we may get there, after all this effort, and find we don't have any place at all to stay, power or no power."

"Exactly."

"Don't you still have friends and relatives in the area?"

"I'm really not sure," Naomi answered. "As I said, most of them left for Missouri—others have died. As for those who may still be around, I have no idea whether they'll speak to me or not. I didn't exactly leave on good terms. And I'm not sure where my brothers and sisters are living."

"What about the person who wrote you that letter?"

"Herte. Yes, she's perhaps the only friend I can count on."

"Naomi, I want you to level with me," I said, speaking up into the dark. "Are we really headed to something real, or is it just a mirage? Will we still be in this car, sleeping on these seats five, ten years from now?"

"Ruth, do I strike you as ideally suited for this kind of life?"

We both laughed.

"I meant what I said when I first told you and Orpah about leaving," Naomi said, her tone now sober. "I'm going because I have roots there. They are my people. And for a woman like me, the prospects are much better in Pennsylvania than they are in Vegas. Still, that doesn't guarantee me much. I just don't see any other decent choice. Even if things don't turn out well—which, let's face it, could be the outcome—a back bedroom in a beat-up Old Order farmhouse sounds a whole lot better than trying to exist on Social Security in a tiny apartment in suburban Vegas. At least I'll have fresh air and the beautiful countryside around me. Green grass and sunshine and dirt under my feet. And values I can relate to. Family. Friends. That would be enough for me."

"Then it's enough for me too," I said, remembering I had also grown tired of the concrete landscape of Vegas.

"I guess you can tell I've come a long way since the days when I couldn't wait to get out of Ephrata."

"You have, Naomi. You've come full circle."

We both awoke to the slamming of a trunk door. That's the price you pay, I suppose, when you're sneaking a night's sleep in a hotel parking lot. It was just growing light outside, the first few minutes of a partly cloudy day. We both sat upright in our seats, blinking the sleep from our eyes, and almost as a reflex I pulled out the keys and started the engine.

After grabbing coffee and a couple of breakfast burritos from a roadside stand, we drove onto the Interstate for day four of our trek eastward from Moab.

As we were leaving central Kansas, right around Topeka, I

noticed hardwood trees begin to appear—clumps of forests crowning the tops of low hills.

"I wonder what adventure we'll run into today," I said. "And I do mean *run into*, unfortunately, with our track record so far. Wild beasts? Tornadoes? Floods?"

"Well, one thing we're bound to run into," Naomi said, "if we keep our noses pointed east. The Mississippi."

"The river?" I asked.

"No, the state," she joked, elbowing me. "Of course the river!"

I glanced at her, recalling the map we had studied earlier. It just didn't seem possible we'd traveled so far and were now approaching this monumental landmark in our journey. I'd heard of the Mississippi—had to spell it on a third-grade test—but until this moment it had seemed more fable than reality.

I pointed ahead. "Hah! Here comes the first unpleasant surprise we're going to run into. A tollbooth."

We had failed to factor into the budget the cozy relationship between the federal highway system and fee-charging local governments. The tollgate ahead, with its sign marked *Kansas Turnpike*, surrounded by another of those sunflower logos we'd seen ever since entering the state, told us we'd have to pay up.

The idea of getting nickel-and-dimed to drive across my own country, at a time when Naomi and I were counting every nickel, filled me with resentment.

We pulled up to the booth, and I looked around. To my disappointment, there was no live human being, only a waving ticket printed with all sorts of city names and the fees associated with them.

"Hello?" I called, leaning out toward the machine and

snatching up the wretched ticket. "Is there someone around I can complain to? Anyone?"

Nothing—just the incomprehensible ticket clutched in my hand.

"Yeah, I need some kind of waiver for very poor people with no cash to spare. Got anything like that? Some kind of form we can fill out? Hello?"

A jarring, rasping sound issued from a hidden speaker, apparently intended to convey the human voice.

"Come on, Ruth," Naomi begged from the passenger's seat. "You're acting like a jerk now. Please, let's go. Don't forget—you can't get pulled over."

I crumpled the ticket in my hand and made to throw the wad at the machine, then decided against it. The madness passed, and I smoothed out the receipt to pay at the next toll and drove on.

"I'm sorry," I said a mile later down the road. "I don't usually act like that. It's just that we already have so many obstacles to finishing this trip; every new one seems like a deliberate attack. We've worked so hard for every one of those dollars. To have some faceless bureaucracy just take them from us . . ."

I decided to change the subject. Or rather, change it back to the subject we seemed to have been on all along.

"Okay, so we're still in Bethlehem, are we?" I asked, looking over at her.

"What do you mean? We're nowhere near . . ." Then she understood what I meant and sighed. "Yes. We're still in Bethlehem. For the time being."

"Why only the time being?"

"Because just a few months after Eli bought the Impala, Bethlehem Steel started to have major problems. And 1977 was the worst year the company had ever seen. I remember

195

the newspaper reporting they'd actually lost something like a half billion dollars. They laid off thousands of workers on the line, including most of our friends. As time went by, things kept getting worse, forcing the company to close its doors completely, one of the worst shutdowns in history. We just couldn't believe it. Back then, they said it was just a temporary downturn. But because Eli was one of the most junior hires, according to the union he had to go.

"Eli took the news hard. You have to understand, up until then, 'getting on' at a company like Bethlehem Steel was supposed to be a gravy train for life. If you worked hard and kept your nose clean, you could honestly expect to make a great wage, with incredible benefits, clean through to your retirement. All of a sudden, that wasn't true anymore.

"To make matters worse, it wasn't a good time to be making a career change in Bethlehem, Pennsylvania. Everybody was going after the same jobs. After Eli had walked the picket line, run out his unemployment benefits, and waited for things to improve, he finally decided to make a total career change. He took a job as a clerk at the historic Hotel Bethlehem. Rather unglamorous, it often involved working nights, but it was steady, was not physically dangerous, and for some reason Eli excelled at it. He had a natural kindness and courtesy about him that fit the job perfectly. Turned out his home-grown Mennonite hospitality was just the thing to put tired travelers at ease."

"You mean Mennonites make good hosts?" I broke in. "Up to now, you made them sound so stern."

"Oh, no." Naomi shook her head. "Opening your home to someone in need is so much a part of Mennonite hospitality it even has a name, Hesed, a mandate straight from God. And Mennonites take direct mandates very seriously."

"So this 'Hesed' made Eli a better hotel clerk?"

"It made him a happier one, more compassionate and attentive. Hotel Bethlehem was like an oasis to us during those years. It was originally built in 1922 and then lavishly restored during the glory days of the steel mill. I loved visiting there, walking through and absorbing the beauty and grandeur of the lobby. Eli received discounts on food and beverages, so occasionally we would splurge on a meal there. He worked such long hours that the hotel became like a second home. Eventually he worked his way up to a front-desk position, and it seemed we'd found a soft landing spot after the loss of his mill job."

"You guys still weren't going to church?" I asked.

"Somewhere around that time, what with the busyness of raising two rambunctious boys and staying afloat financially during challenging days, we gave up on the church altogether. At the time, we justified it to ourselves in terms that were popular those days—'organized religion' had basically failed across the board. It wasn't cool anymore. Being spiritual was in, but not going to an ordinary church. 'That old-time religion' was for just that—old-timers. So we settled into a golden rule, be-kind-to-your-neighbor, John Lennon-ish kind of faith. And for the times, it seemed perfectly all right. It certainly made Sunday mornings easier to manage.

"That is, until a few years later, when the economic depression caused by the problems at Bethlehem Steel caught up with the Hotel Bethlehem. In '84, Eli was laid off. Unemployment had reached historic highs in Bethlehem. By then, Eli was fed up. And I mean with life in general. He now hated Pennsylvania, hated its cold winters, its dour attitudes, its religious quirkiness, its memories of childhood—everything. The place 'constricted' him, he said, as if someone were putting a chokehold on him. I think he was emotionally depressed and felt like a failure. I became quite worried. Eli wanted to keep working in the hospitality business, but someplace drastically different than Pennsylvania. Mel was into trail riding and mountain biking, going all over the place in search of great rides. He'd heard of a mythic biker's paradise called Moab, Utah. So he mentioned it to Eli one afternoon. 'Dad,' I remember hearing him say, 'let's move to Moab, Utah. Arches National Park is there, and it's the best place ever to go biking.' Eli chuckled dismissively and waved him off. But just two nights later he walked over to me, holding open this one page in a hospitality magazine. 'I don't believe it,' he told me. 'Look at this. It's that town Mel was talking about.' I glanced at the photo he held up, and my face couldn't have been too encouraging. It looked like the center of the Grand Canyon to me. Maybe a nice place to visit, but not where you'd want to live, let alone raise your kids.

"Almost on a whim, Eli made a call to the motel mentioned in the article and inquired about a job. The next thing you know, he'd mailed his resume. And I was left trying to talk him out of 'leaving home.'

"But Eli had made up his mind. He accepted the job offer, working as front-desk manager at Greenwell Inn in Moab, Utah. So early in the summer of 1984, we packed all our worldly goods into a travel trailer, hitched it to the Impala, and drove all the way down I-70 to Moab.

"Just before we left, I fetched an atlas out of the hall closet, wondering where exactly Moab was on the map. It was just as I'd expected—in the middle of nowhere. I knew I would hate it.

"But I didn't."

CHAPTER 29

NYSE to Suspend Trading in Bethlehem Steel Corporation, Moves to Remove from List

New York, June 7, 2002—The New York Stock Exchange announced today that it determined the common stock of Bethlehem Steel Corporation (the Company) should be suspended prior to the opening on Wednesday, June 12, 2002. . . . The decision was reached in view of the fact that the Company had fallen below the NYSE's continued listing standard regarding: average closing price of a security of less than $1.00 over a consecutive 30-day trading period and was unable to demonstrate the ability to cure this noncompliance within the required time period. In addition, the Company had previously filed a voluntary petition under Chapter 11 of the Federal Bankruptcy Code on October 15, 2001.

—*The Wall Street Journal*

As we continued our drive, the plains of Kansas melted into the urban approaches to Kansas City. We drove through its downtown, passing by Arrowhead Stadium, crossing the Kansas River, and straight into Missouri, where, with the suburbs behind us, I noticed an almost immediate difference in the landscape. The fields had become thicker and lusher, the trees' leaves shining brightly in the sun, the cornstalks packed together so tightly you could hardly see between them.

Stands of dense forest appeared, bordering the fields as though the farms had been hacked one foot at a time from a jungle of oak and maple. Rather than shoulders of clay or dirt, the highway lanes looked like they'd been hewn out of the fieldstone that lined the roadway in rolling, cleanly sliced sections.

One quaint farm after another bore a strange slogan painted across their barns' sides: *See Rock City.* A very popular amusement park with a down-home approach to marketing, according to Naomi.

As America gradually transformed around me, I grew increasingly content to simply peer ahead and let Naomi's saga roll over me, her words flowing in rhythm with the hissing of concrete and the clacking of tires over highway seams. Her voice, over the hours, became one with the purr of the engine, the unscrolling of scenery, the languid, reflective tone of our drive. She neither sought my approval nor my input on her story as her words traced her progress across this same heartland with Eli, Lonnie, and Mel. My mood softened accordingly and mellowed into a sort of blurry contemplation, a state in which I didn't cast judgment or analyze what she said beyond the surface momentum of her words. It seemed as though she had to continually validate her decision to go back to Bethlehem.

At one point, I wondered, *If Pennsylvania really is as idyllic as she describes it, why did they leave it in the first place?* Then it dawned on me that I was hearing Naomi's confessional. Obviously hindsight made clear that leaving had proven to be a bad decision.

And now Naomi seemed determined to rectify it. By returning—with me in tow.

Midway across Missouri, it occurred to me that I'd never sat that still for that long, nor had I listened so intently to the story of another person, and here it was my good friend Naomi. It struck me then how tragic it would have been had I not joined her on this journey. To think that if I'd stayed put on that bus, I may have arrived at the end of my days without experiencing this level of friendship and knowledge of another human being, my own lost husband included. And yet for Naomi, it seemed the most natural thing in the world.

As I felt the East grow nearer in a softening of weather and terrain, it proved an increasingly odd sensation to relive Eli and Naomi's long-ago drive along this same route, even if they had been traveling in the opposite direction. I felt spurred on by the urgency of Eli. So filled with anticipation, he had made the trip from Pennsylvania to Utah those many years before, driving it in a single, round-the-clock marathon and in the very same car I was now driving. *Surreal.*

"What's hardest of all to understand," Naomi said as she picked up the threads of her account, "is just how thoroughly Eli and I had convinced ourselves that everything in our past was gray and stained, and everything awaiting us out West was fresh and clean and glorious. We indoctrinated each other with romantic notions connected with *going West.* It got to be such a preoccupation that Eli even turned it into a way of speaking. If one of the boys said something negative or defeatist, Eli would admonish him with, 'Now, son, that's

Pennsylvania talk. I want to hear a little Moab in your voice.'

"By the time we had reached Utah, we were a family for whom the whole idea of the eastern United States or Pennsylvania, to say nothing of Old Order *anything*, was absolutely negative, part of our history we wanted to wipe from memory. Like the American generations before us, we were going to reinvent not only our destinies but our very selves in the great West. Eli pumped the boys up with references to climbing mountains and kayaking rapids and fly-fishing for every meal. The two were a little disbelieving at first. After all, the father of their recent memory was a sedentary hotel clerk whose notion of a heavy workout was mowing the lawn in the noon-day sun. The photos Eli and I had produced of the Moab area hadn't helped either. The endless stone vistas may have looked majestic and imposing, but they offered few clues as to how a boy might spend a day of fun in their embrace. I think I told you before that it wasn't until we reached Moab itself, and saw the beauty of the place, that the boys totally bought into their father's enthusiasm.

"But somewhat the opposite happened to Eli, though. By then it was too late. I could see that something had clicked inside Eli, warning him that this experience would not quite deliver on its expectations, just like every other season of his life. Granted, the clouds would part briefly that night at Dead Horse Point, and I'm sure he truly believed that we'd captured a preview of some glorious lifestyle to come. But like I also told you, that only lasted the one night. By dawn the next morning, Eli had faded back into being little more than a sum total of his burdens and responsibilities. A gray man wearing a corporate name tag, spending his hours behind a Formica counter. My heart broke for him every time I walked into that hotel.

"One of the saddest parts was that the land itself didn't

disappoint but delivered according to our highest expectations. Nature didn't fail us one bit. It was the same in Pennsylvania, where the fields hadn't become fallow just because we had walked away from them. Opportunities in Moab abounded to do and to be everything Eli had described to the boys. But somehow our days as a family didn't materialize into times of outdoor fun. There was always a room to clean. Something to repair. A customer to calm. A homework assignment to finish. It's strange how when you live in a beautiful place, you're often kept from enjoying it to the fullest. I'm not quite sure how to explain this, but you sense a reproach seeping out from the neglected area. It's like the splendor is taunting you, scolding you for leaving it alone for so long.

"Eventually the boys found ways of breaking off for long mountain-bike rides and Slickrock climbs, and they toughened into brown, sinewy Moabites like all of their friends. But looking back on it now, those times were also teenage avoidance mechanisms—procrastinations to avoid chores and homework or the need to be around Mom and Dad. Their father would never be a part of that world.

"I saw him once standing there behind the motel counter, waiting on a customer, when his boys whizzed by outside on their mountain bikes without even giving him a glance. He followed them with his eyes through the window, swiping the customer's credit card without even looking, until the boys had disappeared down the road. He kept his gaze locked outside the window as though they would return any moment, but of course they didn't. Then he sighed so obviously that the sadness of it brought tears to my eyes."

"What about you?" I asked Naomi. "How did you deal with life there in Moab?"

"Believe it or not, I started praying again. I'll tell you

about when it began. Back in Pennsylvania, our rejecting the church had felt like a positive choice, something we did that could be changed anytime we wanted. Yet someplace deep inside me never stopped pining for some kind of connection with God. To be honest, it's a little embarrassing to admit now, but I would even occasionally tune in to some of those TV evangelists. Just to hear *something* from the Bible. Even if it came from people who made me want to shut my eyes and just listen to the words. But now, out in a seemingly godless place where no church like ours existed, praying started to become a survival technique."

"No churches at all?" I queried.

"Nothing that felt familiar. There were no Mennonite churches in Moab—that's for sure. What we found was a liberal sprinkling of New Age quasi-churches, a Native American church, which was quite a novelty to us easterners, and plenty of Mormons. . . ."

Her voice trailed off as an old memory seemed to invade her mind.

"Yes, *plenty* of Mormons, some strange ones included. Let me tell you what happened."

CHAPTER 30

"On one of my first mornings in Moab," Naomi continued, her voice sounding far away, "I was busy cleaning out the rooms of the motel—since I was the new housekeeping supervisor—when through one of the windows I saw three women in long, plain-colored dresses walk by. I strained to look closer and saw that their hair was tightly woven into buns and they were wearing little bonnets. I was so enthralled, I thought I'd faint right there on the spot. *Old Order.* They had to be. But I'd never heard of any settlements all the way out in Utah. Could they be with another Order, a group I hadn't heard of? And how could anyone farm the desert soil? I mean, without using a massive, intrusive water diversion system—which would go against everything Old Order people believed in?

"I hurried out into the parking lot, hoping to approach the women before they disappeared out of sight behind the motel office. I found them waiting to cross the street. The nearest woman, who appeared to be in her teens, caught sight of me and smiled. When the pedestrian light said it was safe to walk across, I followed them, trying to keep my distance and avoid looking like I was following them. To my surprise, they entered a nearby self-service laundry. I'd been doing some laundry there myself, so I walked in after them and asked the lone attendant if I could buy a spare box of detergent as I'd supposedly run out. The whole time I watched the women, closer now, from the corner of my eye. It was odd— neither the color, nor the shape of their bonnets, nor the style of their dresses showed them as part of any Order I'd grown up with. In the past, I could usually identify a woman as married or unmarried, Amish or Mennonite, horse and buggy or black bumper, and any one of thirty different Old Order variations after just a second's glance at their attire. But when it came to the three women doing their laundry, nothing of what I saw triggered anything truly familiar in my mind.

"Curious, I finally approached the women. The older two were sitting down, holding up large garments just pulled from an open dryer. They looked up at me with a mixture of goodwill and wariness.

"'Can we help you?' asked the eldest. 'Is something the matter?'

"She probably asked the last question after seeing the nervousness that had suddenly overtaken me. I then knew how all those tourists felt, approaching Old Order families just like my own back in Pennsylvania, feeling both profane and impolite for attempting the simplest of human interaction.

"'Hello. Um—sorry to bother you, but I was just wondering, I grew up Mennonite and . . . I mean, I was just wondering what Order you belong to?'

"'Order? No Order. We're Latter-Day.'

"'Latter Day? I have not heard of that one.'

"'Yes, Latter-Day Saint . . .' She waited for my recognition, then added, 'Mormon.'

"Then the light came on, and with it came embarrassment. *Of course. Utah . . .*

"I shut my eyes, mortified, and made a small wave of my hand. They smiled back, their expressions similar to the awkward reactions I'd no doubt projected as a girl back in Ephrata. All those Englishers passing through who had to be firmly told, 'No, you may not park your Winnebago on our farm overnight.' 'No, you may not take our picture as we work.' And yet I felt the need to make some kind of connection with these women anyway, to find out if, despite their unfamiliar label, they too lived plainly and in harmony with the land, and if their lives were filled with days of simplicity and joy all strung together. I wanted so badly to coax from them a sense of whether God's presence was a constant in their everyday hours, even during the most mundane and sometimes depressing of tasks like sorting endless piles of laundry. The mere sight of them had awakened this dormant desire in me for God again—even though I somehow suspected they weren't even considered Christian by most of the churches I knew.

"Instead, I backed away, offered a quick apology before turning and walking over to the motel, inwardly chastising myself for my pathetic actions."

"I've never heard that Mormons dress like that," I commented.

"You're right," said Naomi. "I would later learn, as the ways of Utah became more familiar to me, that most Mormons didn't dress as these three had. The women were in fact members of an obscure and largely frowned-upon polygamous sect that had filtered into the area. I thought of all three women sharing the same man and shuddered. Just as back home, religious groups had their endless divisions and subsets. But here, those offshoots seemed to have grown far more unusual.

"Anyway, I think it started right then—my struggle to contain growing feelings of regret and longing for the world of my childhood. If I'd been stronger, I would have sat down with Eli that very day. I would have gently taken his hand, looked him in the eye, and told him that we'd made a terrible mistake, a valiant and justifiable one, but a mistake nonetheless. That we'd been on the wrong path ever since leaving Ephrata and the heritage of our youth. That we had to, no matter how inconvenient it might seem, return home right now. That very day." She stared out the passenger-side window.

"But you didn't do it," I finished with a touch of disappointment. "Why didn't you tell him what you were feeling?"

"I think I did seek him out, in fact, after returning to the motel. He looked up at me from a pile of receipts and scanned my eyes for a sense of my errand. Something in his expression caused my resolve to shatter, and just as quickly I was telling myself that my impulse had only been the old voice of fear and unworthiness rising up, poisonous, from my past.

"At least that was the script Eli and I had come up with for ourselves. It went like this—we harbored deeply ingrained programming from emotionally distant childhoods that must be overcome. Self-destructive scripts that occasionally we used when tempted to bolt back for the old ways. The excuse was wearing thin, but it still seemed to work for Eli. And I, unwilling to attack his defenses, still respected his conviction."

"No offense, Naomi," I said, "but that talk sounds like psychobabble to me."

"Yes, I suppose it does. But you have to understand, Ruth, there was a great deal of this 'psychobabble' going around in the seventies and eighties. Some book had told all of us that I was okay and you were okay, and the knowledge had turned us all into navel-gazers. No wonder so many people are messed up today."

Naomi looked over at me, then laughed. I joined her, experienced enough to relate yet too young to truly understand.

I glanced at the car's control panel. We were nearly out of gas. And that wasn't all. The temperature needle had worked its way up the gauge. We had entered some isolated highway town not far from the beginnings of St. Louis, and fortunately a row of gas-station logos loomed ahead. I pulled off the highway, drove into a gas station, and parked at the end of the nearest row of pumps. Naomi and I stepped out and stretched. Pushing the gas nozzle in to begin filling up, I looked behind me. A group of Harley choppers sat on their kickstands, grouped together tightly as if to mimic the space of a single car. Only one leather-clad biker remained. I supposed the others were inside.

"Ma'am!"

The voice was gruff, and loud, and unmistakably familiar. That is, familiar despite its not containing anywhere near the level of hostility and rage of the last time I'd heard it.

I spun around and immediately recognized the face, the gaze, even the peculiar reflection of light from the hairless planes of his head.

"Ma'am, you got fluid leakin' down there." The tone was an impersonal growl.

I gratefully followed his pointing finger with my eyes, away from his. But it was clear. No denying it. No doubt whatsoever.

The biker from Georgetown!

CHAPTER 31

My mind reeled frantically, and the blood in my veins turned cold. Back turned to my nemesis, I hunched my shoulders as if to help shield me from recognition. We'd driven hundreds, maybe a thousand miles since Colorado. How could such a coincidence happen?

Today, in the light of safety and experience, I can tell you the odds were not so great against meeting that group ever again. Fewer than ten major highways feed east to west, and this was the most central one and one of the most heavily traveled. Not to mention that the group had been driving this same I-70 when I'd encountered them.

But such knowledge wasn't in my mind just then. All I felt was an ominous fate. The victim of murderous coincidence.

Desperate to avoid his direct gaze, I left the nozzle to finish pumping the gas on its own and walked over to crouch before the Impala's grille.

"See it?" he said, his tone still a growl. Sure enough, a dark puddle was spreading on the concrete below the front of the engine.

"Lucky thing is," he said, right beside my left ear now, "looks like it isn't oil. That's coolant. You either got a radiator leak or a bad hose."

"Thanks," I said in my best, disguised voice.

"Why don't you pop your hood?" he said.

I wasn't sure what to do. The last thing I wanted was for him to help me with the car, which would only increase the chances of him recognizing me. Nevertheless, popping the hood gave me a chance to duck into the car for a few seconds. While there, I reached under the seat and retrieved the handgun, slipping it inside my waistband and pulling my T-shirt over it. Naomi, opening the passenger's door just then, saw the motion and stared at me, alarmed.

"What's the matter?" she hissed.

I gave her a fierce look, trying to warn her that the real problem was within earshot. "Radiator leak . . ." I said loudly, but before I could explain further, the biker called for me to come take a look.

Keeping my face pointed downward, I went to check out the problem with the radiator. The biker had a thick hand around the radiator hose, shaking vigorously.

"You got a world of problems with this old engine," he said, "but at least your hoses are solid. Must be inside the radiator. Tell you what. You go buy some of that leak-plugger gunk they got inside. I'll bet it'll fix you up."

As he turned away, he got a good look at my face. He stopped and made a small, inquisitive frown. I felt the blood in my veins turn to ice water. Instinctively, my right hand moved to the metallic weight at my waist.

"We know each other?" he asked.

"No, but thanks for your help. I'll take that advice," I said, and turned rather awkwardly for the gas station's door.

Watching from the corner of my eye through the station's glass, I saw he was still frowning in his attempt to place me. He shook his head and walked over to his motorcycle to begin busying himself with cranking up his hog. All around him, his buddies' Harleys were thundering to life.

"Hey, you can't bring that in here! Whatta' you want?"

I turned. The barking voice belonged to the station attendant behind me. He was staring at my handgun, still stuck in my waistband yet visible through my shirt.

Mouth open in shock, I realized what this must look like.

"It's ... it's not what you think," I stammered. "Please. That guy out there, he threatened to kill me just two days ago."

"I don't care about him. Just leave," the clerk insisted. "Now! Before the cops get here."

My eyes followed his index finger, which was aimed down at something behind his counter.

A police alarm.

"Okay, okay. Wait! I haven't paid for my gas, and I need to buy a bottle—"

He shook his head vigorously. "Forget the gas. Just get outta here."

I was now half in the station and half out, the gun still at my waist, when suddenly outside I heard someone let out a shout.

"Hey! I know you! Georgetown!" The biker was yelling so loudly I could hear him above the throb of the Harleys.

Great. The time had come for a quick exit.

I looked over—the Impala was lurching in my direction. Apparently Naomi had seen what was happening and had taken the wheel. With a screech she stopped and somehow managed to throw open the heavy passenger door.

I stepped out, saw the man coming for me, and just before jumping in the Impala, I couldn't resist. Just as he'd done only a couple days before, I made the sign of a gun with my fingers, aimed it at him, and *fired* my thumb.

"Hey, scum!" I shouted, seething. "Go slither back under the rock you crawled out from."

I shocked myself at the anger contained in those words. It felt strangely empowering—words I wish I could have said to the abusers of my past. Years of pent-up anger flooded my mind. I was no longer scared. I was mad.

I threw myself into the car and slammed the door shut as Naomi shot us out of the gas station with a shriek of tires.

I looked over at her. The poor woman was all aquiver with fear.

"Should I get on the Interstate," she asked frantically, "where they know we're headed, or try a country road?"

"We're not going to get lost on some back road. Let's get back on!"

Without the least bit of regard for the traffic signal, or oncoming vehicles for that matter, Naomi turned onto the access road and raced toward the freeway.

For the first time since starting this whole journey, I longed for a working cell phone. To make matters worse, I could see a traffic jam up ahead in the distance.

Naomi reared back in her seat. "Ruth!" she cried. "What do I do?"

"Brake!" I shouted.

"I can't do this! I'm too—!"

Without thinking, and more roughly than I should have, I slid over and grabbed the wheel from Naomi's hands, shoving my left leg under her and forcing her foot off the accelerator where it had frozen. Then I swiftly yanked her over me and slid myself behind the steering wheel just as we were about to ram the back of a semi-truck. I slammed on the brakes.

"Hang on!"

Then we locked up—helplessly skidding toward the rear of the truck. All I could do was to pump the brake pedal, hang on, and hope for the best.

Because of our rush to leave the gas station, Naomi or I hadn't bothered with seat belts.

I could see we were going to hit, and hard. Desperate, I gripped the wheel and pulled to the left, toward the concrete barrier marking the highway's center only two yards away— thinking that striking its flat surface with our side would be better than colliding nose-first into the back of a truck.

With a deafening crash and a spray of sparks, we slammed sideways into the barrier. Naomi's head struck my right shoulder as my left shoulder crushed into the door panel. But somehow I managed to keep the wheel cranked to the left, determined to channel all our momentum into the barrier.

Finally, with a sickening crunch of metal, we stopped. We'd hit the back of the semi before us, but only with a minor bump. I glanced to my right to check on Naomi.

"Are you okay, Naomi? I'm so sorry I had to do all that, but it was the only way."

She looked over at me, bleeding from a small cut at her hairline.

"I understand, honey. I'm okay, just shaken mostly. You did great. We could have been decapitated under that truck. I'm so sorry I froze up like that. . . ." Her babbling words tumbled over each other.

I wanted to hold her, not for a moment but an hour, but I could also hear chaos through the windows and all around us. Trucks braking hard and horns blaring and even the sound of those infernal Harleys, still somewhere behind us. I turned to open my door, but it was wedged against concrete. Naomi and I would have to exit through her door.

"Careful now," I warned as we began to open it.

She climbed out, and I followed. We were hemmed in by halted semitrucks. I could hear the Harleys growling impatiently behind them, with a few of the hogs sounding like they were trying to weave their way through. I glanced desperately around me for any sign of help.

"You all right, missy?"

I looked up. The voice came from above me—the cab of a semitruck.

"No!" I almost screamed. "Those bikers back there are after us! They've threatened my life!"

Immediately the trucker's head darted back into his cab. Through his window I saw a hand reach up and grab a CB mike from its cradle. The truck surged backward, then slammed in place against its brakes, like a thoroughbred rearing back angrily in the starting gate.

"Can you just stay there for a moment?" I shouted up to him.

The face in the cab reappeared. "Lady, I can't *help* but stay here. There's a traffic jam, and your crash hasn't helped it any!"

"Well, if you and the other two rigs could stay put even a minute or two after the traffic starts moving again, you might save our lives from these freaks."

"Gotcha." He yanked down his handheld mike and started talking loudly. Twin blasts of horns announced that other truckers had gotten the message.

Meanwhile, the hogs were revving their motors ever louder, just beyond our improvised wall of steel. Under the truck trailers I could glimpse chrome spokes and black boots.

Then it hit me—was that animal going to park his hog and come after me on foot, right here in the middle of a traffic jam? I thought of the gun now lying on the Impala's front seat . . .

I saw a pair of boots turn toward me, circling the front of the semi. He was definitely on his way.

My mind rushed me away from there, back in time . . .

. . . to boots on wood. The sound of hell approaching. I look up from my bed, past the Motley Crue poster on the wall to the closed, but unlocked, door. *Number Two*. I numbered them to lessen the confusion of all the names and labels rattling around in my head.

Mr. Ratliff.

Ronnie.

State Certified Foster Parent.

Sir.

Daddy. (Right . . .) Devil. Serial abuser.

Cowardly, wife-abusing pedophile.

Abuser Number Two . . .

The doorknob, turning ever so slowly, the way he always announces his coming.

The roll of quarters gripped in my seventeen-year-old fist.

The door cracks just wide enough to show his face, eyelids drooping a little, as they always do this time of night, with a few drinks in him and this activity in mind. When he comes closer, the reek precedes him.

I feel my right hand coil across my chest, my muscles tense, my teeth clench in anticipation. Then, as he begins to crouch down, my fist flies out from under the blanket. Not a punch, but a sideways whack as hard as I can unleash it.

His cheek gives way under the blow, surprisingly yielding. His head reels away and slams into the bedside table. I remember what my self-protection teacher told me, the one brought in from the junior college for the special P.E. section

I took the previous month. I have maybe six seconds before the shock and pain wear off enough for him to retaliate.

I swing my knees out from the outer blanket. I turn away from him, not to leave but to gather strength for another strike.

My karate chop hits him right where they instructed on the chart to hit—base of the neck. Immediate unconsciousness. Whether from the alcohol, the blow to the neck, or crashing into the table, he falls to the wood floor in a heap. I roll him over onto his back and, sure enough, his pants are unbuttoned, zipper down.

I stomp him hard, and that's the blow that whisks me back . . .

. . . to the freeway, outside of St. Louis, with a bully biker coming after me.

What is it I was remembering? What was the lesson of those visions from the past?

Oh yeah . . .

I'm not afraid of you.

I wouldn't go after the gun. I would cross my arms and wait for him, and then if I had to I'd show him all I'd learned about dealing with men like him.

He was almost there. I could see his face now. I stood my ground, took a deep breath.

Then he reached me, and stopped, and spat out a vile curse.

"Hey!"

It was the trucker from before, the one who had called the others on his CB radio. His door flew open and he jumped down to the pavement. The man was built like a pro football player.

"You wanna pick on somebody your own size, cue ball?"

"Yeah!" echoed another voice. "Like me!"

A second trucker stood before his cab, facing the biker. He was smaller but wiry looking, with tattoos everywhere. In his hand was a cell phone, its red light blinking, the universal sign of video recording.

The trucker raised the cell phone, pointing it at the biker. "Say hello to my little friend!"

The traffic around our little arena suddenly shifted and began to move again. Impatient shouts rang out, aimed at the biker. His buddies were leaving.

The man did his outlaw best. Glaring at me, he thrust his middle finger in the air, spun around on his heel, and thrust the finger at the two truckers, then stalked off back to his hog, fired it up, and rode away.

I wanted to shout and dance a jig, but the sight of the truckers running toward me brought me back to reality. I was in the middle of an Interstate outside St. Louis, in a traffic jam at rush hour.

"Let's try to push 'er over a bit, get this beast moving again," the first trucker said. While I stood before them and repeated "Thank you" over and over again, they both squatted down near the front of the Impala and, straining against the car with everything they had, slowly inched it to the right, unwedging it from the concrete median.

"Thank you so much!" I said once more.

My trucker friend walked over and gave me a pat on the shoulder. With a twinkle in his eye, he said, "Young lady, wherever you met that guy, you're never to go there again. You hear me?"

"I promise!" I said.

He laughed as he rushed back to his truck. So did I.

CHAPTER 32

With traffic on I-70 beginning to move again to our right, I walked over to the driver's side of the Impala and winced at the deep dent on its side as well as the disfiguring scrape marks. And my method of stopping had taken a high toll on the car's front end. I tried the door handle, and it wouldn't budge, so I ran around to Naomi's side and climbed over her to the driver's seat.

"Sorry, Naomi, but it's the only way. The driver's door is jammed."

She shrugged. "It's okay. Like I said before, what you did saved our lives. I just hope it starts back up. Go ahead, give it a try."

When I turned the key, the engine chugged four times without turning over. I cannot tell you how many deaths I suffered, how many days I lost from my appointed life span during those moments. If the thing didn't start, we were in a heap of trouble. Not only stranded in the middle of nowhere, but even getting to safety across three lanes of traffic would be a challenge. At last, after panic that I'd turn prematurely gray on the spot, the engine turned over. Yet it sounded rough, as though the fan blades may be broken. When finally I eased the car into drive, checked for an opening in the traffic, and pushed down on the gas pedal, something strange and rather disconcerting happened.

We went forward, but not exactly in a straight line. The nose of the car aimed off to the side nearly ten degrees. Hitting the median had left the Impala massively out of alignment, and to keep the car moving straight now took an enormous level of concentration. Nothing felt or sounded right, like the wheels lumbering beneath us were not quite round anymore.

I instantly regretted all my negative comments about the old car. It occurred to me that the vehicle actually had been a joy to drive. So what if it was thirty years out of style. At least it had driven smoothly and had plenty of power. But now . . .

"Oh, I can hardly look at the road without feeling sick to my stomach," Naomi said. "Do you think this is going to get any better?"

"Not until we find a garage and get it fixed," I said.

"Should we do that?"

"I don't think we've got enough money. Besides the alignment problem, we have a leaking radiator and a busted fan. Our fuel economy has probably been slashed in half. If we fixed everything wrong with her now, we'd not only spend all our money but no doubt exceed her street value by a factor of ten."

"Well, can you get us to Pennsylvania?"

"Maybe. And that's assuming nothing else happens. Especially with the tires," I said, remembering another thing Lonnie had taught me. "With the car so badly out of alignment, they could blow out at any time."

We limped into a service station two exits away from where we'd hit the median, refilled the radiator, and invested in a radiator plugging additive to help with the leak.

And so it was in this condition, rolling at an angle down the highway and left side banged up, that we entered the tumult of downtown St. Louis, gaped at the majesty of the Gateway Arch lit against the late afternoon sky, and gingerly entered a bridge that lofted us over the famous waterway—the mighty Mississippi River.

I must admit that our situation left me a bit too rattled to fully appreciate the view. Yet as we crossed the bridge, buffeted by a strong wind, I was struck that this broad river truly did serve as a worthy divider for the continent. Coming from the arid canyons of the Southwest, I could hardly believe the sheer volume of water all in one place.

"For better or worse," Naomi said solemnly as we reached dry land on the far side, "this is it. We are now in the East."

It's hard to describe, but I felt as though I'd just driven across the boundary of a whole new life. I thought of what lay behind me, and something told me I would never cross this river again. The West—home to every second of my life until then—would never see my face again. The notion, far from saddening me, gave me satisfaction and anticipation.

That thought carried me all the way across Illinois, to the sign that greeted *Welcome to Indiana*. I immediately thought of *Hoosiers*, and with a pang in my heart I pictured Lonnie watching basketball.

Something in the ditch to my right grabbed my attention for a split second. A flash of light. A few seconds later it happened again. Two of the flashes this time. I shook my head.

"What's the matter?" asked Naomi.

"It's weird, but I thought I saw a light blinking in the ditch."

"It's fireflies, sweetie."

"What?"

"Fireflies."

"Really? I didn't think they existed anymore."

"They don't, where we are coming from. But here in late summer and early fall, you can still see them."

I smiled to myself. Somehow, the thought of fireflies struck me as the beginning of a whole new way of life.

"Tell me, Naomi," I said. "What do people in Old Order country do for entertainment?"

"Pretty much what we're doing now, except without all the motion and noise. Certainly not in a crooked car. Sitting together and talking quietly. Maybe not talking at all. But, you know, enjoying each other's company, sharing a dessert, a cup of tea."

"Three weeks ago, what you just described would have sounded boring to me."

"And now?" Naomi said.

"Now it sounds relaxing and inviting—like a long, fresh breath of air. I could use a little peace and quiet!"

We drove on in an easy, satisfying silence. I went to roll down my window to sample the early evening air, but discovered the handle wouldn't budge. Naomi smiled and then lowered her window so we both could feel the wind through our hair.

CHAPTER 33

🛡️ **70**

The Monday kickoff of Bellagio's employee recruitment effort began an 18-month battle for top-notch workers to staff four new resorts on the Strip: Mandalay Bay, The Venetian, Paris, and Bellagio. The properties, with their appeal to upscale travelers, will need as many as 25,000 workers who are trained to serve customers paying more than $200 nightly for hotel rooms. . . . Half of Bellagio's work force, or about 4,250 people, will come from other Mirage Resorts properties, primarily The Mirage, Treasure Island, and the Golden Nugget. The other half is expected to be drawn from new applicants.

—"Recruitment Drive Begins at Bellagio,"
Las Vegas Review Journal, Tuesday, March 31, 1998.

Looking back on it now, those early miles east of the Mississippi were some of my favorite memories of the trip. Simply lapsing into quiet and letting the rhythm of forward motion, the balm of ever-changing landscape, wash over us. At the time, I was a little shocked to find that I could enjoy such things.

It seemed I was changing ever so gradually, mile by mile.

I found that getting used to driving the car now required that I keep my gaze trained on the horizon ahead. If I glanced at the hood at all, I would quickly lose perspective, become rattled and disoriented. It struck me as symbolic—to steer the Impala so at odds with its orientation. It was as if the car had its own idea of where it wanted to take us, requiring me to impose my will upon it and force it, kicking and screaming, into the direction I intended.

And you should have seen the sideways glances we got from those who passed us on the Interstate. With a shake of their heads, they seemed to acknowledge the futility of what they saw. Two women in a beat-up old car, intent on getting somewhere at risk of their own lives, and maybe those of others.

It was late in the evening, my energy spent, when we stopped in Terre Haute at one of the identical clusters of now-familiar hotels and restaurants that crowded so many of the exits—Cracker Barrel, Holiday Inn Express, Bob Evans, Fairfield Inn.

It felt like the ultimate relief to swing that wounded old beast into one of the secluded hotel parking lots, shift it into park, turn off the ignition, and climb into the back seat for a night's sleep.

After the morning stupor had been diluted by harsh, convenience-store coffee and an awful shrink-wrapped pastry, and freshening up as much as possible (what I would have given for a hot bath!) we were on the road again. "So how about telling me some more of your story?" I asked Naomi.

"For instance, what about the boys? When you lived in Moab, were they good or did they get into trouble?"

Naomi chuckled. "Both, Ruth. But mostly they were just lost. Aimless. As a result, they got into drinking heavily, smoking a lot of weed, and chasing women. . . . Sorry, but I'm guessing you knew that. I can't help wondering what their lives would be like if we had all stayed in Moab—probably living like hippies, working in bike or backpacking shops, earning minimum wage and mountain biking on the weekends."

"There are worse things," I noted. "They had good hearts though. Orpah and I saw that in them."

"Yeah, bad boys with good hearts—I'd say that summed up my sons exactly. Of course I adored them, regardless. And they loved me dearly. What mom can resist that? Motherhood has a way of eroding your discernment."

"And what provoked you guys to move to Vegas?"

"The Bellagio, basically. Nearly nine thousand new, high-paying jobs with eye-popping surroundings and opportunities for advancement. And for Eli, no more being the lone man behind the front desk. Actually, Lonnie had moved to Vegas six years earlier—after graduating from high school. Mel went the very next year, and both of them found construction jobs and began enjoying all the wrong things about the town. As you know, they helped build the Bellagio, so when it was about to open they were on the phone with us immediately, urging Eli and me to move to Vegas, too. So we took a short vacation to visit the boys and check out the Bellagio job fair. Eli was offered a great front-desk job almost immediately. Later that evening, Eli dispelled my misgivings by reminding me that he'd lived in another big city, New York, for two years. Despite being miserable without me, in that time he'd met many fine people and enjoyed some fascinating experiences.

Having never lived in a big city, I had to take his word for it. And besides, the pay was good."

"What did you think of Vegas when you first arrived?" I asked.

"I liked it. I mean, it's a grand place for someone who's never been there before. You should have seen us walk into Bellagio's lobby for the first time. I thought Eli would fall over himself trying to take in that ceiling lined with two thousand square feet of handblown glass flowers. I nearly forgot to breathe when I looked up there and saw the colors. We walked on into the conservatory, filled with all these seasonal flowers.

"Then when we stepped outside, the lights were just coming on against those incredible water fountains. I saw the columns shoot up two hundred feet, all in perfect unison to a song by Pavarotti called 'Nessun Dorma'—a fact I later learned from Eli, part of the trivia he had to master to work at the Bellagio. Tears came to my eyes. I was embarrassed until I saw that Eli had tears in his, too."

"It made him sad?"

"No, not at all. For the first time in years, I spotted a glow of pride back in Eli's face. He could be proud of working there, and his boys were proud of him. That meant so much to him. When they got jobs close to the Bellagio, I remember them bragging that finally they'd landed something above their old man. You should have seen his eyes when they said that. And it was good to have everyone together again. I took a sales job at Hermes, the chic Parisian scarf and leather boutique. We couldn't afford to buy anything there, but sometimes during slow hours, Mel would sneak in his camera and take pictures of me in their fanciest clothes and scarves. He and Lonnie would sometimes come by for lunch, and Eli would use his clout to comp us all meals from Mangia, the huge employee buffet where the best food in Vegas is free, all you can eat, twenty-four hours a day. Eli quickly earned respect from managers and co-workers. His Mennonite work ethic catapulted him ahead of others. Almost every night it seemed Eli came home with another story of escorting some celebrity up to his or her suite. It was a thrill. For a while, anyway."

She stopped, and from the sound of her breathing, I could tell that the grief had finally caught up with her again. I reached over and touched her forearm.

"You know what the saddest part is?" she said in a tremulous voice. "Even then, Eli and I didn't know what we had. We thought of our lives as somehow lacking, empty, needing to be filled by something newer and more fulfilling. Still searching, we'd say about ourselves. But now, looking back, I realize I left Pennsylvania as full as someone could possibly be. It's now, going back, that I'm empty."

That last word caused me to glance at the gas gauge.

"Speaking of which . . ."

CHAPTER 34

(70)

> Yet behind a nondescript *Employees Only* doorway near the
> buffet, down an escalator and through a maze of corridors
> and stairs punctuated by office doors and service cubicles,
> lies an on-site employee dining operation as stunning in
> scope and approach as Bellagio strives to be in Las Vegas's
> cavalcade of over-the-top attractions. The dining operation
> is called "Mangia" and it serves to provide food for Bella-
> gio's nearly 10,000 employees 24 hours a day.
>
> —**Mike Buzalka**,
> "Inside Bellagio's Secret Servery," *FoodManagement*, September 2005.

Naomi gave me the bad news right after the next fill-up.
"I've been doing some more calculations," she began, "and
according to this, we made less than half the distance on this
tankful as the tank before."

I was not surprised. "Must be all the damage to the car.
Especially the alignment."

She kept her eyes fixed on her little spiral notebook. "Based on this, I don't know if we're going to make it with the money we have left. It's going to be incredibly close."

"It was always going to be close," I shot back. "Now it's just edging closer to impossible."

She looked at me sharply.

"Are you angry with me, Ruth?"

"I don't know," I said, not wanting to admit it.

"Do you blame me for the wreck?"

Great, Naomi, I thought. *Always the one to barge in and address everything right up front.*

"No, I don't blame you—"

"Because I did my best, you know. My best, I might add, in a situation that I didn't start to begin with."

She was warming up to her subject. "I wasn't the one who walked into a gas station with a gun in my belt. I didn't rile a madman with my gestures and then insult him to boot."

"No, Naomi, you didn't. But you couldn't seem to use a brake pedal. A *brake pedal,* for goodness' sake! You take your right foot, and you push it straight down. How hard is that? Do you think maybe a failure to use the brakes on a freeway might have helped contribute to the crash?"

That was it, the closest thing to an all-out fight we had ever experienced. Buried somewhere inside me lay a sea of unresolved anger. Anger so hot and volcanic that it felt downright dangerous.

"I apologized for that," she said, staring straight ahead.

"Apologizing is nice," I spat out, "but it doesn't erase what happened. Or nearly happened. We came within a split second of having our heads chopped off by the tail end of a Peterbilt!"

"My failure to step on the brake, freezing up like I did— that wasn't a choice, Ruth. It wasn't done on purpose, the way waving a gun was. Or smarting off to the man in the first place, which you told me you did back in Georgetown. Or even trying your best to get us arrested at a tollbooth. Face it—you've made several very poor choices so far on this trip. Some choices that now seriously threaten our ability to make it the rest of the way."

"Yeah, and I chose you as the person I'd follow and stake my destiny on. Is that another one of these bad choices? Is that what you're upset about?"

"I'm not upset—"

"We're both upset, Naomi. It's called fighting."

Yet part of me could hardly believe what we were doing. Up to now, I had never exchanged so much as a cross word with Naomi.

Another part of me was thinking—even as my temper ran away with my senses—*We're finally getting real with each other, that's all. It was only a matter of time. Maybe this will help us get to the bottom of things.* But that was only the thin voice of reason, being mercilessly whipped about by the gale-force winds of my anger.

"No, you're the one who got mad, Ruth," Naomi continued. "Your anger is what started this."

"I'm not mad, I'm frustrated. Frustrated with this whole situation. That we can't just drive across the country like normal folks. No, we have to run headfirst into every stinking problem known to man. And somehow, the people in our lives all played a part in making this the trip from you-know-where. So yeah, I'm frustrated with them, too. With everybody, living and dead alike. Take your pick. I'm even frustrated with Eli!"

"You leave Eli out of this," she said, her voice quivering. "You leave my husband alone!"

"Naomi," I countered, "what kind of man, after thirty-some years of marriage, leaves you saddled with nothing but this heap of a car, a mountain of debt, and hardly enough cash to buy breakfast cereal?"

"He was a good man."

"Yeah, but what I'm saying is that these good people had plenty to do with where you and I are now, today. Same goes for my Lonnie, who wasn't even man enough to quit drinking to save his own life! To spare you and me all this pain. Is that a level of personal strength and integrity I ought to respect?"

Once again, I was feeling deeply conflicted about this confrontation. Even as I heard my voice fill the interior of that car, I inwardly heard another one trying to rein me in, struggling in vain to pull my rage back to earth before I actually inflicted lasting damage. But I blazed on, the volcano erupting.

"And you, Naomi—you think you're the victim in all this? Think about it. You're the only one who saw things straight, years ago—so what kept you from saying something? From giving your husband the advice and feedback he needed to hear? You spout all this stuff about how much you pitied Eli, how pathetic his life was, but what did you *do* about it? Except keep to yourself probably the only solution that could have turned things around. What's the virtue in *that*?"

"I've never said I was innocent. But I was in pain myself, Ruth," she answered meekly. "I thought you'd experienced a little of that yourself."

"Pain?" I repeated adamantly. "Of course I know about pain. But you could have helped change things if you hadn't chosen to stay silent. You chose to keep your thoughts to yourself. You and your dumb silence! Which doesn't give you much ground to criticize me, or anyone else, for making bad choices. We *all* made them!"

"My point exactly, Ruth. We've all made mistakes. Past

and present. And yet you're the one who's so frustrated by it all."

"I'd say we're both plenty frustrated. I'm just wondering if what you're really mad about is my being here in the first place. My choice to become your permanent appendage, to crash your trip home and spoil your pity party. You don't even know where exactly we're going to stay, or who will be there!" I was twisting the knife even further. "How long has it been since you actually talked to anybody in Bethlehem? And if they're such good people, then why weren't any of them at Lonnie's funeral?"

There. I'd said it.

"First of all, I didn't *ask* you to choose me!" Naomi's reply was in a voice so controlled it felt like a shout. "I never asked you to come racing down the street and barge into my car, telling me all this stuff about me being your home and coming with me! I was going alone. Whether I made it or not, I wasn't dragging anyone else into my mess."

"So now you feel you have to take care of me, look after me?"

"Exactly! It's like becoming a mother all over again. And I don't have the strength for it. To start caring again, start worrying, working for your future. I'm through with that. Caring about so-called loved ones only brought me unspeakable pain. I'm done with it. Or at least I thought I was, until you showed up!"

"Who are *you* really mad at, Naomi?"

"Oh, hush. You know who, and you don't have to make me say it."

"You're going to have to sometime. Because you and I can't keep on arguing like this."

"He abandoned me, Ruth!" she cried.

"Who abandoned you?" I asked, not recalling anything

about Eli walking out on Naomi. "Eli?"

Like the air let out of a balloon, Naomi answered, "No, not Eli. God . . ."

Now the car grew quiet. No sounds but the car's struggling motor and the highway beneath us. We rode like that for some time. The awkward silence held reign until I dared ask, "But didn't you abandon God, along the way?"

"No," said Naomi, shaking her head. "I was abandoning legalism. Blind tradition. Enforced conformity. My spiritual straitjacket. But I didn't intend to abandon Him. I didn't leave Him. He left me."

"Really? Then tell me, why are you going back to Bethlehem? Why not go somewhere else instead? I mean, if you didn't leave anything back there, then why are you so anxious to return?"

"I told you. I have nowhere else to go."

"You know what? The floor I worked back in Vegas was full of women who'd been abandoned in some way or another, whose hearts had been broken. Husbands who died, husbands who left, husbands who got sent to prison. Those women were alone, many of them single mothers with young mouths to feed. And do you know what they did every morning? They didn't sit around moaning that they had nowhere to go. They went to work, smiled at the world until their cheeks cramped, and did what needed to be done. So if you want to go back to your people, back to your home because it's the only good thing you've ever known, or because you changed your mind about the Old Order, then great. Own it. Get real about it. But don't insult us both by saying you have nowhere else to go."

Naomi turned to face me, her gaze level and clear. "Fine. I will. I'm on this journey because I *want* to return to my people, to the values I grew up with, because it's the only place, the only time when I remember my life feeling real. When I understood where I belonged in the world. When I knew the people and the land around me and felt connected to something lasting and good. Maybe it was God."

"Good," I said. "Finally, the truth."

"And you?" Naomi said. "Why are *you* on this trip?"

"It's simple. I'm the one who really has no place else to go. If it wasn't for you, Naomi, I would have left Las Vegas a long time ago."

That charged statement, which Naomi understood at once, ended both the conversation and the conflict. We lapsed into another silence, one completely different from any on the trip so far. It was the kind of interlude I was quite familiar with from my days with Lonnie.

The after-fight breather.

I'm sure you all know something of what I'm talking about. This break comes when you're so spent, your nerves are so frazzled, your communicating ability so depleted from the verbal sparring that all you can do, short of physically leaving the other's presence, is to sit quietly and recover.

I recall trying to read Mel poetry in the hospital, and now snatches of an Emily Dickinson poem I read to him seeped into my mind.

"*After great pain, a formal feeling comes / The Nerves sit ceremonious, like Tombs ... / A Wooden way / Regardless grown ...*"

I know it may sound odd, someone like me recalling poetry back then. But I think hidden within every soul is a secret yearning for beauty, and a love of poetry was my secret. I could relate to Dickinson; her words had a way of reaching my core, and I just knew what she was writing about. The first time the words left my lips, sitting and reading them aloud to

Mel, I could hardly finish them. They were too raw. Too close to my actual experience.

At last, I turned to Naomi with a faint smile. "You fight pretty good for an old lady, you know that?"

"*We* fight pretty good. For two women who love each other so much. Besides, I'm not old," she chuckled.

It was her way of making up. And she was right—we'd managed to have a tussle without tearing each other to shreds, and that was a good thing. All the credit for that went to the affection we'd never stopped feeling for each other. As well as Naomi's character, I'm sure.

At least it was all out in the open now. Naomi was going back to her roots. I knew she would never embrace the Old Order "legalism," as she called it, but she was returning to her Mennonite values. I always knew family was important to her; I just didn't know *how* important. Perhaps that's why I was so drawn to her.

Regardless, I can't remember now how long that "formal feeling" lasted, at least in actual time. I do recall that, in cold geographical terms, it lasted us all the way into Ohio.

The Buckeye State was a gradual change from its predecessor. The forests grew dense, their hardwood trees taller and thicker. Beyond Columbus, the ground became hillier as we approached the beginnings of Appalachia.

Overall, I was finding it an unexpectedly strange experience to see the country fly by in a single, unbroken pass. Conditioned by book learning alone, I'd always pictured the states of America according to the choppiness of maps and atlases—two-dimensional, separated by boundary lines and different colors. To view them all as one land, each state seamlessly flowing into the next, with bodies of water as nature's only real divider, gave me a whole new perspective.

As we drove on, Naomi became more industrious, cleaning the Impala's interior, arranging her things in the back seat, continually checking the map, writing in her notebook, fixing her hair.

Outdoor temperatures on that particular early fall day soared into the mid-nineties. And it was on that day that the dying Impala chose to inflict perhaps its cruelest upon us. The temperature on my side of the car—where the earlier impact had made it impossible to lower the window—became nearly intolerable. So I decided, despite the cost to fuel efficiency, to briefly turn on the air-conditioner.

What was I thinking?

The small vent shuddered in its attempt to cough up some kind of relief. All it eventually produced was a few moments of moldy smelling mist followed by blasts of air considerably hotter than the heater setting would have generated.

Did I mention that since we were saving on the cost of lodging by sleeping in the car, Naomi and I hadn't really bathed since Georgetown? Naomi reassured me by saying that when growing up she'd survived just fine with the traditional Saturday evening bath, but somehow that admission didn't satisfy me. If I'd thought of a safe way to do so, and if the car wasn't already damaged enough to attract unwanted attention, I would have smashed the window altogether just to get a little relief from the oppressive heat.

The result was that I drove through Ohio with my hair damp from sweat, my body stuck to the seat, gripping the wheel in an effort to keep the misaligned Impala on the road, and doing everything I could to keep my mind off the fact that I was melting and in desperate need of a shower.

Naomi tried to help by first offering to drive, which I refused, and then by stating that because of the time of year it was and with our passing just south of Lake Erie, we might receive the gift of a rain shower.

The thought that we had now entered the Great Lakes region had a surprising effect on me. Suddenly the words *back East* were no longer an abstraction. Although the landscape's gradual changes had lulled me into unawareness, we had arrived nonetheless. Yes, this was a real place—with its own skies, lakes, hills, trees, its own roads, stores, restaurants, and people.

After the glancing wounds of our fight, Naomi began to address other issues of mounting interest. My curiosity about the ways of the Old Order increased with every mile closer to the Pennsylvania state line.

"Don't worry, Ruth," she laughed after my tenth question in a row on the subject. "I have no intention of waltzing in there and trying to rejoin the Stauffers right away. Even if they'd want to restore me that quickly, which I seriously doubt. I may not rejoin them at all. I may just stay churchless, if God keeps His back turned away from me. Or I might look into one of the other Mennonite congregations. We're just going to have to feel our way back into Ephrata, and make one decision at a time."

"So there aren't any utilities at all in the farmhouse?"

"The house had gas for the stove, a propane refrigerator, and hot and cold water. No central heat, no electricity. But what state everything's in, or who might be living in it—we won't know until we get there."

We truly didn't know what we were getting into. All we had was the hope of what our move might bring us later on, down the road a bit. *A better life.*

Naomi's reassurance of Mennonite and Old Order hospitality did help to calm my fears. But more practical questions, such as the absence of any electricity, began to plague my big-city mind.

"How did you see at night?" I wondered.

"My papa would light two or three kerosene lamps—one in the living room, another on the dinner table. I know that sounds kind of austere, but now that I look back, I see how it all promoted family togetherness. We didn't scatter all over the house doing our own things. The youngest children cuddled next to my mama while the older ones sat at the table and did homework, read, or played games. Papa usually sat in his chair, reading. We were all within fifteen feet of each other. Of course by the time I was a teenager, that togetherness drove me crazy. Some nights I felt so hemmed in, I wanted to scream and run all the way to . . . You see, that's what prevented me. Where would I have gone? My whole world was Stauffer Mennonite."

"And that's what we'll do, when we get there? Sit around and read at night?"

She smiled indulgently at me. "No, my dear. We might sit on the porch and enjoy gazing out at the fields and up at the stars, taking in the night air. Oh, and go looking for fireflies! Or we might, when through cleaning up after a satisfying, home-cooked dinner, just sit together and have a long, heartwarming conversation, or even sing. Or we might read a good book together, out loud. You know how much I have always enjoyed reading. Remember, we had no TV; reading was my escape and entertainment. There's more to do than you might think."

I sighed and tried to picture a life filled with such evenings. "What you're describing sounds as foreign to me as life in another century, or on another planet. I have to admit I'm a little scared of that simplicity. Part of me thinks it could be wonderful, but another part is wondering if after some time I'll go out of my mind. I'm afraid I'm too used to all the technology and conveniences, to spending my time in crowded rooms, always in the fast lane with everything whizzing by around me and blowing my hair back. Then again, I know I need to reconnect back with myself, with my life. I've lost touch so completely I don't even know what I'm about, except surviving. And maybe that's what Vegas did to me. It kept me in survival mode for so long that after a while I stopped questioning it. I didn't know any different."

"The Old Order has a Pennsylvania Dutch word for how they treat other people," Naomi said. "I've told you about Hesed. A very important term for them. It means caring. Just caring for other people. After we get there, we may be dependent on Hesed for a while. Assuming they're in a frame of mind to extend it to us."

CHAPTER 35

70

It wasn't until we left Ohio and crossed the narrow finger of West Virginia's northern panhandle that I realized how much of a toll our marathon journey was starting to have on me. I began to reel from a kind of nervous exhaustion the likes of which I'd never felt before. My head seemed to buzz, to defy clear thinking. My bones ached, as did my eyes—tormenting me with all sorts of fanciful yet disturbing little shapes dancing in and out of my field of view.

We needed to reach our destination, and soon. And the Impala was nearing its end, more erratic with each mile added to its odometer. Once again, I pictured Naomi and me coming so close and yet not making it there after all. The ultimate indignity. Would we find ourselves hitchhiking across our final state? Surely Naomi wouldn't allow herself to get this close and not complete the last leg, even if she had to trudge the last few hundred miles on foot.

After gritting my teeth through a series of broad turns

down increasingly steep and wooded valleys, we seemed to burst out into free air, with the rich blue waters of the Ohio River beneath us and the beams of the old Fort Henry bridge that whisked us across into Wheeling, West Virginia—a jumble of antique buildings passing by quickly before the highway lofted us upward again, through a short tunnel, then up a long hill of sharp curves that kept me riveted to scenes beyond the windshield.

When we reached the top of the hill, I looked out over a sweeping panorama of thickly wooded hills. I thought of what I'd always heard about the Appalachians and recalling the sound of Loretta Lynn singing the word *holler*, I finally understood.

The sun set on us as we began the unrelenting climb through steep, lush valleys. Fearful memories of Vail and Loveland's mountain passes and steep descents returned to torment me. No longer a novice, I knew that a long climb meant only one thing—a corresponding descent. And with a car half as maneuverable as it had been in Colorado, that could spell disaster.

With a thick fog of exhaustion continuing to dim my senses, having Naomi entertain me with stories of Old Order life and the joys of Lancaster County now escalated from being a pleasure to a reviving necessity.

I may have been only semiconscious during most of the evening drive, but both of us were determined to reach Pennsylvania before retiring for the night. Our entry into the Keystone State descended into a nightmare of trying to stay focused and awake, mentally straining toward the head-clearing timbre of Naomi's voice the way a drowning person reaches for the elusive ring of her life preserver.

I hardly remember stopping to eat our by-then-traditional meal of convenience-store bean burritos, microwave popcorn, and bottled water. It takes effort to even recall the next morning, when Naomi told me it took her a full minute of vigorous shoulder shaking to rouse me in a Wal-Mart parking lot. I do recall, now that I think about it, becoming excited all over again at the realization we were now in Pennsylvania.

Naomi, more than excited, was electrified. As we continued east, each town and landmark she remembered from her childhood, and she talked about them all without pausing, sharing story after story of what it was like growing up in Lancaster County. It seemed as though every barn reminded her of something and launched her into another tale. Then she would just as quickly fall silent, only to brighten up again at the sight of the first rustic fruit stand along the roadside.

"We're getting close," Naomi said. "We could see a horse and buggy any moment now."

"If this car doesn't make it," I replied, "we'll be looking for a horse and buggy of our own!"

The main contrast to Naomi's sunny disposition was the condition of our car, along with the finances we'd hoarded to nurture it along. We had awakened with a half tank of gas, and enough money to fill the tank. The Impala's shimmying and bad alignment had now made simply steering a muscle-straining job. The radiator—which had temporarily improved after dumping in a sealant powder—was now leaking again and required that we fill it up with water at regular intervals.

And yet, with every passing mile, our sense of determination deepened. We had made it all the way from Moab, Utah, and we would not be turned back from reaching our goal. Even as we climbed into the Alleghenies, I no longer allowed myself the luxury of appreciating the landscape around me, lush and wonderfully rolling though it was. I concentrated instead on shepherding our car as efficiently as possible up the long hills, then coasting as long as possible down the other side. I'd given up on keeping an eye out for troopers in my rearview mirror. The fact that I had a suspended license had now faded into oblivion, along with other data from my past.

It seemed the urgency of this trip had erased my entire sense of identity. I was no longer Ruth Escalante Yoder of Las Vegas, Nevada, recent widow of Lonnie Yoder, ex-perennial victim and abuse survivor, employee of one of the city's most upscale drinking establishments. No, those facts belonged to some other person, of another time. I was now Ruth, a person in glorious transition. Someone between lives. A woman in anticipation.

And also a woman in a state of great anxiety and stress....

We entered the Allegheny Mountain Tunnel, which ran through the top of the range, then on its eastern side began a long, winding descent toward pastoral Pennsylvania. While we coasted its other side, I granted myself permission to gaze out at our surroundings. I was amazed that anyone could build such substantial farms on the crests of forbiddingly steep valley walls. I peered down at the densely wooded bottomlands and marveled that the pioneers of old had ever penetrated such a place. Thinking back on the beginning of our journey, I tried to picture Las Vegas, a city hundreds of miles from the nearest naturally occurring leaf-bearing tree. Or even Moab, where the West's largest rivers could flow mere yards away from some of the driest patches on the continent.

I'd come a long way, baby.

We both had.

CHAPTER 36

Pennsylvania—one week since leaving Moab

Three miles beyond Harrisburg, after we'd left I-70 for good and turned onto the Pennsylvania Turnpike, Naomi glanced out her window and made a peculiar sound, a sort of close-mouthed sigh. Then I felt her hand grip my sleeve and turned; she was pointing off to her right. I leaned forward and saw a hulking, white barn.

"What is it, Naomi?"

"Did you see the star and moon shapes nailed to the far corner?" she asked in a breathy voice.

"No, I didn't notice."

"Those are hexes. I take it you didn't see the buggy, then."

"You're kidding . . ."

"No," she answered, shaking her head with a wonder-filled smile. "I'm not. That was an Amish farm. We're in the country. I can feel it."

And I could feel the thrill in her voice, just speaking those words.

"But that place was huge," I pointed out. "In all my life, even back in California when I was a little girl, the only farms I saw that size were the corporate operations. Not family farms."

"I know. You probably thought an Old Order farm would be a tiny plot of land with a mini-sized barn. What you don't realize is that if you treat the land right, year after year, and your family works it faithfully from generation to generation, following carefully the rules of stewardship, it'll yield incredible results."

"What about the land around your family farmhouse," I asked. "Has it been sitting idle all these years?"

"No, it hasn't. Eli leased the fields to one of his brothers, Hans, for cultivation. I think they had an understanding between them that, in exchange for Eli not asking for lease money or any produce that would result from Hans working it, Hans would take care of the farmhouse and land until the day we returned."

"Oh yeah," I said, mentally revisiting Naomi's stories. "I'd forgotten that Eli made that strange remark, all those years ago. In the back of his mind, maybe he was considering coming back, too."

"I'm sure of it," Naomi said. "The place was in his heart."

"Are you worried he may not have kept up his end of the bargain?"

"Who? Hans? Not at all. Hans is a very conscientious man. A hard one but true to his word. The only thing that has me concerned is that he stopped writing shortly after Eli died. We'd made an effort to keep up with him and receive back news of the place. Then all of a sudden it quit. And that's not like him."

Naomi fell into a pensive mood for a moment, and I could tell she was mulling over a somber set of possibilities. I was consumed enough with the challenges I knew about, so I didn't press her to share her thoughts with me.

I looked out at an expansive wheat field, at the deep blue sky beyond, which seemed to frame perfectly the immaculate crop below it like some heavenly seal of approval. Rising from the rows at a distance stood a pearly white silo and barn and a three-story house.

"The houses are big, too," I commented.

"Remember, they don't send away their older generations. A lot of times, after the younger ones take over, they'll build what's called a *Dawdy Haus*, a separate dwelling, small but quite comfortable, for elderly parents or grandparents."

I nodded, processing that small but significant fact. I could see now why Naomi might want to live in the bosom of such a culture.

Glancing over again, I saw a small, golden cloud rise from a field, surrounded by odd-looking machinery, a cluster of young men, and a string of square bales trailing behind them, across raw earth.

"It's harvest time, isn't it?"

Naomi nodded. "With the fall comes the harvesting of crops."

I sighed, an unexplainable feeling of satisfaction welling up inside me. *It's getting closer,* I told myself. But just what *it* was, I couldn't say precisely. Perhaps the ethereal sense of home I'd described to Naomi on that first dawn as we glided down from the Rocky Mountains.

But it was more than that, deeper. It was all of those good feelings and positive attributes that advertisers try to shamelessly evoke, then imitate and try to resell you in so many home products, using words like *down-home* and *goodness* and *hearth* and *all-natural*. I wondered—did this mean I was becoming sappy, or gullible, or even old-fashioned? I examined my heart and concluded that if it did, then those qualities weren't as regrettable as I'd once thought. Because the sense of home and belonging I'd begun to feel was nothing short of wonderful.

Strangely, at this moment I thought of Orpah. What was she doing just then? It was even stranger that Naomi and I had hardly mentioned her name since Moab. I guess we had been too preoccupied with our string of moment-to-moment crises to discuss Orpah's absence.

I glanced down at the car's control panel. We were on our final tank, at one-third full and draining fast. I breathed in heavily and felt my stomach churn.

.We hadn't eaten since early morning.

As for the Impala? It's hard to describe the contrary motions and disquieting noises coming from the engine, radiator, undercarriage, and who knew where else. Maintaining a forward course was a major challenge. I was amazed at the skills I'd reluctantly acquired as I fought to control the ungainly contraption without being arrested.

I considered then how things would go once we arrived. Would the Impala get us to where we needed to go? I mean, we were arriving to Ephrata on fumes, and we didn't have the money to fill it up again. Let alone buy food. Or pay for any utilities. Or even think of paying the back taxes that Naomi had mentioned.

I forced myself to think of two things. First, we'd made it to Pennsylvania by focusing on a single mile at a time, not worrying about everything else. Secondly, I was with Naomi, who more than ever, more even than when I'd spoken those words, was my home. My center of gravity. It sounded cornier than it should have, especially coming from a hard-bitten, former Vegas waitress, but it was true. We had each other.

Whether *each other* was enough, and whether it would survive the challenges of the upcoming stage in our journey loomed as our sixty-four-thousand-dollar question.

CHAPTER 37

With the gas-gauge needle pointing just above the *E* and the red warning zone, that afternoon we crossed over into Lancaster County, Pennsylvania. Harboring an old memory of farming from my childhood, I could only marvel at the meticulous condition of the fields and farms. Perfectly straight rows of corn and wheat stretched on and on, acre after acre, punctuated by fringes of forest—oak and maple trees glowing in red and gold amidst the sunbeams. Clearly we were driving a land cherished by those who lived and worked and raised their families there. I was in awe as I tried to take in the contrast between what lay before me and the landscapes I'd been accustomed to—the miles of arid desert surrounding my Vegas home.

I forced my eyes away from the gas gauge—it didn't even wiggle anymore. For her part, Naomi appeared to have entered a state of perpetual tearfulness and nostalgic reminiscing. When we turned twenty miles later onto a county road that went by the name Reading Road, her emotions only intensified. She was now on home ground, surrounded by sights long buried deep within her.

"This is the road from Bethlehem," said Naomi with a tone of reverence. "The same road that Eli and I came back on to say good-bye to my papa."

Then she pushed herself back in her seat and pressed a hand over her mouth, tears trickling down her cheeks. I looked ahead, and somehow the image awakened something inside me as well, even though I'd never seen such a thing before.

Don't laugh, but it was only your basic, family-sized *Dachwaggeli*—square, plain, black, and pulled along by a stout brown mare. But what that sight meant to Naomi, I couldn't begin to say.

We traced a slow turn around the horse and buggy, careful to keep our distance. When I drove by the bearded, blue-shirted man steering the buggy, I chuckled as I imagined what he must be thinking—getting passed by such a swaying monstrosity of an automobile. No doubt he had all the more reason to reject gasoline-powered travel.

The immaculate farms, which miles ago were scattered around the landscape, grouped closer together now. I saw first one, then nearly a dozen fields in the process of being harvested by threshers of varying levels of modernity. All around us was hard work and the rhythms of a life unchanged for centuries.

We were in Amish country.

As soon as the realization struck, I felt a more pronounced shimmy run through the steering wheel and into my hands.

The Impala was nearing its end.

The irony of the moment became most obvious after I'd pulled over onto the shoulder and heard the horse and buggy pass on the left. Seeing them clop away, I didn't know whether to laugh or cry.

We barely heard the engine shut off; it expired without even one of the gasps and sputters that had accompanied most of its final miles.

I took a deep breath, turned and gave Naomi a weary smile.

"Well, that's as far as she goes," I said. "We got pretty close, I take it."

She nodded, laying a hand on my shoulder.

"You did an incredible job, Ruth. Thank you for bringing us all this way."

"How far are we from the farm?"

Naomi peered through the windshield.

"Let's get out and look around," she said at last.

We slid out on her side, into a warm, soft breeze laden with the smell of fresh hay and a faint hint of manure.

With her face toward the setting sun, Naomi closed her eyes and tipped her head back.

"Thank you," she whispered. "Thank you for letting me come back here."

"You talking to me," I said, "or to God?"

She smiled without looking down or cracking her eyelids. "Both, I guess."

I chuckled. "I thought you were mad at Him."

I heard a vehicle approaching from behind and stepped aside for safety. Then, hearing it slow down to an idle, I turned to see a boxy gray van. As it inched toward us, a blond-haired woman leaned her head out the window.

"Hey, you folk needing some help?" she called.

"We've run out of gas," I replied. "But it's worse than that. As you can see, the car's old and may have gone her last mile."

"We got a towrope," the young woman said. "We can pull you somewhere."

"We don't want to impose," Naomi said. "Thank you, but we'll figure something out."

"Ya sure?"

"Yes, thank you very much."

The woman shrugged, and the van drove on.

"Why did you do that?" I asked Naomi crossly. "What's wrong with accepting a tow?"

"Nothing," she said. "I don't know why I did that. Some prideful old piece of my stubborn papa coming out, I guess."

"Well, now we're stuck with waiting."

Naomi pointed ahead, staring.

The van had stopped a few hundred yards away, its brake lights glowing red. It then swung back and headed toward us again. Just opposite where we stood, it pulled over. Now the driver, a middle-aged man, leaned out the window with his eyes directed at Naomi.

"Ma'am, we don't mean to pry, but my wife here is dying to know if you used to live around here and went by the name of Dimples Yoder?"

Naomi went still, staring at the man and not saying anything in reply.

"Ma'am?"

"Naomi?" I said, walking over and touching her on the shoulder.

Without answering the man's question or responding to my touch, Naomi walked slowly toward the van window.

"Who are you, miss?" she asked the young woman, whose head now leaned over the driver's shoulder.

"Emily. Emily Gautner," she answered with a German accent. "I know it's kind of silly, ma'am, but when I was younger, my family had this wonderful housekeeper everyone called Dimples. Dimples Yoder. They called her that because when she smiled, which she did almost all the time, it made the deepest dimples in her cheeks. She and her family moved away, and after a few years, I never heard talk of them."

"You're Herte's Emily." Naomi said the words flatly.

"Yes!" the young woman cried. "Oh, my goodness! Is it really *you*?"

The passenger door flew open. Emily, clad in a simple flowered dress, ran over and engulfed Naomi in her arms.

"Oh, my goodness, Dimples! Where did you disappear to?"

Naomi took a half step back, smiling at Emily. Our hair was a mess, our bodies needed a bath, and here she was meeting an old friend. For a moment, I felt embarrassed for her.

"Please, Emily," said Naomi, "don't call me Dimples. I'm not that woman anymore."

"Well," said Emily, "where's your husband and those two boys of yours? I've got four of my own, you know. Sitting right there in the back of the van—."

"To answer your question, Emily," Naomi interrupted, a little abruptly, "God turned His back on me." Bitterness bubbled to the surface.

An awkward silence followed as Emily seemed to be processing the fact that Naomi was truly no longer Dimples, no longer Old Order, or even Mennonite.

Speaking to no one and everyone at the same time, Naomi vacantly continued. "I've come back today empty—empty in every way. Family, finances. Spiritually, emotionally. Every way . . ."

"So, Naomi," Emily said softly, "where *are* Lonnie and Mel, if you don't mind my asking. And Eli?"

"They're gone. All of them . . . passed on." Naomi paused once more, a dazed look on her face. A moment later her countenance brightened, and she gestured toward me and said, "I'm sorry—this is my dear, sweet daughter-in-law and friend, Ruth."

Obviously reeling from hearing the sad news of Naomi's family, Emily said, "Naomi, I'm so sorry for your loss." Then Emily extended her hand to me and I shook it. "Pleased to meet'cha," she said. Poking a thumb over her shoulder, she added, "That's my husband, Stefan."

The man sitting behind the wheel of the van turned and touched the brim of his straw hat.

"Please, ladies," he said with the same thick accent as his wife, "let us tow you home or wherever it is you're headed. It's no trouble at all. You know it's gonna be evening soon."

Naomi glanced at the car, then at the lowering sun, then back at Stefan, and nodded, thanking him and Emily for their help. I simply smiled in gratitude.

Wreck or not, this was no place to leave the Impala. Not after all we'd been through together.

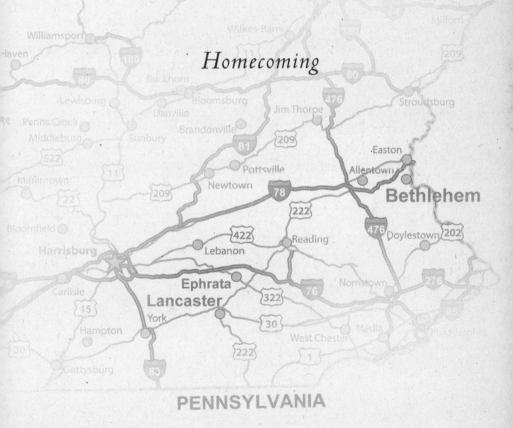

PART THREE

Homecoming

CHAPTER 38

Lancaster County, the Kauffman farmhouse

So the Impala did take us all the way home—or close enough.

The last few miles proved some of the most harrowing of all. The towrope Stefan Gautner produced from the back of his van was strong enough for the task but hardly long enough. Only eight feet in length, it left me with little reaction time in the event of a sudden stop, and I didn't have any power to assist the brakes.

But Stefan was quite able, towing us slowly and cautiously along the unpaved road, which at times sent the Impala jerking sideways. I steered with both hands tightly gripping the wheel, leaning toward the windshield should anything unexpected occur. The closest I came to hitting the back of the van was when approaching the farm—I didn't know we'd arrived. We had coasted down a straight stretch of road when all at once we turned onto a narrower, even bumpier road and entered a lush valley, bordered by stands of hardwood forest.

I first caught a glimpse of the idyllic farmhouse through a cluster of oak trees, and the sight was beyond anything I'd imagined. All of Naomi's accounts of her homeplace still hadn't prepared me for the experience of seeing it for real. As we drew nearer, she too looked mesmerized by it all, occasionally taking a quick breath and wiping at her eyes.

When brake lights flashed red in front of me and caught me unaware, I slammed on my brakes in a frantic attempt to avoid hitting the van.

We stopped just inches apart.

I followed Naomi out her door. With her eyes glued to the farmhouse, she walked slowly, her feet scattering a thick carpet of red leaves as she moved forward.

What stood before me, nestled in this lovely valley, was a graceful-looking postcard of a farm. For a long moment I just stood there and stared.

Finally I walked up alongside Emily, and from a distance we watched Naomi's thoughtful approach toward the farmhouse.

"So Naomi really hasn't been back here to visit—not once in all this time?" Emily asked quietly.

"Not since her father's death," I said, "and I don't think she ever thought she'd be coming back here, until recently."

"Where has she been all this time?"

"Out West. Utah for a while, and then Nevada."

"No one will believe she's actually back," murmured Emily.

"Honey, we should get going now," Stefan called. I silently marveled at this calm perfection of a husband. Was this the kind of men they routinely turned out around here? He hadn't made a false or less-than-confident move since pulling up beside us to offer his assistance. I nodded at them with a smile, then shook their hands.

"It was very nice meeting you. Thank you so much for

your help," I said. "I don't know what we would have done without you."

"Oh, don't you worry about that," Stefan said. "This is one of the best places on earth to find yourself in need of help. Lots of folk would have stopped."

"Well," I said, "I'm glad it was you two."

"Thank you, Ruth. I'm sure we'll see you again real soon."

Stefan said good-bye, smiling and touching the brim of his hat again, and they both turned and walked back to their van and waiting children.

"You take care, Naomi, you hear!" Emily called out as she climbed in.

But Naomi didn't hear her. She was now at the door of the farmhouse.

After the van pulled away, I hurried toward the farmhouse and Naomi. The place seemed to welcome me, unfolding around me as I approached. Beyond the house, I noticed several outbuildings, many trees in full autumn color, a wide patch of lawn, and one massive oak tree—its base surrounded by a blanket of red and orange leaves—that kept the front of the house shaded. On the front porch sat a pair of old, spindly wicker rocking chairs. The yard seemed somewhat kept up, but the house—judging from its front steps and porch littered with leaves, the dirty windows, the chipped paint—looked a bit neglected. It was obviously empty, and no doubt had been so for some time.

Naomi stood facing the front door, perfectly still.

I walked up to her and asked, "Naomi, are you all right?"

She shook her head.

"What is it?"

"How could I forget?" She turned to me with a forlorn expression. "I don't have a key to get in. I should have contacted Hans."

I tried opening the windows that looked out over the porch, but none of them would budge. I walked around the perimeter of the house and tested all the windows within reach. Again, all were locked.

"Ruth, are you a good climber?" Naomi asked.

"I guess so. As a girl, I enjoyed a good climbing tree."

"I remember now how my old bedroom window never closed right. It's something I never told my parents, because it came in handy in my teenage years. It's right there on the second floor, above the porch roof," she said, pointing.

Before she was through with her sentence, I was standing on top of the porch's railing where the porch met the house, pulling myself up between wall and post. It was awkward, and my strength wasn't what it once was, but in a graceless scramble I managed to flop myself over the edge onto the porch roof. Careful not to lose my footing on the rather steep incline, I slowly made my way over to face the second window. I shoved the heels of my hands up against the bottom sash and lifted. It shook and slid upward about an inch.

"It's open!" I called down.

"Great!" cried Naomi.

I inched forward, giving myself more leverage, and moved the window up a foot and a half. Grasping the inside frame, I pulled myself in, preventing a fall to the floor with the palms of my hands. Now in a crouch position, I looked around as my eyes adjusted to the dim light of the room.

The stillness around me was astonishing. Looking back on it now, I realize why. There was no motorized vehicle in use within at least two miles. No electric motor, TV or radio, or any sound whatsoever.

As I stood, I realized I was alone in an Old Order farmhouse, and it was utterly silent.

CHAPTER 39

The bedroom was empty and fairly small. The walls were painted a pale blue color. I smelled old wood and dust, and a mildewy chill hung in the air. I stepped slowly into a narrow hallway. To the left were more doors to other rooms. At the end of the hall and to the right was a staircase. I headed toward the stairs, floorboards creaking under my feet, dust fluttering upward in late-evening shafts of golden sunlight.

I walked down the stairs and entered a room that was larger than I would have expected in an Old Order home. Half hidden by shadow were the kitchen and dining area—open cabinets, an old refrigerator, exposed water pipe, a peeling linoleum floor. A long, roughly hewn wood table sat at the center along with three chairs. In another corner sat a large, box-shaped appliance that appeared to be some kind of space heater.

For a house that had stood like this for who knew how long, it seemed to be in fairly good shape—a sound structure, the floors and walls appearing level. Granted, I had spotted what looked like a box of rat poison in one corner, and the place overall was in need of a thorough cleaning, but other than that, it showed great potential.

I hurried through to the front door to open it for poor Naomi, who no doubt was standing and waiting anxiously. After spending a moment fumbling with the old and unfamiliar lock mechanism, I finally swung the door open.

"Why, Naomi, I'm so glad to see you! You're welcome to come in," I joked.

She laughed and stepped inside. For some reason, I felt the need to take her by the hand. She indulged me, and together we walked deeper into the house. I kept silent as she looked around, taking in every inch and detail of her childhood home.

"When I was little," she said, "we called this place the *schtupp*, which means the stove room. It held a lot more than that, but on a cold winter's night its most important feature was the gas space heater over there. The house wasn't heated otherwise. I think I told you that earlier. Over here was Mama's big cupboard. They took that with them to Missouri."

"I thought the house had no electricity," I said.

"It doesn't."

"Then what about the refrigerator?"

She smiled. "Propane."

"Really? A gas-powered refrigerator? I didn't know they existed."

"They do around here," she said with a wry grin.

We stepped into a hallway leading to a couple of bedrooms in the back. "It's plain," she said, "and it seems so small now. Growing up here, even with all my brothers and sisters around, this place felt bigger than a palace. Some days it never even occurred to me to go outside, and Mama had to shoo me out like some lazy tomcat."

"It's not in bad shape for having been empty so long," I said. "Although . . ."

Naomi looked at me. "What?"

"Well, we're in desperate shape, Naomi. The car's dead, and we're out of money. No food. No jobs. No one's expecting us. The list goes on and on. And it will be chilly tonight, and there's no heat—I mean, apart from that old heater there, which I'm afraid to light. Am I leaving out anything?"

"Yes, I think you are," said Naomi. "Think back to Moab and what we said to each other when we first started this trip."

"We have each other," I said, remembering.

"That's right. We made it here, a huge accomplishment. We have hope. We have our health. And most of all, we have each other. I say that's enough to make a pretty good start."

"Good point," I conceded. "All of them."

For the next hour I began the difficult process of picking up and cleaning what I could while Naomi took time to walk through the house and familiarize herself again with the place and with all the memories it held for her. As she moved, she grazed the walls with her fingers, stopping and starting unpredictably, every so often closing her eyes as if doing so might help to remember more clearly. For the most part I remained in the great room, listening to her slow footsteps echo through the floorboards and among the rafters.

It was nearly dark by the time Naomi joined me. She found an old broom and began sweeping the room's hardwood floor. She had launched into telling another story about this very room when we heard the sound of footsteps on the porch. The front door stood open to let in the fresh air as well as whatever remained of the natural light.

"Knock, knock!" came a matronly voice.

Standing in the doorway was a plain-clothed man with a

pepper-and-salt beard. Beside him stood a kind-looking woman wearing a flowered-print dress and a bonnet over her thick dark hair.

"Are you Naomi?" The woman's voice was a high-pitched squeal.

"I am," Naomi answered, moving closer. Then her gaze shifted to the man, and she smiled. "Oh, Hans! Hello—how are you?" Naomi gave them both a hug.

"I am well, Naomi," he said. "I heard word in town that you had come back to the house, so we decided to come see for ourselves."

"And to bring you these," added the woman, holding out a large basket and pulling back a towel, revealing four small loaves of bread, some smoked ham, cheese, and assorted fruits and vegetables.

"Oh, thank you, my dear!" said Naomi. "We haven't eaten very well lately, so this will be such a treat."

"Naomi," Hans asked, "were Tillie and I married when I saw you last?"

"I was wondering the same thing. It seems I remember you two courting, but I don't recall a wedding."

"And now our youngest boys, Isaac and Jacob, are almost marryin' age," Tillie said proudly. Then looking at me, she asked, "What about your children, Naomi?"

"Yes, my boys," Naomi said with a heavy sigh. "My two sons, Lonnie and Mel, both recently passed away. As did Eli, three years ago."

Hans closed his eyes and took a deep breath.

"I'm sorry, Hans," Naomi whispered.

"I'm sorry too," Hans said. "I wish I'd known."

"Oh, my," Tillie said, leaning toward Naomi with a stricken expression. "I am deeply sorry, Naomi. Nobody knew . . ."

Though Naomi had corresponded with Herte over the years, it was clear the woman had not passed any news on to others—knowing Naomi, I assumed it was at her request.

"No, they didn't. By the way, please forgive me, but this is my daughter-in-law, Ruth, the wife of my son Lonnie." The man and woman both greeted me with kind words, and afterward Naomi said, "Ruth has been a dear friend and companion to me, especially during this difficult time. If it wasn't for her, I would have never made it back here."

"Have you returned to settle things and put the land up for sale?" Hans asked.

"I've returned for good, Hans," Naomi said evenly. "I've decided to live out my remaining days right here where I grew up . . . Lord willing."

I couldn't help notice the way she tacked on those last two words, *Lord willing*. When it came to matters concerning God, Naomi seemed to be constantly contradicting herself.

Tillie turned to her husband and grinned, but he didn't make eye contact with her.

"And the farmhouse?" Hans asked, his eyebrows arched.

"We intend to stay in the house," Naomi answered. "To fix up the place and then live here together. And thank you, Hans, for watching over the place—for your wonderful care of the fields and the house, too."

"Just as we agreed," he said, smiling now. "Our arrangement was most generous, and I was glad to honor it."

"And I hope we can continue," Naomi said. "We'll stay in the house, but for now you can continue to farm the fields."

Tillie looked happy to hear this, taking up her husband's hand and patting it.

"Thank you," said Hans. "We appreciate the offer. Is there anything I can do for you, Naomi?"

"Yes, there is. I was wondering about the state of the utilities with the house."

"Let's see. I've kept the well pumps running, because I sometimes use them for irrigation in the higher corners of the fields. Of course, that means gas. I also kept the space heater functional, because I let the Aid Society store canned goods in here during the winter around Christmastime. So the propane tank should be in working order and still have plenty of gas in it."

"That's wonderful news, Hans," Naomi said, flashing me a smile that clearly said, *See? Already things are looking up—even if just a little.*

"Does that mean," Hans asked, hesitating, "you're hoping to spend the night here . . . *tonight?*"

"I made the decision to come back here on sort of an impulse," Naomi confessed. "So nobody knew I was coming. And to be truthful, after all these years so many people have moved away, or passed on, or left the farm, I wouldn't know who to call on. But anyway, we wanted to get a head start on cleaning the place, making it livable again."

"Well," Hans said, "while Tillie catches you up on the news of who's around still and who's moved on, I'll get the heater and other things up and running for you and . . . and Ruth, is it?"

CHAPTER 40

As Naomi and Tillie talked and Hans helped with the utilities, I ran out to the Impala to retrieve our blankets and other things from the trunk. With my arms full I started back toward the house. I saw Hans march out and unscrew a valve on the water pump, then appear to replace something with the hose, like a coupling, perhaps. He worked with quick, aggressive motions, appearing a bit irritated for some reason.

I entered the house to find Naomi engrossed in the life stories of her countless relatives and friends in the area. While I finished sweeping the floor of the schtupp, Hans reentered the house and began firing up the space heater. He accomplished this task in just a few minutes. I was already impressed with these Old Order men. Of course that's coming from the widow of a man who, although he could weld steel girders and restore old cars, wasn't all that handy around the house.

Wiping his hands clean with a rag, Hans turned back to the women.

"Naomi, there is something important I need to ask you,"

he began slowly. "Are you aware of the tax situation on this property?"

"Yes," Naomi replied. "Being the owner, I know about my obligation with that, and it's something I'll have to take care of at some point, once we're settled."

"Well, according to what I've been told, something must be done quickly toward paying off the property tax balance. I mean, maybe it's none of my business. . . ."

"What do you mean?" Naomi prodded.

"Since I've been farming this land for over twenty years now, I'm hoping . . ." He paused, then rushed on. "Before letting it go to the government, you might let me know. Give me a chance to make other arrangements."

"I'll be sure to do that, Hans," said Naomi, sounding perplexed. "Right now, I'm not sure which way it's going to go. But I'll let you know as soon as I find out. All right?"

The smile returned. "Wonderful," he said. "And it's so good to see you back." He placed his hand at the small of Tillie's back and started ushering her out. "By the way, will we be seeing you in church this Sunday?"

"Pike Meetinghouse?"

"Oh, no. I left the Stauffers years ago. Tillie was raised Eastern Pennsylvania Mennonite. Which I understand was the church you attended for a while before moving to Bethlehem."

"You're right, Hans. And to answer your question—yes, you may see us out there very soon."

Even with the various appliances now running—the refrigerator, the water pump, the space heater—it was a blissfully quiet evening. And thanks to Tillie, we had something to eat. She'd even thought to bring along plastic dishes and eating utensils.

The experience of eating freshly baked bread, smoked ham

and tasty cheeses, succulent fruit and vegetables—after going without for so long—was heavenly and one of the most satisfying dinners of my life. Earlier I'd found two candles in the Impala's trunk, so we placed them on the table. Behind our backs, as a night chill rose remarkably quickly, the space heater ticked, then groaned, then came to life. A most heart-warming sound.

We sat at the table devouring what lay before us while Naomi shared the news and gossip she'd just heard from Tillie. It was a difficult mental challenge, because with several generations and intermarriages and comings and leavings, the discussion covered the equivalent of a small town's population. And it was doubly brain numbing for me, as I had no clue who these people were, let alone being able to organize them in my head. But to see Naomi so enthused and bright-eyed, and about the subject of her own family no less, warmed my heart.

At a break in the conversation, we looked down from our feasting and saw it was nearly gone.

"Can you believe we ate a basketful of food?" I said.

"You mean, can I believe I ate one quarter and you ate three-quarters of that basket? Yes, I can believe that, you glutton!" Naomi teased.

"Right, I suppose I ate more than my share. Sorry about that. Guess I was hungrier than I thought."

We both burst out laughing, then abruptly stopped to listen to our echo throughout the house.

Naomi stood and picked up a teapot, tea bags, and mugs, which I'd brought in from the Impala's trunk. Setting the pot on the space heater's ceramic lid, she boiled the water and made us both chamomile tea—a tea she said was an old remedy for a good night's sleep.

We gathered up our quilts and mugs of hot tea, walked out on the front porch, and after cleaning leaves and cobwebs from the wicker rocking chairs, prepared ourselves for what Naomi called an "evening sit." I wedged the quilt around my limbs for warmth and reveled in the feeling of having nowhere else to go, nothing else to do.

A half-moon floated just above the far tree line, its light causing the leaves of the large oak tree in front to cast their shadows on the ground below. A pair of white-tailed deer appeared off in the distance but quickly bounded away into the woods. I don't know that I'd ever seen a deer in the wild until that evening. And the breeze—just cool enough to bring a chill to the exposed surfaces of my face—was laden with that hint of woodsmoke I love so much.

The essence of fall.

"We made it," Naomi murmured, looking over toward me with a smile.

I held up my mug and we clinked them softly for a toast.

"To the Impala," I said whimsically. "May she rest in peace."

"To I-70," said Naomi.

"To Brantley's one and only truck stop," I came back.

We chuckled into the night.

"You know what I hope for you, Naomi?" I offered. "I hope this evening, as wonderful and surprising as it's turned out, doesn't wind up another Dead Horse Point for you." I smiled as I held up my tea mug.

"Thank you, Ruth. Here's to *us*."

"Right. To *us*!" I said.

"May we enjoy many, many peaceful years out on this porch, rocking in these chairs and enjoying each other's company."

We downed the rest of our tea and settled into the most exquisite silence we'd shared yet. As I gazed at the autumn sky, I'd never seen so many stars, all shining so brightly, in my life. And I'd never known such solitude. Again I drank in the exquisite silence—no cars, trucks, televisions, stereos, construction crews working, telephones ringing—none of the background noise that had become so part of my life that I'd hardly noticed it. Except now, in its absence. The only sounds now reaching my ears were that of the breeze, the leaves rustling about, and the regular creaking of our wicker chairs.

I sat and felt time flow at a rhythm that resonated not only outside of me, on the clocks of the world, but inside me, at a cadence that was in sync for once. That was my first night on what would become our familiar front porch. I had arrived. *Where*, I was still not entirely sure. But I definitely had arrived *somewhere*.

For some reason, my dear family, at that moment I thought of my old life back in Las Vegas. I thought of the famed Strip—the polar opposite of what surrounded me on that porch. I thought of the huge hotels crowded close together, the frantic movement all hours of the day, and the blinding, multicolored lights of the casinos, as well as everything that went with it all—the glitter, its grand purpose to amuse and entertain. Which perhaps it does, though in a very fleeting sort of way. I don't know. But I remember occasionally stopping in Vegas and looking around, and seeing mostly facsimiles or façades of *real* places, of buildings and landmarks elsewhere on earth, and then feeling let down, anxious and displaced, but never able to pin down what it was exactly that nagged me so.

Well, finally I knew.

Something about that night on the Kaufmann family farm in Lancaster County, Pennsylvania—on that modest porch and in that creaking rocking chair—told me that I, Ruth Yoder, had found my place in the world. And that, despite my never having set foot there before, it was a place that definitely felt like *home*.

CHAPTER 41

That first morning I awoke feeling stiff, groggy, and very disoriented. For the last week or so I'd opened my eyes to the same odd angle on the Impala's front seat, looking up at its dashboard, smelling the same mustiness of old carpet and motor oil. Before that, it was Naomi's lumpy couch at her apartment, and before that an accursed vinyl chair in the Las Vegas hospital. But the farmhouse at dawn was entirely different. The smells of old wood and dust touched my nostrils, and instead of car doors slamming and nearby freeway traffic, I was greeted only by the twitters of birds outside the window and the light snores of Naomi not far away.

The awareness of where I was brought a sense of accomplishment, followed by a hazy notion of farmland. Of simple things. Then faces. Emily. Hans. Tillie.

We made it. We're home.

I got up from the kitchen floor, where we'd spent the night next to the heater, and stretched my arms and back. My mind went to the few items left in the basket of food brought by

Tillie the evening before. Despite my eating a considerable amount, I was extremely hungry again. I looked down and saw Naomi's eyes half open, looking at me.

"Good morning," she murmured.

"Morning. Hey, are you as hungry as I am?"

She nodded.

I stood and walked over for a look at some bread and two apples in the basket, then went to stare out the front window. The valley below us was transformed, flooded now with warm sunlight instead of afternoon shadows. The rusty majesty of the woods on the far ridge made me want to spend the day outside, strolling around among the trees' lower branches. I felt like the carefree kid I'd never been but always longed to be.

"We've got to get some more food in here," I announced at last.

"I'm all for that," Naomi agreed. "And furniture, starting with beds."

"Right—which means we need money," I added. "I have to get into town, see if I can't find some kind of job."

We finished up the food, and the next task was to get cleaned up. Thanks to Hans's help with turning on the gas for the hot water, we would be enjoying our first full bath in several days. Granted, it took Naomi and me half an hour to clean the first-floor bathroom to a level either one of us would call tolerable. Two small bars of soap and half a bottle of shampoo were all we had left—not much, but enough to do the job. It felt so good and invigorating to be rid of all the grime and sweat from our journey.

Wrapped in a towel Naomi had brought along, I stepped out of the bathroom, and there stood Naomi, smiling and holding up a beautiful, ankle-length dress of pale lavender covered with tiny purple blossoms.

"This is my birthday dress from when I was young," she said. "For some reason, I never had the will to part with it. All these years I've lugged it from one place to the next, and when it came time to move back here, I couldn't bear to toss it out."

"It's lovely," I said, caressing its lace collar. "I wish I could have seen you in it."

"I'd like to see *you* in it."

"Me?"

"I think you're petite enough. It's worth a try, because if you're really going into town, looking for work, you can't go in those nasty jeans you've been wearing."

And so that's how I happened to walk into Ephrata looking like a proper Mennonite woman—wearing a long plain dress, with my body fresh and clean and my newly washed hair woven into a tight bun, all with Naomi's help.

What seemed most out of place were my Hispanic features, my darker skin—not exactly Pennsylvania Dutch. In any event, I certainly felt like a thoroughly Old Order young woman as I launched out on my three-mile walk into Ephrata, empty-handed and with no idea where to begin my quest.

Naomi had gladly stayed behind to continue cleaning the house. I waved good-bye as she stood on the porch bathed in sunlight, dappled by the shade of countless oak leaves. For the first time in all the years I'd known Naomi, I would have described her as *radiant*. And for the first time in many years, I would have described myself as *expectant*. Expecting something good to happen instead of something bad.

After sitting in a driving position for so many consecutive days, it felt good to engage my leg muscles in the long walk to town. Surrounded by rows of late-season corn, I followed Naomi's directions to the unpaved road, then a paved one called Red Run Road. Minutes later I reached another, Hahns-town Road, and headed south. On that road I was overtaken by someone driving a large gray van. Had I been in another part of the country, the prospect of being accosted by a non-descript van would have filled me with fear and provoked a mad dash to escape. But here in Lancaster County, I merely glanced at the bumper and saw that it was painted black. Black-bumper Mennonites, though the precise name escaped me. The vehicle pulled to a stop alongside me, and a bon-neted, middle-aged woman leaned her head out the window toward me.

"Are you in need of a ride, miss?"

"Will you be going into Ephrata?" I asked.

The woman cocked her head and squinted at me for a better look. "Believe so," she said. "What are you, if I may ask?"

"What *am* I? I'm sorry, but what do you mean?"

"What Order, miss."

"Oh." I looked down at my dress. "Not much of anything, I suppose. My dress was given to me by a Stauffer friend."

"So you're Mennonite?"

Not wanting to be dishonest with the first person I met, I said, "No, I don't suppose I am."

"Oh." The driver's expression changed. "Well, are you a Christian?"

"I'd say so, ma'am," I said, though keenly aware that I'd hardly thought of such matters in a very long time.

"Hop in, then."

A teenage girl moved from the front passenger's seat to give me room, which I thanked her for profusely.

"So you're headed to Ephrata?"

"That's right," I answered.

"Whatcha looking for?"

"Work. I thought I'd look up an employment agency, something like that. This is my first day here."

"Where'ya from?" piped in a high-pitched child's voice from the back.

"I'm from—" I stopped and thought through my response—"out West. Nevada, actually."

"Oh, what's that city out there that's so foul? The one our pastor believes is the pit of hell."

"Ah," I said, chuckling. "That would be Las Vegas. I must admit, that's where I'm from."

"Really? Well, if I may say so, young lady, you look mighty good and plain for one hailing from such a city as that."

"Why, thank you," I said. Ironically, I was indeed thankful.

"Now, when we get to Ephrata, you'll want to talk to the folks at Mennonite Community Services. It's an aid office and food pantry and employment service and secondhand-goods warehouse, all in one."

"That sounds perfect, ma'am. I'd greatly appreciate it."

We drove into Ephrata, a charming town of boxy-looking brick homes and buildings.

As we pulled over in front of a low-slung building with a sign that read *Mennonite Community Services*, I thought of Naomi's mention of the car-driving Mennonite group. "Are you all Weaverland Mennonites?" I asked.

"That's us," the woman said.

"Thank you for giving me a ride, even though I didn't turn out to be an Old Order girl."

"Actually, that's why we gave you a ride," the woman said, shaking her head and smiling. She didn't explain, and I didn't ask.

I waved good-bye to the Mennonite family, who drove away with a "Lord bless ya" drifting off on the wind.

CHAPTER 42

Inside the Mennonite Services building, an attractive older woman with the signature bonnet sitting behind a desk fielded my question about possible work in the area. "You've come at a very tough time, miss," she said, frowning in an effort to think of possibilities. "You see, it's not only harvest time, but this week we're gearing up for the biggest event of the year—the Ephrata Fair. It starts next Monday night and runs through the following weekend. Unfortunately, all my Help Wanted tickets have already been filled for that. I'm sure there are plenty of jobs hauling and such, but those are usually taken by men, and the employers often don't list them with me. I'm afraid there aren't any jobs available for a young woman anywhere in town."

"I can do farm work," I suggested, trying not to seem too desperate. "I grew up pulling vegetables in the Imperial Valley."

"The where?"

"Never mind. But I can do farm work. I'm a hard worker."

"In *that* dress?"

"Please, ma'am. I really need something, and soon."

She thumbed through some papers on her desk, paused, then looked up at me and said, "I'm pretty sure it's the same at the Green Dragon. You heard of that, sweetheart?"

I shook my head. That response apparently clued her in to the fact that I wasn't from the area. Her demeanor changed somewhat.

"The Green Dragon is a huge farmers' market, auction house, and flea market just outta town. Owned by a gentleman who is also Mennonite. At least in his blood. Except for during the Fair, they are open on Fridays only, and they draw scads of folks. You may wanna go out there and ask around. There are so many folks there selling their stuff, you never know what you could find."

"Thanks anyway," I said, thinking that *Green Dragon* was a strange name for something Mennonite. "Could you give me directions to this Green Dragon?"

"Well, it's out of town to the north, right on—" The woman stopped and looked at me again. "Why don't I drive you? Considering how little help I've been, it's the least I can do."

I really didn't know how to respond to this strange kindness. This would have never happened in Vegas. What was that word Naomi had used? Hesed? If my initial reception was a true representation of the Bethlehem and Ephrata area, I had a feeling I would like this place—my new home.

I accepted with gratitude, and she drove me in her Volkswagen Beetle into the countryside just north of Ephrata. There, right after passing through a covered bridge, we turned into a parking lot adjoining a dozen white buildings. A large green dragon towered over the complex, breathing fire and promising the best bargains in Pennsylvania.

I exited the car with the woman's genuine best wishes and began walking toward the biggest building I could see. Inside was a long open space lined with three rows of stalls and displays and signs and smells that promised every sort of merchandise imaginable. I saw a sign marking a purveyor of smoked meats and cheeses, fresh lamb and pork. Another announced fine Amish pastries, another fine candies, and still another farm-fresh produce.

Since it clearly wasn't a selling day, few of the displays were more than half full. The aisles were free of shoppers, but a steady stream of people bearing boxes and racks of merchandise filed busily back and forth.

Feeling determination well up inside me, I marched up to a produce vendor, who had just arrived with a tall stack of empty lettuce boxes.

"Sir, do you have a minute?" I asked the man—probably not Mennonite, judging from his jeans and cowboy hat.

He merely nodded, eyeing me up and down.

"I've just arrived in town and I'm looking for work."

"I'm sorry, but we're staffed up for the week."

"If you don't have any paying work, how about if you let me help you guys out in exchange for some of your culls."

"Some of our *what*?"

"Your culls. Your castoffs. The merchandise that's a little bruised, a little old, maybe?"

He frowned thoughtfully, apparently considering my offer.

"I grew up pulling produce out in California. I'm strong and I can work hard."

"Really?" He eyed me again. "I would have figured you for being a local."

"It's just a dress I borrowed from a friend."

"Well, I suppose if you can empty the back of my truck and bring everything to the booth over here, I'll give you a case full of questionables. That's what we call 'em."

"Great!" I said, grasping his hand and shaking it. "Where's the truck?"

It turned out the man's truck contained only eight more boxes. I marched down the loading ramp, dolly in hand, only to be met with the suspicious stare of a man wearing a green apron.

"Can I help you?" he asked as I, undeterred, began lifting the boxes.

"The man inside," I said, "I didn't catch his name, but he's letting me help out with these boxes in exchange for some of your older vegetables. Your culls . . . I mean, the question-ables."

"Are you Mennonite?"

"Only by marriage," I replied.

"So why are you wearing that?" he asked, pointing at my dress.

"Oh, just for fun," I said breezily. "It's comfortable." I grabbed a box, a heavy one at that, and placed it onto the dolly. He gave me a suspicious look and walked away.

It turned out that Naomi had a far more productive morning than she'd expected. Less than an hour after my departure, a pickup truck had approached the farmhouse, carrying her old friend Herte as well as some old chairs, bed frames, and household goods. Alerted to our presence and our need by her daughter Emily, Herte had stopped by the Mennonite Services building—just minutes after I'd left there—and ransacked the place in order to make a surprise call on Naomi.

Herte was now in her mid-sixties. Animated by that spry energy of the happily retired, she bounded up the porch steps and almost knocked Naomi over in her rush to wrap her in a hug.

The two spent hours visiting even while unloading and installing the various and urgently needed housewarming items Herte had brought over.

In the course of their conversation, Herte found out that Naomi was unsure about the tax status of the property. The woman promptly ordered Naomi into the truck, and the pair made the thirteen-mile drive into Lancaster proper, the county seat. There Herte led her friend through the county apparatus, eventually to discover a state of affairs that made every other dark cloud look positively cheery by comparison.

Naomi owed $24,849 in back taxes on the farm. And while the grace period for their payment hadn't actually expired, it would do so soon. Time, procrastination, funerals, grief and loss were all conspiring to grab away from her the one thing on this earth she most cared about—her childhood home.

To make matters worse, a lone document seemed to indicate that a Hans R. Yoder of Akron, a nearby town, had legally paid the taxes on his own behalf, then recently filed a notice of intent to satisfy the entire lien and purchase the property at fair market value upon the expiration date.

Later, Naomi told me she felt as if she'd been kicked in the stomach and fought nausea all the way home from Lancaster. No wonder Hans was so eager to inform her of the problem with the property taxes, requesting that she contact him if she found herself unable to come up with the delinquent amount.

Of course Naomi had no money and no plan for acquiring enough to satisfy the claim on her farm, especially with such little time left in which to pay it. The cold reality of it all made her feel as though her return home had been a childish fantasy, nothing but a fool's errand.

She worried about how she would break the news to me.

All the way to Lancaster County she'd bragged about the inherent kindness of her people. And although legal, Hans's plan to obtain the farm for himself seemed so ruthless.

In light of this development, the farmhouse went from comfortable and healing to painful and sad. So much so that, on the way home, Herte asked if Naomi and I would like to move into her house, occupying the same spare room Naomi had lived in while keeping care of Herte's house and kids so long ago.

Naomi considered the offer seriously for several moments, but then the same stubbornness that had launched her on her journey home and enabled her to reach her destination compelled her to stay put and fight it out.

We would continue to live on the Kauffman farm.

For the time being, anyway.

CHAPTER 43

With 400 vendors to visit, it's easy for one to spend the day at the Green Dragon farmers' market. Arrive early and watch the Amish, Mennonite, and 'English' farmers bid on hay they will take home to their horses and cattle. There are seven large market buildings. In fair weather, outside vendors offer everything from china and crystal giftware to novelty T-shirts.

Regular market-goers—those ones wearing comfortable shoes and carrying cloth or wheeled tote bags—return time and time again to their favorite stands. Specialties include doughnuts, whoopie pies (Amish dessert) and over-sized cookies at Dutch Maid Bakery. We also like the beef jerky, hog maw (old-fashioned farm dish) and other meats at New Holland Meats. Or for lunch we might take a counter seat at Jake & Leola's Restaurant (look for the big birch beer barrels). But usually we snack as we walk, buying hot pretzels, a sandwich, or Knepp's Caramel Corn—the kids

> love watching the popcorn being stirred in the large copper kettles.
>
> The myriad offerings at Green Dragon on a recent Friday included hardware sold by the pound: Japanese parasols, antique dishes, cell-phone accessories, tin cookie cutters of various shapes, handmade pillows, NFL and NASCAR collectibles, old books, Amish-made oak furniture, and pet tags that are engraved while you wait.
>
> Finally, don't miss the market stables where the Amish park their horses and buggies for the day.
>
> —"For Different View of Dutch Country, Visit Ephrata," Joanne E. Morvay, *Baltimore Sun*, May 13, 2004.

Green Dragon, Ephrata

My day at the Green Dragon proved to be one of the most productive and promising to come my way in a long time. In payment for unloading his truck and a few other tasks he assigned to me, the produce vendor gave me a cardboard box filled with vegetables and fruit—carrots, potatoes, squash, apples, pears, and peaches. Many of these appeared to be of prime quality. Later the vendor led me over to the middle of the larger of the buildings, had me stand on a makeshift platform of wood crates, and introduced me to everyone in a loud voice.

"Hey, everyone!" he said. "Listen up! This here's Ruth, and despite her small size and cute little dress and all, she can outwork most of the men in this building. She's here to work in exchange for a few extras—your questionables and whatever else you decide. So how about you guys give her a shot at doing some labor for you? You won't be sorry you did."

His bit of good-natured humor kept it from feeling humiliating. Regardless of how self-conscious I felt, I was grateful for the help. Desperation and hunger are fertile ground for nurturing a humble attitude.

The announcement was met by the echoes of several jocular taunts, a clear sign I'd provoked some male defiance. I played along by lifting an arm like a bodybuilder to show everyone I was a good sport. It worked. Before long, I had four vendors competing to employ me, and I asked them to wait their turn.

I ended up putting in a half hour with Samuel the butcher, an hour with Amos Martin's family of Mennonite bakers, and another half hour with Elizabeth Witmer at her flower stand. So I would return to Naomi not only well stocked with food, but bearing fresh-cut flowers to decorate the dinner table.

But the whole day almost fell apart in one awful moment.

I was engaged in the delicate task of moving an enormous stack of egg cartons up a twin set of stairs with Amos Martin. The precarious tower of cartons was quite heavy, probably around sixty pounds. As Amos started backing up the first steps and I lifted my end of the load to keep everything level, all speech ceased in the building. I don't suppose anyone at the Green Dragon had seen a woman carry such a load. The pounding of blood in my veins and the hard breathing of physical strain was broken by the sound of footsteps behind me, followed by an outbreak of laughter.

A hand planted itself on the inside of my calf.

I was shocked. Had I been in a bar back in Vegas, this would have been a nonevent. But this sort of thing wasn't supposed to happen in Lancaster County.

"Hey! Get away from her!" Amos valiantly shouted from where he stood on the step above me.

More laughter from several of the men rang out from behind us. The hand on my leg moved, caressing now. It was a coward's gambit, betting that I wouldn't drop my fragile load just to stop him touching me, or even turn around to find out who was responsible.

From somewhere around me I heard several guttural sounds coming from the men, the kind lofted into the smoky darkness of a strip show.

Still reeling from the effort of keeping the cartons level, my consciousness was snatched away to another place, another time. . . .

This time on my bare thigh, and the hand is gloved in latex because it belongs not to an abuser but to a man of medicine—someone who, it has been promised, will make everything better again, taking care of the nausea that no fourteen-year-old girl should ever have to suffer, and the fatigue too, along with other strange, disturbing symptoms. A man who stands at the same galling vantage point as the monster, but I've been told this is okay, this is good.

He speaks, and I can't tell to whom his words are intended because of the drugs they've given me and the odd, disoriented way he looks at the walls while he talks. But now, even though I only hear them weave in and out of my consciousness, I know the words can only be meant for me.

"Surely you don't want his baby, the child of your attacker, do you? No, of course not. No, not at your age, not ever. . . ."

But I cannot even begin to process the meaning of his question, because trauma has channeled all of my focus to that one raging spot on my thigh where a man's hand lies, casually placed, arrogantly oblivious, another unthinking violation by the powerful and the entitled—a convenient perch for the fingers awaiting the upheld tool a nearby assistant is sterilizing, which will soon turn what Mama used to call my "special places" into a place of death. . . .

Go away, my present, woman's mind shouted at the painful memory. *Leave at once!*

"Amos, how much do all these cartons cost?" I asked through clenched teeth.

"My cost? About thirty bucks. But don't worry—he'll pay."

He'll pay.

That's what I earnestly wished, although my life experience said otherwise. My memories of such encounters featured mostly unmitigated surrender, turning away with awful cheek-stinging humiliation.

The hand on my leg withdrew, yet something told me the affront wasn't over. I turned and spotted a utility mirror on the wall, installed there to help haulers see around corners and prevent collisions. My harasser was a man I recognized only by his bloody apron. He belonged to a delivery crew for a local meat processor, made up of an obnoxious pair whose truck had been parked out back. They were not Mennonites, I would later learn, or even Pennsylvania Dutch. Just average, American good old boys.

My instinct proved right. He had withdrawn his hand only because he'd moved in closer to perform certain lewd motions.

I turned back to Amos.

"I promise. I'll clean up."

I extended my right leg, cocking it back at the knee to bring my heel swinging behind me with as much force as my aching muscles could muster, almost causing our teetering load to slip from my hands. I felt my heel strike and heard a deep exhaling sound behind me. In the mirror I could see the man wince and bend forward at the waist. For good measure,

I raised my knee high and stomped down on the man's foot as hard as I could, feeling his foot crunch under mine. The man groaned and cursed behind me.

A high-pitched cheer went up and echoed across the place—the women who worked there every day, who'd probably endured such treatment in silence.

I shot out my right hand and grabbed him by the neck, in that vulnerable spot I was taught about just above the Adam's apple. The egg cartons began to sag and fall from my left hand as I shoved his face forward with my right. My hands flew toward each other, forcing a union of meaty face and crushing eggs by the hundreds.

I stepped back and allowed the weight of all twenty-six dozen eggs down upon the creep's head and upper body.

Then I strode away—amidst a renewed chorus of male and female cheers—over to where I knew a pile of cleanup rags awaited me.

CHAPTER 44

I still couldn't decide whether my retaliation had been the right thing or whether I'd just given my rage a field day at some jerk's expense. I tried to bury my still-raw emotions by concentrating on the task at hand—cleaning the floor of crushed eggshell, yolks, and slippery whites. I didn't mind the work; it was my salvation.

But what proved most rewarding was the exultant smiles of the women who got down on their knees next to me, gleefully joining in the cleanup.

While I labored over the concrete floor, I noticed a rugged-looking, gray-haired man enter the building and sit down with the men who were eating at a nearby table. I saw him glance my way, then look again as I worked. He called to a young man. I discovered later the older one was the owner, the younger man one of his managers.

"Isaac, who's that new young woman working over there, the one with the dark complexion?" I heard the man ask.

"I don't know, but she's one hot pistol—I'll tell you what," Isaac replied.

"It's called a *woman*, Isaac," the owner grumbled. "Show some respect."

"I will—believe me."

I couldn't hear much more of the conversation, but the bits I did catch sounded like Isaac went on to tell the owner what just happened, what he described as the "butcher and egg incident."

It was sometime later before I heard the details of the conversation. "And you don't know any more about her than 'one hot pistol'?" the owner had said. "If that's true, then you're losing your touch, Isaac."

"I don't know as much about her as I'd like to, boss," said Isaac. "She just walked in off the street. She's been doing odd jobs here and there, pickup work for some of the vendors, all morning. Working for food, I hear. Doesn't seem too hung up on money. A real hard worker, and very strong for her size."

"No one knows any more than that?"

"Keith over in produce thought he heard her tell someone she'd just gotten into town from out West. That's about all."

"She's a brave young woman," the man said. "You put those looks together with a knowledge of how to work and the spunk to stand up for yourself, and you've got yourself a keeper."

"You got a point there, boss. You want me to call her over here, have ourselves a little talk?"

The owner nodded.

And that's the first I came to realize what a stir my actions that day had caused. Isaac approached me, asked me if I had a minute, and then led me over to where this nicely dressed older man sat at one of the lunch tables, speaking into a cell phone.

"Boss, here's the young lady you asked to speak with," Isaac said.

Putting his phone down on the table, the man turned, smiled, and extended his hand for me to shake. "I'm sorry, miss, my name is not 'Boss,' but Salmon. Bo Salmon. I hope you'll call me Bo."

"Thank you, Bo," I said. "I'm Ruth."

"Ruth. . . ?" he said, obviously asking for my last name.

"Yoder."

"Ruth Yoder. Nice to meet you. Well, I heard about what happened to you this morning. I want you to know something. That call I just hung up from was me firing that meat vendor, effectively immediately."

"Immediately?" Isaac said, his eyes wide.

"Yeah," Bo said, turning to him. "Time has come for us to go with the Witmer Brothers. Now, Ruth, would you like to sit down and have lunch with us?"

I shook my head. "I'm sorry, sir, but I'm skipping lunch—."

"Not if I have anything to do with it, you're not. Not after spending all morning working hard and putting disgusting losers in their place. Please, sit down. Lunch is on me."

I shrugged. "All right. Thank you, sir."

After Isaac fetched me a shrink-wrapped ham sandwich from a cooler, as well as a bag of chips and ice-cold can of Coke, the man sitting across from me looked me straight in the eye and said, "I suppose you know you're the Green Dragon's mystery of the day. A young lady in Mennonite clothes, with a Pennsylvania Dutch name, who tells folks she's from out West, handles labor like an Old Order woman, but who's not afraid to stand up for herself with the men. From what I hear, that's the gossip so far."

"I'm impressed," I said, "since I've only been here a few

hours. But I've heard it said that a lady should always keep a little mystery about her. What exactly is it you want to know?"

"You're right. It's none of my business, and I'll admit I'm mostly just curious here," Bo said with a grin. "But I'm wondering where you're from exactly, Ruth Yoder with the Mennonite getup. I'm dying to know. You don't really have a Pennsylvania Dutch complexion, you know."

We both laughed.

"I don't think you'd believe me if I told you," I answered, still taken by the man's warmth and directness.

"Why don't you try me?"

"I grew up in California, mostly. San Joaquin, Imperial Valley."

"Of course," he said. "Famous growing areas. You grew up on a farm, did you?"

"You might say that."

"So are you Mennonite or not?"

"Not. Or maybe by marriage—or at least used to be. No, I would say I'm a lapsed Catholic with a soul somewhere in transit."

"Still in transit. Well, I like the sound of that. It certainly describes me. So, Ruth, I hear you're looking for work."

"I am. Any work available. The truth is I can take anything. I've been a field hand and a waitress, and just about everything in between. I can handle a crowd, a rude customer, a runaway car, and a trayful of drinks."

"And pick up heavy loads of produce from the looks of it."

"Ah, yes. I forgot that part."

"What does your husband do?"

"Excuse me?"

"I see you're wearing a wedding band."

A bit flustered, I said, "Oh, right, the ring. My husband

passed away not so long ago. I guess I haven't thought to take it off my finger just yet."

"I'm sorry to hear that," he said, and he seemed sincere. "It's all the more reason for me to say what I'm about to say."

"To say what?"

"First, Ruth, I'd like to apologize. I work real hard to make the Green Dragon a safe place for everybody. And if I'd been here earlier, when you were being harassed, that guy, besides never setting foot in here again, would have had me personally to deal with. I like most of the folks who rent stalls from me and work around here. In fact, I more than like them—I depend on them for my business. But clearly, some of them require carefully watching. Others might toss you a few rotten carrots for a half day's work, and you're worth a lot more than that."

"Thank you, sir," I said.

"As a matter of fact, I want you to work for me," he went on. "There's something about you. . . . Well, I don't know how to put it."

A chuckle nearby quickly stifled when Bo said, cocking his head sideways, "I know a lot of folks are going to think I only hired you because you're so pretty. But don't fool yourself. We work hard here. And *pretty* can wash out at the Green Dragon as quick as anything else. In fact, pretty might be more of a liability than an asset. But what I see in you goes deeper than that. You seem to have a double dose of character. And integrity. I need folks with those qualities right now, while we're preparing for the Ephrata Fair and our second biggest selling day of the year. So if you'll promise to show up tomorrow and dump the dress—since we already know you're no Mennonite—and trade it in for a work shirt and a pair of blue jeans, you've got yourself a job."

CHAPTER 45

My new protector and friend made a show of turning around and wagging his finger sternly at the group gathered around us.

"And the rest of you'd better shape up, because my guess is Ruth will be threatening your job security if you're not careful," he said. His laugh was joined by the others. He turned back to me. "Is it a deal?"

"Deal!" I said, trying to hide my elation.

"Great," he said. He lowered his voice. "Before you leave today, Isaac's going to pay you the wages you've earned, then take you around and fill a couple more boxes with prime produce and goodies. The good stuff. My employees don't go hungry. Isaac, plenty of eggs and cheese along with the veggies. And payment goes on my tab."

So Isaac took me around with a pushcart and filled not one but three cardboard boxes with food beyond what I'd already accumulated.

He wheeled all four out to the parking lot and turned to

me for directions to my car before I even thought to tell him I had none.

"No car? How did you get here?"

"I walked into town, then hitched a ride with someone."

Isaac shook his head and chuckled. "You're full of surprises—that's for sure. So how are you planning to get here tomorrow?"

"Well, I'm not exactly without wheels," I answered. "It's . . . it's out of gas. I was going to take what you've just paid me and buy some." Of course I didn't tell him that the car's problems went *way* beyond a lack of fuel. Oh, and that I didn't have a driver's license.

"Fair enough," he said, pushing the cart of food to his pickup truck, where he loaded it and then drove me home.

On our way we stopped at a gas station. He took out a large fuel can and filled it with premium unleaded—another gift from the Green Dragon—then placed it in the back of the pickup. As I told him the last of my directions to the farm, he furrowed his eyebrows and frowned at me. "That's funny," he commented, "'cause my father works some fields out here—land owned by a couple who've been gone from these parts an awful long time."

I turned to him. "You mean the Kauffman farm?"

"That's the one."

"Your father's Hans Yoder?"

Isaac half snorted, half laughed. "Last time I checked, he was. But you can't be the lady in question. You're too young."

"No, I'm the lady's daughter-in-law."

"Ex-daughter-in-law, I gather, from what you told Bo."

"I suppose, technically speaking. But we're still family, and she and I are the best of friends."

"I'm sorry. I didn't mean to be callous. Although I must admit, I'm a little relieved. You see, this is the second time you've thrown me for a loop today. The first was when you explained the reason for your wedding ring. I'm a bit relieved because, well, frankly, I'd worked up half a mind to come calling on you sometime, as they say among us Mennonites."

Thankfully, we were pulling up to the back of the farmhouse, so I didn't have to respond. Naomi was outside hanging laundry on the clothesline. I saw my jeans and other clothes, all washed and drying in the sun. I'd need them to wear to work the next day.

Before stepping out of the pickup, I patted him on the arm and said, "Isaac, thank you for the ride and everything. It's been only a short time since I lost my husband, and I need time to adjust to a whole new life here. I hope you understand."

Staring straight ahead through the windshield, he nodded, and that was it. I thanked him again, then got out of the truck and hurried over to Naomi.

"Did you have a good day?" she asked, her gaze fixed on Isaac and the box he was unloading.

"I sure did! That's a new friend—Isaac. That box he's carrying over is the first of four."

She stepped closer to look into the box. She turned back to me with wide-eyed amazement.

"Ma'am," Isaac said as he brought the box to a corner of the porch.

"Oh, could you be so kind as to take that into the kitchen?" I said. "Thank you, Isaac."

"Where did you get all this food?" Naomi asked.

"At work," I answered triumphantly.

"And where would that be?"

"Well, before I tell you, let me tell you about Isaac. You won't believe who Isaac's father is."

"I give up. Tell me."

"It's none other than Hans Yoder."

The change in Naomi's demeanor was as sudden and dark as the Colorado sky. Her smile vanished, her eyes narrowed, and her face paled.

"What's the matter?" I asked.

"I know why Isaac's really here," Naomi said, her tone cold. She turned away abruptly.

"Naomi!" I scolded, trying to keep my voice down. "What on earth's gotten into you? You're being rude. He's here because my boss told him to."

"Your *boss*?"

"Yes. How do you think I got all this?" I waved my arm toward the pickup where Isaac was headed for another load. "I worked for it—worked hard all day. The owner of the place was so impressed he asked Isaac to fill up those boxes with produce, and he was nice enough to drive me home when he found out I had no ride. They even bought us some gas for the Impala."

I turned to Isaac, who was shoving the last box onto the porch. The can of gas sat on the ground near the steps. He was back to the truck and climbing into the cab when I called out, "Isaac, thank you—"

The next thing I heard was the slamming of the pickup's door. "Sorry!" I called toward the departing back bumper.

I turned back to Naomi. "Great!" I fumed. "First batch of really good news, and you had to give him the cold shoulder."

I stalked past her, up the porch steps and into the house. She followed.

"Ruth, I'm sorry for the way I treated Isaac. But before you pass judgment, wait until I tell you about *my* day!"

I stood in amazement, looking at all the furniture. When I asked about it, Naomi explained Herte's gift. I moved to the dinner table and began sorting the various kinds of food between boxes.

Staring at the name printed on the boxes, she fingered the emblem stamped next to the name in the shape of a salmon.

"Tell me again who your new boss is? Your new job?"

"I worked all day at the Green Dragon, and my new boss—the one who made all this happen—is a wonderful older man named Bo Salmon. He's the owner."

Naomi closed her eyes and sank into a chair by the table.

"What is it, Naomi?" I laid a hand on her shoulder and looked into her face with concern.

She reached up to pat my hand. "I'm not sure, Ruth, but this may be very good news."

CHAPTER 46

"Bo is short for Boaz," Naomi told me. "A good Mennonite name."

"Well, I just hope when I show up tomorrow, I'll still have a job. Bo Salmon may be the owner, but Isaac is the manager in charge. The two seem to be tight."

"You're right about that, Ruth. Bo is his second cousin."

"How do you know?"

"Because Bo is Eli's cousin. Do you remember the story I told you about that cousin who took Eli and me into his basement right after we'd both left our families?"

"That's him?"

"One and the same. Bo is an important man in this community and back then probably the best ally I had. He's known around here for lots of reasons, the least of which is owning the Green Dragon, the biggest farmers' market within a hundred miles of here."

Naomi went on to tell me all about Bo, including the story

of his mother, Rae Salmon, a German woman with a dubious past who married one of Lancaster County's most famous sons, Luke Salmon.

According to Naomi, Bo's father, Luke, had defied the Mennonite ban on fighting the Second World War, finding himself not only excommunicated by his church but in one of the deadliest jobs—a turret gunner on a B-24 bomber flying over Germany. On his fourth mission, a night raid, the plane's left wing was blown apart by antiaircraft fire and the plane crashed near Celle, a scenic, medieval town in north-central Germany. Luke, the sole survivor of the crash, was hurrying down a cobblestone street when he came across a fairly tipsy woman of ill repute. Whether she knew who Luke was or mistook him for a potential customer is a matter of debate, but one thing's for sure—to avoid capture by the Germans, Luke holed up in her attic.

Soon after the accident, a pair of SS officers began searching for the lone survivor, canvassing the entire village. Eventually they came to Rae's door and questioned her. She said she didn't know anything about an Allied pilot, but that she had seen a stranger heading in the direction of the thick woods that backed up to the village.

After the Nazis left, she went to the attic and told him in broken English that she'd heard news of how the Allies would soon overthrow the Third Reich. She pled with him to convince the Allies to spare her and her aging parents. Luke agreed. He gave her his red pilot's scarf, after signing his name and squadron number on it and telling her to present it to the Allies when Celle fell. Then they waited another day—until the SS had finished searching the woods—and in the dead of night Rae snuck Luke out the back of the house dressed as a priest, and he escaped from enemy territory.

Luke's escape back to the Allied lines became legendary, and so did the story of what he did after V-E Day. He went searching for Rae and found her in a refugee camp, where he proposed marriage to her and brought her with him back to Pennsylvania.

Upon his confession to the congregation, Luke was forgiven of the sin of taking human life and settled down with the remarkable, intelligent, and vivacious wife who would go on to win over the affection and friendship of everyone who met her. Even years later, when reports trickled back from Germany of Rae's checkered past, the news did not dim her popularity in the community. Rae had become a shining example of charitable and civic virtue, helping the poor and raising untold sums for worthy causes of every sort.

It turned out that Luke and Rae's son Bo was much like his father, early on showing signs of the same independent spirit, the same stubborn streak. The strapping, farm-bred eighteen-year-old was walking home from the store one night and came upon a drunk shouting insults at his mother, who sat on a park bench waiting for her son. In defiance of his church's every rule, Bo engaged the notorious brawler in a fistfight and sent the man to the hospital with a shattered nose, two black eyes, a concussion, and a broken collarbone.

"Like father, like son," the men of Ephrata noted, shaking their heads. It turned out, though, the very Mennonite leaders who felt duty-bound to call Bo to task were congratulating him under their breath. The general Mennonite population of Lancaster County experienced the same ambivalence when Bo, just like his father before him, became popular with the larger community for his controversial actions. But unlike his father, Bo refused to confess before his church. His pride wouldn't allow him to repent of something he felt had been morally justified. Following his excommunication, Bo moved into a strange no-man's-land of quiet admiration from most, mixed with official alienation by the church. He remained tied to his heritage and was still on speaking terms with friends and family, but eventually he tossed his own life to the winds, attempting to numb his feelings about this strange situation by drowning them in a bottle.

None of this diminished his naturally strong business sense, however. In fact, he made a career out of marketing and preserving the very heritage from which he was estranged. Though not a farmer himself, while a youth he had set up a roadside stand to sell produce on behalf of local farmers. Later he purchased the Green Dragon site, an already established yet struggling farmers' market, swiftly turning it into one of the most profitable enterprises in the state of Pennsylvania. He'd made himself into an anomaly among the Mennonite community—a friend, yet not belonging. In the process, Bo was known as one who stood up for the rights of small farmers against the encroachment of the Philadelphia weekend elite and their never-ending appetite for rural real estate, even lobbying for the relaxing of restrictions on organic farming and labeling. It was said Bo could have been elected governor if he'd had the inclination to enter politics and run for office.

Bo had remained a bachelor, partly because of his excommunication status, partly because after a lifetime of courting and losing several beautiful and available women, he'd weathered an incredible streak of bad luck with the opposite sex. For all his outward charm and leadership ability, Bo Salmon was at heart an intensely shy and insecure man. Perhaps it was the curse of being the son of a truly unique and remarkable woman that he could never find the likes of her. Though his mother had been a prostitute and his father an unlikely war hero among a family of pacifists, apparently that gave Bo all the excuse he needed for his own eccentricities. He had extended the usual years of a young person's rumschpringe well into middle age, some Mennonite faithful had sagely noted.

"Rae Salmon would die," said Naomi, finishing the story, "and her husband a few years ahead of her, without knowing if her family line would continue or not. Ironic, if you think about it."

"And that's the man I had lunch with?" I asked, bewildered. "Who asked me to work for him?"

"Yes, Ruth, and that's why it's such good luck, not only that you're going to work for him but that you made a good impression on him. We could hardly gain a stronger ally! And after what I learned today, we'll definitely need the help."

It was then that Naomi told me her news of the farm's enormously high tax bill and of Hans's double-dealing—resulting in Naomi's rudeness to Isaac.

We went on to share an evening of joy mixed with concern, even as Naomi cooked for me her best dinner of creamy mashed potatoes, honeyed ham, boiled string beans and bacon, yeast rolls, sweet corn, and baked apples. All for just us two. We ate in a newly refurnished kitchen complete with checkered tablecloth, a vase of freshly cut flowers, and cushions on the seats.

Once again the evening was crowned by a time of quiet spent rocking on the front porch, ending only when the air became too cool for comfort. When we moved inside, I sat down to read the newspaper I'd picked up earlier, the *Ephrata Review*, by the light of a kerosene lamp.

With my eyes beginning to ache, I shut them and my mind drifted back over the events of the last weeks. At last, after trying in vain to take in the enormity of all that had taken place, a sober realization dawned on me.

I was a pretty dim prospect. I had secrets to keep. Both of us did.

I looked over at Naomi. "You know, overall it's been a pretty good first day," I began.

"I suppose," she said, smiling. "If it weren't for what I

learned about our tax situation, it would have been a *great* day."

"Yes, and as fortunate as we've been in getting here, we can't forget the fact that we have pasts—like me, a former cocktail waitress with a police record, a recent widow. We're going to have to keep a lot to ourselves—I mean if I want to keep this new job of mine."

"You're probably right, Ruth. But not everything to do with our pasts is bad, you know. The best part of mine was meeting you. Let's leave all that where it belongs—behind us. I don't feel any obligation, and I have no intention of revealing every detail of my life since leaving Lancaster County for public scrutiny. There's no reason to. None of those things define who we are. What we make of this moment, of this day, tells the latest and the truest story about us. The only one that needs to be told."

"Well put," I said with a yawn, the day's labor catching up with me. "A new start—that's what all this is about."

Just moments later we each crawled into actual beds, with real mattresses and warm flannel sheets. In other words, *heaven*.

The next day's work would prove altogether different. Early in the morning I poured the can of fuel into the Impala and somehow managed to keep the thing moving forward all the way to the Green Dragon. A punch card awaited me as well as a burgundy apron with my name inscribed alongside the Green Dragon logo. All of the men on the premises, from longtime vendors and visiting delivery drivers to Bo's own staff, treated me with hushed deference, which I found intoxicating. My workload had changed dramatically, too. Starting out as essentially a glorified beast of burden, today I'd been shifted to the responsible position of coordinating all the new stalls and products to be offered during the Ephrata Fair for an expected influx of about three hundred thousand visitors.

Nothing in the Greater Bethlehem area came even close to the size of this annual fair.

It was fascinating work, helping to organize the various craftsmen and artisans at the Green Dragon—many featuring products and traditions I'd never heard of—so that all would run smoothly and efficiently once the Fair got under way.

Even more interesting, as days passed, Bo walked through the complex on a daily basis, checking on things, answering questions, giving directions. He'd previously been somewhat of an absentee landlord, I was told, contented to leave day-to-day operations of the business to managers like Isaac and spend his own time out on the golf course or with his prized horses. Other of his employees just shrugged at the change. I found myself watching his progress through the building with some fascination.

I guess most in the area would have called him a backslid Mennonite, but he continued to be just about the kindest and most fair-minded man I'd ever met. I began spending more and more time in conversation with him.

You will remember that he had no idea I lived with Naomi on the Kauffman farm. During an afternoon break, he began telling me some of his life story—most of which of I'd heard before, from Naomi. At the point where he broached the subject of running into trouble with the church over the encounter with his mother's harasser, I decided to interject.

"Bo, I thought you were excommunicated for harboring a couple of youthful fornicators in your basement."

These were the same words Naomi had used when telling me of his kindness to her and Eli. Now, hearing them come at him from the mouth of an outsider, he turned and gave me the strangest look.

"What . . . what are you referring to?" he sputtered out. "Who's been talking to you?"

"Oh, someone from your past," I answered airily. "One of the few people more notorious among the Old Order than you."

A questioning stare was his only response.

"My mother-in-law," I finally said with a little smile. "You mean, I haven't mentioned her yet?"

He shook his head.

"Her name is Naomi. Naomi Yoder."

"Eli's wife? She's come back?" He looked astounded at the news. His hand covered his mouth in both shock and amazement.

"She sure has."

"You're one big bundle of surprises—you know that?" he laughed. "So Naomi's back, and you're her daughter-in-law. If that doesn't beat all!" Turning serious, he asked, "How's Naomi doing? Where has she been all these years? And where is she staying?"

It was my turn to laugh at his barrage of questions. "First, she's fine," I answered. "She's had it really tough the last few years, but I'll let her tell you about that herself.

"To answer to your second question, she's been living out West. Utah for a while, then Nevada. And third, she and I are staying at her family farm."

For a moment Bo simply stared at me. Finally he said, "Unbelievable. You know, Naomi has always been one of my favorite people. I've never stopped praying for her and Eli."

I gave him a sideways glance as if to say, *Really? You prayed for them?*

Suddenly his face brightened. "I have to see her. Come, let's go."

That is how, only a few days after starting my new job at the Green Dragon, I found myself walking with Bo across the parking lot over to his oversized pickup. Soon we were speeding down Reamstown Road.

His enthusiasm and fondness for Naomi were evident as he talked about her and the many years since he'd seen her.

The fall day with its piercingly blue sky and air crisp and refreshing invited me to lower the window as we drove. The pungent smells of hay and ripe fruit were an intoxicating change from the big city.

Bo seemed a bit unhinged by the surprise of my revelations, alternatively laughing to himself and shaking his head.

"You know," he said at last, "folks in Lancaster County are known for being distant with outsiders, for not talking to anyone but church members and kinfolk. I've wondered how easily you've managed to break through those barriers. Now I know. Why did you keep me in the dark?"

"At first I had no idea who *you* were," I admitted. "Naomi figured it out when she saw the name on the produce boxes that Isaac brought to us. I've been waiting for the right opportunity."

Bo raised his eyebrows and gave me a quizzical grin. "Well, anyway, I can't wait to see her."

We bounced onto the road that led to the Kauffman farm and reached the house to find Naomi waiting for us, apparently drawn outside by the sound of the truck coming up the drive.

With the energy of a man far younger than his years, Bo leaped from the cab and stood for a moment by the door. But Naomi was quickly across the few steps between them. "Cousin Bo!" she cried as they embraced.

"I'd just about given up on ever seeing you again," he said, still holding her, tears in his eyes. "I hoped and prayed for so long. After all this time I was starting to resign myself to never knowing."

"I'm so sorry," Naomi said as they broke apart and she led him into the house. "I never intended to stay silent all this time. You know how a list of oughta-do's can sometimes build up in your mind until they've all turned into impossible hurdles? You mean to do it once and for all, but then time passes and life intervenes, and before you know it the delay has grown so absurdly long that it's easier just to wait for another day."

"I know," he said. "And another day never comes. Then tell me, where have you been? Where is Eli? And your boys? Ruth told me . . ."

He must have remembered the somber tone of my words earlier, because he stopped and stared into Naomi's face.

Even though Naomi had answered this same question from others, something about phrasing the words for Bo appeared to break her spirit. Her lips began to form the words, but then she looked down at the floor and shook her head, reaching out and grasping my elbow for support. She motioned for Bo to have a seat at the table. Bo and I sat down on either side of her.

I bent forward and whispered, "Do you want me to tell him?"

She whispered, "No," then raised her eyes to his, her cheeks flushed. "They're gone, Bo. Dead."

"What? All three?" he said, incredulous.

"Yes, all three. One by one, God took them and left me alone. Apparently as punishment."

"Well, alone except for Ruth," Bo said after a pause and a nod toward me that immediately filled me with gratitude. "And I for one don't believe God 'punishes' like that."

"Maybe I shouldn't say it that way," Naomi admitted, looking at me with a weary smile. "I keep telling everyone Ruth has been so good to me. I don't know what I would do without her."

"And Naomi," I added, "has been the only family I have ever really known. That's why I couldn't bear to be parted from her."

"But what happened to them?" Bo asked.

As Naomi explained it all, I began to see how completely she and Eli and their sons—from the perspective of those who had known them—had vanished from the earth. From the Ephrata point of view, the family had simply melted into the fabric of greater America, little more than a cause for a shake of the head and shrug of the shoulders. One of life's inscrutable mysteries.

"Both the boys got good construction jobs," she said in a low monotone, as if her real self were now removed a step back from the conversation. "But before finally meeting two wonderful girls, they had already sowed the seeds of their own downfall. Lonnie, whom Ruth married, developed a drinking problem which he never conquered. Mel caught hepatitis during a period of drug abuse. His widow, a beautiful girl named Orpah, almost came back with us."

Naomi glanced at me as if to seal my agreement not to mention Orpah's occupation. Or my own, for that matter.

"Eli was the first—a heart attack at his work. A hotel . . . in Las Vegas," she continued numbly. "He collapsed while checking in a guest. Lonnie quit drinking after meeting Ruth, but seeing his brother dying in a hospital pushed him to relapse. One time too many. He crashed his car on the way to tell his brother good-bye. They . . . they died on the same day, Bo."

Bo, obviously moved, turned to me and said in a thoughtful tone, "So, Ruth, you've only been a widow for a little while."

"A little over six months," I said. He shook his head.

"This all happened in Las Vegas, then?" he asked, looking at Naomi. "Not in Utah where you first moved to from Bethlehem?"

Naomi nodded. "We had some good years in Moab, and our sons enjoyed the outdoors there. But better opportunities opened up, so after the boys graduated from high school they moved to Las Vegas, and eventually Eli and I followed."

Bo shook his head, looking amazed. "I've got to hand it to you, Naomi. You went all the way. Traveled as far from the Stauffer Mennonites as possible, geographically and otherwise.

I mean, in many ways Las Vegas is farther from Lancaster County than China."

"I know that, Bo," she said. "You have no idea how much I know that. For the first several months I was there, it felt like I was awakening after a sharp blow to the head. Wandering in a daze and coming to myself as someone living on another continent, like I'd actually awakened at the far ends of the earth."

"What was life like there?"

"Well, you have to understand, Eli and I didn't move there to gamble and join the never-ending party. We moved there because of a job opportunity. Our slice of the American pie. Hope of a better life for our family. You remember that after the steel mill closed, Eli went tó work at the Hotel Bethlehem. Eli had invested much of his career in the lodging business, going on to manage the Greenwell Inn at Moab, and Las Vegas offered the best opportunities for lodging jobs in the country."

Naomi went on to describe the lavish lobby of the Bellagio where he worked. Then she said, "Lancaster County and its Old Order residents have one set of values. We found another set in Vegas—self-indulgence, fast money, tolerance of every human vice you could imagine. And yes, those affected me. I found myself, day after day, becoming so far removed from the values I grew up with." She shook her head. "It got to the point I couldn't recognize my true self and what I really believed anymore."

"You were very far removed," Bo agreed. "I often imagined you living in some big city. Philly, Pittsburgh, maybe even New York. But *Vegas*? Wow. I never would have placed any Stauffer there, no matter how badly they wanted to distance themselves from the Old Order."

"We didn't mean to, Bo." Naomi said, a sad look in her eyes. "We thought we were making the right decision for our family. Times were hard in Bethlehem and Ephrata. We thought our family would do better someplace else. But instead . . ."

She buried her head in her hands, sobbing now.

I put my arm around her, and I heard Bo take a deep breath.

After a few moments Naomi lowered her hands and looked up. "I wouldn't have imagined it either," she continued in a shaky voice. "Eli and I didn't set out to leave Bethlehem and wind up in Las Vegas. It just seemed to happen one move, one choice at a time, gradually. You rationalize, you surrender your standards one little piece at a time. Then one day you wake up and you're shocked at where you find yourself. And by then you're so far from home that you despair of ever finding your way back."

"But you have, Naomi," said Bo. "You've found your way home, and in spite of everything you've been through."

Naomi nodded. "I suppose . . . yet so much has changed, so much lost."

"You know," said Bo, "for years everyone in the community suspected I was the only one who knew where you'd gone. Maybe because my house was one of the last places you and Eli lived before leaving for Bethlehem, I don't know. But folks around here thought I was keeping a tight lid on what I knew. I tried telling them I had no idea, that I wished I had the faintest notion where you were, but I just didn't. And yet I don't think my protesting ever satisfied anyone. Then, like you said, time passes and pretty soon the people who wondered about you became fewer and fewer."

"Bo," said Naomi. "For so long now I've been out of contact with people from here, even my own family. Can you tell me anything at all about my kin?"

He did indeed have news to share of those in her family who had moved to Missouri. For the most part, all had gone well. The farms given to her brothers and sisters had proven fertile and productive. In a development that would have far-reaching implications for everyone, her mother had met and been courted by a widower, a wealthy and successful farmer whose wife had passed and left him with five teenage children. They were married, and the two families blended.

The news was bittersweet for Naomi. She was truly happy for her family, but it meant only a handful of Kauffmans were now left in the broader Stauffer community.

"Once or twice a year I would receive a letter from one or the other of your sisters," Bo went on. "They would ask if there had been any news of your whereabouts. Eventually they married and gradually stopped writing. Later, I started receiving these little notes from your mother, addressed *Boaz Salmon, Ephrata, Lancaster County, Pennsylvania.* She always made the sweetest attempt to keep up with me and my doings. Then she finished every letter with an inquiry about you— had there been any word of where her Naomi had gone? Had the authorities declared you missing, or worse? Had any mail come that might bear a clue of where she could find you?

"I always answered her, even though the nature of my report never changed. And it wasn't only for your sake, Naomi. After all, she was a friend. Now, assuming she's still alive, I can hardly wait to contact her again! Just think what it will mean to her to learn you are here!"

"I so wish I could see her again," Naomi said. "But I have no idea whether a ban was ever put on me or not."

"You were never baptized," he reminded her, "so you were never an actual church member and therefore couldn't be shunned or excommunicated. You were beyond the reach of their discipline. From the tone of all those letters, I think she'd be overjoyed to see you again and know you're all right. So, what do you plan to do about church?"

Naomi looked away. "I suppose it's possible, Bo . . ." I was surprised at her words. She had never confessed to me even the slightest inclination to make any kind of overtures to the church here.

"You and me are alike," said Bo, "in that we're both a little too questioning of Old Order ways to go back that far."

"You must know I've lived the last few years telling myself that God has turned His back on me. It truly does feel like He abandoned me, to let such a calamity befall me as losing my three beloved men."

"And yet it seems that He watched over your trip home, right?"

She laughed, but not without a touch of bitterness. "It cuts both ways. Sometimes it struck me as proof of His abandonment that we ran into so many obstacles. But when we overcame them all, got here and look back on it? Yes, it seems as though He was there with us, helping us through each one. Wouldn't you say, Ruth?"

They had been speaking without my participation for so long, I was startled by her question. I gathered my wits and thought about it.

"Well, it's sort of strange," I replied. "In the past, I never gave God much thought. At the same time, I've never questioned the notion that He exists, or even that He cares about me. Yet I'd have to say that God never seemed more real than at some of the lowest points of our traveling here."

CHAPTER 47

Lancaster County has been called the "Garden Spot of America, a kind of Eden on the East Coast, the idyllic farm country where the Amish retreat from the modern world" (*Boston Globe*, Michael Grunwald). The county also produces hundreds of millions of dollars in farm products and hosts thousands of tourists every year, who come to enjoy the area's beauty and experience a piece of American history.

But Lancaster is beginning to take on the cast of the rest of suburbia. While an agricultural protection program is in place, the county has lost about 4,800 acres to development each year since 1980—or 68 square miles over a ten-year period—to house 60,000 people, according to the National Trust for Historic Preservation (NTHP). To add insult to injury, Wal-Mart has proposed building five stores, which the Amish and other dedicated citizens are trying to prevent from happening. Lancaster County has in fact been named one of the most endangered historic sites in the world by the NTHP because of the devastating effects of sprawl.

—"Sprawl: The Dark Side of the American Dream,"
Sierra Club, Environmental Update, Stop Sprawl, Report 98.

"To answer your question about reconciling with my old church," Naomi told Bo, "I will need to think about it, even pray about it. But I can't predict the outcome, or the timing."

"Fair enough," he said. "I'm no great church person myself, but I know how wonderful it would be to have you back. What healing it would bring. You know, shortly after your family left Bethlehem for Moab, I finally made a confession and returned to the church."

"You?" Naomi was obviously astounded. "The rebel? I can hardly believe it."

"It was time. I realized I had a drinking problem and that I couldn't handle it alone. I didn't rejoin the original Stauffer group, mind you. I've learned too much to settle for the Old Order. I joined the so-called liberal, Conservative church you and Eli joined when you were with me. That's why the chrome on my truck isn't painted over," he added with a chuckle. "Many of the folks still act a little awkward around me, like they expect me to knock their blocks off at the least provocation. But it's okay. I've come to believe you can be reconciled to God and still not be totally accepted by everyone in the church."

"What about a wife?" Naomi asked carefully, her voice rising with the question. "Have you ever married?"

He shook his head. "No, I have not. For a while, after returning to the church, it seemed like I was being tried on for size by every eligible older woman and widow in the county. But there was always the question of whether they were impressed at the money and the success of my business or me. Somehow, none of them worked out. I've concluded I've become set in my ways, a little too cantankerous for my own good. Too contented with work and my friends, I suppose."

"Where are my manners?" Naomi interrupted with a glance toward the window. "The sun's near the horizon. It's time for supper. Bo, would you please stay and eat with us?"

He laughed. "It looks like we've just about talked the afternoon away. Actually you beat me to the punch, Naomi. I was hoping to talk you both into riding with me into town and treating you to dinner at Lily's. What do you say?"

Naomi and I looked at each other and both nodded in unison. "Thank you," Naomi said, her eyes bright with anticipation. "That sounds wonderful!"

"Then Lily's it is!" He stood and led us outside to where his truck was parked.

Once out on the front lawn, Bo stopped and took a long look at the fields surrounding the farm. "Naomi, have you spoken with Hans yet . . . since coming back?"

Naomi was climbing into the truck and said nothing in response. But she picked up the topic again after we were all in the cab. "Why do you ask about Hans?"

Bo paused before replying, clearly meaning to choose his words with care.

"Maybe I can help you with your answer," Naomi said after Bo's pause had grown lengthy. "Herte took me to the courthouse the other day, where I learned what Hans has been up to . . . besides keeping up the fields quite faithfully."

"Oh?" Bo said. "And what exactly did you find out at the courthouse, if you don't mind my asking?"

"That Hans has been quietly paying the taxes for several years. Apparently he intends to take the land for himself after my grace period expires, which will be soon."

"I didn't know that part," Bo admitted. "But I did know that Hans has been working for years now as a broker for a huge Philadelphia real-estate-development company. The same one that turned a sizable chunk of Lancaster County into residential neighborhoods in the last three years. I also know that Hans has been pledging to add the Kauffman farm to the largest development plot the county's ever seen."

Naomi stiffened in her seat and grimaced.

"How do you know all this?" I asked.

Bo turned the truck to the right, off the main highway toward town, then glanced at me before answering. "I do volunteer work with a couple of conservation groups. Stopping urban sprawl in Lancaster County is our number-one goal. We want to preserve the culture of the old ways. Here," he said, swerving again onto a side road and pointing. "Take a look at that."

On the right side of the road, as far as the eye could see, lay the greenest, most picturesque farmland. Then Bo gestured to his left with a disgusted jerk of his thumb. Lots of privacy fencing and endless rows of identical-looking houses went on and on, stretching to the dusky horizon.

"Lancaster is just pretty enough, rural yet close enough to Philadelphia and a lot of major cities, to make a perfect target for commuters. And a few years ago we found ourselves in the crosshairs of greedy developers and speculators. One newspaper estimated that southeastern Pennsylvania was losing an acre every hour to development. That's one acre of farmland, twenty-four times a day, 365 days a year. So far, Lancaster County's been losing 2,500 acres of prime farmland a year. I'm not against progress, but this kind of unplanned, careless growth is ruining everything that makes the county special. Here. Look at this."

We pulled up and stopped in front of a white covered bridge.

"The old Keller Bridge," Naomi murmured. "I remember it from my younger days."

"That's right," Bo said. "It's been here for over a hundred years. Only there's so much sprawl around here that traffic over the bridge has quadrupled in the last four years, and that much use is causing it to break apart. If you pried loose a few boards and looked under there, you'd see an underside being split from one end to the other. Last I heard, they're considering tearing it down, or maybe moving it two miles away, where the congestion hasn't caught up yet."

"That's awful," I said. "Is that the best anybody can do?"

"Well, we're trying our hardest," Bo said. "We fight back through tougher zoning laws and getting farmers to donate some of their land as conservation easements—legal trusts that make sure the land will never be developed. And we've done okay. Lancaster County has more farmland protected from development than any other county in the state. But the big boys are ruthless in fighting back. One of their tactics is hiring trusted community leaders to be their front men. Guys like Hans."

"Your farm," Bo told Naomi as he leaned over to look into her face, "is the last major piece of a huge plot Hans has been helping this large company to put together for a long time. If he succeeds in taking it out from under you, it will be a major setback for many of us in this part of the county. It could mean the end of our fight to hold back development and create a sanctuary for preserving our culture."

All at once I felt something rise in me, and to my surprise I felt a sob in my throat. Bo and Naomi turned at the odd sound I made and frowned.

"Ruth, are you all right?" he asked.

"I'm fine," I said, wiping my eyes and half chuckling at my sudden emotion. "I don't know why it struck me like this. It just occurred to me—"

"What?" Naomi said.

"We . . . we can't let this happen! We just can't." After taking a minute to compose myself, I continued, "We can't let this place be changed like this. I left the city behind, and I couldn't bear to see it follow me here. I can't tell you how much I love how real this place is. Nobody trying to fool me, to sell me anything, to cover anything up. Just God's green earth and four seasons, everything following their own schedules. Honest work. Simplicity. You can't possibly know how refreshing, how healing that's been for me. What if they turn it all into just another cookie-cutter rehash of every other suburb in America? It just can't happen!" I was a bit embarrassed at my outburst. After all, I was the new kid in town and didn't really have a say in what might happen.

I looked over at Bo and saw he was appraising me with a strange expression and flushed cheeks. "No," he said, so low I barely heard him. But I heard enough to know the word had been spoken with deep emotion behind it. "No, I won't let it. *We* won't let it." He pulled away with a loud roar and loose gravel flying back behind the truck's massive tires.

"Tell me," Naomi said, "how is it, if you're so appalled at what Hans is doing, you're okay with employing his son as your right-hand man at the Green Dragon?"

"That's a good question," he said with a chuckle. "A couple reasons, actually. One is that Isaac thinks for himself, and I'm hoping to steer him away from his father's selfish mindset. The other is, as the old proverb goes, 'It's good to keep your friends close, but your enemies even closer.' Although Isaac is not yet an enemy, I'm determined to keep it that way by being there as an influence in his life. He's a good kid. So right now, whether friend or enemy, I'm keeping him close."

After parking the truck at Lily's on Main, we walked toward the restaurant's entrance, and Bo turned to me. "I noticed Isaac seems to be quite interested in you, Ruth. Not that you're out hunting for a man, I realize. I know it's too soon after your loss for you to even start thinking like that. But many of the available women in our county would dearly love for him to look their way. That's all I meant."

"I understand, Bo," I said as we seated ourselves at a table. "I'm flattered but certainly not interested. You're right—Lonnie's passing is still too fresh. I can't believe Isaac would be interested either, after seeing the rather unladylike way I behaved the other morning."

"Oh, you have to know that everyone was completely enthralled after that happened. The story of your handling that creep has already traveled all over Ephrata. In fact, that same afternoon an older woman came up to me at the post office and said, 'Heard you had yourself a commotion out at the Dragon.'"

I shook my head, taken aback by how fast news spread here.

After chatting about the food and my unfamiliarity with all its nuances, our server took our order and brought a basket of rolls. Bo took a bite of a still-warm roll and immediately grew serious again. "Naomi," he said, "I don't mean to pry but was just wondering—what's your plan? What do you intend to do about the farm?"

Naomi's face noticeably saddened. "I'm not able to redeem the back taxes, if that's what you're asking. We limped back here with pennies in our pocket and that's about it. I got a letter from Herte that economically things were better now in Bethlehem—."

"Herte. I should have known," he interrupted. "You know,

she never once let on." Bo smiled at the thought.

"She was always a very discreet friend," Naomi added. "She's been kind enough to bring over much-needed furniture and things for us to use at the farmhouse."

"Well then, that settles it," said Bo. "We have to do something. We can't just let Hans take over the farm. But if the worst happens and you two need a place to stay for a while, maybe for the winter, you know you're both welcome at my house. I wish this wasn't the week of the Fair. I'm so busy with preparations that it's going to be a challenge to think of a plan right now."

"I'm sorry to have brought you into this," Naomi said, looking worried. "We would understand if you're unable to—".

"Don't worry about that," he said quickly. "We'll figure out something. There are other ways to get to Hans than just money, you know. He's very proud of his status in the community. Shaming is a very powerful tool in this culture, and it may be time to expose what he's been doing."

"It's probably time I start talking to God about all this mess," Naomi said slowly, "instead of all the complaining I've been doing lately. He may be the only one who can salvage the situation."

"Perhaps," said Bo, "His hand's been more involved with your story than you think. I can't get over the fact that you came home right before your farm's grace period was set to expire. Just when your people needed you most, at just the right time, with only a week left."

To be honest, I was shocked by the spiritual overtones in Bo's language. Shocked and comforted, I guess. Bo obviously ignored many of the Old Order's legalistic notions, but I got the distinct feeling he was more in touch with God than merely observing a bunch of rules. There was a deeply spiritual side to this so-called rebel.

After we finished our dinner at around nine o'clock, Bo drove Naomi and me to the Kauffman farm. With a gentlemanly escort to our door, Bo said his good-byes and drove away, leaving us both with a great deal to think about.

"You were awfully quiet," Naomi said to me after his headlights had faded in the distance.

"It wasn't my moment," I said. "This was your reunion, and I was glad to listen."

Naomi gave me a searching look. "Did you notice the way Bo darted his eyes back and forth—looking at you and then quickly away? The rest of the time it seemed like he totally avoided you."

"No, I did not," I shot back. "As you know, it hasn't been that long since my husband passed. Bo's probably twice my age, plus he's related by blood to Lonnie. So let's just drop it, okay?"

"Fine," said Naomi with a smile. "Consider it dropped."

CHAPTER 48

My work, as much of an unexpected surprise as it was, proved fascinating and a welcome distraction from our mounting anxiety tied to the tax debt and the farm. I had the impression, despite my protestations otherwise, that Bo was maintaining a careful arm's-length reserve with me.

A series of cold nights taught me—and reminded Naomi—just how bone-chilling Pennsylvania could be that time of year, and how inadequate an Old Order home was without preparations against howling winds and subzero windchills.

Still, we were sorrowfully counting down the days before having to give up the farm the Kauffman family had owned since the mid-nineteenth century. Every dawn was a new grief for Naomi, a fresh reminder of all she stood to lose.

Together we racked our brains for ideas, brainstorming and making lists of possible ways to save the land. We even sank to our knees and spoke desperate prayers together. But no solutions came to mind—besides simply waiting and putting our trust in others.

It seemed more than ironic to think we could succeed in our perilous journey, find friendship and work in Ephrata, only to lose ownership of the one anchor that had brought us here in the first place—the farm.

We occasionally comforted ourselves with the fact that we had at least Bo's hospitality to fall back on.

The night of the Ephrata Fair's opening parade, Naomi and I drove into town to witness the festive procession of marching bands, floats, decorated fire trucks, new and antique tractors, and vintage automobiles that packed the town's central square.

It was a picture-perfect setting of charming small-town America, decorated with suspended lights by the thousands, banners and flags held high in mittened hands over wind-reddened cheeks. As the day turned into night, the more spectacular and heartwarming it all became.

Clutching a cup of hot apple cider and hearing families on every side of us—Old Order and modern folks alike—cheer a marching band's rendition of "America the Beautiful," I turned to Naomi and shook my head in wonder. I felt as though I were in the middle of a Norman Rockwell painting.

Bo came by and stopped to chat with us for a moment, then hurried on to his parade duties as a leading town father.

I didn't know how to describe the feelings I was experiencing, but the same satisfying thought continued to echo through my mind. *It feels like I've truly come home. Finally . . .*

The next day, the Dragon's now-familiar aisles and stalls, which had seemed only half full on my first day there, now bustled with energy, overflowing with an abundance of produce stacked high. Vendors were anticipating large crowds and brisk business.

Most of my time was spent dealing directly with Isaac—an unsettling experience, given his interest in me and what I knew of his father's intentions. Since I didn't know whether Isaac realized everything his father was up to, many of my encounters with him included attempts to glimpse in his eyes any sign of suspicion or coldness. Strangely, I saw none.

Only that unsettling attraction for me.

As I went about my duties, I found the thought of a man's romantic intent toward me quite annoying. Only Lonnie had ever breached my angry defenses toward men. Suddenly I missed him all over again.

The distractions and stresses of our cross-country drive had succeeded in keeping my load of grief at bay. Then the challenges of adapting to a new and daunting reality concerning the farm had achieved the same effect. At least for a time. But as a semblance of routine began to settle in over my work environment and living conditions at the farm, I could feel the possibility of certain other emotions begin to emerge and threaten once again.

How could I become so lonely, and so quickly?

Strangely it wasn't the young and available Isaac who crept into my thoughts. Rather, it was the grounded and wise Bo. Even though he was considerably older, and even though I would have never given such a man a second glance back in Vegas, I found Bo's grizzled good looks and affable personality somehow appealing. He seemed to embody many of the same qualities I found so remarkable in Naomi.

Greatest of all was his sense of centeredness. Bo was comfortable not only in his own skin but with his own life, his place in the world, and in his restored faith in God. To me, those points made him much more appealing than some hard-bodied, clean-jawed younger man.

I found myself looking forward to Bo's visits to the Dragon and seeking out his company when he arrived. I could feel his own discomfort, though he never said a thing. As soon as he left, I was inwardly chastising myself for daring to harbor an attraction for another man so soon after losing Lonnie.

My confusion seemed to increase by the day, even as my grasp of the job grew accordingly. The diversity and quantity of goods being sold at the Dragon staggered my imagination, with thirty acres of craft goods, clothing, foods of every type, and live auctions. I discovered I wanted to keep working there even if the current crisis dislodged Naomi and me from the farmhouse.

Because the prospect of our staying put seemed more and more unlikely as winter drew near.

CHAPTER 49

That year's Ephrata Fair was the most successful of its long history. Bo took time off on the first day of the Fair to shepherd Naomi and me through the crush of it all. Downtown streets, closed to motorists, overflowed with a record number of revelers who crowded around the food and amusement booths lined up along the sidewalks. At one corner a Ferris wheel rose into clear blue skies from a bustle of carnival attractions. At the opposite corner a stage had been set up, featuring local Beach Boys imitators among other musical groups of the area. At nearby Grater Park a tent city was erected to show off a variety of agricultural exhibits, celebrating the town's rich farming heritage.

The Fair's crowds pressed into the Green Dragon's parking lots to browse—and buy—from the colorful and varied displays. All the work and preparation was fully rewarded as visitors took advantage of the Dragon's full range of products for sale. My satisfaction over the day's success was enhanced by the presence of Naomi. Although my duties kept me confined for most of the morning, Naomi roamed freely and seemed to thoroughly enjoy herself. She had visited many times as a younger woman, but the Green Dragon of decades ago, she told me, was no match for what she experienced that day.

Shortly before lunch she reappeared at my small booth, a broad smile lighting up her face.

"I forgot how much fun the Fair can be!" she exclaimed. "It's all so Ephrata—the smells, the accents, the foods. Come, I want to show you something special you'll only find from a Pennsylvania Dutch butcher."

My responsibilities allowed me only fifteen minutes, but after seeing Naomi with me, Bo said I should take whatever time we wanted.

Naomi's eyes seemed to shine brighter with every booth we passed. At that moment we were more like girlfriends than mother-in-law and daughter-in-law, partners in the pain of widowhood. Rather than order lunch, we sampled the countless foods offered by booth after crowded booth of local delicacies, including something delicious but unnamed from the butcher.

She smiled at the passing of certain faces, brief glimpses of people she might have known years ago. She marveled equally at the number of folks who saw me and smiled or waved, mouthing "Hi, Ruth!" through the clamor of voices. Naomi was clearly pleased that I had embraced my new life in Pennsylvania already, even making some friends since our arrival.

At other times, the day's festivities aside, I could detect the shadow of concern flit across her features. Would we lose the farm? Would all this hometown happiness prove to be a cruel mirage for us? Would our poverty banish us from Lancaster County altogether, leaving us with just these memories for solace?

This combination of bliss and worry continued through

the second day of the Fair at the Dragon, whose numbers turned out to be higher still. Bo was ecstatic at the year's success, which made it hard for me to read whether he still intended to "do something" about Hans's plans to buy our farm out from under us. He seemed distracted by the sheer size and busyness of it all. I hoped he hadn't forgotten, and debated bringing it up and reminding him of his pledge but decided the subject might not be well received in the midst of the Fair.

The lessons learned during our drive to Ephrata seemed to have taken root within me.

Stay on the highway, and don't leave it for anything less than an emergency.

Don't worry about the miles down the road.

Keep things pure and simple, and believe the road ahead will take care of itself.

Bo retained me at the Green Dragon after the Ephrata Fair. In fact, he kept me on through the barley harvest, then the corn harvest a few weeks later, then the final wheat harvest after that. Before I knew it, over two months had passed since our arrival in Ephrata.

The last night of the wheat harvest and the Green Dragon's most successful season was marked by a huge Pennsylvania Dutch potluck dinner—which took on a whole new meaning in the heart of Mennonite and Amish country, a land known for its hearty, home-cooked food. "Just wait!" I'd been told at least a dozen times before the final Friday workday ended.

The Dragon's parking lots had hardly begun to thin with the exit of visitors' cars before they started filling up again with the return of employees' vehicles filled with home-prepared foods of every kind. The main exhibit hall was swiftly evacuated and set up with a long line of folding tables that soon held platters, pans, casseroles, baskets, and Dutch ovens, each with its own heavenly fragrance.

A broad cross section of merchants and artisans from every walk of life—potbellied Amish bakers to Old Order Mennonite butchers to slightly less Plain of Pennsylvania Dutch extraction to mainstream folks who embraced all things modern—lined up for the dinner.

Over the course of a loud and raucous few hours I managed to return twice to the table, sampling such wonders as oyster pie, thickly noodled chicken-corn soup, chow-chow vegetable salad, red beet eggs, yeast sticky buns, and hot potato bread dripping with fresh-from-the-creamery butter.

It seemed for Naomi—who had brought a platter of goodies to add to the potluck—the experience of trying as many dishes as possible had everything to do with taking in the smells and tastes of her childhood. With every forkful and spoonful she would close her eyes, then spend the next few minutes regaling me with another anecdote out of her endless reservoir.

CHAPTER 50

By meal's end Naomi no longer appeared to be the tired, prematurely aging woman who had left her Las Vegas apartment to make the agonizing drive to Moab, then across a continent to Pennsylvania. The years, along with their cares, seemed to have faded from her face. As a result, former friends began to identify her, sometimes making long, careful inspections before approaching.

The first person to notice her came just as I had finished looking over the dessert table, then selected a slice of shoofly pie and cracker pudding as well as a piece of old-fashioned crumb cake. The blond-haired woman, bright-faced and similar in age to Naomi, sat down beside her with an expression of curiosity.

"Are you Naomi. . . ? I'm sorry, I've forgotten your married name."

"Yes, I am Naomi Yoder. And I'm sorry, but I don't recall your—."

"Yoder—that's it!" she exclaimed. "I'm Sydna Massey

from the Weaverland Order. We started in third grade together, and I think we went on through sixth grade."

The flurry of recollections and laughter lasted almost half an hour.

During that time Isaac stepped up to the podium and officially opened the evening's program, raising a glass of what looked to be beer, or maybe red wine, for it was dark in color. "Everyone," said Isaac, "please, if I could have your attention. Thank you. And thank you for coming to this celebration banquet. Here's to you—for a job well done, for all your hard work in making this harvest season the best yet! This is in honor of all of you, to your health and happiness, and also to our boss and friend, Bo Salmon, who makes all this possible." He turned and raised his glass to where Bo was seated near the front. "Thank you, Bo, for providing a great place to work."

Bo stood, faced the crowd and lifted his glass, and following his lead, everyone—whether water or soda or something stronger—clinked their glasses and took a sip.

Earlier, when I had seen the kegs of beer—what Naomi called "lager"—hauled into the building and set up, along with dozens of bottles of wine, I was surprised. I thought I'd left the whole alcohol thing back in Vegas, and that once in Pennsylvania such things would not be seen again. Yet here it was, with at least some of these folks drinking to celebrate the end of harvest time ... although I noticed, as the evening wore on, most everyone was being careful not to overdo it. Naomi explained how an occasional glass of wine or beer was part of the culture in some Amish and Mennonite communities, and a few farmers even brewed their own. "And of course there are a lot of folks who are not Amish or Mennonites here at this occasion," she added. She also told me that drunkenness was very seldom a problem among the Plain people, although among the young during their rumschpringe both drug and alcohol abuse were raising their ugly heads. I guess I still had a lot to learn about these folks.

The time came for Isaac to announce the traditional gag awards to staff and vendors who had experienced some kind of amusing, insider adventure. This generated a lot of raucous laughter and friendly ribbing. Just when I thought he'd finished, he looked straight at me and proclaimed, "And now I'd like to call up to the podium our most recent new employee, Ruth Yoder of Las Vegas, Nevada."

Even as I slowly stood with a smile frozen on my face and heard an outbreak of applause, I quailed inside. How had Isaac learned about Vegas? I'd been intentionally vague, saying only that I'd come from "out West." I knew the city's name had never left my lips. Unless of course Bo had told him. . . . Dismissing a wave of anxiety in order to play the good sport, I left my smile in place and walked toward the podium.

"For those of you ladies who've longed to even the score," said Isaac, "tonight's final award recipient proves that revenge may just be everything it's *cracked* up to be." His winking emphasis on the word caused a wave of laughter among the crowd. "So without further ado, lest I make our recipient impatient and wind up with, uh, *egg* on my face"—another round of laughter—"the Green Dragon hereby presents the Sweet Revenge Award to Ruth Yoder!"

The standing ovation I received seemed quite genuine, but what touched me most was the fact that the first ones on their feet, their clapping hands held high, were the Dragon's female staffers. My friends.

I received the plaque inscribed with my name from Isaac, then reached for his handheld microphone. "Do I get to make a little speech?"

"Yeah! Speech! Speech!" chanted the crowd.

"You all probably remember," I began, "that I showed up here without any money, in a borrowed dress, without even a ride home. But since that first day you've all made me feel at home, like family. That's a testimony to the kind of place this is. You guys took me in, in every way, and I've held down enough jobs in my time to know how rare that is. When I realized my job would end tonight, I got a lump in my throat. All I could think was, *What about next year?* I don't know what the future holds, or whether I'll be here in a year's time. But I know I'm going to fight to stay, and Lord willing I'll be back here again to help Amos Martin get his eggs up the stairs, and not scrambled next time!"

My friends all cheered again. A thrill ran up and down my spine. I stood there grinning, hardly believing the words that had just tumbled out of my mouth. *Lord willing. . . ?* I had begun to take in the culture here. Though I didn't know exactly what it was, something very spiritual was happening to me. And I liked it. It felt like *home.*

I handed Isaac the microphone and returned to my seat, my head spinning and my heart spilling over from the crowd's warm response. Naomi met me with the rib-crushing embrace of a woman reborn.

Out of the corner of my eye I noticed Bo quietly exiting the building through a side door. I couldn't imagine why he'd leave now with the celebration not yet over.

I was just about to ask Naomi about this when a woman appeared at our table. She wore the plain blue dress of a Stauffer Mennonite. "Did I hear correctly that you are Naomi Kauffman?" she asked almost timidly.

Naomi smiled and nodded. "Hello! Actually it's Naomi Yoder now."

"It's . . . I'm Lettie," the woman said, and her voice broke.

Naomi's jaw dropped, and her eyes grew wide as she threw

herself into a long hug. When they finally drew apart, Naomi looked at me and explained, "Lettie was my childhood friend in the Stauffers. We were bosom buddies!"

Lettie vigorously nodded her agreement. The two spent the next several minutes catching up. It turned out Lettie's son had a stall at the Dragon, selling assorted farm-style foods.

I suddenly found myself fighting feelings of melancholy. The good-natured spirit and warmth of this harvest celebration had truly swept me up, and now that it was over I felt bereft once more.

I hadn't been told until just recently that indeed many of the jobs in Ephrata ended abruptly after this evening, the celebration of final harvest. After tonight the next season to anticipate on the calendar was the coming of winter and the holidays. And given our looming crisis with the farm, neither prospect was one I relished facing anytime soon. Jobless.

I wondered again why in the world Bo had left so abruptly. I felt myself longing to speak to him. I hoped he had some plan or magic solution that could take away the strong sense of foreboding I had about the future. But it was more than that, I had to admit in the privacy of my heart.

Those few Dragon employees I asked in passing didn't know why Bo had taken off or when he planned on returning. After being assured he would surely show up to deliver his usual final speech of the night, I settled in to finish my dessert.

About a half hour later, just as it became clear the evening's energy was beginning to wane, Isaac took to the microphone again. "Excuse me, everyone. I know we're all eagerly anticipating hearing from Bo . . ."

Expecting this to be his introduction—for those who hadn't seen Bo leave—the crowd began to clap.

"However," Isaac continued more loudly until the crowd quieted down, "Bo put a lot more energy than usual into this year's event, and so he's had to leave early with his apologies. But he asked me to be sure to thank you all again on his behalf for your hard work and dedication, and for making this year's harvest season such a big success—a record season!"

More applause erupted.

Slowly, reluctantly, the crowd began retrieving food containers, then dispersed across the Dragon's thirty-acre complex.

"I can't believe all the people I've seen tonight!" Naomi exclaimed, looking happier and more vibrant than I'd ever seen her.

"Yes, but what do you think happened with Bo?" I asked. "He just up and left, and then never came back. And we were hoping to talk to him about the farm, remember?"

"Well, let's go find him," said Naomi. "He lives right on the far edge of the Dragon property, you know."

Somehow I had missed that piece of information.

Together we walked out into what had turned into a cloudy night. The wind had picked up, and just then a smattering of raindrops hit the pavement.

"My goodness," said Naomi, "looks like quite a big storm is cookin'!"

"That reminds me," I said. "Why didn't you bring the pie you talked about? I noticed you brought a dessert, but not your famous apple pie."

"I baked it," answered Naomi. "Then at the last minute I decided to leave it in the car. There just are so many around here who bake wonderful apple pie—"

"Didn't I hear tell your pie was the best there is?"

"Oh, Bo was just exaggerating."

"Well, he certainly seemed to like it."

We were in the parking lot now—a large, dimly lit space

occupied only by a few lingering vehicles of dinner attendees.

"You're right," she said, pointing to a solitary house at the far end of the lot. "Let's get the pie and bring it to him. That's one way to start a conversation."

"Sure. Unless he really is exhausted and wants to be alone right now."

Naomi stopped and turned to me, her hair blowing this way and that in the wind. "No, Ruth. After seeing Bo's actions tonight, my guess is his problem is you. I bet his stomach is tied in knots right now. No, wait, hear me out," she said, moving closer to me. "He's one very confused and heartsick man. It's rather obvious—he has feelings for you. And I know you feel the same about him. There's no use denying it, sweetie."

"Fine, I admit it," I said loudly into the late-autumn night. "I *feel* something. Something inappropriate. Something untimely. Yes, Bo definitely seems to act strange around me, just like you pointed out. But what about Lonnie? I loved your son, Naomi, more than I can say."

The spark was back in Naomi's eye. "Ruth, I know it hasn't even been a year since we lost Lonnie, but I want you to hear it from me." She took my face and held it so we were staring directly into each other's eyes. "Ruth, I give you my blessing. You have my permission to love Bo. I think you and he belong together, and that waiting for the sake of waiting makes no sense. And one thing more you need to know. You will always be my daughter-in-law and my dearest friend. And besides, Bo's family!" she finished triumphantly.

"Then there's the age thing—"

"Oh, puh!" she interrupted with a term probably from her childhood, "Bo's heart is young, and you will have many good years with this good man."

I felt my throat constrict, tears edging my eyes. "Thank you, Naomi." I hugged her for the gift she had just given me.

When I drew back, I looked down at myself and chuckled shakily. "But I can't go over there dressed like this. I mean, just look at me—I look like a Mennonite woman who's just finished a hard day's work—or in this case, a harvest-end's potluck."

Naomi looked me up and down. "You're right," she agreed. "You can't visit Bo wearing that crumpled dress. It was fine for church, but ..." She paused, then said, "Let's quick run home so you can take a bath, freshen up. I also have the perfect perfume for you—."

"I've got that little black number we brought all the way from Vegas—the cocktail dress we rescued from final oblivion under the wheels of an eighteen-wheeler. . . ." We looked at each other and both shook our heads at the same time. "No, Naomi," I said, "that's from another life. Not the way I'd like. . . ." I drifted to another stop, but Naomi seemed to understand perfectly.

"Then why don't you put on that new outfit you came home with recently?" she suggested. "You'd look absolutely beautiful in it with your golden skin tone and dark hair!"

Naomi was referring to a long colorful skirt and Spanish-styled peasant blouse given to me by one of my co-workers, a woman who ran a booth filled with handmade ethnic clothing and accessories such as turquoise jewelry. The woman said she'd seen the "butcher and egg incident," thanked me for standing up for women at the Dragon, and to express her gratitude wanted to offer me the clothing.

So we did just as Naomi suggested. We hurried to the Impala, got in and raced—well, I should say rumbled—toward home as quickly as we could, the rain coming down steadily now.

CHAPTER 51

After showering, drying my hair, applying Naomi's perfume, and dressing in my new skirt and blouse, I presented myself to her in the kitchen. I did a little twirl around the table, and Naomi clapped with pleasure and approval. I was ready for this visit with Bo. We would begin by talking to him about the farm and what we could possibly do to prevent losing it. We simply would see how things went from there.

We approached Bo's house by way of the Dragon's parking lot. The Impala was now the only car in sight . . . or so we thought at the time. After we parked, Naomi boldly led me around to the front of the house, where a large picture window faced a nearby stand of trees. A single light shone in the window.

Huddled under an umbrella with Naomi's fresh apple pie in hand, we stepped up to the front door. As Naomi reached over and pushed the doorbell, a smile playing on her lips, I sensed determination and purpose building within me. And confidence.

A very surprised Bo opened the door. "Ruth . . . Naomi!" he stammered. "Please, come in out of the weather!"

"Hello, Bo," we both said in unison while I shook off the raindrops from the collapsed umbrella.

"We thought you could use a little company," Naomi began as we moved inside. "Plus, there are some things we need to talk with you about. Oh, and we brought pie—apple, your favorite, if I remember correctly!" She lifted it for him to see.

He glanced at the pie and smiled crookedly. "I . . . I don't know what to say. I'm so glad you've come, and in this rain even. Please, let me take your coats." When I removed my long raincoat, a recent acquisition at a little shop in town, and handed it to him, his eyes went wide. "Ruth, I don't think I've seen you wear that before, but you look—you look wonderful tonight. Really wonderful . . . I mean, *stunning* and—"

"Thank you," I said to keep him from embarrassing us both. He kept staring into my eyes, seemingly unable to arrive at his next word.

He finally chuckled, sounding just a bit forced. "Yes, well, I guess it's true—there *are* things we need to talk about. I'm sorry I left early tonight. You were probably wondering what was going on. Well, I can explain, but first, come and sit down while I go fetch some plates and forks. I think I even have some vanilla ice cream in the freezer. What would you two like to drink?"

Somehow the word drink made our eyes move in unison to a nearly empty wine goblet on the little table next to an overstuffed chair.

"Oh boy," he said and groaned. He turned to Naomi, looking stricken. "I know what this looks like, Naomi," he said, shaking his head. Turning to me, he said, "I've had a drinking problem in the past, and when I got back home tonight I just felt I didn't have the courage to face—"

"Bo," we both said at once, then I nodded to Naomi to finish.

"That's between you and your Maker, dear friend," Naomi said calmly. Then she picked up on his previous question. "On a night like this," she said, "I was thinking a nice cup of hot tea. Any kind is fine." The awkward moment was over, and we joined him in the kitchen to help serve up the pie and pour the tea.

As we sat down in the living room with our plates and cups, we discussed the farm and told Bo about our hopes for his plan to keep Hans from taking it away. The whole time, though, I couldn't help feeling Bo was giving us only part of the plan, as if there remained some critical piece he was reluctant to divulge for some reason. Still, Naomi appeared relieved for his having given the subject significant thought, and both of us were confident that Bo would do all he could to help us with our situation—before the deadline came and before winter hit Lancaster County.

Naomi started gathering up the plates and bringing them into the kitchen. When I moved to help her, she gave me a rather direct message without saying a word. Bo and I, sitting together on the living room sofa, fell easily into satisfying conversation, our words coming out almost in a whisper as we shared things about ourselves. It felt like we had known each other for years, not just months.

Naomi appeared in the living room doorway to announce she was tired and would be heading back to the farmhouse in the Impala. She asked Bo if he wouldn't mind giving me a ride home when we were finished visiting. Bo said he'd be glad to, and he thanked Naomi again for coming over and for her thoughtfulness in bringing the pie, which he loved. Then Bo looked her straight in the face and said, "Naomi, I really don't want you to worry about this land or about Hans. I foresee everything working out just right in the end." I could tell he hoped she wouldn't ask for any details, and she must have caught that too because she smiled, nodded at us both, and picked up her purse.

"Please, Naomi, take the umbrella," I said. "And be careful—the roads can be slick in all this rain, and the storm looks to be getting worse." Just as I finished the sentence, lightning flashed in the picture window, followed by a deafening thunderclap that seemed to shake the house to its foundation.

Naomi didn't look worried. She simply smiled once more and said her good-byes, giving Bo a kiss on the cheek and telling me she'd be fine and "there's no need to hurry home." Before I knew it she was gone, and Bo and I were alone.

"Ruth," he said slowly, turning to me, "I don't know how to begin."

"I do," I said, shocked at how brazen that sounded. But immediately he reached over, gently took my hand, and pulled me close. My heart leaped in my chest; my knees felt weak.

"Ruth, I need to explain the extra drink or two. First of all, it was a mistake. Others may be able to—I cannot. But you should know that after you gave your speech, I was nearly beside myself. I was churning inside with emotions as strong as those that drove me out of the church years ago. I felt like I needed some bolstering to get me through the night, the next day, and the day after that. . . ."

He was quiet for a while, then went on to tell me that as a lifelong bachelor, he now found himself overwhelmed by his feelings for me and feared being in the same room with me, as though he might say or do something he'd later regret. Therefore he'd thought the best thing to do was to leave the banquet. He was also saddened knowing that with the harvest season over now, so would be my employment at the Dragon, along with his excuse for spending time with me.

"And, Ruth," he said, "you can probably tell how nervous I am talking so frankly like this. If you wouldn't mind, I'd ask if I can just tell you everything at once, and then you can ask questions or comment."

I kept back a knowing smile—wasn't it just like Bo to want to organize this discussion, emotionally fraught as it was.

At my nod of agreement, he took up his tale again, telling me the most painful thing of all—his feeling that since I was a recent widow, he couldn't risk asking if he could court me. He could sense I was still grieving, still healing emotionally, and he was sure it would be wrong in every way, and possibly wreck any chance he might have with me in the future.

He turned to me on the sofa, still holding my hand. "What I can't understand, Ruth, is why something tender and warm seems to flow between us every time our eyes meet."

"Maybe because it's supposed to," I whispered.

We fell into a long embrace. I could hear him whispering, "Ruth, Ruth," into my hair. When finally we pulled back, he said, "Ruth, I know I'm much older and that you could have your pick of much younger, better looking, stronger men, and I—"

"Shush," I said, placing a finger on his lips. "It's you I want, Bo Salmon, and only you. Our age difference doesn't matter to me—really it doesn't."

He gazed into my face as if he could see into my soul, then finally smiled before bending his head to kiss me. "I love you, Ruth," he said when he again could speak.

"I love you, too," I told him. "It's taken me a while to admit it, but even Naomi's helped me to see what's real—what my heart's telling me—and that, although it's not been all that long since I became a widow, it's okay to open my heart again and love another man. She's my best friend and mother-in-law, and as I'm sure you could tell tonight, she's more than okay with us being together and gives us her blessing. I guess I needed to hear that from her before I could express to you my true feelings."

"You don't know how relieved I am to hear you say those words," said Bo, capturing me again to his chest. "The torment I've been feeling, not knowing if we'd ever be together, or if you would move on and that would be that. I don't think I could have handled such a hard reality—you know, not being a part of your life."

As we sat there together on the couch, the kisses created more enraptured moments. My head was snuggled against his shoulder, "just like it belongs there," he whispered. For a long time we just held still and relished the sense of truly coming home.

Bo began caressing my face, gazing into my eyes, kissing me tenderly. As his hands moved over my body, I knew we were both responding to our newly awakened love in a way that would be very difficult to stop. A part of me said one thing, but another voice was far more compelling.

Then came a clap of thunder so loud I cried out, and Bo leaped to his feet and went over to peer out the window. One of the tall pine trees in his front yard had taken a direct hit and was split in pieces all over his lawn. I went to stand beside him and saw the largest part of the tree trunk had fallen across the driveway.

"Oh, brother, I don't know if I can move that to get the truck out." He looked kind of sheepish as he started for the kitchen. "I'll get my rain gear and see if—"

"Oh, no you don't," I challenged. "You're not going out in this storm. I don't want to lose you when I just found you,

Bo." My arms circled his neck, and he grinned crookedly before kissing me once again.

"You're right—it's probably not safe even to drive you home in this. You might just have to stay the night. Not exactly kosher, is it?"

This was all so new to both of us that we were still a bit awkward, and certainly the weather situation was not helping.

"I'd call Naomi and explain," he told me, "but as you know, there's no phone at the farmhouse. What do you think?" he asked as he flipped on the TV to see what the weather people were saying.

Every local station showed a screen filled with multicolored maps, angry-looking radar images, warning messages streaming along the bottom of the picture as adrenaline-charged meteorologists repeated the names of counties affected by the storm system passing through. The severe storm warning with hail was going to be on for at least another two to three hours.

"I agree," I said, shrugging. "It's simply too dangerous to be out there right now. I'm sure Naomi will understand if I don't make it home tonight. She'll know it's because of the storm." I couldn't look at Bo in case the smile I was trying to hide crept out. "And she'll know I'm safe with you."

At that point I realized that what I said was totally true— I felt safe with Bo. Safe enough to honestly express my feelings. Safe enough to trust my future in his hands.

Bo's eyebrows went up. "I don't know how safe you'll be with me, Ruth," he muttered under his breath. "Just so you know," he continued, looking directly at me, "I'm not trying to pull anything here. That sofa pulls out into a bed, so you can sleep right here in the living room. I'll go to my room down at the end of the hall." He pointed with a bemused expression on his face. "But I'll be honest with you—I'm not *that* old. I mean, I am tempted, and you are a beautiful woman, therefore we best say good-night right now. Actually, maybe you should take the bedroom so you can lock the door," he offered, his tone both light and serious. When I shook my head with a little smile, he said, more to himself than to me, "Besides, there are some important things I need to take care of at the courthouse early tomorrow morning, and Isaac's supposed to drop by to go over the week's numbers. Which means we need to get you home long before he arrives, or anyone else for that matter. Let's not give the community anything to wonder about and add to the gossip mill."

"I understand, Bo," I said. "And I appreciate you wanting to protect me. I guess I'm just so delighted things are working out for us to . . . to be . . ." I couldn't quite bring myself to say the word *married* since Bo had not used it yet.

He reached over and took both my hands in his. "Ruth, my love, I want you to be my wife. Some things I need to get settled tomorrow, but then I will ask you properly."

My hands tightened on his and I felt tears fill my eyes. He looked at me carefully, then leaned in and whispered again in my ear of his love for me.

"When I do ask you to marry me, Ruth, would you like me on one or two knees?" he asked playfully.

"Oh, I think one will do just fine," I joked back.

But then I was once more in his arms, and I could feel his heart beating against mine as our lips met.

The thunder was not only inside the house, it was inside my heart—lightning flashed in my emotions. My passion inside felt as out of control as the storm raging outside. Then his embrace tightened as if to pull me into himself.

CHAPTER 52

It was an awkward morning for me. When I slowly stepped from the bathroom before the sun was up, dressed again in the skirt and blouse I'd worn the night before, I noticed Bo was in the kitchen, and I could smell coffee brewing. I approached him tentatively, feeling shy for some reason, as if last night was only a dream and now in the morning I was left unsure where things stood between us.

He looked over at me with the same questions in his eyes, then held out his arms and smiled warmly at me. "Good morning," he said in a low voice as he moved toward me and wrapped his arms around me. Everything was all right.

"Morning," I said back. "How are you?"

"I feel great—and well, not so great," he quipped, giving me a firmer hug and shaking his head with a rueful expression. "Could've used a bit more sleep. . . ."

Over his shoulder I said, "Looks like the storm's finally passed, and it's left an awful mess. Branches down everywhere. Thanks for letting me stay over, Bo," I said, moving out of his embrace. "It was very kind of you." The rather formal words belied my playful tone. I gave him a kiss on the cheek. He leaned in for another kiss, but I held up a hand. "Um . . . don't you think we'd better get going? You know, before Isaac shows up."

He chuckled. "You're right. Here, have some coffee first, then let's go." He poured a hot cup of coffee and handed it to me. "But before I drive you back to the farm, we need to stop by the Dragon. You're sure not going home empty-handed. I have some things for you and Naomi—fresh fruit and veggies. Lots of both! And if any nosy person wonders, it's an early morning pickup—groceries, that is." We laughed together comfortably. I could hardly believe how relaxed and close I felt with him, though we really hadn't known each other very long, and certainly not with any kind of understanding.

He reached out his hand and lightly touched my arm. "Ruth, thank you again for coming over, for your openness. You're a woman of character and substance. I tried to tell you that the first day I met you. And after last week, half the town knows it for themselves."

We both laughed again, and then I said more soberly, "Even though I was once a cocktail waitress in Vegas? A woman with an arrest record who hasn't hardly a dime to her name?"

"That's right," he said, also serious. "None of that matters to me."

Then came the tears. His words were sinking all the way to my marrow, touching my wound in the deepest parts. He'd seen something of worth in me. Somehow he'd seen things I myself couldn't even glimpse.

"I told you last night, and I meant every word. *I love you*, Ruth. End of discussion."

"Are you really sure?" I asked stubbornly, still full of

questions why a man like him—leader in the community, with wealth and businesses requiring a small army of employees who revered their boss, a very attractive man in every way—would even consider me.

"I should be asking you that," he said. "Are you sure you want me, Ruth?"

Before I could answer, a muffled sound from outside startled us both.

Checking his watch, he said, "Oh man, it's almost six thirty. Isaac said he'd come by around eight to go over the totals for the week."

"Well, come on—let's go!" I said. I rinsed out my coffee mug and set it in the sink, then rushed to pull on my raincoat.

Bo stepped over and looked out the living room window, moving his head back and forth, then nodded. "I think we're okay—far as I can tell, there's no one out there. But we still have to hurry. We'll run out to my truck, then drive over to the Dragon, where I'll load the back with some good stuff for you to bring home. I also have your pay for this week's work to give you. I intend to see you soon, but it's possible I'll get tied up with some stuff the next few days, so just in case, I'm going to send you home with your pay."

We would need to get to the manager's office, which was in a part of the Dragon complex I knew fairly well—down a narrow hallway behind the back wall of the Building 2 exhibit area—to get my pay.

I followed Bo as he darted out the side door of the house. The morning air, chill with the approach of winter, struck my face and spurred me on. He was already struggling with the errant tree limb in the driveway, and when he had it pushed out of the way, he quickly was into the garage and backing his shiny new pickup out. I waved him off when it looked like he was going to climb out to open my door, and I scrambled in.

Soon we were heading to the nearest Green Dragon building. Shivering behind Bo as he fiddled with his oversized key ring and hurriedly unlocked the door, I pressed up against him, and his long arm circled me as he pulled us into the entrance.

Flipping on a row of light switches as he passed, Bo took my hand, and we began running together along the building's length. After checking for any sign of Isaac at about the half-way point, we made another dash toward the door near the building's other end, where he switched off the main lights. That door, thankfully, led to the manager's office and the safe. After unlocking the small cubbyhole, he opened the safe with four practiced turns of his index finger and thumb, then plunged his hand inside. When he withdrew it, his fist was clenched around a thick wad of bills.

"How much was it?" he asked, out of breath. "Do you remember?"

I shook my head. I told him that based on the previous check, it would be somewhere around five hundred.

"Yeah, but I promoted you, remember? That would have doubled it." He began counting, and somewhere in the middle he lost track, crumpled the remainder and put the entire roll in my hand. "Here. A bonus for an exceptional job under extreme duress."

"What duress was that?"

"Your boss's overwhelming crush on you, how's that?" he said with a sly grin. "Look, as of today I can't guarantee how long you and Naomi might need to manage on what's here. Winter's on its way, and it's supposed to be a hard one. Please, just take it."

For some reason I don't recall now, I didn't argue further but curled my fingers around the bills and shoved them into my handbag. Then I followed Bo to the nearest exit, where he eased the door open and peered out toward his truck. "Ready?" he said.

I smiled and hugged him around the neck. "Ready," I whispered.

Somehow, in the light of a brand-new day, I loved him even more. I loved every crease and laugh line on his face, the crinkles around his bright, clear eyes.

We grasped hands and ran for the truck, laughing like high schoolers the entire way.

Minutes later, after Bo had loaded two boxes filled to the brim with fresh produce into the back of the pickup truck, we were on our way to the farm.

We talked briefly about our visit the night before and the storm that had kept me overnight.

"I'm going to make an honest woman of you, Ruth," he assured me as he reached across to squeeze my hand.

When we came to the drive that led to the farmhouse, suddenly Bo stopped the truck, turned in his seat and once more took hold of my hand, looking me in the eyes, his expression earnest.

"Now you listen to me, Ruth. You must have faith in me— and in God. Stay at home and wait until you hear from me. I'm going to take care of this thing with Hans and the land, and make everything right. You understand?"

He'd said it with such determination that for a moment I believed maybe, just maybe, Naomi would be able to keep the farm after all. And me— well, my future was beckoning to me with a promise I could hardly allow myself to consider. I gave him a weak smile in response. He leaned over and kissed me.

"Just remember," he reassured me, "how much we love each other. I won't let you down. Now, instead of getting together with Isaac, I'm headed straight to Lancaster. I need to go to the courthouse."

Bo stopped the truck at the front of the house, grabbed the boxes of produce from the back and stacked them on the front porch with a quick apology for leaving them there. "I've got no time to lose," he said over his shoulder as he ran back to the truck. I called a shaky good-bye, and then he sped away. Quite out of character for me, I hadn't asked him what exactly he intended to do at the courthouse once he arrived there. *I guess we'll know soon enough,* I thought as I lugged the first box through the door.

While Bo was on his way into Lancaster, near the turnoff on Highway 322 he and Isaac crossed paths.

They stopped to talk, and Bo later told me that Isaac appeared not his usual self and did not seem surprised when he told Isaac their meeting would have to be postponed due to urgent business at the courthouse—something, Bo explained, that had come up at the last minute that he needed to take care of right away. Isaac's demeanor could only be described as distant the entire time they talked.

Later we learned that, while watching Bo drive away, Isaac pulled out his cell phone and called his father, giving him a complete report—that he'd seen Naomi and Ruth go into Bo's house the night before, then only Naomi come out and leave just when the storm hit. So he staked out the place all night, sleeping on and off in his car outside Bo's house and waking up to watch them scurrying into Bo's pickup in the morning. He had followed them to the Kauffman farm, then left and turned around so he would meet Bo out on the highway when he left the farm. Isaac warned his father that Bo was in an awful hurry to get himself to the Lancaster County courthouse.

Naomi was sitting at the table with her hands around a cup of tea, obviously waiting for me. She jumped to help me with the produce.

"From Bo," I explained as I put the first box down. Having expected me back late the night before, her face was full of questions and more than a hint of worry.

I pulled her out onto the porch and we sat down facing each other, both of us wrapped in wool afghans.

"All right, Naomi—yes, everything is *all right*," I told her as I began to recount my evening with Bo, the one that turned into my night with Bo. But whenever I came to the details she wouldn't let me tell any more—as if she was protecting my privacy about whatever happened.

"So, tell me," Naomi said when I finished, "what do you think Bo meant by saying he would make everything right? I'm still not clear if or how he intends to fix things with Hans. . . ."

I shook my head, "I'm not sure either, Naomi."

After a moment I told her, "Bo said some rather extraordinary things about me—said I was a woman of character, and that my past mistakes don't matter to him—or to God. That the Lord forgives and loves me. And that he loves me, just like that—'I love you, Ruth.' I can hardly believe those words coming from anybody, much more someone like him." I pulled the afghan more closely around me and just sat perfectly still, savoring the thought.

Then I remembered the piece of all this that Naomi was vitally interested in exploring. "As far as his 'making everything right,'" I continued, "like I said, I'm not sure what exactly he was referring to. But he said he was going straight to the courthouse in Lancaster and that he'd come see me as soon as he could. In the meantime, I'm to just hang on and trust him. Trust him and trust God," I finished, trying to get my tongue and my mind around the unfamiliar words.

"Ruth, I think I know this man and what he stands for. Bo is a man of honor. If he says to wait and let him take care of things, whatever that means, then that's exactly what you should do—what we both should do."

I nodded slowly.

"Yes. The key now is to wait for him to come back and see what he has to say."

I looked at her, reached over and took her hand and thanked her for her friendship and guidance, especially in the last twenty-four hours. "Naomi, I'm so happy and excited and exhausted, I don't know what to do with myself!" I laughed out loud.

She joined me in laughter, hugged me, then pulled back. "Well, how about we start with breakfast? We've sure got some food to eat up."

That's when I remembered the money Bo had placed into my hand and I had thrust, uncounted, into my purse. When I dug the rolls of bills out and showed it to Naomi, her eyes grew wide. It was more money than we had seen since leaving Vegas.

"I earned every dime of this," I declared. We giggled like schoolgirls and began counting it.

CHAPTER 53

Lancaster Highway

You will soon realize that I've had to piece together little bits of information to tell you this part of the story. But I'll give it to you as accurately as I can.

Hans Yoder was usually a highly prudent driver, one who obeyed the posted speed limit. Though a lapsed Weaverland Mennonite, he was a respected member of the local Eastern Pennsylvania Mennonite Church, and he never wanted to endanger the horse-and-buggy folk. He also never wanted to be accused of indifference to the laws of the state—clearly a sin. Perhaps most of all, he detested the reckless, arrogant speeding often seen on the roads with the youth in the area— whether one holding the reins of an Amish courting buggy or at the wheel of a car during rumschpringe, that unusual Plain tradition of teens trying out modern life before committing to their heritage and faith. Hans tried to set himself apart as a good example, an upstanding citizen, when behind his own steering wheel.

But he threw all such considerations to the wind as he

floored the accelerator of his plain Ford pickup and traced the thirteen miles between Ephrata and Lancaster in less than fifteen minutes. Foremost in his mind was a throbbing determination to stop Bo Salmon before he ruined everything. Before he dashed years of careful planning and for the worst possible motives—infatuation with a wayward woman. Hans had done his homework. Isaac had been a big help, feeding him information on a regular basis, piecing together Ruth's full name and then feeding it to a search engine at the local Internet cafe. A modest fee to one of those enhanced personal searches told him all he needed to know.

Maiden name.

Ethnic origin.

Previous employers.

Arrest record. DUI. Suspended license.

Hans knew it all. He wasn't sure even Naomi knew all the dirt he'd dug up. And he was poised to use it.

He wove through downtown Lancaster—somewhat flooded due to last night's storm—to the courthouse and found a parking spot only four removed from Bo's familiar truck. Seeing it there, with Bo nowhere in sight, filled Hans with foreboding. Bo had indeed come early, no doubt determined to accomplish something quickly before the lines grew long.

Hans glanced at his watch. It had taken him ten, maybe fifteen, minutes to get on the road following Isaac's phone call, plus the time it took to get there. Was he already too late? Without breaking into a run, he began walking as rapidly as he could toward the courthouse. He entered and started climbing the stairs to the second floor, heading straight for the deeds and licensing office.

There stood Bo, just as Hans had feared.

"Bo!" he called.

Bo looked over and didn't hide his consternation at seeing his kinsman there—in the same place, and at such an early hour. "What a coincidence," he said in a tone that made it clear he considered their meeting anything but.

"Actually, Bo, I was looking for you," Hans said as pleasantly as he could. "I was hoping we could have a few words together."

"Maybe just a few," he answered guardedly. "I've got a very busy day ahead of me."

"I know. That's what worries me. What are you up to this morning?"

"I'm sorry, Hans, but that's none of your business."

"But you see, I think what you're up to *is* my business. Are you going to try and pay off the taxes on the Kauffman farm, Bo? Because I beat you to it. I did it a year ago. My claim matures Monday at noon. After that, it cannot be redeemed back by the original owner. You can forget it."

Bo turned to face him. "I'm not here to stake some kind of claim for myself. I'm here to pay off Naomi's tax debt on *her* farm."

Hans shook his head. "How?" he demanded. "How can you do that? Naomi—or maybe Ruth, if she really did marry one of Naomi's boys—could pay it. And you know they don't have the money it would take."

"You forget, Naomi is my kin, too. Not close enough that I could redeem it myself, but you're a fine one to be talking, Hans!" Bo had all he could do to keep from shouting at the man.

Hans shot back, "I'm the sort of kin that sticks around, that stays through thick and thin, instead of running off to some sleazy place thousands of miles away, then comes begging to a backslid relative when her luck runs out."

Bo took a deep breath, keeping his voice even. "I may have

backslid," he said, "and I may not have always done what was right, but with the Lord's help I'm back on track. People know where I stand. You, now, you're always in church on Sunday, smiling at everybody, but Monday comes with backroom deals and conspiring to line your own pockets by selling off the family's land. Is that something to be proud of?"

"What I'm doing *is* something to be proud of," the man spat out. "What about contributing to the economy? A *real* economy, instead of this—this shadow of the real thing we get from Old Order freeloaders who never pay their fair share of taxes and force us to live as tourist guides, off the droppings of the gawkers who drive out here to fawn over how backward we are!" Hans had worked up a real head of steam, and his fists were clenching and unclenching at his sides.

"Do you realize, Hans, that if you put half as much energy into farming as you did into pulling other people's land out from under them, you'd be the biggest landowner in the county by now?"

"Bo, you can't do this." Hans had turned to pleading now. "You can't hand over a prime piece of Ephrata farmland to a derelict church reject and a Mexican with a criminal record!"

Bo slowly lowered the papers he was holding, the muscles tensed in his face and neck. The two people he cared about most in the world were being slandered. "Hans, who are you talking about?" His tone was even, but Hans caught Bo's underlying meaning.

"You know who I'm talking about," he said with some bravado.

"Maybe, but I want you to say it. I want to hear you speak their names."

Hans noted the tension in Bo's posture, but then what was this antagonist going to do? Mennonites don't fight. Nonviolence was their most cherished virtue. Then he remembered

Bo's checkered background on that issue. Maybe he ought to be careful.

But they were standing in the middle of the county courthouse. An armed sheriff's deputy was within sight, sitting behind a desk.

"Naomi Yoder," Hans finally said with a sneer, slow and measured so as to make it sink in. "And Ruth Yoder—born of illegal immigrant parents, later ward of the state, convicted with a DUI, twice, then charged with third-degree reckless indifference resulting in death less than a year ago, although charges were dismissed because of insufficient evidence. Bo, you're starting to hang your hat in the gutter now? Or is this just your mother's influence rearing its ugly head? I heard she spent last night with you, Bo. That true?"

"What? How did you—?"

"Isaac saw you! He called me on his cell. Naomi and Ruth paid you a visit after the banquet—am I right? Ah, but only the older one left that evening. The young one stayed on till morning." He laughed derisively. "So much for discretion."

Bo's voice came out just a hair away from exploding. "You coward! How would you like to continue this conversation outside, just you and me. But you probably don't have the guts for that, do you?"

"You don't think so?" Hans snarled with a glance at the deputy. The officer was busy with some paper work and didn't seem to be paying a bit of attention. Hans didn't know what he should do next.

While he hesitated, Bo grabbed Hans's arm and marched him downstairs from the courthouse's second floor and out onto the lawn.

As soon as the sun hit his face, Bo charged the man. At that moment Bo craved nothing less than to give Hans the thrashing of his life.

But Hans ducked out of the way with surprising nimbleness, swiveling quickly to strike Bo from behind as the bigger man went barreling past, falling face-first on the turf.

The advantage was too much for Hans to pass up. As Bo struggled to get to his feet, Hans stepped closer to kick his cousin in the side and drive him back down. But Bo caught Hans's boot in both hands, twisted the leg savagely, and tossed Hans aside, yanking off the boot in the process.

Hans fell backward, the back of his head striking the edge of the concrete sidewalk. Rolling away and clutching his head with a high-pitched shout, Hans came up with a handful of bright red.

When the sheriff's deputy reached the pair, there stood Bo, unsteady on his feet and holding a boot, and Hans, with one very noticeable white-stockinged foot, wincing and howling like a newborn calf—and looking very much the victim with blood smeared on his hand and across his face. It seemed rather obvious who the aggressor must have been.

The deputy already had his handcuffs at the ready. He cuffed Bo's hands behind him, then led him right back into the courthouse. In Bo's distress, he made the mistake of protesting his innocence too vehemently and maybe even giving the deputy a little push.

Bo was still huffing and grunting in rage many minutes later as he sat in a holding cell in the courthouse basement, signed in on charges of assault, disturbing the peace, and resisting arrest by one very angry young deputy.

Hans gladly signed the complaint.

Finally, Bo was calm enough to ask for his phone call, for access to an attorney and a chance to post bail.

But this happened to be a very slow day—clerks out with the flu, deputies busy with other pressing duties, a judge who would call in sick later that morning.

Bo eventually got his one phone call, after demanding his rights for almost an hour. It turned out the attorney he knew for this sort of work was out that day and unable to be reached.

Bo, calmer now, kept picturing me, waiting faithfully back at the farm, believing in him. He could hardly bear to think of it.

He had been a lot of places, but he'd never been in jail. He sat on the bench in his cell, head in his hands, utterly miserable. He'd screwed this one up big-time.

Then there was Isaac—his longtime employee whom he'd taken under his wing—who had now betrayed him. The thought made Bo feel nauseated. And Hans, Isaac's father, was still out there, free to make even more mischief.

It would turn out to be the longest weekend of all of our lives.

CHAPTER 54

Kauffman farm

For the first three hours I was both keyed up and apprehensive. Then came the noon hour, and my imagination began conjuring up all sorts of wild scenarios. The afternoon consisted of one mind game after another as I kept glancing out the window or walking onto the porch, checking the drive that led to Red Run Road, hoping to see or hear Bo's truck approaching the farm. As time went on, I could hardly believe how mercilessly the doubt excavated my most deeply buried fears, dating back years and covering countless painful experiences with other men I'd fallen for. It went back all the way to my childhood, replaying my mama and papa's broken promises, my time in foster homes. If my own family could abandon me, give me away to a foster family, whom then could I really trust? And whether it was broken families or men I'd opened my heart to, the outcome was usually the same—me waiting in vain, feeling my hopes crushed once again with the setting of the sun.

It felt like the hours themselves were mocking me, allowing their tortuous crawl to afflict my every moment with reminders of how unworthy I was. Was Bo going to honor his promise to me? Or had the light of day and time for reflection brought him to his senses?

Of course every time I glanced at Naomi, I was reminded that we had pinned all our hopes on Bo for keeping the farm. Monday's deadline was approaching like a merciless locomotive of fate, bearing down on us without an ounce of pity or consideration. Monday was D-day, the final judgment in court.

Naomi, bless her heart, said not a word of reproach about our situation, or Bo.

Just as we did during the drive from Moab, we alternated between periods of deafening silence, avoiding the subject of Bo's disappearance and its likely consequences, and times of intense discussion. Through it all Naomi seemed serene, as though she believed without a doubt that Bo would pull through and come to do the right thing by me, by us. That indeed Bo's rushed errand to the courthouse had to do with the issue of the farm and our crisis of ownership, and that he had things under control. And of course he loved me without a doubt and wanted me for his wife.

But when the evening shadows had grown long and the sun was no longer visible, Naomi came over to me at the window and said, "Ruth, I think it's time we prayed about this whole thing."

"You mean together?" I asked.

"Yes, together, and right now."

We sat at the table opposite each other. Naomi closed her eyes tightly and clasped her hands, and I followed suit. She began to speak, pleading for Bo's safety, for God's hand on whatever Bo was up to, for success and a swift resolution to this painful dilemma. She asked for the farm to somehow be delivered into our hands as a gift for her later life, her uncertain future, and maybe even for heirs that might follow after.

That one took me a while to figure out. I shook my head slightly, wondering how she could be so hopeful when things looked so bad. She then spoke of me, asking that peace and assurance fall over me like a soft rain.

I prayed as best I could, awkwardly since up until then I hadn't practiced it very often. I mostly asked God to look after us, to somehow work things so we could keep the farm, and not let all the miracles and hard work of getting us the farm go to waste. I couldn't quite bring myself to pray about Bo with all the uncertainties I was feeling.

I did somehow find myself with a sense of peace when we were done, though our prayers didn't produce Bo at our doorstep, nor even lessen very much of the anxiety of that day. When night fell, however, that peace fell away and I began to slip into a state of panic. I didn't eat. I became very quiet. Naomi tried her best to engage me in conversation, but it was no use. Eventually I retreated to the porch with an afghan, taking a seat in my rocker and staring into the darkness, continuing to pray silently while fighting back tears.

Believe it or not, the next day, Saturday, was worse. From dawn to dusk the waiting intensified into a physical test of endurance. I had to force myself to stay home, to resist driving into town and asking around for news of him, or even more risky, driving over to his house to see if he was home. Though I hadn't missed a telephone much before, I sure wished the farmhouse had one right then.

I had to admit to myself that I really didn't know Bo all that well. It had all happened so fast. And my past history of bad choices in the men department only fanned my doubts and misgivings.

Ultimately the only scenario that truly mattered to me was Bo speeding up to the farm with wonderful news to share. No, I couldn't risk leaving and in the process miss him, even though that left me stuck, feeling powerless and helpless, cut off from whatever it was Bo was doing.

To pass the time during those agonizing hours of waiting and wondering, Naomi and I dove into doing housework, beginning with the great room, scrubbing every inch of floor and wall with a soapy solution. After a quick lunch we moved to the front porch and swept off the fallen leaves, then raked the entire front yard. Every bit of physical labor was a way to silence, if only for another moment, the inner voices assaulting my mind with endless lists of my shortcomings.

At last it was evening again. With dinner eaten and cleaned up, the whole affair carried out without a word spoken between us, it was Naomi who finally broke the silence.

"I know God hasn't yet seen fit to answer our prayers," she said matter-of-factly, "but I've been thinking for some time about reconciling with the church. I don't think I can go back to being a Stauffer Mennonite. But maybe the church we joined in Ephrata after first leaving home, a conservative Mennonite and one of the Eastern Pennsylvania group. It's the church Bo belongs to now, and my friend Herte, and a number of people I knew growing up. Anyway, I think I'm going to go to services there tomorrow."

"So you and God are on speaking terms again?"

She nodded. "I believe our praying together yesterday changed something in me," she said, looking pensive. "I truly believe that God cares, that He wants me to keep on seeking Him and not to give up, to be honest with Him about what's bothering me, no matter what it is, and go to Him with it . . .

instead of complaining to others." She paused, then chuckled almost to herself. "It's funny, but I guess I don't feel so angry and abandoned anymore."

"Despite what we're facing on Monday?" I asked.

"Yes, Ruth," she said confidently. "For some reason, even despite what we're facing on Monday." She shook her head slowly, then said, "Oh, I'm not saying I don't wonder about what's going to happen, and I am tempted to try and figure things out myself. But, Ruth, I want you to know that even if Bo is not able to keep this property from Hans, I still want the two of you to be together. And I will count on the Lord to take care of me and my future," she finished determinedly.

I took a deep breath and thought a moment about what she'd said. Then I said, "If it's all right with you, I'd like to go to church with you tomorrow."

Perhaps for me, one reason for going to church was the hope it would distract me from my third day of waiting and the anguish that went with it. But it turned out my going to services was a bit more than that. Quite a bit more.

Naomi and I rose with the dawn and began preparing ourselves for a Plain sort of Sunday. We enjoyed an ample breakfast, after which we each bathed and readied ourselves for church. Our Mennonite-style dresses had been ironed the night before. At midmorning of a beautiful Indian-summer day we climbed into the car and began as leisurely a drive as the old Impala could manage. We must have passed fifteen Old Order horse and buggies and half a dozen crowded meetinghouses. After two days of being sequestered at home, it felt wonderful to be moving through such lovely farm country. Eventually Naomi directed me toward the south, leading to Highway 322, the old Turnpike. As we approached it, she motioned for me to pull over and stop beside a white clapboard building, shaded by a pair of oak trees and flanked by dozens of black buggies.

She breathed in deeply and shook her head "This is it, Ruth. Not the church we're heading for today, but the church I attended as a girl. This is the Pike Meetinghouse, where the Stauffers started back in 1845. It's called 'Pike' because the road used to be known as the Harrisburg-Downington Turnpike. We were the Pike Mennonites—also called Pikers." We looked at each other and chuckled at the sound of that name.

"Do you have relatives in there?" I asked.

"I'm sure I do," she said. "But I doubt I'd know a single one of them."

We sat and gazed around in silence. Hardly anything moved except for the twitching of horses' tails and the cool breeze ruffling oak leaves and the nearby lilac bushes. After several minutes had passed, a young boy in black pants and vest, a blue shirt and a black wide-brimmed hat came walking out of the building at a brisk pace.

"Call of nature," Naomi commented wryly. "It feels like I'm looking back through a time machine. Almost nothing has changed from this picture in going on two centuries."

Deep in thought, I finally asked, "Do you really think they're closer to God than others because of living so plainly?"

"That's a good question," she said, "and a tough one to answer. I'd venture that they have fewer temptations. But they're still human beings. They still have a rebellious nature inside of them that needs to be surrendered. They still sin. Still make major mistakes. But they're good people, too. Doing their best, working hard, caring for one another, respectful and loving toward God and others."

I knew right then that I wanted to be one of those "good people." Like Naomi. I reached across and patted her arm. She sighed and nodded in response as I started the car and pulled back onto the road.

At last we turned onto the highway and followed it back into Ephrata, parking in front of an ordinary brick building, this one surrounded by cars, although rather older and plain-looking sedans and family-type vehicles. Humble and weathered enough that the Impala didn't appear excessively old-fashioned or rundown in their company, although its size and ornamentation did make it stand out, I'm sure.

We stepped out and joined a couple walking toward the entrance, the woman clothed much like we were, the man in a dark suit. Mine was the same dress of Naomi's I'd worn the first day of work at the Dragon.

We walked through a narrow lobby, then through a set of doors into the back of a large, down-sloping sanctuary. A group of around 150 stood holding books and singing. Their song was accompanied by piano and organ, its melody spare but beautiful in a way I couldn't quite define. I glanced around. For a former Catholic with only a handful of Masses to reference from my childhood, the room's relatively low and wide dimensions seemed utterly new and strange. I stepped forward and felt something that can only be described as a peculiar energy in the room.

CHAPTER 55

A dark-suited man looking to be in late middle age stood behind the pulpit, directing with his hands while everybody sang. Without losing rhythm or saying a thing, he nevertheless took note of our arrival, nodding his head, smiling and looking our way as we walked down the aisle. Heads turned and eyes stared curiously as we moved toward the front of the church. I wanted to find seats near the back, where there was plenty of empty space, but Naomi apparently had other plans.

I touched her elbow. "Where are we going?" I whispered.

She pointed with her chin down to the second row, where Herte was beckoning us to come. Try as I might, I couldn't seem to ignore all those stares directed our way. They were not hostile, mind you, merely inquisitive. Suddenly it became clear the expressions were those of recognition. These were people who had known Naomi at one time, although many years ago, in another lifetime.

I overheard a few of them whispering to each other, "Is that really her? Naomi Kauffman? Naomi Yoder?"

We finally arrived at Herte's row. I followed Naomi, taking the outermost seat by the aisle. Beside me, Naomi and Herte stood whispering, and then the two embraced. I could see that Herte's eyes were filled with tears.

The song ended, and everybody sat down. The man at the front began to speak. It took me several minutes before I realized this was in fact the sermon, as his words were quite ordinary sounding and casually delivered. I didn't really focus on what he was saying until his message was well under way.

With a slight accent, which I figured out hinted at his Mennonite German heritage, the man was speaking about the "idolatry of the world," and how their ancestors had left everything they knew back in Europe—possessions, social standing, national pride, native roots—all to leave that idolatry behind. They'd come to Pennsylvania for the promise of a life of plainness and simplicity before God, free from the enticements of wealth and vice and greed and all of the world's distractions. And by all accounts, he said with a noticeable touch of pride, they had succeeded in building the foundations for that kind of living. Simple, well-constructed farms on well-tended earth, beautiful thriving families, congregations of faithful followers. A good name in all the land. They'd even paid a high price for following God's commandment regarding the killing of another human being.

But then his words turned a corner. I could feel the audience around me sitting utterly still and focused on this man with an evident heart for God and these people, though I wouldn't have been able to describe it as such at the time.

"Is it possible," he asked, his voice rising in anticipation of his point, "that we've become so pleased with our works, so engrossed in the nurture of farm and family and the manifestations of our plainness, that we have made *them* the idols instead? After all, is not God alone the true source of our deepest joy and satisfaction?"

I thought of how his words might relate to me. Had I turned the farm and its beauty, its feeling of warmth and security, into an idol? Had I made survival and my own personal grief and past pain into idols?

"Only each of us can answer this question in our own hearts," the preacher said. "Yet I challenge us to all ask the Lord to show us where we might have misplaced our highest priority, our deepest and most precious love. Let us also ask ourselves if we have made it too easy to turn our hearts toward these, our own idols-in-the-making, when He has not done what we wanted Him to. How do we react when He chooses not to answer our prayer the way we hoped? When God in His sovereignty doesn't grant the thing we want the most? It might even be something entirely worthy. The healing of a loved one. The blessing of children. The restoration of a broken dream."

He paused there, looking down at the podium. Finally he raised his head again, and something in the intensity of his gaze told me he wasn't finished but had a most important point still to voice.

"And when He lovingly answers *no* to even these," the preacher continued, "do we simply turn away from Him?"

I turned to Naomi with a stunned look. She gave me a brave smile and took my hand in hers.

A moment later the sermon came to a close, ending with an invitation to a time of reflection and prayer. The preacher left his place behind the pulpit amid a silent congregation.

The silence continued, and over the ensuing minutes deepened into something palpable, like the feeling of an unseen presence. I had never experienced anything like it before.

There was a stirring beside me. Naomi was rising, letting go of my hand. She stepped around me and walked the few feet to the end of the aisle. She lowered herself into a kneeling position on the floor, her head bent low, her hands clasped.

When I had gotten over the shock of seeing her there, I tried to imagine how many old hurts tumbled over each other in her mind as she prayed. Only in coming here and seeing the sights of her childhood could I appreciate everything she'd lost in all her years of running from her strict childhood, from a God who she felt did not care about her. And only now, hearing what I'd just heard, was I beginning to understand what might lie at the root of it all.

Then it gradually dawned on me that I must respond, too. It was an urging as real as the physical ache in my chest, as sharp as the point of a knife. Clearly I was facing some agonizing questions of my own—about a man in whom I'd placed my trust, and possibly my future. And things did not look good. How would I respond to what Monday might bring? As vague and unformed as was my awareness of God, I wondered if it could withstand the realization of my worst fears. Where would I turn if Bo broke his promise to me? To Naomi? To these people around me?

I heard a voice deep within me, whether in actual words or merely impressions I couldn't have said. What I could tell was that it was the voice of truth, and it was loving beyond my own capacity to understand. It wasn't directing me to respond as much as simply *beckoning* me—extending an invitation for my allegiance, my total surrender. Not to look to man, even a good man, nor to people, even good people, but only to Him. To God himself. To trust Him with my future, with everything.

I got up and moved next to where Naomi knelt. I lowered myself to my knees and bowed my head. *God, thank you for being so patient,* I prayed, my heart beating hard at this unfamiliar circumstance and the fact I was speaking to the Almighty. *You know I haven't done this very often—spoken to you. But it's become obvious I've got a lot to learn about what it means to have faith . . . how to follow the right path, your path. I admit, I don't know how. Please help me. . . . And no matter what happens tomorrow or the next day, even if Bo proves false, even if we lose the farm, even if all these wonderful times are suddenly taken away from Naomi and me . . . like our loved ones were back in Vegas, I'll still trust you. I'll still follow you. . . .*

I knelt there and kept praying for a while longer. Finally I stood and saw that Naomi was rising, too. Herte was also beside her and, as I turned, I noticed I'd become surrounded by most of the congregation, kneeling at the front in one large group.

Eventually everyone made their way back to the pews and there was some sort of benediction, which I did not tune in to very well, and the service was over. The well-ordered rows immediately broke into families and small clusters, talking amongst themselves.

I glanced toward Naomi. The sound of an urgent voice beyond her alerted to me to the fact that Herte was speaking to her in an animated manner about something important.

Naomi stopped and looked at me, her face pale and very serious. "Nobody knows where Bo is," she said in a low voice. "He . . . he seems to have simply disappeared."

Something blinding flashed before my eyes, wiping out the world for a split second. A feeling of nausea threatened to overtake me, and the scene around me began to tilt. Suddenly I was back where I'd always been, before this encounter with God or whatever it was, and all the mind games messing with my reality in this odd place began to suffocate me like an old blanket. *Ruth, what are you doing? Why is the God of the universe going to pay any attention to you, a Vegas cocktail waitress? And are you going to believe all those fairy tales about a prince on a big white horse? Just like all the men who never showed, all those who broke their promises, who hurt you over and over again? Get real! Men disappear, and they don't come back. Even your own father failed you. That's the way of things.*

And that's probably God's story, too. Floated off somewhere, never to come back. At least for the likes of you. . . .

That was it. I began striding out of the church. I could hear Naomi just behind me, trying to catch up, calling my name as we rushed across the church parking lot.

"Ruth, are you all right?"

"No, I'm not all right!"

"Don't worry, sweetie—they'll find him," she panted. "He hasn't been gone all that long, you know. Who knows what he's been doing? But I'm sure he will show up soon—."

"Sure," I said, whirling around to face her. "They'll find him. He's probably not even 'missing.' The question is, does he still care about me? Does he want anything to do with me?"

"Please, Ruth, it'll be all right—."

"You don't know that!"

I grabbed the Impala's passenger door open and scrambled in. While I scooted across the front seat, Naomi squeezed in after me. I settled in and started the engine, and fighting the urge to floor it and squeal out of there, I shoved it into drive and headed toward home.

"Naomi, I just can't do it anymore," I said after a few long and tense moments had gone by. "I've run out of strength."

"Can't do what?" she asked.

"Wish so hard all the time. Hope against hope that everything will turn out for the best. That some wonderful, happy ending is waiting for me, for you, maybe just around the next corner, even though we're living in the real world and not in some make-believe romance movie. That all the odds against us will not in the end ruin our chances at a better life."

Naomi looked at me, frustration in her eyes. "Ruth, I have no idea what you're talking about. Wish so hard for what? Hope for what?"

"Do you really think a couple of women without a dime to their name can just show up in Lancaster County and basically start squatting on a multimillion-dollar farm and be able to keep it?"

"But . . . but it's *mine!*" Naomi protested.

"Really? Tell that to Uncle Sam. Or how about the notion that if I just bat my eyelashes at the town's biggest catch, the most eligible bachelor, that true love's gonna make him gallop over and sweep me off my feet into a glorious future of prosperity and happiness. Naomi, it's all nonsense. It's not reality. And I've run out of strength to keep trying to make it become real!"

"Is this about what I just told you? About Bo?"

"Of course it is. I saw the look on your face. The fact that you were surprised by Bo's taking off made me realize what a dreamworld we've been living in all this time. I'm accustomed to men breaking their promises to me. Apparently you're not."

"Okay, Ruth. But what about this? 'I'll go wherever you go. We'll have each other. I'll just fit in and make it work. I'll make your people mine as well.' How pie in the sky is that?"

"Sure," I answered slowly, "the way you say it."

"Except it really is coming true! You did come with me, and you helped me reach our destination when I never would have alone. And my people have embraced you as one of their own. And we've stayed together through it all and been each other's rock."

"Yes, and the whole thing's about to unravel, starting tomorrow morning. The deadline's up. The alarm clock's ringing, and they're coming to roll up this cute dream of ours and take it away."

"Ruth," said Naomi, softly now, "I'm so sorry the news about Bo affected you this way. I understand—you feel hurt and rejected. It was a kick in the gut, and naturally it took some of the steam out of you. But I for one still have hope, and I'm not about to give up. I remember growing up, my daddy used to quote this old Pennsylvania Dutch proverb. 'The grand essentials of life are something to do, something to love, and something to hope for.' Ruth, I'm not going to apologize for putting my hope in something. That's only human. And there's nothing naïve or unrealistic about hopes coming true. They come true all the time, every day. Unless of course you let them die."

She took a long breath, then said, "And I know this is going to sound preachy and another unrealism for your list, but something deep and satisfying—and, yes, *real*—happened to me there at the front of the church. You can believe me or not, but it's possible God has plans for us we haven't even imagined."

I stubbornly refused to answer, but I sure was thinking.

CHAPTER 56

And it did feel like something had died as we pulled up to the farm, as if the last shred of hope for some satisfactory explanation had now been stripped away as the countdown to hard, cold reality was narrowing down to its last hours.

I hardly remember how I spent the rest of that Sunday. I know I cleaned up lunch after Naomi and I had finished. I recall resting out on the porch, wrapped in my afghan, watching the last of autumn slip by as a now-overcast sky brooded over the land. What was once a cool breeze now turned to biting cold, stinging my cheeks and hands. But still I sat there, numb. My mind kept repeating the phrase, *"Nobody knows where Bo is."*

Despite my anger at Bo, I was worried, too. It didn't seem like Bo to just disappear, with no explanation. Even Naomi said so—for whatever that was worth.

Freezing, I finally left the porch, moved back inside, and went straight to bed.

The next morning I got up and walked into the kitchen somewhere near seven o'clock. Naomi was already dressed and sitting at the table. Spread before her was a breakfast of oatmeal and scrambled eggs and strong coffee. Beside the coffeepot lay a stack of papers, legal documents I recognized immediately. Naomi had lovingly reassembled them after our open trunk had tossed them onto I-70 and I had risked my life dodging trucks to save each one. My marriage certificate. The death certificates of Eli and his two sons. And their original deed to the farm.

I took a seat at the table, groggy.

"Good morning," Naomi said. "Hungry? There's plenty here, and everything's still hot."

"Not really," I said. "Just coffee, thanks."

She picked up the coffeepot and began pouring me a cup, then handed it to me, her expression kind but determined. "Ruth. I'm going into Lancaster."

"Why?"

"Because I want Hans to look me in the eye as he takes my farm. And if there's a judge to be spoken to, who might want to hear from the owner before he turns it over, to hear whether I have hopes or plans of redeeming the tax lien, then I want to be there to say my piece."

"That's awfully brave of you. If I were in your shoes, that courthouse is the last place I'd want to be."

She reached over and took my hand in hers. "Ruth, I don't know what happened to you at the church yesterday. I mean, one minute you were praying, the next you were all upset and running for the car. But personally, I was telling God that I was back. Not just here in Pennsylvania, but back home with Him. And not just back to join the church. I may not—no, I will not—embrace all of the Old Order ways, but I will embrace their values. Mainly, though, I'm here to follow Him again. No matter what. I realize now that finding my way back to what really matters *is* the happy ending to this story, not whether I keep the farm or not, and not whether I keep living in Lancaster County. Being in that old meetinghouse yesterday made me see it's not about geography. The preacher there helped me see this even more clearly—that my coming home wasn't to a place, or even to a group of people. I was coming home to my faith, to my values. To the things that are really important to me—all of it centered around God. Without Him, it's all just a bunch of empty nostalgia and old dusty platitudes. And idolatry, as it turns out."

"So you're happy either way? No matter what happens today?"

"I'm not sure *happy* is the word. But, yes, I'm fine with it. The story of my life won't begin or end in that courthouse today. I think that's why I can stand to be there when the decision's made final. No matter what happens, I'm following Him."

"Even if He lets you down and doesn't answer our prayers?"

"No matter what happens," she repeated. "I trust Him . . . that *He* knows what's best for me. It's all in His hands."

I took a sip of my coffee and pondered her words for a moment, at the same time feeling disappointed with myself for the way I'd reacted at church yesterday, the things I thought. "Well then," I said, "I guess if you can follow Him there, I can, too. You know, I told God pretty much the same thing yesterday. But then, after hearing the news about Bo, I freaked out and allowed it to rattle me so badly that I forgot what I'd just prayed. When will I ever learn?"

"One thing I've been discovering lately is that we follow God one choice, one moment, at a time, Ruth. Now, please, eat something, then get dressed and let's go. Together."

Unknown to us, nearly half the folks of Ephrata were heading for the Lancaster County courthouse that morning. Bo's attorney had returned home from a trip to Philadelphia late Sunday night, waiting until then to check his messages. Furious that a client as prominent and solid as Bo Salmon had been allowed to sit in jail over the entire weekend, he got on the phone and woke up every friend of Bo's he could think of and urged them to be at his arraignment in the morning.

As a result, the word of Bo's whereabouts spread like wildfire, along with the rumors as to *why* he'd just spent the weekend in jail. Since we had no phone, we found out later that Herte had stopped by the farm to fill us in on what she'd heard, but by then Naomi and I had already climbed in the Impala and were on our way toward town. Without a moment's hesitation, she simply assumed we'd heard the news from someone else, turned her car around, and headed to Lancaster like seemingly everyone else.

Walking from the parking garage to the courthouse building, we noticed at once that the sidewalk facing the entrance was unusually crammed with people. "Those two women over there," Naomi said, pointing, "they were in church with us yesterday. I wonder what's going on." Then she remembered the custom of carrying out auctions on the courthouse steps. Only this time it was her own property at jeopardy.

The old courthouse building was made of stone and soared upward four stories, topped by a copper dome turned green. We had approached a sign listing the locations of various offices within the building when out of the corner of my eye I saw a man in an orange jumpsuit being escorted from a blue van marked *Lancaster County Prison* by a tall peace officer.

Something about the jumpsuit man's stature and his

manner of walking nudged me to look closer. I focused on the face.

And then I dropped my keys to the pavement. My heart began thumping, and I found I couldn't breathe.

"What is it?" Naomi asked.

"It's Bo!" I said, pointing. "I don't believe it! He's been arrested."

Naomi looked over to where I pointed. "Oh, my goodness!" she cried.

This explained why he'd been unable to follow through with his promise of coming to see me. He couldn't leave. He hadn't failed me! He'd been detained the whole time!

Suddenly I felt stupid. So much wasted anguish and distress. All the bitter voices in my mind left me in a single, liberating rush. Naomi had been right. Hope was worth having, worth protecting.

But what was he in jail for? Why had he been arrested? I'd actually grown accustomed to bailing Lonnie out of trouble and had certainly spent my own nights in jail. But Bo?

Then another crisis loomed before me. If Bo was in jail, then he couldn't have taken care of the property problem—*if* that was his intention. So much remained unknown, with our fate still up in the air.

Naomi took me by the arm. "Come on! We're going to follow him."

At that point I wasn't sure whether she was referring to God, or Bo.

CHAPTER 57

Conflicting emotions assaulted my senses, my thoughts doing cartwheels as I moved almost automatically, following the officer who was escorting Bo. Soon it became clear that the people crowding the sidewalk were going the same direction, toward the door through which the officer and Bo had just disappeared. After waiting awhile in a long security-check line, we entered the large courtroom where Bo now sat waiting. The place was packed with people. As Naomi and I walked toward the last occupied row, she spotted Hans there. He was clutching a fat manila folder, and he had a gauze bandage wrapped around his head.

"Hello, Hans," Naomi said curtly. "Are you here because of Bo, or do you have some other business at the courthouse today?"

"Hi, Naomi. Mornin', Ruth," he said, sounding smooth and professional. "You know very well why I'm here. How about you, Naomi? Any large payments you'd like to tell me about?"

"One show at a time," she said, looking forward as the judge entered the room.

"Yes," said Hans. "And in the first show, I'm the victim."

"All rise!" said the bailiff in a booming voice.

Everyone stood as the judge, looking irritated, took his seat behind the bench and then motioned for those in the court to do likewise. He directed his glare toward the two tables facing him. At one table sat a pair of dark-suited men, with Hans sitting in the first row behind them, and at the other table, Bo and his lawyer. The courtroom fell immediately silent.

"My goodness," the judge said, moving his attention to the crowd. His expression changed to a look of sincere surprise. "Look at all these people. Welcome, folks. I assume you're here this morning to witness the proceedings surrounding the tussle that recently took place, as friends of one party or the other."

I glanced at Naomi. At that moment it dawned on us that Bo must have gotten himself involved in some kind of altercation.

The judge continued. "Prosecutor, you can cool your jets this morning, because I'm not even close to a finding of fact sufficient to level a charge. So this is nothing more than an informal session with the purpose of determining the facts of the case. I've known the defendant thirty years, and I'm not about to consider serious charges until I've heard firsthand just what sort of incident we're talking about and what brought it on." Taking over for the lawyers, the judge looked over at Bo and asked, "Now, Mr. Salmon, did you strike the individual, Mr. Hans Yoder?"

"I tried to," answered Bo, "and I definitely wanted to, but I tripped and fell after he ducked out of my way. I grabbed his boot, but I never hit him, and I didn't put that cut on his head. On any other day I would have walked away from this fool. But on this day, I was here at the courthouse on account of a good friend, someone he insulted, regarding something very important. I'd like to offer this as proof."

Bo's lawyer stepped forward, holding up for the judge a sheet of paper. The judge took it and started reading. "Remember," he said, "this is informal. We're not dealing with submitting any evidence at this point. Right now we're just giving the story of what happened, what was the cause behind it, who did what to whom and why? Understand?"

The opposing lawyers replied, "Yes, Your Honor."

The judge returned to reading the document given him by Bo's lawyer, then after a silent pause looked up.

"This is missing a signature, you know, Bo."

"I know that, Your Honor. That's exactly what I was trying to obtain when all this happened."

Slapping the document down on the bench, the judge said, "This is mighty convincing in my book. I don't need to hear anymore; this matter isn't going any further. Mr. Salmon has served enough time during his bungled incarceration this past weekend, and Mr. Yoder will have to go through life with a nice little scar on his head. But I think both of you have suffered enough for the stupidity of throwing a few shoulders around—if you can even call it that—on courthouse property." He banged the gavel.

Hans stiffened in his seat, turned, and gave his lawyers an angry look. Bo nodded as if in relief.

Suddenly Hans leaped to his feet and ran out of the courtroom. Naomi looked at me and said, "Well, that was subtle. Three guesses where Hans is headed to now." Implying the other end of the courthouse, where tax matters were settled.

"Do you want to follow him?" I asked.

She shook her head and pointed ahead. Bo and the judge hadn't moved.

"Your Honor?" asked Bo. "I'm deeply grateful. But with your help I'd like to complete this matter and follow through on that . . . evidence. Before it expires."

"Is the other party here in my courtroom by any chance?"

"I think so, Your Honor . . ." I heard Bo begin, and then he swung around and I saw him frantically scanning the crowd.

I had no idea then what Bo was up to, or even that he was looking for me. At the time I didn't know what they were referring to with this so-called evidence, what exactly was written on that sheet of paper. Before I had time to realize I should probably signal him, he spotted me and Naomi. At the same time Naomi began waving to him. By the time he smiled and waved back and started striding toward us, I was convinced he was coming to speak with Naomi about the farm.

As he approached us wearing that bright orange jumpsuit, I was overcome with my feelings for the man. Knowing he hadn't intentionally broken his word of three nights ago, little else mattered at that moment. He drew closer, we locked eyes on each other, and a shiver ran up and down my back. Now I knew for certain. Nothing had changed.

"Ruth," he said, "would you come with me a moment? There's something I need to say to you." He took my hand and led me out into the aisle, where all of a sudden he dropped to one knee.

Instantly I felt all the disappointment and despair of the last few days completely leave my being, replaced by pure anticipation. That and utter joy.

"Ruth Yoder," he began, his eyes gazing straight into mine, "if you'll forgive me everything that's odd and mismatched and inconvenient and rushed and maybe even inappropriate about this moment, and marry me and be my wife, you'll make me the happiest man alive. I love you. . . ."

From his smile, the look in his eye, and the trembling of his fingers as he held my hand, I could tell he'd meant every syllable of his speech.

I forced my mind to focus on my response, realizing that even if I'd waited until the time was perfect, until my grief was spent and a proper courting had been observed, this was the man I would have chosen. "Yes!" I said, then broke into laughter.

As soon as the word was spoken, a great cheer immediately rose up and filled the room.

Bo rose to his feet and wrapped me in his arms and kissed me.

Then, taking me by the hand again, he began to lead me down the aisle, back toward the judge, who still held Bo's document. Naomi followed close behind us, and halfway to the judge's bench I reached back and grasped her hand with my free hand as we completed our rush down the aisle.

"Now, you know I'm not used to doing this, so don't expect anything fancy," the judge said. "Just the basics."

"That'll be just fine, Your Honor," said Bo.

"All right then, you two," he said, then handed the document back to Bo. It was a marriage license, dated last Friday.

Naomi motioned to Herte, who stood near the front of the crowd. We needed two witnesses, and I couldn't think of two better people than Naomi and Herte.

Bo handed me the license and turned so I could sign it against his back. I leaned forward and whispered, "Bo, we will have a somewhat fancier church ceremony sometime, won't we?"

His shoulders shook. "I promise," he laughed.

"I mean, I know you Mennonites like plain," I joked, "but, honey, this is *plain!*"

After Bo handed the license over, we took our positions, standing side by side and looking up at the judge—Bo in his prison garb and me in the jeans and T-shirt I'd thrown on that morning.

"All right. Please join your hands." He looked at the document we had just signed. "Ruth Escalante Yoder, do you promise to take this man, Boaz Salmon, as your lawful wedded husband, to have and to hold, from this day forward, for better or for worse, for richer or for poorer, in sickness and in health, till death do you part?"

Every word of that vow whisked me back through the last year's memories. *Husband* . . . Losing Lonnie. *Poorer* . . . Sleeping on the Impala's front seat, counting our last few bills and coins as we journeyed to Ephrata. *Death* . . . Racing down Loveland Pass at seventy miles an hour and seeing terror flash through Naomi's eyes. *Do you part* . . . Pleading with Naomi that morning in Moab to take me with her.

Finally I returned to my senses and the present moment. I glanced at Naomi and saw joy in her eyes.

I looked into Bo's eyes and saw there all the love, gentleness, kindness, and passion I had always wished for in a man. Surely even if I had waited another year to grieve Lonnie's death, I would have chosen him. I would have accepted his proposal. "I do," I said.

I'd never felt words resonate through my soul with such certainty and confidence.

"And you, Boaz Salmon, do you take this woman, Ruth Yoder, to be your lawful wedded wife, to have and to hold, from this day forward, for better or for worse, for richer or for poorer, in sickness and in health, till death do you part?"

Bo smiled and said, "I do, Your Honor. I do!"

I felt transported. Was this really happening to me? Tears began streaming down my cheeks.

Naomi was handing me a tissue from her purse when Herte said, fairly loud, "What about rings?"

The judge shook his head. "No. There's no absolute legal requirement for rings, and obviously these folks don't have any handy at the moment. So let's keep going, shall we? I'm sure Bo will take care of this detail in the near future. Right, Bo?" he said with a wink.

"Of course, Your Honor," said Bo.

"Well, then, by the authority vested in me by the Commonwealth of Pennsylvania, I declare you two to be husband and wife. Bo, you may kiss your bride."

Bo engulfed me body and soul, sealing the ceremony with a passionate kiss. Afterward he grasped my hand and pulled me away. "Thank you, Your Honor," Bo said. "But we have one more extremely important matter to take care of before we can start our honeymoon."

CHAPTER 58

At first, still in shock by all that had just taken place, I couldn't recall what that pressing matter was. Until we reached the courtroom doors, and Bo pushed us through them, mimicking the hasty exit of his cousin just minutes earlier.

Bo led me down the stairs to the second floor, another mad dash that included many others following behind—not only Naomi and Herte but half the people in the courtroom, it seemed, so consumed now by curiosity that they came along to see where we were going.

We burst into the office of the Recorder of Deeds—a wide, low-ceilinged room. Bo didn't hesitate but rushed me over to the shortest line of people who stood waiting beside a long partitioned divider. Three people were waiting before us, but Bo forced our way to the front, excusing himself and explaining loudly, "I'm so sorry, sir, ma'am, but this is an emergency! We must cut in line. Please forgive us." Two of the people took one long look at the words *County Prison* on his orange jumpsuit and quickly left the line for another. The third was an older gentleman who gestured for Bo to go ahead and walked around behind us. "Thank you!" Bo told him.

We reached the front, and I saw why he had risked such rudeness.

In the row beside us, just about to complete his business, stood Hans.

"You're too late, Bo," said Hans. "I'm just minutes away from being through, and there's nothing you can do to stop me."

"Oh, really?" Bo said. "What makes you so sure?"

"Because only a direct family member can redeem the parcel from the tax sale. I see Naomi here, but we all know she's penniless. Ruth is a direct relative, as Lonnie's widow, but I don't believe she has a dime more than Naomi does. That leaves me and a claim I made a year ago that matures in just a few minutes' time. Since I filed my claim first, no one but a family member like Ruth or Naomi can preempt my claim to the farm. So let me complete my transaction and be done with it already."

"You're wrong, Hans!" Bo snapped. "Ruth has more money than you know about."

Hans sneered at me. "Everybody knows you're dirt poor."

"You left the courtroom too soon, Hans," Bo continued. "You missed our wedding. I am now the proud husband of Ruth Escalante Yoder Salmon."

Bo shoved the marriage license forward so Hans could see it for himself.

"And I think she now has plenty of money to redeem the property."

For a moment a charged silence reigned over the room. Hans stood there dumbstruck, staring down at the paper, opening and closing his mouth again and again yet producing no sound. Then several peals of laughter rang out around the room, followed by a round of applause.

Bo looked at me. "Honey, now why don't you and Naomi step up and tell the nice man there that you want to settle your tax bill." Naomi rushed forward and planted a kiss on Bo's cheek, hugging him and thanking him over and over.

Arm in arm, Naomi and I approached the clerk's window, laughing and crying both, our hearts pounding.

"I'd like to pay off all outstanding taxes on the Kauffman farm," I said in a shaky voice, "in Ephrata Borough," I added, trying to make this sound as official as I could.

"I'm sorry, ma'am," the clerk said, "but are you directly related to the owner of record?"

"Yes, I am," I answered.

"Because the taxes were past due and have already been paid by a third party, I'm going to need you to prove that for me."

I held him in a blank stare. Then I heard Naomi cry out beside me, "Oh, I have that! I actually have it!"

She pulled out the stack of legal documents she had carefully kept with her all morning. She handed me one. Bo handed me another. It felt strange, looking at two marriage licenses, both of them bearing my signature, both of them separated by so much time. So much life.

The clerk instructed me where to sign. I filled out the check Bo provided and handed it to the clerk, feeling a tingle in my fingers. As he stamped and stapled a brand-new document, then handed it to me with a resounding, "It's all settled, ma'am," something settled into place deep within me. I turned to Naomi and we embraced. I brought my mouth close against her ear.

"*Thank you*, Naomi. Thank you. You've been better to me than . . ."

Although I couldn't get out the rest of the sentence, Naomi knew how it ended. It seemed as if she always had.

EPILOGUE

My dear family,

You all know what has transpired in the many years since that day at the Lancaster County courthouse. Bo wasted no time moving out to the Kauffman farm and restoring it beyond anyone's imagination to charm and beauty. And of course we prevailed on Naomi to live there with us, though she tried to tell us newlyweds needed their own space.

"Okay, Naomi," my organizer of a husband finally told her, "we'll fix you up your own apartment with its own entrance, kitchen, sitting room, and we'll work it right into our remodeling plans. It will be our version of a Dawdi Haus," he added, referring to the Plain folks' tradition of adding a self-contained unit onto the family home for aging parents and other seniors of the community.

A year later, in our bedroom there, Naomi midwifed at the birth of my first son, the one who is father, grandfather to most of you reading this.

The birth of our beloved son, Obed—a good Bible name,

we agreed, and unique—seems as likely a place to draw the line and declare this tale finished as any other. To all of you who waited, who heard me declare years ago I would write it and took me at my word, I apologize. Please forgive me. I discovered far more worth telling than I had ever dreamed.

From here on it becomes a story with which most of you are familiar. But in the interest of your children who will come along later and read these pages, I will give a little account of that which followed.

Shortly after Obed's birth, a procession of horse and buggies appeared along the road leading to the Kauffman farm. The first person to descend from the buggy was an old woman—Naomi's mother. I can't describe the emotions of that moment when mother and daughter embraced for the first time since Naomi was barely out of her teens. Her mother had brought her brothers and sisters, along with their families. Bo had written them after our marriage, inviting them to come. They decided to wait until our baby was born.

The reunion for Naomi was beyond words. During the five-day visit she would often pause, put her hand over her heart, and whisper to no one in particular that she was now "restored." I knew what she meant by this. Naomi no longer felt bereft of family and loved ones. God had restored to her the joy of being at the heart of a large and growing family.

Naomi's kin left far too soon, but from then on a steady procession of cards and letters flowed between our homes.

Hans's scheme to patch together an immense parcel for big-city developers failed completely. He spent his remaining days as a local farmer and mostly kept to himself until the very end.

Isaac was immediately fired by Bo and moved off to become an office manager somewhere in Florida.

As the years passed, the family grew, and I began to

experience for myself the Old Order's familiar blessing of a large and loving family. Bo proved to be a warm and tender husband, and when age finally forced him to leave the helm of the Green Dragon, I was by then at home with every nook and cranny of the place and so took over the management of it myself. Bo still hung around the office, quietly helping out where he could and not looking over my shoulder too often. Obed grew up at the Green Dragon, probably spending more time there with us, running around the huge complex, than at home.

Then Naomi passed away, gracefully in her sleep. Only eight months later, in the heat of summer, Bo died of a heart attack while attempting to help unload cattle at the Dragon's holding pens.

That's when the mantle fully came to my shoulders and I came to be known in Lancaster County as "Aunt Ruth," as if I'd been born and raised here. Ironically, I now found myself matriarch of the area and sole owner of its largest tourist attraction, the Green Dragon, as well as its loveliest, completely restored Stauffer Mennonite farm. To those who meet me for the first time and assume I was born to prosperity, pastoral beauty, and comfort, I only smile and keep the truth to myself.

The deepest joys of all this are understood only to me and God, who has graciously made himself known more deeply with every passing year. I marvel at His grace and creativity, that He could take a pair of broken-down Las Vegas widows with checkered pasts—at least in my case—and usher them into such a place of honor, responsibility, and privilege.

Just two days ago my grandson Jesse, Obed's oldest, visited me, holding the eighth precious bundle he has presented me with so far. But when I held and caressed this latest one, a beautiful boy Jesse and his wife have named David, an almost physical charge went through me. I can hardly explain it, except to say that I sensed, as rich as my own story has been, this little David would carve a path that may change the world and resound through many generations to come.

If I have disappointed any of you with what I've shared about my life, let me offer some small comfort. Should any of you stray from the right path in life, you are never beyond hope. The way can be found again. The right values can be re-embraced. The one true God can be discovered, most eager to restore His fellowship with us.

Any life can be redeemed, no matter how wayward or wandering its journey.

You too can find the road home.

Author's Note

Writing a book is always a journey, but usually merely a journey of the mind. The research for this novel involved a literal journey. The authors wanted every possible aspect of the story to be truly authentic, and the only way to insure that level of realism and accuracy was to take a cross-country road trip. Piling editors, writers, drivers, and laptops into a rented RV, we literally drove "The Road Home." From Las Vegas through Moab, Utah, then on to Bethlehem, Pennsylvania. A seven-day, several-thousand-mile research expedition, complete with breakdowns, a 2:00 a.m. interstate-wreck-induced multi-hour traffic jam, and various sundry additional insults to sanity provoked by many days of travel crammed into a small space. . . .

All with one purpose in mind. To insure that what we wrote actually existed (or some reasonable semblance thereof!) Almost without exception, if a road or a place is mentioned, it actually is part of America's landscape. The Green Dragon is much as we described it, the motel in Moab, the blown-glass ceiling in the Bellagio, the All Aboard Inn, Reading Road—all can be found just as we described in the story. The Kauffman farm does not exist by that name, but others very much like it can be found in Lancaster County. Of necessity some things had to be changed, some names altered.

(Whether to protect the innocent or disguise the guilty, you decide!)

Perhaps the most amazing thing is that running parallel with the biblical geography of Bethlehem, Ephrata, and Moab, halfway around the globe here in the USA are contemporary places with the same names.

This fact inspired me to ask, What if the story of Ruth took place in the twenty-first century...?

—Tommy Tenney

For more information, see
www.TommyTenney.com

A reading group discussion guide for
The Road Home is available at
www.bethanyhouse.com/theroadhome

About the Authors

TOMMY TENNEY, a prolific author with more than three million books sold, penned the mega-bestseller *The God Chasers*. His books have been translated into more than 40 languages and nominated for multiple awards, including the Gold Medallion Award and Retailers' Book of the Year. A few years ago, Tenney became fascinated with the story of Esther, inspiring the novel *Hadassah*—as well as the major motion picture *One Night With the King*—followed by its sequel *The Hadassah Covenant*. In the wake of the Esther novels' success, Tommy was drawn to Ruth, particularly her struggles and their similarities to our world—full of regrets and restoration. He is a highly acclaimed speaker with a decade of pastoral experience and twenty-five years of passionate and effective ministry in over 150 venues around the world each year. He and his family live in Louisiana.

MARK ANDREW OLSEN is a full-time writer who collaborated with Tenney on bestsellers *Hadassah* and *The Hadassah Covenant*, and now *The Road Home*. His novel *The Assignment* was a Christy Award finalist. In addition, he is the author of supernatural thrillers *The Watchers* and *The Warriors* (to be released in spring 2008). Mark grew up in France, the son of missionaries, and is a Professional Writing graduate of Baylor University. He and his family live in Colorado Springs.

More From Bestselling Authors Tommy Tenney and Mark Andrew Olsen

Both a Jewish woman's memoir and a palace thriller full of political intrigue and suspense, *Hadassah* brings the age-old story of Esther to life. This historically accurate novel, layered with fresh insights, provides a fascinating twist on a pivotal time in religious history, and readers will find it bursting with page-turning drama. *Hadassah* is also now a major motion picture called *One Night With the King*, featuring Peter O'Toole and Omar Sharif.

Hadassah by Tommy Tenney and Mark Andrew Olsen

When an antiquities expert uncovers ancient documents bridging the centuries, he also finds a conspiracy that has tragic implications for modern-day Jews in Iraq and Iran. And Hadassah, the wife of the Israeli prime minister, may be the only hope her people have. As a history-altering truth thunders across the centuries, can this explosive discovery once again save a people?

The Hadassah Covenant
by Tommy Tenney and Mark Andrew Olsen

Also From Tommy Tenney

Watch for Tommy Tenney's inspirational study of the biblical story of Ruth, *Finding Your Way*, in January 2008, published by FaithWords and available wherever books are sold.